No Warning Could Have Prepared Me To Face What Filled Most of The Right-Hand Corridor.

Or, rather, *who*. A pulsating mass pressed against floor, wall, and ceiling, as though the being had forced itself to fit within our parameters. Five long, fibrous-appearing arms lay in parallel along the near wall, as if we'd surprised them reaching toward our cabin door. There were no other obvious features of body structures. With the exception of the arms, the whole seemed insubstantial, as if darkness had been poured into this shape and left without form, only a glistening, as if wet or coated in the finest possible scales.

Morgan's arm lifted into a valiant, if improbable, barrier between me and our latest uninvited guest. I put my hand on his wrist and gently brought it down. *Rugheran,* I sent to him, as tightly as my mind could focus. Despite this care, the flesh—if that's what composed this being—quivered in response.

"I think it likes us," I ventured hopefully.

"It could learn to knock, too," Morgan muttered under his breath, but I heard the growing wonder in his voice as he surveyed the being stuffed into his ship. "Rugherarn. Sira. Do you realize what this means? First contact . . ."

Novels by
JULIE E. CZERNEDA
available from DAW Books:

*Coming soon in hardcover from DAW Books

TO TRADE THE STARS

The Trade Pact Universe #3

JULIE E. CZERNEDA

DAW BOOKS, INC.
DONALD A. WOLLHEIM, FOUNDER
375 Hudson Street, New York, NY 10014
ELIZABETH R. WOLLHEIM
SHEILA E. GILBERT
PUBLISHERS
www.dawbooks.com

First Printing, June 2002
2 3 4 5 6 7 8 9

DAW TRADEMARK REGISTERED
U.S. PAT. OFF. AND FOREIGN COUNTRIES
—MARCA REGISTRADA.
HECHO EN U.S.A.
PRINTED IN THE U.S.A.

For Scott Aleksander Czerneda

What should I give you, as you venture forth? I'd give you kindness and a generous heart—but you have those. I'd give you warm wit and wisdom—but you have those, too. I'd give you a sense of justice and chivalry—but no warrior imagined or real could have more. (And you're already tall enough to reach all the cupboards, thank you, so no more height.)

Which leaves me, Scott, with just this riddle to send with you. What will you have wherever you go, yet never need to pack? Home. Heart. Family.

Always.
Love, Mom

ACKNOWLEDGMENTS

The end of a beginning. That's how it feels to write a finale to the story begun by my first novel. Who knew it would lead to this? Well, Sheila Gilbert, my friend, editor, and publisher, who once more found what this book needed to be its best. And probably Roxanne Hubbard, who again fit a friend's needs into her busy life. Thanks, Luis Royo, for capturing Sira from the beginning. And thank you to all the fine folks at DAW, who treat their authors like family.

Many people have given their enthusiastic support to my work. Debby de Groot, Kate Lennard, Wendy Bush-Lister, and Peter Robb at Penguin Canada made me feel like royalty. Then, the Palm eBook guys, the nicest people you could meet. Hi Mike, Jeff, Lee, Joth, and Hayden! To sign a book for the charming Martin H. Greenberg, then meet the Tekno Books folks in person? A high point of the year. Thanks also to Gordon Van Gelder, Laura Ann Gilman, Wen Spencer, Kathryn Helmick (Hi Kat!), Jim Seidman, Larry Smith and Sally Kobbe, Frank Hayes, Patricia Bow, Russell Martin, Michael Green, David Shtogryn, Jana Paniccia, and Don Hutchison.

I was Guest of Honor at Willycon 2001, Wayne, Nebraska. My thanks and Roger's for a fabulous time to the SFFC, Ron Vick, Stan Gardner, and Kelly (Pancake Man) Russman. Hats, fame, and bowling! Thanks also to our friend, the amazing Frank Wu.

Happy hunting, Hounds of the IPU. I've sprinkled this book with nuggets just for you. My special thanks to MT O'Shaughnessy (Uriel) for his friendship and inspiration, and to Kristen Britain, convention queen and buddy. Thank you, Tim Bowie and Ruth Stuart, for allowing me to use your names as well as your good natures.

It's been another year where kindnesses flooded in, but the production people will protest if I thank everyone I should. Still, there are four absolutely dear ladies whose generosity and affection I must acknowledge: Carol Bennewies, Donna Beuerman, Barb McGrath, and Cheryl McGrath. See you in July!

Thank you, Jennifer, for putting up with my writing while you were home—and for braving the bookstores! Scott, thanks for all those names—and making me lunch! Mom's back—until the next book. And Roger? Come here.

Prologue

A KITCHEN can be a dangerous place for an argument. This one, in the rear of *Claws & Jaws—Complete Interspecies Cuisine*, looked like a scene from a low-budget horror vid. Knives protruded hilt-first from cupboard doors. What appeared to be body parts from several different species had been tossed in every direction, their flight paths marked by bloody trails of red, ocher, and corrosive green. And what had been done to the salads . . .

Suffice it to say the regular staff had long ago run and, in one case, slithered out the service entrance to where they could listen at the door in relative safety. Now, they exchanged worried looks as the argument grew suddenly—and ominously—quiet.

They weren't the only ones.

A cautious eye, gleaming black, peered over the edge of the mammoth, steaming hot stove. It was followed by another.

And another.

And another.

Until dozens formed an anxious, beadlike row.

"But, Chef Neltare," a voice more accustomed to booming than pleading emerged faintly from somewhere behind the eyes. "Whatever name we use for your new pâté . . . I can't add it to the menu. Not on Plexis. I mean—think of the clientele." There was a clanging sound, as though pots had fallen loose inside a cupboard. It had an overtone of distress. "We can serve Humans liver pâté—we certainly can't serve them Human liver pâté. You do see the problem."

The Neblokan standing in the middle of the aisle between the stove and the sous-station glared back, his shoulders forward and flared to their maximum width. While it wasn't a particularly impressive display— evolution and culture conspiring to produce a species prone to the "find a crevice large enough to hide your head and hopefully more" philosophy of conflict resolution—this Neblokan had the bottomless courage that came of knowing oneself to be indispensable. There were, after all, only three Trade Pact Certified Multi-Species Master Chefs on Plexis.

And the other two had already quit.

"You try to confuse my genius with mere semantics?" the Neblokan shouted, reaching for another bowl of doomed salad. "I'll leave today! Now! Before supper! You will have not only no Master Chef, but no clientele at all, Hom Huido!"

"No! No. Please. Believe me, Chef Neltare, I mean no insult. There simply isn't a restaurant on the station that will allow sapient-based dishes to be served. The Food Inspectors alone—" A huge shape rose from behind the stove, head plates pulsing with agitation. "Perhaps—a special menu? To highlight your

vast and undeniable talents in some, ah, less controversial way?"

"Semantics, I tell you! I spit at semantics." A bile-
yellow glob sizzled across the stove.

"I assure you, Master Chef, semantics are very
much the issue here," the Carasian took a careful sidestep to move clear of the stove and into what had
seemed a generous aisleway, until he narrowed it with
his bulk to barely passable. Seen in the light, his
gleaming black carapace and jointed arms were
streaked with a granular pink substance of highly suspicious origin and several wilted sprigs of garnish.

Huido Maarmatoo'kk, owner of the famed *Claws &*
Jaws, as well as what he hoped would prove a growing
number of franchises throughout this quadrant of
space, lowered his great claws to the floor in a concil-
iatory posture he trusted the Neblokan could read and
thus forestall any further launches from the menu. The
incensed chef had already accounted for most of
tonight's entrées. "I understand your species' culinary
traditions are more—" the Carasian struggled to find a
word in Comspeak to encompass proudly cooking
one's parents for the ceremonial first feast of the next
generation and settled for: "—*liberal* than those of
other Trade Pact species. Still, you did pass the Trade
Pact Certification. You *did* pass, didn't you?" This with
a suspicious rumble.

Chef Neltare looked shocked. "The certification
cannot be counterfeited!"

"Then how did you miss learning that most non-
Neblokans abhor cannibalism!" Huido restrained the
urge to snap his lower pair of massive handling claws

with considerable difficulty, and continued in what he hoped was a more reasoning tone. "Chef Neltare. It's not as though we're talking about beings eating one another for survival. Try to imagine how those beings would feel to discover they'd violated their principles for an overpriced appetizer."

The salad bowl lifted threateningly. "Are you implying my appetizers aren't worth the price?"

Huido switched tactics. "I have enough trouble getting truffles—how can you possibly obtain the—" even the usually callous Carasian hesitated, "—raw ingredients?"

"Hardly a problem in so vibrant a community as Plexis," Neltare boasted. "In fact, today alone I was paid quite handsomely to take the ingredients for my new pâté—as well as a rib dish I modestly believe will be a marvel." The being's amber pupils glowed beneath their sequined eye ridges. "I hardly thought you of all beings would balk at this, Hom Huido. You've done it before, after all. Everyone says so."

Wondering if he'd ever live down having served that Clansman's corpse to a delegation of vastly impressed Thremms—a secret spread so far around the station as to have become legend, thus resulting in shiploads of vastly disappointed Thremms and a welcome decrease in uninvited Clan—Huido's sigh shuddered through his body. The resulting vibration slithered free the topmost plates in the clean stack, most crashing to the floor. Huido calculated the cost of the nonrecyclable porcelains and winced. "All I know, Master Chef," he said, almost to himself, "is my life is being ruined by success. I've hardly time for the pool anymore. And your novel approach to broadening the menu at the *Claws & Jaws* will be the ultimate straw, as the Humans express it."

"Humans. Brain-dead pests with no taste buds," the Neblokan muttered, the gleaming blue wattle beneath its chin swelling with displeasure. Then, perhaps realizing criticism of a species that included the giant Carasian's dearest friend was likely unwise, given the ringing snap of a great claw, the being added in haste: "Except Captain Morgan. An epicure, of his kind. Remarkably cultured—"

Forgetting he was trying to reconcile with the being, Huido lunged forward, claws snapping in unison, sending the chef dodging behind his side of the stove. "Don't talk to me about that unreliable excuse for brexks' fodder! Too busy for the Pocular run, is he? Too busy to help his brother keep up with business or to see what a disaster he's left behind! Too busy in his own pool to care about mine! Does he even call?"

As this last was delivered in a deafening bellow quite probably heard all the way into the dining hall, if not out into the Plexis concourse itself, the now-cowering chef didn't bother to answer.

Chapter 1

Chapter 1

"**D**ON'T they ever knock?"

We were alone. *Now*. The Council representative who'd mistakenly 'ported into our cabin, setting off Morgan's complaint and the *Fox*'s alarms—including some which should give said representative a well-deserved headache—had left as quickly as he'd appeared. With a little help from me.

And after one look at me or, rather, where I was.

I gazed at my hand, fingers spread over the warmer skin of Morgan's stomach, fascinated anew by the firmness of muscle and curve of rib—both of which had moved quite abruptly in reaction to our visitor, as had his shoulder beneath my cheek. I shifted to nestle even closer. *I've tried to convey the concept, my love*, I sent into his thoughts, uninterested in speaking aloud in this moment before we had to stir, this moment before the universe demanded its share of us. How quickly I'd come to love waking together, lingering at the edge of peace.

Morgan chuckled into my hair, his arms gathering me in a brief, tight hold. No need of words, spoken or sent. My gentle, passionate lover, my Chosen, was also

Captain of the *Silver Fox*, Karolus Registry. Lingering lasted only until he began to think of the day ahead and his starship.

Our starship, I reminded myself proudly.

For among the fundamental changes in my life: from the protective seclusion of a Chooser, to Choice with this Human; from being little more than a rumor to my kind, the Human-seeming Clan, to Speaker for their Council; and from being alone and hunted, to companionship and happiness—I counted becoming a partner and crew on this small ship as wondrous a change as any.

I'd been right. Morgan rolled away with a practiced twist to slide his feet to the floor in the narrow space between our bed and the fresher stall, leaving me cold along one side until I snuggled under the portion of sheet warmed by his body.

Temporary refuge. The sheet disappeared as suddenly as the Clansman had. "Time to get up, Lady Witch," Morgan informed me, a laugh beneath the words. "We have bills to pay."

I didn't need to look to know the sheet was no longer in the cabin, though I hoped it was still on the ship. My Human's Power left a tingle in the M'hir between us, just as his triumph left a surge of joy for me to share. "Show-off," I said, pretending to grumble.

"Practice, practice, practice," he said, knowing full well I was proud of his growing ability to move objects through the M'hir. My kind, the M'hiray branch of the Clan, had believed this was solely their talent.

They'd been wrong, I thought contentedly, following Morgan into the fresher. *About so many things.*

INTERLUDE

"You know they're wrong. This is impossible." Barac sud Sarc, former Clan Scout and presently serving as Mystic One for the powerful Makii Tribe of the Drapsk, ran one hand through his thick black hair and glared at the image hovering a hands' breath above the carpet. "I tell you, Rael, it can't be done their way!"

"Tell them, Cousin, not me," Rael di Sarc, also Mystic One for the Makii—though the Heerii claimed her, too, through some unfathomable confusion of Drapsk internal politics—appeared more interested in scrutinizing the delicate lacework tattooed from her thigh to ankle, revealed by the slide of blue issa-silk from her long legs. She was beautiful, of course, as all Chosen Clanswomen were; her green eyes and fair skin, her lustrous black and living hair a legacy of her Serona lineage. Beautiful and no fool—Barac knew Rael well enough to take her apparent inattention as its opposite. He also knew why she was reluctant to discuss their situation: she didn't like admitting failure. Proud to a fault, like all their kind.

"Come back to the capital," he compromised. "Talk to me."

"Where I'll trip over them at every turn?" Rael had recently moved from their luxurious apartments in the Drapskii capital to an equally luxurious, but isolated, suite in a small border town near the mountains. The reason given, and accepted by the Drapsk, was that the greater distance enabled the two Clan to further experiment with their Power. A lie. Rael was as fond of the beings as he was—hard not to be fond of creatures so devoted and earnest—which only made it harder for either of them to contemplate disappointing them.

Not to mention that Rael was perturbed by their hosts committing *grispsta* if, as she'd complained to Barac, she so much as winked. An exaggeration, but there was no denying the Drapsk fascination with the Clanswoman. The closer they could be to her, the happier they were. If she tried to walk anywhere, they crowded lifts and corridors until her steps took on the semblance of a dance in order to avoid contact. Whenever she grew frustrated enough to 'port away, the little beings trembled in ecstasy and sent her extravagant gifts—which would have been more pleasing except for their tendency to deliver those gifts in person. At any time of day.

Finally some benefit to being the lesser in Power, Barac smiled to himself, since the Drapsk treated him with the same casual courtesy as they did each other. He carefully kept the amused thought private. Rael wasn't one of those Clan who relished any opportunity to flaunt her superior strength, but old habits died hard.

Old habits. Barac took a steadying breath. Arguing with Rael was about as productive as arguing with Drapsk. Their species' approach to just about everything might be diametrically opposed, but as individuals? Both were as stubborn and set in their orbits as this planet's moons. Still, he had to try. "We've been here almost three months, Rael," Barac reminded her, keeping his voice calm and persuasive. "Three months without a hint of success. And you know why as well as I do. They won't let us do anything without their failsafes and gadgets in our faces. They're obsessed with keeping us safe. We have to do this our way, or we'll be here the rest of our lives."

"You unChosen are too quick to dismiss the value of safety. I, for one, approve the Drapsk's caution—"

"And you Chosen are famous for avoiding risk of any kind!"

His outburst, a surprise to them both, drew the hint of a smile. "Are we, now?" Rael murmured, but not as though offended. "Perhaps that's because we have much to protect, Cousin. Our Joined partner, our potential as child bearers, our links of Power to our offspring—"

Barac had never met Rael's Chosen, though he could sense, if he strained, the Power laced around their Joining through the M'hir. Janac di Paniccia lived on Omacron III, the only non-Human world inhabited by Clan; a verdant planet made irresistibly attractive by its inhabitants' high proportion of weak telepaths, individuals easy to manipulate, if inconveniently short-lived and fragile. Janac was a dabbler in the culturing of rare orchids, if Barac remembered correctly.

Not a Clansman known for controversial views or even personal Power, though he must have enough to match his Chosen. Barely enough, as Rael had elected to retain her House name and her father, Jarad di Sarc, had refused Janac his. Mind you, Jarad was consistent. He'd refused the same honor to Pella's Chosen, Dasimar, ending the hopes of that Joining reflecting status on the House of sud Annk. Barac supposed the quietly xenophobic Council was grateful Sira's Human hadn't been interested in assuming his rightful designation of di Sarc.

Irrelevant details. To be so Joined was the heart's goal of every Clan. To never feel that completion of self, know that living bond through the void? Barac had almost convinced himself the aching hunger within his soul was fading with time; suddenly, all his desire surged forth, as eager and hopeless as always.

His cousin felt it; she had the grace to gesture appeasement with one long white hand. Courtesy or pity? Barac controlled his resentment and continued, willing to trade on her sympathy. "The Drapsk idea of risk has nothing in common with ours, Rael," he said firmly. "They admit they don't know how we interact with the M'hir or how Sira was able to begin the reconnection of Drapskii within it. How can they know what's dangerous to us or not? Their caution smothers our ability to find these or any answers for ourselves."

"And how do you plan to convince them otherwise?" the Clanswoman asked, arching a well-shaped brow.

"Come back. Help me talk to Skeptic Levertup. He's the worst of them."

He saw her shudder delicately, black hair lifting from her shoulders in echo. "He's your Skeptic," Rael reminded Barac. "You deal with him."

Barac allowed a little of his frustration to leak into the M'hir and touch his cousin's outer thoughts. She scowled, slamming down her shields until almost invisible to his other sense.

"They can't detect your image 'port, Rael," he assured her. "And they can't eavesdrop."

"I'm aware of their limitations, Cousin." Rael looked up and met his eyes. Hers, dark and expressive, were unexpectedly troubled. "It doesn't matter. Don't you see? The Clan Watchers are bad enough. To have Levertup and his kind recording each and every time I use the M'hir? Making lists—having meetings about this level or that power flux? There's no privacy anymore, Barac. I can't be what I was. Not here."

Barac made a throwaway gesture. "You can't be what never existed, Rael," he said very gently. "It was all a lie. The Clan were never alone in the M'hir. We never owned or created it. As for the Watchers?" He hesitated. It was unseemly and potentially dangerous to talk about Them. They tended to notice. Barac went on recklessly: "Maybe they approve—"

"Or don't care," Rael almost whispered, her voice trailing away. They were both less relieved than unnerved by the continued silence from Those Who Watched.

There were two, distinct and opposite, kinds of Clan Watchers: those who guarded the unborn and those who guarded the M'hir itself. The first were known, being posts of honor within a House: individual Clan assigned to act if a Joining between a Chosen pair was severed during pregnancy, to attempt to save the mind of the infant despite the loss of the mother's into the M'hir.

The other type of Watcher, the feared and disembodied voices of the M'hir, seemed not to know themselves. Oh, there were plenty of theories, none provable. Scholars hypothesized that, in some individuals, a portion of the mind lingered within the M'hir waking or sleeping, forming a complex awareness completely separate from the individual's consciousness, possessing the knowledge of that individual but none of the personality. Some went so far as to speculate the Watchers were the next step in the evolution of the Clan, the M'hiray, beings closer to a true and continuous existence in that other space.

Most Clan, though they wouldn't admit it, believed the Watchers were their dead, whose minds, once dissolved into the M'hir, were locked in an endless vigil guarding that space.

No matter if ghost or unconscious state, the numberless Watchers were lightning-quick to sound the alarm to Council if Clan or alien transgressed borders or behaviors they themselves established—a territorial instinct ruling Clan Councils had found very useful indeed.

As part of his final testing to become a Scout, Barac had touched the thoughts of a Watcher, a process; he'd been told, of assessment and identification. Its strange, almost hollow questioning had left an intangible echo within his mind, as if dreamed rather than experienced.

He shook off the memory. "Sira believes Copelup. He claims the Watchers don't touch the M'hir in a way that lets them encounter the Drapsk or their machines." Barac himself doubted anything could miss the metallic stench of Drapsk technology, including that surrounding the mind-deadeners they supplied the Enforcers.

"Proving only that all we know, Cousin," Rael said sharply, "is what the Skeptics choose to tell us. Which is either insufficient, confusing, or completely incredible. And, don't forget, your Levertup is one of those who doesn't believe the Watchers exist." Rael pursed her full lips in an impression of the little Drapsk, lacking the characteristic ring of fleshy tentacles but otherwise matching his scornful expression perfectly. "'Figments of untrained imaginations. Proof, Mystic One. Show me proof!'"

Barac chuckled. "Visit me, Rael," he coaxed. "I promise not to inflict Levertup on you. It's almost time for supper here. You must be as tired as I am of eating alone."

That confession drew a smile from her. "Alone? Surely our kind hosts never leave you bereft of companionship."

"You know what I mean."

Rael's smile widened, and Barac felt a teasing sting of Power against his. "A First Scout, weary of the alien? Who'd have thought?"

"Then you'll come?"

He watched Rael's image stand, her feet on a floor he couldn't see.

"I'll be there. For supper only. Arrange it for two

hours from now." He tasted suspicion suddenly. "You promise—no Drapsk?"

Barac gave her his most sincere smile as he watched the Clanswoman vanish.

Almost immediately, a stern, high-pitched voice rang out from under the bed platform. "I am not pleased you are using falsehood to lure her here, Mystic One. Not pleased at all! What will her reaction be? Have you thought of that? She tends to highly emotional responses, you know."

"My dear Copelup," Barac said soothingly, hurrying to help the small being extricate himself. It had been a tight fit. "We agreed it was time to bring Rael back. Trust me. I know my cousin. She'll understand."

Three of the Drapsk's distractingly red and mobile tentacles disappeared into his mouth, the rest forming what could be described as a stylized mustache over his upper lip. There were no other features on the round white globe that served the Drapsk for a face. Copelup's antennae, bright yellow and plumed, rose to a quivering height Barac thought might express determination. Or the Drapsk could be reading an olfactory message wafting through the room on one of the omnipresent drafts.

He could also, Barac decided glumly, simply be stretching, after being folded so long under the bed. After three months living with the species, the Clansman was only sure that Drapsk were never obvious.

The tentacles popped out again, a cue sometimes signifying the Skeptic had reached some decision, or had given up the effort. "I most certainly hope so, Mystic One," the Drapsk stated primly. "And may I remind you, in any discord between our Mystic Ones, my esteemed colleagues—including Levertup—will have no hesitation in supporting the other Mystic One's position over yours. No matter who is right. I trust you will not be offended."

Barac, unChosen and sud, lifted his shoulders and let them drop. "Why would I be, Copelup?" he said, tasting the bitter, accustomed truth. "Among my kind, who is right always depends on Power."

Chapter 2

"WE can always depend on Huido—and his need for truffles," I offered, trying to hide a smile. One of the unexpected results of our time in the jungles of Pocular had been the introduction of the rare Merle truffle, a native edible fungus I found less appealing than C-rations, to the *Claws & Jaws*. Huido had somehow turned the black lumps into a must-have delicacy for several species on Plexis. Or so I was told. The Carasian certainly imported enough of them to keep Withren's people, the Fak-ad-sa'it, busy digging in their meadows, at a price that made it worth their time.

Morgan grunted something incomprehensible, keeping his attention firmly—or at least ostensibly so—on the display in front of us both. As this was an alarmingly symmetrical comparison between operating costs (rising) and our credit (dwindling), I found myself in the novel position of feeling I might know better than my Chosen, Master Trader or not. Ferrying dried fungi to Plexis wasn't glamorous, but if Morgan hadn't canceled that lucrative contract, we wouldn't be sitting here worrying about the critical refit suddenly needed by the *Fox*'s aging translight drive—as if her ailing starboard thrusters hadn't been enough.

My amusement at this turn of events was likely rippling along our link despite my best efforts, but I couldn't help it. A routine cargo run was as new and exciting to me as everything else Morgan and I did together, with the bonus of being safe and profitable at the same time. What more could one want? Apparently, Morgan saw a lack in that life I could not. Or Humans were simply every bit as restless a species as I'd been told.

It's not . . . "that, Sira." Morgan's mind voice slipped into speech—a habit of which he was largely unconscious. It was a sign he was absorbing some of my Clan ways, even as I took on more of his Human ones. A fair trade, I thought, smiling to myself. Of course, among Clan, such slips were a sign of deliberate secrecy—it being supposedly easier to hide the truth out loud—or a disrespectful reversion to childhood ways. Being quite foolishly fond of the sound of my Human's voice, I chose not to correct him.

"It's not? Were you not the one who said you'd had enough of the—monotony—of running between Pocular and Plexis?"

Morgan turned to look up at me, an impish grin lighting his eyes. Endlessly fascinating, how their remarkable blue varied with his mood. "I believe I used somewhat stronger language."

"So did Huido," I remembered.

A raised brow. "Who had no problem finding another carrier the next day. Probably an entire fleet, by now, seeing how enthusiastically the Fak-ad-sa'it have embraced the concept of hunting prey that doesn't hunt back. We spent more than our share of time plying back and forth to fill Huido's menu, my Lady Witch." Morgan's eyes grew solemn. "And more than enough findown on Pocular, don't you think?"

"Oh," was all I managed, surprised again by his empathy. Nightmares visited me on that world, nightmares I couldn't stop. We'd never discussed it—I now understood there hadn't been any need. I drew my hand in the air to gently trace the lines of unseen tension around his head, neck, and shoulders, drawing them down and away with a touch of Power. "So, Master Trader," I asked him, mouth close to his ear, "where do we find our next vastly profitable cargo?"

Morgan's hand slipped warm and strong behind my neck, his head turning so my last words brushed against his smiling lips.

My hair enclosed us both.

"So?"

"So . . . ?"

"So—what next?"

At Morgan's sudden smile, I took a firm step backward and finished fastening my coveralls. "You know perfectly well what I mean, Human. If we aren't reconsidering Huido's contract, what are we going to do?" I didn't bother saying what we both knew: that only Huido would chance a cargo with us, given the present state of the *Fox*.

Other opportunities had been as far apart as their star systems. We'd made some successful trades on our own, keeping afloat, but Morgan's former clients seemed to have vanished in the last couple of months. Certainly none appeared to have shipments needing the famed luck of the *Silver Fox* and her Captain.

Was it my presence? Gossip spread translight, especially among Traders. We hadn't bothered fabricating a life history for me, which meant that, so far as Morgan's business associates knew, the Human might have grown me in a tank. Morgan had shrugged when I'd voiced this suspicion. The *Silver Fox* would find new clients, if that was the case.

I walked over to the table, tracing its edge with my fingers as I let myself be frustrated. I might be the acknowledged leader of my entire race, but, to date, that lofty accomplishment had produced only visitors with complaints, most arriving when and where we least wanted them. Payment? The Clan, with the exception of the self-styled and unstable society on Acranam, existed as independent families; no one "paid" another of our kind for service. That was what Humans were for.

My House, di Sarc? It was wealthy, but its more portable riches had left with my father, the exiled Jarad di Sarc; no one on Council, including its newest Speaker, was inclined to invite him back for an accounting. I'd last seen his Chosen, my mother, Mirim sud Teerac, at the Clan gathering on Camos. She'd been compelled there, like all our kind, by the Watchers, but hadn't spoken to anyone, including her daughters, disappearing at the end to wherever she now chose to live. I presumed she had the wherewithal to keep herself however she wished. If her lifestyle didn't involve replacement parts for starships, it didn't interest me.

There had been other assets, legitimately mine and so Morgan's as my Chosen. Property. Business interests. The sort of thing less than easily pilfered by someone disgraced and perhaps fearing reprisal, but now all gone, sold to pay a debt. My Human hadn't commented when I'd entrusted the substantial sum to Sector Chief Bowman. He knew how I felt about those twenty-two shattered lives. The Human telepaths had suffered because of an experiment I'd started without compassion or compunction—that they'd been victimized by others of my kind made no difference to my guilt. I'd been the one to put them on a list, ready for use; it was only just I help their families with the cost of caring for their mindless husks.

In that, the Clan way was cleaner. When the mind was lost in the M'hir, the body was sent to follow. But the Human med-techs refused to believe the Clan Healer, Cenebar di Teerac, that these individuals would never recover, that their personalities had been erased forever.

Courtesy of my father, who saw any mingling of Clan and Human as obscene. Especially mine with Morgan. My fingers became a fist.

Mind-speech, soft and familiar, wove peace into my troubled thoughts: *What's done's done, chit. Enough dark memories for one morning.*

I focused on the here and now, smiling up into Morgan's perceptive eyes. The Human hardly needed the invisible link binding us to read my mind. "My apologies, Captain. Where were we?"

He beckoned me to follow him out of our cabin. "I've had an idea. What do you think of setting course for—" The beginning of his announcement took us into the corridor; its abrupt end was ample forewarning all wasn't as it should be.

Although no warning could have prepared me to face what filled most of the right-hand corridor. Or, rather, *who*. A pulsating mass pressed against floor, wall, and ceiling, as though the being had forced itself to fit within our parameters. Five long, fibrous-appearing arms lay in parallel along the near wall, as if we'd surprised them reaching toward our cabin door. There were no other obvious features or body structures. With the exception of the arms, the whole seemed insubstantial, as if darkness had been poured into this shape and left without form, only a glistening, as if wet or coated in the finest possible scales.

Morgan's arm lifted into a valiant, if improbable, barrier between me and our latest uninvited guest. I put my hand on his wrist and gently brought it down. *Rugheran*, I sent to him, as tightly as my mind could focus.

Despite this care, the flesh—if that's what composed this being—quivered in response.

And more. A blurred mix of /joy/satisfaction/~!~/ curiosity/ flooded my mind, effortlessly breaching any shielding or defense I might believe I possessed, reaching Morgan through our link in the M'hir. For that was the rightful place of the Rugheran, the species owning a physical connection to the M'hir greater than any my kind had imagined possible, traveling inside it like birds through air. I'd met one once, at the Drapsk

Festival. My hair lifted from my back and shoulders, as if the Rugheran's message instilled it with static. I grabbed it with both hands to keep it out of my eyes.

"I think it likes us," I ventured hopefully, unsure of Morgan's reaction to this latest intrusion.

"It could learn to knock, too," Morgan muttered under his breath, but I heard the growing wonder in his voice as he surveyed the being stuffed into his ship. "Rugheran. Sira. Do you realize what this means? First contact . . ."

I opened my mouth to contradict his humanocentric view of things, given the Heerii Drapsk had found the Rugheran homeworld and I, another non-Human, had already had a more-or-less successful encounter with a member of the species. For all I knew, I thought with sudden suspicion, this one. Then I closed my mouth, alarmed to see Morgan on the move. He stopped closer to our latest guest, his hands low and held open in a gesture a smart primate might deduce was non-threatening, but of what use to greet an amorphous M'hir being I couldn't begin to guess. But he was a Master Trader and had dealt with aliens long before I'd ever left the Cloisters. I trusted his instincts.

And my own. "Keep out of reach of the arms, Jason," I said, watching those appendages warily. They hadn't moved, but I'd held one on my shoulder and knew their speed and strength—and substantial weight, for all they appeared flimsy.

He nodded, standing still. "Can you communicate with it?"

"Communicate?" I considered the mass of dark

flesh doubtfully and raised one brow. "And say what, exactly?"

"Hello."

I'd decided several weeks ago—following a memorable misunderstanding about Morgan's attachment to some dusty antique entertainment vids which no longer fit our reader—that it could take lifetimes to fully understand Humans, if it were possible at all. Still, I kept trying. "Hello?" I echoed. "Why? It's hardly necessary to exchange inanities with a creature that may not even have language."

Morgan didn't bother to look at me, but I felt a touch of impatience. " 'Hello' is necessary. It represents fundamental acknowledgments." He lifted his right hand, raising a finger for each as he itemized: "One, both parties recognize the existence of the other; two, we're both prepared to communicate; and three, there's a mutual agreement not to run away screaming."

His last point cued me to something I'd missed until now: a sliver of fear coming from my Human, a perfectly natural anxiety about this huge "thing" on his ship and its intentions. He was trying to hide that fear from me, and perhaps from himself, but it was real.

"A Rugheran can't survive long away from its kind," I said, keeping my voice as matter-of-fact as though I reported on some valve or part on the *Fox*. "I suggest we assume the 'Hello' part of this conversation had occurred and move on to the next."

"What does it want?"

"The last one wanted me to send it home—" Before

Morgan could begin to speak his instant concern, I continued, "—but that hardly seems likely this time. Maybe it wants to trade."

That straightened Morgan from what was beginning to look ominously like his defensive crouch. "Trade," he repeated softly, as if the word had a flavor. "But for what? You said they live in the M'hir."

"Actually, they live on a planet not too far from . . ." *Ettler's Planet*, my mind voice continued after I shut my mouth on the words, betraying me completely. My hair fell limp and defeated around my shoulders, a stray lock landing across one eye. I shoved it aside.

"And you were going to tell me—when?" This in full "Captain Morgan" voice, the one usually reserved for the first moments after I'd done something memorable, like dropping the old vids into the recycler. His blue eyes were glacial.

The Rugheran obligingly sent another wave of /joy/satisfaction/~!~/curiosity/ sloshing through the now-strained link between us.

As if it knew.

INTERLUDE

"We might as well close, Hom Huido. For tonight, at least. Don't you think that's best?"

Over two dozen eyes stopped their restless examination of an equal number of simmering—and dented—pots to focus on the slight Human standing just out of reach, arms trembling beneath a tray crammed with cocktails. The somewhat random garnishing of each drink implied excessive speed in their manufacture. "The desertion of one fish-faced idiot will not shut down the *Claws & Jaws*, Ansel," the Carasian rumbled irritably. "Keep the drinks flowing until I can get something on the tables. They'll be happy enough."

"Until we run out of liquor," Ansel muttered to himself. He seemed to hesitate, then ventured timidly: "Do I have permission to open the vault if we do?"

The Carasian's left and right upper handling claws almost dropped the spoons they held. "You do not! Get out there—and start putting extra ice in those drinks before you bankrupt me worse than that creteng excretion of a chef!"

Ansel left, moving as quickly as possible through the bustling crowd of sous chefs, bakers, cleaners, and anxious servers, the latter lurking in any available space that kept them out of the dining room. Things were, to put it mildly, getting ugly out there. Chef Neltare couldn't have found a busier night to abandon the restaurant, or a touchier crowd to leave foodless than this already dissatisfied group of theatergoers. Opening night for *Hamlet the Scat* had flopped like the spectacle it wasn't.

Unfortunately, a gold air tag guaranteed a paying customer, not one with patience.

While things simmered, including a pot of prawlies that had finally given up trying to squirm to imagined freedom, Huido poured a beer into his upper left handling claw, transferring the soothing, cool liquid into his mouth with a practiced slurp. Single greatest invention of the Human species, he reminded himself. He'd managed without a Master Fool at the stovetop before now. Mind you, then most of his customers had worn spacer coveralls of the faded variety and tended to order any food that went well with beer. And rarely tipped.

He sighed, a rain-on-plas sound. The staff could keep up using some prepared courses. He need only offer a couple of the favorites as specials to appease his fussier—and most prone to gossip—clients. Give them something memorable and expensive—the two-hour delay would soon be forgotten.

With luck.

Something he'd been running short of lately.

"Excuse me. Hom Huido?"

One eye swung back and down to target the source of the quiet voice: Ruti, one of the more recent additions to his kitchen staff. Small, yet sturdily-built, with bright dark eyes and short, even darker hair, she passed well enough for Human to those without his finer senses. He remembered vividly when she'd arrived—yet another of those days when the universe begrudged a simple restaurateur any peace. . . .

"Hom Huido. Come quickly. There's someone to see you at the service entrance."

"Deal with it. I'm a little busy, Ansel," the Carasian rumbled, one clawtip entering the code to his private apartment. His staff knew better than to interrupt him when the restaurant wasn't open, especially since the installation of a proper pool—and the arrival of its delectably insatiable inhabitants.

Ansel, normally the most easily intimidated being on Plexis, grabbed Huido's nearest handling claw and began to pull. While the gesture had as much effect as if the Human tried to move a bulkhead, the Carasian was surprised enough to send a few eyes his way. "What's the matter?"

"You have to come yourself."

More eyes reluctantly left their lustful fix on the code pad to join the cluster studying the Human. Definite agitation. "Has the accountant missed a payment to the station?" Huido asked reasonably enough. Plexis wasn't patient when it came to fees or taxes. Her collectors tended to be opinionated and prone to blustering—until one of the staff brought Huido. Some weeks, he sighed to himself, it seemed he was constantly in demand to intimidate some biped or other—not that the activity lacked charm, but there was only so much time in a day. More eyes shifted back to the door.

"No. No. You must come!" Ansel dashed away, as if certain this uncharacteristic secrecy would pique the Carasian's curiosity.

It did, although Huido rattled and clanked warningly behind the Human. The Carasian could move relatively quietly on his spongy feet, but preferred not to waste any opportunity for self-expression.

When he reached the service entrance, however, the familiar and ominous tang of Clan *grist* stopped him in his tracks. The source was a small being, deceptively Human-looking, standing just inside the doors to the serviceway behind the restaurant.

Ansel, the doddering old fool, had both hands on her shoulders, looking pleadingly his way. "This is Ruti," the Human said quickly, in a low voice though it was too early for the kitchen staff to be at work. "She's all alone." Ansel paused, wrinkled eyelids blinking furiously as was his habit when troubled. "She doesn't even have luggage, Hom Huido," he concluded, as if this was the hallmark of imminent tragedy.

The child, for it was apparently such, ignored Ansel, gazing up at Huido with no particular expression on her face beyond polite attention and a natural enough caution, considering she confronted a being who looked better suited to knocking down trees than slicing onions. "Carasain. You're the friend of Sira di

Sarc." Statement, not question. "I claim refuge in her name."

Typical Clan arrogance. Huido was tempted to point out the absence of an air tag on her cheek to his servant, abundant proof this Ruti had found her way onto Plexis without passing through any air lock or alerting security. Only the Clan disregarded both physics and bureaucracy. Then again, poor Ansel probably wouldn't care, obviously afflicted by his species' excessive parental instincts. To his credit, the elderly Human knew the appetites of the underbelly of Plexis too well to believe it safe for anyone alone.

Huido, on the other claw, knew the Clan well enough to dismiss that particular worry. Morgan had told him how the Clan maintained few family ties, deeming them unnecessary. More significantly, even young members of that species possessed mental abilities they willingly used to smooth their lives while disrupting others'.

Huido did not fall into the trap of judging one species by another's standards. On the other claw, he usually knew precisely what to do with the Clan—offer the high end of the menu or the exit—but this one?

"Are you going to make me stand here all day, Hom Huido?"

Ansel gave him that pleading look; the child, a challenging one. The Carasian's first impulse, to send her back out the door, faded as he focused on her face and sampled her *grist* more carefully. Something was wrong with it. Ah. He'd smelled this particular underscent before.

Rage.

It didn't take much to guess she stood in the service entrance of the *Claws & Jaws* against her will, despite her Power.

"Come with me," Huido grumbled, turning to lead the pair to his apartment, cursing himself all the while for having hearts far too soft for his own good. He keyed in the code, careful neither could see it, then dismissed Ansel with a claw snap once the door opened. "In here," he told the Clan child. "Mind where you step."

The doorway led to another, the space between the two merely a featureless box. A relatively new innovation, and one capable of charbroiling the uninvited, but Huido didn't bother sharing that information. He hurried his unwelcome guest through the outer room he kept for entertaining, taking her through a second locked doorway to his inner sanctum.

As they entered, Huido kept a pair of eyes on his guest, interested in her reaction, but most glanced wistfully at the waves tossing against the imported rocks which formed the division between the pool and the small irregular patch of dry floor.

Rows of shiny black eyes began appearing in the froth, as his always-alert wives floated closer and closer. It wasn't so much curiosity at the alien visitor in their haven as appetite.

Something he'd willingly share with the Clan child, if she seemed any kind of threat.

"Sit here." As Ruti obediently found and sat on the only piece of Human-suitable furnishings, an easi-rest Huido kept for the only other being permitted into his sanctuary, the Carasian arranged himself comfortably on a rock carved specifically to his bulk, his claws resting on the pebbled floor. "You do realize I know what you are."

She nodded, slowly. They stared at one another for a moment, the Carasian being naturally well-suited to the task and the Clan child seemingly determined to keep her poise. Suddenly, she drew a sharp breath and her dark eyebrows met in the middle. "Your mind is utter chaos," she stated with disgust.

Huido rattled contentedly. "So I'm told. Now, why would Sira send you to me—"

"I didn't say she did." Quick and angry. "I doubt the First Chosen of di Sarc knows I exist. But I've tasted her memories. We all did, that day on Camos when she forced her strange ideas into our minds: the Clan being doomed, needing aliens, joining the Trade Pact. I may never have met you before, Hom Huido, but I 'remember' you. A little. Enough to know where you are is—it's somewhere safe." Her voice turned almost sullen. "That's why I came here."

No missing the rage, adult in size and almost painful in intensity. Huido felt echoing vibrations through the floor. His wives could detect the child's *grist* as well as he; their reaction was to tap the rocks to summon their mate. At this truly glorious stage of their lives, any strong emotion aroused their passions. He shifted, his immediate and healthy response making the rock seat less than accommodating. An unexpected complication, if not entirely unpleasant.

"So may I stay?"

"This isn't a hotel. Any why should I let you bring whatever trouble follows you to my pool?"

Her eyes slid past him to examine the water, then back. "I know this isn't a hotel," she said, her voice almost firm enough to be convincing. "But I'm not being followed by any trouble, Hom Huido. The First Chosen of—of my House sent me to this station, expecting me to find a place to stay for the next few weeks. That's all. But I didn't know what Plexis was like, that there'd be questions and air tags. I tried to obtain one—I'm not a fool—but these beings began asking for information I'm not allowed to give. Then I remembered you." The last word didn't break, not quite, but the hint of imminent panic was there.

A young Clan who didn't know Plexis. "You're from Acranam," Huido said with no doubt whatsoever, using his greater claw to snap a signal to quiet his amorous wives.

"Yes, but how—"

"I know Acranam. Too well." The Carasian heaved to his feet. "I will not tolerate a threat to my blood brother or his mate."

"I'm no threat—" She half stood, as if to run away or, more likely, disappear into thin air. "All I know of Sira or her Chosen is from her sharing. I was too far back in the crowd to even see her for myself. Why would I mean harm to them?"

"Then stay."

Ruti blinked at that, tossing her head as if confused. "But I thought you said . . ."

"The *Claws & Jaws* is a fine restaurant, without servos or automated pap. My table settings are works of art, not that recycled junk, which means dishes that need washing. If you aren't above such a task, Ruti of Acranam?"

Confusion turned into something else. Huido had fully expected offense and outrage—this looked more like the dawning of hope. "And stay—here?" she repeated, as if uncertain. "I don't understand."

"If you are no threat, I gain a dishwasher. If you are?" Huido tilted his head from shoulder to shoulder in a shrug. "You stay where I can watch you."

Perhaps to a Clan, such frankness was reassuring. Regardless of why, Ruti had smiled and nodded.

Since that day, Huido had almost forgotten Ruti's existence. She'd moved in with the other permanent staff, in return for cleanup in the kitchen and running errands for the rest. He'd expected protest over the work—at minimum, some signs of Clan xenophobia— but in all this time, she'd seemed content, setting to work with a will. No one had complained of her. Indeed, no one mentioned her at all.

Huido, unfamiliar with younger humanoids, had wondered if this was normal.

Still, he himself was guilty of ignoring the Clan child, so smoothly had she blended into the daily routine of the kitchen. Had he also neglected a potential threat? Of all the days for more trouble to arise—he drew air to bellow, then stopped.

A few more eyes followed the first, studying what Ruti was patiently holding up for his inspection. "That's a soufflé," he said slowly.

Her face was usually pale. Now, twin spots of red

highlighted her cheeks, either heat from the nearby overworked stove or embarrassment. "Yes, Hom Huido. With trumquins. There was an order for one. You were—busy . . ."

Huido turned down the stove so he could give this amazing development his complete attention. "You can make a soufflé—with trumquins. Do you also know which customers can eat one of those without melting their digestive tracts and leaving me at the mercy of their surviving kin?"

The dish was heavy, despite the apparent fluffiness of its contents, but her grip didn't let it waver. "Scats and Whirtles, Hom Huido. I have been paying attention."

"While mopping the floors."

"Yes. I've—"

He lowered his voice to barely audible and interrupted: "Paying attention, is it? You little Clan sneak. You've been prying inside the head of the Neblokan chef all this time, haven't you?"

Dark brows creased together, but she didn't deny it. "Noisy creature," Ruti told him, her voice pitched as low and aimed at his elbow. "It would have been more work to keep out his thoughts. But he knew the craft. Almost as well as I do. I cooked at home."

"You're telling me a Clan does manual labor."

"Cooking isn't manual labor," Ruti said firmly and with every indication of sincerity. "It's an art form. My—House—is renowned for our ability."

"Would this have anything to do with why you chose my door to haunt of all Plexis?"

Definitely a glowing pink blush this time. "It might."

Huido snapped his claw to bring the nearest server rushing over. "Take this trumquin soufflé over to the table—?" he paused.

"Twenty-five", Rubi supplied without hesitation and with the beginnings of a smile.

"Twenty-five. And keep an eye on the Whirtles to make sure they don't die before paying their bill."

The server looked askance at Ruti, but hurried off with the dish.

"Maybe this isn't going to be a total disaster of a day after all, little Fem," Huido pronounced. "What other useful tidbits did you steal from that excrement's excuse for a brain? Everything you'd need for a promotion from washing dishes, I assume?"

Ruti really did have the kind of smile Humans called mischievous.

For her sake, Huido hoped she'd learned very well indeed, given the Carasian now understood why the last available Master Chef on Plexis had so abruptly lost his good sense and decided to serve his fellow beings a little too literally.

Clan were infamous for manipulating others to get what they wanted.

Huido's eyes focused on Ruti, delivering multiple images of her confident expression.

Did she know Carasians never forgave being used?

Chapter 3

THE *Fox* was free of visitors, if not their conse-quence. The Rugheran had stayed only a handful of seconds longer, the reason for its departure as much a mystery as the reason it arrived in the first place. Let alone how.

Which hardly mattered to me. Morgan was not happy. His displeasure sent a discordance through our Joining, like a sound that, however faint, clenched one's teeth. Perhaps this explained why most Clan pairs lived as far apart from one another as possible, something I didn't want for us. But how would it be to have this intimate connection to the feelings of an-other, if that other had no warmer feelings than this to share?

There could be nothing worse, I thought, then looked at Morgan's grim face and knew I was wrong. It was infinitely worse to be connected, with love at its core, and have wounded one another.

"A new sentient species," he was saying, in a clipped, angry voice. "A chance to be the first to trade with them. Explain to me again why you decided not to mention knowing their location?"

"Why?" I countered, rising to stand. We'd taken our argument into the control room, sitting like civilized beings, he on the pilot's couch and I on what had been the copilot's when the *Fox* operated with a full crew, but was now mine. I wasn't feeling particularly civilized after half an hour of debate. "I've told you why and you aren't hearing me. The Rugheran homeworld is not just close to Ettler's Planet. It's close to Acranam. Too close! It's within their range. Many of them wouldn't need a pathway to reach it."

"Since when do Clan care about aliens—"

"The Clan care about you!" I protested, cutting him off in midsentence. "And where do you think most of our enemies are now? Acranam!"

"Sira . . ." He somehow put a world of frustration into my name, then leaned forward, fixing me with those penetrating blue eyes. "Why are you so worried? You're their leader—"

"No, I'm Speaker for the Clan Council. The same Council Acranam rejects. Jason, don't you see it? There's no way I can guarantee my safety from them, let alone yours. We can't trust them."

"Then we'll be careful," Morgan countered impatiently, throwing up his hands. "Traders always are— or they don't last long. Thanks to you, we know what, or rather who, to avoid: the Clan. Nothing new in that, my Lady Witch. I don't see the problem."

"I do." I sank back down. "I see so many, Jason, and so much to fear. I'm not like you, not anymore," I said, knowing he felt the despair suddenly filling me, but unable to hide it. "I can't take risks. Not with so much to lose."

Sira. Just my name, but with it an upwelling of joy to catch my breath in my throat. Aloud, though his eyes gleamed, "I would never put you—or us—in jeopardy. But there's a difference between a foolish risk and a calculated one. The *Fox* is a trader. *We're* traders, Sira. The Rugheran homeworld is the chance of a lifetime—do yo know how long it's been since a new system was added to the trade routes? New materials, new forms of art, information, culture—it's the reason I chose this life in the first place. To roam the stars and discover what's out here! What could be better?"

"We don't know if we can talk to them," I protested, even as part of me responded to his enthusiasm—shared it. Perhaps I was, slightly, curious myself.

A flaw to be resisted, like a fascination with cliffs.

"Trust me," Morgan urged. "Trust yourself. Don't you see it? No one but you and I together could do this! Why else did the Rugheran come to us?"

"Good question," I muttered darkly.

Morgan leaned back, his couch curling to accommodate him. "Did you sense any harm from it?" he insisted, a rather premature note of triumph in his voice.

Mine was decidedly surly, but I didn't care. "How should I know? Maybe the happiest Rugherans are the hungry ones."

"We can take the *Fox* to Drapskii," my Chosen continued, warming to his theme. "Get her refitted there—I assume our credit's still good with the

Makii—while we talk to your friends about the Rugherans."

I saw another possibility and brightened. "We could leave the *Fox* and take the *Makmora!*"

My Human's lips pressed together in a straight, thin line, then pushed out again. He seemed to be waiting, his lips repeating their interesting new movement, nostrils flaring slightly each time.

He didn't need to speak, and I didn't need to dip into his thoughts. Ossirus give me patience.

"Of course, who needs a mammoth freighter with four hundred beings on board dedicated to preserving our lives at any cost when we could go by ourselves in the *Fox*. Alone." I'd meant it to sound light and humorous; my voice broke shamefully at the end, making it anything but.

I stared at my hands involuntarily gripping one another, holding in my presence within our connection just as tightly. "What has happened to me?"

"What's wrong?" he demanded, sitting up straight.

"I've—I've become a coward," I said it with a kind of sick wonder, the way one might confess an addiction, as if it must belong to some other, weaker self. "I'm terrified of everything outside this ship, Jason. Is this being Chosen? I knew I'd become more cautious— it's only reasonable—but this . . . ?"

Hands wrapped around mine—warm, strong hands. I raised my eyes to meet Morgan's. He crouched on his heels before me, eyes full of compassion. I felt his Power trying to offer comfort as well, but kept myself and my misery impervious. He nodded, as if acknowledging my need for my own pain, then spoke in a quiet, steady voice, words that didn't make sense at first. "I can't know what you should feel as a Chosen Clan, Sira. But fear? It comes with the territory. You aren't alone in it."

Locks of my hair slipped over my arms to stroke his cheeks, then rested on his shoulders in quiet curls of red-gold. "I don't understand," I answered numbly, ready to admit when I was lost.

Morgan's thumbs rubbed gently over my clenched fingers. "Perhaps, in this, a Human has the advantage, my Lady Witch," he mused slowly. "Humans are brought up with the literature and legends of love. We hope it lives up to its promise; we dream all our lives of finding that one great love. And we're warned of its cost if we do."

I mouthed the word. "Cost?"

"To risk love is to risk loss. The greater the love . . . ?" He brought my hands to his lips.

"The greater the loss," I finished reluctantly. No wonder Humans seemed to live under a shadow at times. "You aren't reassuring, Jason."

"I can't be. If I measured my love for you in terms of that fear," the Human said so quietly I had to strain to catch the words, "I wouldn't be able to take another breath, dooming us both." His eyes devoured mine. Louder, firmer: "Sira. Accept, as I do, that what is *now*—" his fingers tightened on mine, "—is what matters. It's all we can control. It's all we should try to control. Do you understand that?"

In words? Slippery, misleading things. But there was more. Morgan's thoughts abruptly whirled around and through mine, providing a maelstrom of concepts. I gasped under the impact, fighting not to keep them out, which I could have done with ease, but to sort them into coherence. The harder task. The worthwhile one.

I fixed my eyes on his, turning my hands so our fingers intertwined, willing to also grasp what he offered—no matter how alien—if I was able. "You'd prefer I'd be as willing to spend my life now, as I was before our Joining—despite knowing you'd die as well." I shook my head in disbelief. "How can you feel that way?"

"Because otherwise, you turn us into different people." Morgan's hands loosened and withdrew. "And risk losing more than our lives." His eyes were somber now, as though my reaction pained him in some way I couldn't feel.

What I did feel was the cold emptiness of my hands and frustration with his Human mysticism. "Only death loses this," I said roughly, then widened my awareness of our link through the M'hir until close to drowning myself in Morgan's thoughts and feelings, involuntarily matching the rhythm of my heart to the slower, stronger beats of his. It caused him discomfort—the Human mind had never adapted to such a link with another's, let alone the M'hir itself.

At the same time, it exposed me to depths I would never reveal to anyone else.

Explaining, I supposed, why he smiled. "This is what makes us the same as other Joined pairs," my Human said, with a nod. Then he raised one hand, and lightly ran his fingertips down the side of my face, as if needing the touch to know its shape. With the touch came an inner warmth, a caring so deep tears welled up in my eyes and tumbled over my cheeks before his fingertips rested on my lips. "This," Morgan went on, more or less steadily, "is what makes us different. Love came first. Now, do you understand?"

I wasn't sure. The Council preferred any M'hiray Joined to live apart, unless performing their function to produce offspring. The distancing enhanced their Power through the M'hir, an enhancement which perhaps not coincidentally enriched the food source for the living things within the M'hir itself. An uncomfortable, possibly unsafe thought, that somehow our pairings were being distorted by the needs of others.

Togetherness such as ours was brand new, yet ancient. Those who dared, said the Clan had been like this once, with pairings built from more than the instinct for Power. The evolution of our kind into the M'hiray, those who could enter the M'hir, had changed that; selection for Power had ended it.

"You're warning me that while our Joining will last until death, your—love—might not?" This would have sounded better if I hadn't hiccuped over the last word. "That if I change in some way, you no longer care—"

"No, never!" Morgan denied hastily, looking quite reassuringly horrified. "I'm only saying we're both afraid of taking chances, because we'd lose one another. That's natural, Sira, but we can't allow it to influence our decisions about how we live." He hesitated, then went on in an earnest tone: "We can only live now, Sira. And living includes taking worthwhile chances."

"You want me to be a cliff dancer," I said with sudden, rather alarmed, comprehension. I felt him remember the little animals who lived near my former home, the Cloisters, how their mating behavior included a daring and sometimes fatal display along the sheer cliff face. It seemed only those most willing to tempt their fate were able to attract mates.

"Not quite," he said, smiling slightly. "A cliff dancer with an antigrav harness. And a partner."

I could manage that, I thought cautiously, drawing a deep breath. Then I gave my Human a stern look: "As long as you remember the first one to fall takes the other as well."

You don't become either coward or cliff dancer in one conversation. As we set course for Drapskii, I considered both. Morgan gave me room for my thoughts, busying himself with records from historical first contact situations, his presence becoming a distant glow of happy preoccupation.

I stayed on the bridge, nominally in charge of the *Fox*, which gave me a chance to talk to the ship. It didn't matter that I spoke and my respondent blinked a few lights in an order totally unrelated to my meaning. I'd seen Morgan do the same and seem comforted. It was my habit now as well.

As long as he wasn't anywhere nearby to catch me at it.

"You'll only get a minor refit," I insisted, having already enumerated the list of what had to be done and what could be left until we had a bit more in the holds for credit. The Makii would likely give me anything I asked, but being indebted to the Drapsk had its own price. "If we ask for all the repairs you need," I warned the *Fox*, "they'll doubtless smile, suck a few tentacles, and suggest I be a Mystic One while the work is underway. You don't know them like I do. It's amazing how many polite and inevitable ways they can find to interfere with a straightforward, common-sense plan."

A soft beep seemed to answer.

"No, really," I assured the ship. I lay back on the copilot's couch and let it curl up under my knees. "I love them dearly, but getting anything done around the Makii is like building a tower of feathers on a windy day. You'd better supply glue."

Beep.

"Yes, they mean well, but if Copelup even suspected I was heading toward the Rugheran system—"

BEEP!

The ship had never interrupted me before. I glanced at the com panel and realized I'd been so preoccupied I'd missed an incoming signal. Not surprising, since we were translight and such signals were notoriously expensive propositions for the sender—unless the sender was close by. Interesting choice: urgent or we had more company.

I lunged for the board, summoning Morgan as I did so, having learned not to simply *reach* and 'port him to me when something like this happened. The last time, he'd been using a plasma welder to fasten two critical parts. Needless to say, it was a good thing the *Fox* had automated fire control in the main holds.

Coming, he replied.

"This is the *Silver Fox*, Karolus Registry, Sira Morgan speaking," I told the com, quite pleased by the professionalism in my voice. At the same time, I sent a tendril of Power searching outward, as Morgan was doubtless doing. Nothing. So. Urgent it was. But who?

A blast of static, until I refined the settings. Then a woman's voice came through the speakers, clear, crisp, and familiar: "Bowman. Sorry for the intrusion, Fem Morgan. We need to talk. Would you prefer us to dock or—" the suggestion of a throaty chuckle "—will you 'pop' over yourselves?"

Much as I admired Sector Chief Lydis Bowman, and valued the work of her Trade Pact Enforcers, I scowled at the panel. So much for my scan of our surroundings. Her ship, the *Conciliator*, could be right beside us but, because she and her people had mind-deadening implants, they would remain invisible to my other sense. It was more than disconcerting—there was something ominous about any technology able to counter my Power.

"I'll check with Captain Morgan," I said primly. "He should be here any moment. *Fox* out."

"Well," I told the now-silent ship, sighing fatalistically, "if you think the Drapsk can interfere with a straightforward goal—just wait until you see what Bowman can do to one."

INTERLUDE

"It's straightforward enough, Rael," Barac said, waving his curved Drapsk eating utensil in emphasis. "If this is Drapskii . . ." he stabbed a hapless vegetable and held it in midair, ". . . and this is the M'hir . . ." his other hand flailed a napkin in the general direction of the vegetable, but about an arm's length apart ". . . all we need to do is get them closer together." The Clansman draped the napkin over the vegetable and beamed across the table. "Simple."

"Simple," Copelup echoed enthusiastically, then hurriedly sucked all six tentacles as Rael's fierce glare swung back to him.

Barac had half expected his cousin to simply 'port away the instant she'd seen he'd lied and a Drapsk was joining them. Instead, Rael had set herself to eating her meal with the grim determination of someone tricked into an unpleasant social gathering.

Mind you, if she'd spoken one word, both Barac and Copelup would have been less prone to play with the vegetables.

"You have the technique from Sira," Barac went on valiantly. "Surely we can give it a try, Rael—"

The Clanswoman put down her utensil, lining it up precisely with the other six, then spent a long minute shifting her wineglass to more exactly fit the previous impression it had left in the woven layers of flower petals serving as a tablecloth.

Copelup's antennae sank lower. In fact, his entire body seemed to slump. Barac kicked the being's nearest leg under the table. The last thing they needed was for the Skeptic to hide himself in a ball of comatose Drapsk. Copelup responded to the contact with a sharp "yip" of surprise, all his tentacles flaring out in a ring of outrage. "Mystic One!"

"Which is," Rael spoke slowly, as though begrudging the need to speak at all, "the crux of our problem with your people, Copelup. We are not mystical beings. You persist in seeing us as more than we can possibly be, without paying attention to what we truly are. Barac and I came here to do a job and you turn us into some sort of idols. I, for one, find this— unwelcome."

The Drapsk leaned slightly forward, as if intent on more than Rael's words. "You are not idols. Our reverence," he paused, then went on almost reluctantly, "is not for you."

Barac felt and shared Rael's startlement. Getting real information out of a Drapsk was next to impossible. "If not for us, then for what?" he prompted, tempted to kick Copelup again in case it helped.

Copelup's antennae dipped, then rose. "It is essential that Drapskii be reconnected. It is essential that our Mystic Ones complete their task—"

The same old litany, Barac thought, grinding his teeth. "Yes, yes. We know all that—"

Rael's raised hand stopped Barac's disappointed outburst, then lowered to reach across the table, coming to rest lightly on Copelup's tiny fingers. "If not us, then what?" she echoed Barac's own question, her voice low and intent. "If you want me to stay, speak of more than what we know, Copelup. Please."

The Drapsk hesitated, sucked a tentacle for a moment, then sighed. "The Makii, all Drapsk, idolize not who you are, but what you might accomplish. You cannot comprehend how important it is to us that this world become part of the Scented Way once more."

"Then help us understand. Why is it so important?"

They'd asked this question a thousand times, in as many ways as they could, Barac thought glumly. The only difference now was that Rael's Power had a dangerous feel to his deeper sense. She was preparing to leave if Copelup failed her this time—not just this room, but this world.

Perhaps the Drapsk had his own way of gauging their kind. Copelup put his other hand over Rael's. "We haven't been completely open with you, my dear Rael. It grieves me to admit I was among those who felt no alien could be trusted with the truth. I've come to see otherwise. Your sister's influence—" His antennae fluttered eloquently. "I still cannot tell you everything you'd like to know, or need to know, but I will tell you this."

The Drapsk actually stopped and swung his antennae in a complete circle, as if scanning the room for eavesdroppers. Barac found he was still gripping his utensil with its pinioned vegetable and replaced both in the bowl.

Apparently satisfied, Copelup continued, patting Rael's hand in emphasis with each word, a familiarity she endured with unusual restraint. As desperate for information as he was, Barac decided. "We didn't lose the Scented Way, my friends," the Drapsk told them solemnly. "We were driven from it—at terrible cost."

"Driven?" Rael's horrified expression likely mirrored Barac's own. "By what? Those creatures Sira showed us?"

"I thought they only harmed Choosers," Barac blurted, then subsided as both Rael and Copelup turned to him, the former with a scowl.

"The life you have seen so far is a mere shadow of what dwells within the Scented Way," Copelup elaborated. "There are countless others who exist only there, as well as many who live there only in part, as do your own species, coming and going as they please. Some of those are—unpleasant."

"Are you saying you have an enemy trying to stop you reconnecting to the M'hir?" Barac demanded. *No wonder they've been cautious to the point of paranoia*, he sent to Rael.

She didn't reply, beyond a sense of impatient agreement. "You might have told us this at the beginning," Rael said coldly, reclaiming her hands from the Drapsk.

Copelup sat up straight. "The other aliens we've engaged as Mystic Ones have been more happy in that role," he protested. "You are the first to be uncomfortable with it—to ask all these question. Why?" He seemed sincerely puzzled.

Rael's hair twitched at is ends. Barac could feel the effort she expended to keep her temper. "Besides the fact that we're the first real 'Mystic Ones' you've had," she said icily, "it's probably because we don't trust aliens either."

The Drapsk hooted with laughter, covering his bud of a mouth with both hands as if this wasn't appropriate at the dinner table. Rael's generous lips began to twitch, then widened into a grin. Barac felt the easing of her tension as a lightening within the M'hir and slumped back in his own chair.

Personally, he didn't see anything amusing in the idea of a war within the M'hir.

Chapter 4

"NOW, Chief. Why the urgency? A war broken out?"

"Not that I'm aware of," Bowman said calmly, offering me a tray of tiny pastries, each curled around a different sweet filling. She'd insisted on making our meeting a luncheon and refused to talk business until the meal was concluded, claiming it spoiled her digestion. We'd reached this tray, cups of spiced sombay, and the limit of my patience at the same time.

Not that Morgan and I were displeased to share the Sector Chief's famed table—it was more that the quality of food always seemed related to the unpleasantness of her news, explaining why today's superb meal wasn't sitting particularly well in my stomach.

Bowman put down the tray and patted her lips dry, a signal to her two Constables, Terk and 'Whix, to clear the table. Business at last. And serious business, given she relied on her most trusted underlings to do the service. Unlikely waiters. Russell Terk was Human, Morgan's height but almost twice as wide through chest and shoulders—older than my Chosen, I thought, but

I'd been wrong in such estimates of his variable species before. I couldn't tell if Terk was annoyed to be taking my plate or pleased to obey his commander; his heavy-featured face, below limp pale hair, rarely showed more than a dour watchfulness, as if he expected the worst at any minute.

Terk's partner, P'tr wit 'Whix, couldn't have been more different. 'Whix was a Tolian, an attractive, graceful being with faceted emerald eyes to either side of beaked mouthparts. Tall, slim, feathered (which couldn't have been comfortable under his uniform), he had an implant in his throat to allow him to utter the Trade Pact's common language, Comspeak. He was unhappy about something. I couldn't read his features or body posture, but Morgan had sent me the significance of that oh-so-flattened head crest.

I did know Tolians were a precise and methodical species as a whole, so it wasn't hard to imagine that 'Whix was once more disturbed by the haphazard Human approach to things. For his kind, he must be remarkably adaptable to still work with Terk.

Or Bowman. I surveyed the Human female without making it obvious. As usual, she wore her uniform with little care for its formality, pushing up the sleeves and leaving the collar open. Her short black hair wasn't so much trimmed as it appeared to have been ordered to stay out of her way. Morgan had heard there were implants in both of her eyebrows: one a comlink and the other a recording device. Certainly Bowman had a habit of tapping her forehead at the oddest times, but then again, she also tapped the nearest surface when making a point in conversation. I refused to believe there were implants in the plates and tabletop as well.

A resourceful being, however. She'd been the first of her kind to learn of the Clan Council and be allowed to keep that knowledge. That leniency had been my father's decision, part of his practice to collect Humans of influence, seeking to manipulate them with information carefully tailored and supplied. Bowman's acquisition had proved to my advantage, however, not his. She was no one's pawn and hadn't taken well to Clan interference—my father's interference—on Camos or in my life.

Bowman was also a policy maker within her beloved Trade Pact. Those policies had included, surprisingly enough, the survival of the Clan as well. I raised my cup to my lips and met Bowman's fiercely intelligent eyes through the steam. So far, I thought.

"You want to know why we've matched course?" Bowman said bluntly. "I have some questions, Fem Morgan, questions not being answered by your representative to the Trade Pact, Councillor Crisac di Friesnen."

Explaining a certain annoying visitor to our cabin, Morgan sent, raising one brow at me. He was right, of course. Crisac had been the only one of the original Council willing to deal with other species—that didn't make him good at it. If Bowman's questions had disturbed him, it was entirely likely he'd stall in order to rush a message to me.

There was something to be said for only delegating to the competent.

I'd like to know who gave Crisac the locate, I sent back

to Morgan. It had to be someone who'd been in the
Fox—or could home in on the signature of my Power
in the M'hir. A short and personal list.

"I trust you'll answer my questions, Speaker?"
Bowman said, interrupting several dark thoughts
about my relatives and their lack of courtesy.

"Questions? After such a fine meal?" said Morgan,
as he theatrically leaned back in Bowman's well-
designed dining chair. An illusion of ease. I laid my
palms flat on the tabletop and studied them, feeling
Morgan hovering closer than usual in my thoughts, a
presence as real as if he'd physically moved to stand at
my side.

With that security, I looked up at Bowman and
replied calmly: "I'll do my best, Chief, but I've hardly
been keeping in close contact with the Clan. Morgan
and I have been busy the past three months."

Terk coughed suddenly. Morgan gave the other
Human male an inscrutable look, then said: "Trading,"
as if some explanation was required. "Access the *Fox*'s
logs," he told the Constable, a definite note of challenge in his voice, "if you want details."

Before I blushed—judging by the warmth of my
cheeks, that concern probably came too late—or Terk
made a comment I imagined he'd regret, I jumped in.
"You have questions about the Clan, Chief Bowman?
What have they done now?" I'd known better than to
expect bringing my kind into closer ties with other
species, especially Humans, would go smoothly. Still,
this was annoyingly early for trouble.

And trouble it was, judging by her frown and stern
tone: "The Clan joined the Trade Pact. You yourself

signed the treaty guaranteeing mutual noninterference in the politics and internal affairs of other species—"

"I'm fully aware what I signed," I interrupted, then paused, noticing what I hadn't until now, though Morgan undoubtedly had. Bowman's constables wore their usual red-and-black uniforms, but the gray gleam of adaptive body armor showed at collar and wrists—the sort of armor, Morgan had told me, that repelled the force of a blast or projectile with messy results to those nearby. They were armed as well, and not as discreetly as Morgan. Very odd dress for a gathering of allies, let alone one taking place on the safety of Bowman's own ship. I swallowed, well aware the rich lunch had indeed been a warning. "You feel you have to protect yourself from us—from me," I said with disbelief. "What's happened?"

"What's happened?" Bowman's eyes were suddenly as cold as I'd ever seen them. "We can no longer trust our mind-shields, Fem Morgan. Which puts us at a serious disadvantage dealing with any Clan—even you."

"Yours is working fine," Morgan drawled, a not-casual reminder of his own abilities. He nodded at Terk and 'Whix. "And theirs." I didn't need to confirm my Human's findings; the three were like dimensionless ghosts to my deeper sense, something I'd become used to—a protection they'd grown to take for granted, it seemed.

"I've a brain-wiped operative with my med-techs to prove otherwise, Captain Morgan," Bowman countered harshly. "As I said. Someone's found a way past that protection."

"Why would you imagine that 'someone' is Clan?" I lifted one brow, feigning a composure I didn't feel in the least. "I'm quite sure it's not."

"Why? Because we're suddenly all friends?" This came from the always cynical Terk, of course. The Human, I'd concluded long ago, was sure of only one thing in life—no one but Bowman could be trusted.

"Because the Clan wouldn't bother," Morgan answered for me, a nice touch of exasperation in his voice.

"Let's be frank with one another, Chief Bowman," I offered, before Bowman could argue—or Terk, already drawing a deeper-than-normal breath. "You have very few of these artificial shields—and even fewer beings willing to risk the surgery to implant them. It's easier, and far more prudent, for the Clan to simply avoid or ignore those wearing them. No offense."

"None taken." Bowman tapped her finger on the table, habit again, rather than emphasis. "But the fact remains, Fem Morgan, that I have a constable as good as dead, attacked in a way that suggests Clan involvement to me."

"And I'm sorry. But—" I hesitated, seeking Morgan's approval. He nodded, eyes somber, knowing what I planned to reveal. "These shields of yours hide your thoughts—your minds—from those with Talent. That's all they accomplish, Chief. They aren't the protection you believe."

She leaned forward, her forearms on the table. I had her attention—hers and whomever was eavesdropping through her implants. Bowman was never really alone. It paid to remember that. "What do you mean?" she asked.

"Even I—a Clan Adept—can't simply invade and influence any mind I want. That's a myth," I told her, then licked my lips before adding honestly: "and a very convenient one for the Clan, who have felt it prudent to be feared rather than understood. In reality, just as only some have the ability to invade minds, only certain minds are susceptible to that invasion."

Terk almost spat the word: "Telepaths."

It seemed tactful to nod, although I could have corrected his assumption. Within those species who produced telepaths, there were other receptive minds—those without enough Power to be detected or used, but enough to be malleable by the skilled. That detail wasn't likely to reassure them, something I considered highly important at a luncheon with body armor and disrupters on display. "The Talent is like a door that swings both ways," I said instead. "It's no different for the Clan than for Humans. As your own telepaths have surely told you." She didn't quite nod, but something in her eyes acknowledged I was right. "Frankly, Chief, instead of relying on these devices, you would be safer to simply ensure that any beings you put in critical posts aren't Talented. That would make it highly unlikely either Clan or Human telepaths could influence their thoughts without being detected."

"Unlikely." Bowman didn't like the word.

I smiled and shrugged. "I won't lie to you, Chief." Just won't tell the whole truth, I added to myself. "We can't replace a particular memory with another the individual will believe. However, with skill and power, perhaps drugs, it is possible to extract information from a—less receptive—mind and temporarily block the memory of the invasion. But it isn't subtle. There's always significant damage." I was living proof. "Still, if done to someone who wasn't with others familiar with that being's normal behavior, others who could spot inconsistencies, it might succeed."

As I'd hoped, Bowman understood the value of what I'd given her. She nodded slowly, then tipped her palm toward me as if offering something in return. "The shields were and are an experiment," she said, frowning to quell Terk's involuntary protest. "One which we are continuing to assess. I understand what you are telling me about the vulnerability of telepaths, Fem Morgan. We were aware of the—special—risk to them and initially tried the implants as a protection. Unfortunately, there were problems."

"What sort of problems?" Morgan demanded, suddenly still. I knew he suspected worse than that, as did I.

"The shields work both ways, don't they?" I guessed. "They crippled your telepaths."

Bowman gave another brief nod, her eyes somber. "And it turns out to be impossible to remove the devices without causing permanent harm to the brain."

Not only the telepaths, then. She, Terk, and 'Whix would have to keep theirs until there was a new removal technique, or they died. Foolish, foolish beings. I controlled my revulsion with an effort. "What about

your constable? The one who was harmed. A telepath?"

"Why? Could you help her, if she was?" Terk came
close to the table as he spoke, the questions quick and
furious—and unapproved, judging by the darkening
of Bowman's expression and 'Whix's sudden panting.
The Human ignored them both, staring at me with a
wild look on his face. "Will you try?"

Morgan sat straighter. "I thought you said she was
brain-wiped—"

"And so quite beyond help. Thank you," Bowman
said in a voice that snapped Terk and 'Whix into parade stance, though the Human's deepset eyes continued burning into mine. "Fem Morgan. I appreciate
your candor on this matter. While I won't say I'm convinced there has been no Clan involvement," she nodded graciously, "I will pursue other—possibilities.
However, we need to set aside, for the moment, the
question of who might be able to attack a shielded individual. I'd like to move on to the business that
brought me to you, Captain, Fem."

"That wasn't it?" I protested rather weakly. Morgan
had the nerve to wink at me, finding, as always, something amusing in my being surprised.

Bowman, on the other hand, had assumed that
predatory look I knew all too well. "There have been
some disturbing reports from Acranam."

Acranam? I tightened my defenses out of sheer reflex, then felt Morgan do the same. "May I ask how
you could possibly be hearing reports from a Clan
world?" I asked stiffly, quite aware Bowman knew
Acranam had been a thorn in the Clan Council's side

since the hidden enclave had been revealed, and equally aware that any reports I had from that world ranged from unreliable to outright deception. And this—this Human?—had a source of information I did not?

Bowman's lips quirked, as if my reaction wasn't unexpected. We'd come to know one another well over the past year. "I've remained interested in Acranam, Fem Morgan, given its history of welcoming, shall we say, less savory sorts. Without going into technical details, my people keep an eye on shipping coming and going from that system. It's been nothing more than regular freighter traffic, the occasional private yacht, until a month ago." At Bowman's signal, 'Whix handed me a sheet of plas containing a list of ship names. "Within a day, seven ships landed and took off again: four Human-registered, two Ordnexian, and one Scat."

I slid the list over the tabletop to Morgan, whose lips tightened as he read the names. "No one I'd want in orbit with me," he commented.

"I agree." Bowman's voice grew serious. "So why were they there? I thought your Council put a stop to Acranam's trade with pirates."

Careful, Morgan sent, his eyes shadowed. I understood the warning. The moment I'd signed the Clan into the Trade Pact, our relationship with Bowman had fundamentally changed. She was no longer the distant observer, watching the Clan in order to warn others if our kind disturbed Trade Pact commerce or stability. Now, we had put ourselves under Enforcer authority.

A threat, perceived or real, from the Clan wouldn't produce a cautionary report.

Bowman would act.

"The Council doesn't rule Acranam," I told her truthfully enough. The Clan who remained there still preferred an ofttimes paralyzing form of group consensus. As a result, they were agonizingly slow making decisions; once decided, they could be frustratingly stubborn. "Of course," I couldn't help but add, "it's inaccurate to say the Council rules any Clan. We, like you, monitor adherence to certain—laws—that protect us. We have never desired a government. Clan don't value—unity." I felt Morgan's amusement at this.

Bowman wasn't deflected. "Except on Acranam."

"Except there," I admitted.

"So they could still be trafficking with pirates, selling their abilities to them without your knowledge or the Council's."

"Yes, but—"

The Chief leaned forward, her eyes intent on mine. "Would Jarad di Sarc be involved? He had connections with Acranam, did he not?"

My father's name, from this Human, offended me. A wholly Clan reaction I concealed from the Enforcers, if not from Morgan, whose face immediately assumed that frustratingly bland look of innocence. I wasn't sure if he was amused or dismayed, too busy trying to sort out my own feelings.

Not love. Jarad and I had never felt warmth for one another, unless you counted pride of possession and moments of common purpose. Not hate. I understood all too well what had driven him to try and control my destiny, the living legacy of the House of di Sarc. I felt pity, I decided, for the waste of such power. "Jarad is not on Acranam," I said flatly, though Bowman had no right to the knowledge. "He has been defeated in Challenge and chose exile."

"Is he guarded?"

My hair writhed in outrage at the question, obviously startling everyone but Morgan who'd either expected it or was, as usual, too self-controlled to show any reaction without reason. "There is," I said icily, while fighting my hair back to my shoulders, "no need." One did not speak of Those Who Watched to non-Clan. I could barely bring myself to speak of them to Morgan in anything more than the most vague terms. As for Jarad, only the Clan Council knew the Watchers had moved of their own accord to forbid his movement through the M'hir after he'd appeared on Garastis 17, one of the oldest of the Inner Worlds. It was an ability and a response unheard of before this, and the entire Council shared my apprehension about its meaning. No, I decided with a shudder, I wouldn't be sharing this information with Bowman. "Trust me, Chief," I told her, "Jarad di Sarc is not involved in any of this."

Her keen eyes fixed on me, but she nodded once in acceptance. "Then when you next contact your Council, Fem Morgan, I trust you will inform me if they have any information about this—traffic—on Acranam. Especially if it concerns Trade Pact interests in any way."

"Naturally, Chief," I said sincerely, even if I was sure she didn't fully trust me. I smiled to myself. While it wasn't something Bowman needed to know, I considered her my staunchest ally, after Morgan, in the ever-shifting power struggles within the Clan. My relationship, however unofficial, with such a powerful alien puzzled and terrified others of my kind. It was a relationship I chose not to explain to them, based as it was on Bowman's continued faith in my good intentions.

Of course, as Morgan was fond of saying: the best way to keep faith with Bowman was to keep a good distance.

All I wanted now was to hurry back to the *Fox* and find out for myself what was happening on Acranam. They had shut down their dealings in stolen information, but not because I or the Council had ordered it. Only their former leader, Yihtor di Caraat, had had the ability to scan nontelepathic minds at that depth. With his destruction, they'd fallen back on the wealth he'd accumulated and attempted to develop an export trade in rare drugs from Acranam's forests. Morgan didn't expect the colony to last another decade.

Knowing the Clan and labor of any kind when there were Humans to do it for them, I gave them less. So this news of Bowman's was every bit as alarming as she thought—just not for the same reasons.

"I will contact the Council, Chief Bowman," I said, burning with impatience to do so, but keeping that, too, I hoped, from all but Morgan. "As for your concern about your shield device, I'll ask, but I doubt I can help there." I stood, Morgan doing the same, only to be stopped by Bowman's lifted hand.

"And now there's something else again?" Morgan

asked sharply. "This is proving an expensive lunch, Bowman. What is it?"

"You and I should speak in private, Captain—if you don't mind, Fem Morgan."

I began to bristle, then felt Morgan's amused thought: *Go. Let her think we can be dealt with separately.*

With a smile that was far more gracious than I felt, I concentrated on the *Fox*'s control room and *pushed* . . .

"Humans," I told the ship. It was sufficient explanation.

While I wasn't overjoyed to be separated from Morgan at Bowman's whim, I hurried to our cabin, grateful for this chance to contact the Council without him close enough to hear every thought. While I firmly believed in telling my Chosen everything, I'd learned there was always a better time and place for that telling than during a conversation with the Clan. It wasn't Morgan's fault—it was theirs. If my kind suspected Morgan might be listening, they were impeccably polite—and never completely honest. And if they were sure he was there, they gave annoyingly monosyllabic answers to any question.

I closed the cabin door behind me, ordering on the lights, but dimly, so I wouldn't be distracted by the colors gleaming on every surface of our cabin. Morgan's tendency to add new creatures and plants without advance warning had startled me more than once.

We'd had to move out the desk to make room for two of us to inhabit his cabin. The original table had gone as well—replaced by a smaller one with two chairs that obligingly tucked underneath unless required. The bowl of flower petals remained, a fragrant reminder of worlds beyond the metal and plas of the *Fox*. I pulled out a chair, sat, and pulled the bowl closer with both hands, bending to inhale the petals' scent. The name of this particular plant eluded me, though its distinctive aroma carried memories of an evening spent trading with the Nenemans. A successful night for the Morgans, I recalled fondly, although sitting on the Nenemans' floating couches had made me queasy. Our last success, given the return trip had revealed the growing cracks in the *Fox*'s translight drive.

Which I couldn't deal with now.

I considered the seven other Council members—the First Chosen of Lorimar and Su'dlaat, older Clansmen from the Houses of Sawnda'at, Mendolar, Friesnen, and Teerac—then nodded to myself. I pictured Tle di Parth in my thoughts before pouring Power into a sending through the M'hir. An odd choice, perhaps. Tle was the newest, least experienced member of the re-formed Clan Council. She was also an enemy, being of the House of di Parth—a House whose leader had conspired against me and mine, losing his life at the hands of my father. The Clan didn't forget or forgive.

What mattered most, however, was that Tle was another too-powerful Chooser; she faced the doom I'd predicted and proved with my own existence. I had no doubt she would do anything to save herself and our kind from it. In a sense, she *was* me, before I'd met Morgan and learned alien ways. It was always—refreshing—to deal with her.

As long as mine was the greater Power.

Greetings, Speaker and First Chosen of the House of di Sarc. To what do I owe this honor? No delay. The line of Power binding us through that other space crackled and thickened as she poured her own strength into our communication. And more, as Tle probed for weakness in my shields—that politely aggressive reaffirmation of our mutual status from a Clanswoman at the peak of her abilities, determined to demonstrate those abilities at every opportunity.

I did enjoy Tle di Parth. *I understand the Council has been unsuccessfully trying to contact me,* I replied. *There's such a thing as a translight com, you know.*

Confusion, quickly hidden. I knew full well the Council members wouldn't attempt to reach me mind-to-mind unless it was a dire emergency. Being the most powerful of my kind produced that caution, though I'd never acted against any of them. But to 'port, unannounced, to the *Fox?* The echo of Morgan's plaintive "They could have knocked" came to mind, carefully private. It was so typical of the Clan to risk lives rather than use alien technology. It would have been Crisac's decision, not Tle's, so I relented, sending: *Is it about Acranam?*

Acranam. Who else? Tle let her revulsion into the M'hir. I ignored it. Many Clan resented how Acranam continued to refute the Prime Laws, most especially Council directives concerning Candidates for Choice. As far as I could tell, Acranam was simply proving our survival as a species was impossible. They wouldn't admit how many unChosen had been killed by their Choosers, but the Watchers had felt only one Joining since Acranam had been established, and that recently. This implied any planet-born offspring came from already Joined pairs; the irony was lost on no one that those pairs would have been preselected by the Council.

On my order, the Council stayed away from Acranam's affairs, beyond ordering any Choosers be sent offworld to protect their remaining unChosen. We had no need of conflict between ourselves, when all were faced with the same doom. Not so long ago, I'd confessed a sympathy for their independence to Morgan.

Had that restraint been a mistake? We had no records concerning those living on Acranam—bizarre as it seemed, our best information was a list of those Clan who had died over the last two and a half standard decades. The Clan practice of pushing bodies into the M'hir for disposal left no way to check who had truly died and who had preferred exile on Acranam with Yihtor di Caraat—with his promise of free Choice.

The source, I judged, of Tle's distaste for anything about that world. She wasn't getting any younger, waiting for completion. Acranam's wasting of potential Candidates for her Choice must rankle.

Not a Human compassion. The Clan version. I smiled, seeing no humor in the expression reflected by the mirrored tiles of the fresher stall, understanding Tle di Parth very well indeed.

But not enough to permit her reaction to waste my time. I sent a flash of impatience, reinforced with sufficient power to sting, then repeated my question: *What about Acranam? Have they returned to crime?*

How did you?— She wisely stopped to send a wave of appeasement, then continued: *Yes, Speaker. They again flout the Council and the Prime Laws. We wouldn't have known except that the fosterling was discovered in one of the holdings of sud Eathem, a House tied to that of di Caraat before its fall.*

Fosterling? Like a sudden cold rain, I felt the truth slipping through me. *Acranam is dispersing its children.*

Tle's confirmation was reticent, unconvinced. Probably Sawnda'at's influence—he was prone to avoiding conclusions even when the facts nipped his ears. *We know of only this one, Speaker. Surely the Watchers would have warned us—*

The Watchers should have screamed an alarm in every Councillor's mind for even one child. Stretching the mother-child link through the M'hir created a thunderclap in that space; the force of that thunder increased exponentially if the link began a totally new pathway. Which left, I realized, bile rising in my throat, only one possibility. *The Watchers would know if Acranam dispersed children through the M'hir,* I told her. *But not if they traveled from their mothers by starship.*

As Tle seemed stunned by this heretical notion, I allowed her time to absorb it, busy thinking it through myself. Bowman had listed seven ships. Seven fosterlings? There could be that many. I might have found out for sure during the enclave on Camos, to which every member of the M'hiray had been drawn by the Watchers, but my mind had been on survival, not a census. Others might have paid attention. As a matter of courtesy, I'd never asked Chief Bowman what she learned that day. She'd promised not to make any recordings, and I really didn't want to know if that had been a lie. But she did have other sources of information—information she'd probably gladly exchange for our help with her schemes.

Which I wouldn't do. The Drapsk, as I warned the *Fox*, were trouble enough.

We should have known, I decided. I should have. It was our way to send children as far as possible from their mothers at a certain age. Given the length of time Acranam had been a colony, their first generation would be more than ready to be fostered.

Disturbing that Acranam was taking this step on its own. The Council, much as I hated to admit it, did serve a useful function by arranging all fosterings. Locations were carefully selected in order to enhance pathways useful to all Clan, not just a few. Foster families were selected for their stability and Power. Raising and educating a child with the Power inherent in my kind took more than kindness.

More than disturbing. By dispersing their children outward in secrecy, Acranam's Clan stood to gain seven pathways known only to themselves. There was a reason pathways were forged for all—it permitted the weakest of us to move freely through the M'hir, letting us be a species, no matter how far apart. Each generation had sustained existing pathways as well as built new ones. But as the M'hiray continued to produce Choosers too powerful to Join and mate, like me, we faced a future of fewer and fewer children—a future in which many Clan would eventually be unable to travel through the M'hir, isolating us from each other, dooming our kind. The link from child to mother was a precious resource for all, yet Acranam chose to keep it to themselves. One of their attempts had already failed. The others could all succeed, to Acranam's gain.

What do we know about these ships? Tle's question interrupted thoughts growing darker by the minute. She'd recognized the danger as well. *We must know their destinations, if we are to find the pathways from Acranam. It should be possible to have scouts coerce or bribe their crews.*

Unlikely to be that easy. *For all we know, the children could have 'ported from the ships once within range of maintained M'hir pathways. That could have been overlooked by the Watchers.* Or been hidden by them, I thought to myself suddenly. After all, they'd kept silent about Morgan, something I'd always assumed meant they couldn't sense the Human in the M'hir—it being incredible they wouldn't react to an alien presence in that hallowed space. Now I wondered how far to trust that assumption—or the Watchers. Their notion of M'hir and the Clan's place within it had seemed indistinguishable from the Council's. But was it always? I thought uneasily, keeping that worry to myself.

So Acranam's brats could be anywhere?

I turned the bowl slowly with my fingertips, beginning to feel the faintest drain from maintaining this link. Tle, the weaker, would suffer first. I withdrew some of my Power and was satisfied by her renewed effort. *No. Not "anywhere," Tle. There is only so much distance possible between mother and child—farther than that,*

and their link dissolves forever. Find out what you can from
sud Eathem and their fosterling.

As you wish, Speaker. Definite fading now.

Before I released Tle, I thought about Morgan and
added, with a firm reinforcement of my own Power:

And tell the others to use a com next time.

INTERLUDE

It was no wonder the Clan scorned technology—from coms to starships—when they were capable of this. Jason Morgan watched Sira disappear from sight, fascinated, as always, by the Clan ability to sidestep space. Oh, he'd managed parlor tricks under her guidance—moving objects across short distances, hiding things in the M'hir for a moment or two before bringing them back—but not to push himself through that otherness. Yet. Sira, honest to a fault, didn't promise he ever could. She didn't discourage his efforts either, merely noting it took some Clan years to perfect the technique and he had the disadvantage of biology.

"Neat trick." Terk's dry comment brought Morgan's attention back to the Enforcers.

"If you want to talk about Clan abilities, Chief Bowman, you should have kept Sira here, not me," he observed dryly. "So, what's up?" He didn't commit to a chair, preferring to prop one hip against the table. It meant Bowman had to look up to meet his eyes, but Morgan considered that hardly sufficient advantage over someone who'd faced down the Clan and made

Sector Chief in the same year. The short, stout, almost placid-looking woman before him was never, ever to be underestimated.

Perhaps she thought the same of him, getting right to the point. "There's been an incident on Plexis."

Morgan had considered numerous possibilities, but this was a surprise. "Plexis? What's that to do with me? We haven't been back in months." Then he narrowed his eyes. "Huido? He's all right, isn't he?"

"As far as I know. 'Whix? Get the report from Plexis security for the Captain." As the Tolian moved over to a wall console, Bowman continued: "We don't get involved in criminal investigations, as you know. There are, however, certain individuals we prefer to—" She paused, as if looking for a polite word.

"To spy on," Morgan supplied helpfully. "Why Huido? He lives in that restaurant. Mind you, he's picky about sharing his recipes, but I'm sure if you asked—"

"We weren't watching your friend. After the regrettable lack of cooperation we encountered from Plexis last year, I instituted a regular sweep through their security system—to notify us of anything which might be of concern to the Trade Pact." Morgan grinned at that, having experienced firsthand the pompous secretiveness of Plexis' head of security, Inspector Gregor Wallace. Bowman didn't quite smile back. "A recent sweep triggered an alert. A name of interest came up—associated with a murder investigation presently underway on the station."

"Who?"

"Naes Fodera. You do remember it?"

Morgan eased his weight more to his feet, careful not to make the instinctive move obvious enough to stir Terk's interest. No gain pretending he didn't know. "Fodera was on Sira's list. A Human telepath."

"The only Human telepath from that list unaccounted for," Bowman added, all trace of good humor vanishing from her face. "As you'll recall, two refused the Clan's offer to take part in certain—experiments. One of those, Matthew Jodrey, was subsequently kidnapped and tortured to death by your old friend Ren Symon. The other, Fodera? Like Symon, Fodera simply disappeared from sight, despite our best efforts to track him down. Until now."

Morgan concentrated on keeping his face expressionless, using even more effort to keep his reaction to that name, Ren Symon, from boiling across his link to Sira. He'd put his desire for vengeance, that *rage*, behind him. Or so he'd thought. "Where is he?"

Bowman made her own decision as to which "he" Morgan meant. "Fodera, or what's left of him, currently resides in a sample vial on Plexis. Oh, and I believe there's a bit of him hanging in a freezer. Seems your friend Huido was trying to dispose of the body in the same memorable way he disposed of that Clansman."

Morgan didn't bother to protest—if Bowman went after an answer, she'd dig for it until the answer gave up. Obviously, uncovering Huido's and Barac's earlier indiscretion hadn't bothered the Sector Chief, her focus always on what disturbed the balance of the Trade Pact, not crime.

Even if it were murder. "Does Plexis think Huido killed Fodera?"

'Whix offered Morgan a data cube. "Here is what they know—and don't know. Thus far, Captain Morgan, there is no motive, very little body, and nothing to prove this was more than a misguided attempt to recycle protein. If there hadn't been an informant, a disgruntled former chef, there would likely be no case at all."

"All moot. The investigation has been declared within my official interest. Plexis will keep their hands off." Bowman's tone contained a confidence Morgan, knowing the station from a somewhat different viewpoint, didn't share.

"This is the real reason you chased us down, isn't it?" he said more than asked. "And why you wanted to see me alone. You believe Ren Symon had something to do with Fodera's death. You're trying to drag me back into all this—to help you find him." Morgan almost spat the last word.

Bowman steepled her fingers and regarded him without flinching. "No denying you could be of use. But you've made it abundantly clear, Morgan, that you want nothing to do with our investigation into Symon's band of disenchanted telepaths. Frankly, if they'd stuck to species-specific criminal acts, I wouldn't care about them either. But I don't believe Symon's plans have ever been that small in scope. Do you?"

"I don't think about his plans or him," Morgan ground out, sensing Terk coming to alert at the hostility in his voice. "Leave me out of this. Leave Huido out of this!" Heaven only knew what was leaking through his link to Sira.

Too much, Morgan realized belatedly, as the lithe form of his mate rematerialized, her hair whipped into a frenzy as if she were some avenging goddess come to his rescue, her expression equally wild. The M'hir seethed and burned with power.

He winced.

Which might have been at the thought of explaining Huido's current predicament to his beloved.

Chapter 5

THAT night, my dreams were crowded with evil Huidos and Human heads on platters. To make things worse, I awoke to find myself alone.

I stroked the sheet beside me. Warm. Morgan hadn't left long ago. My seeking thought ceased almost instantly. My Human was troubled and, if he sought time to himself, I would obey his wish.

I'd been wrong to 'port to Bowman's ship—I knew better than to act by reflex rather than sense. Normally, I would have delayed at least an instant, knowing Morgan's capabilities and awaiting a true summons. Glumly, I decided the combination of Enforcers in body armor, what Bowman and Tle had to say, and the Rugheran's surprise visit had seriously shaken my confidence. In other words, more Chosen cowardice.

One could hate biology.

More important than my personal embarrassment was that I'd cost Morgan a chance to extract further information from Bowman. Of course, left alone, he might have agreed to something he shouldn't. For a being without Talent, I thought, the Chief was exceptionally proficient at manipulating others.

I carefully avoided thinking about the Carasian. Strong emotion was the most difficult to keep from my Chosen, and I experienced plenty whenever I considered Huido and his latest culinary masterpiece. It wasn't, however, the outrage Morgan assumed.

It was foreboding.

Like Bowman, the murder of a strange Human—even if our friend was suspected of the crime—didn't matter to me so much as its consequence. We were going to Plexis.

Which meant someone had known exactly how to lure Morgan there.

Just when the Acranam Clan had exerted themselves, in secret, to be able to travel from their system? Coincidence, I'd found in my lifetime, didn't exist when it came to matters of power.

I pulled the covers over my head, as if that would help.

Troubled or not, I drifted back to sleep. Morgan didn't return, but my awareness of him—perhaps heightened by my earlier, anxious thoughts—increased, saturating my dreaming mind until, abruptly, it was as if I looked out his eyes, felt what he felt. He seemed to sense me only as my sleeping presence; I remained unsure if I dreamed or floated closer to consciousness.

It had to be a dream, I decided, moving with Morgan as he strode down the ship's corridor to the air lock, lights night-dimmed. We'd connected the *Fox* to the

Conciliator, a gesture of trust to Bowman and convenience for Morgan. That much of what I saw I believed. By why was Morgan here?

. . . Time dilated, or I lost the threads as my resting state deepened. Perhaps this was simply a stranger dream than most.

"Are you sure you can help her?" Terk's rough growl had no place in my sleep. I became almost too alert, losing my sense of Morgan. Deliberately now, I calmed myself, seeking the dreamscape.

"No." Morgan's voice had an odd reverberation within my thoughts, as though heard and felt at the same time, but slightly out of synch. "I'll do my best. And Bowman won't hear about this from me, Russ. You know that."

"Bowman can have my badge, for all I care."

. . . I'd lost minutes again. Morgan was now looking at a Human female seated in a chair, her body held in place by restraints. Her head had been shaved and metal disks were leeched to her scalp, trailing wires that disappeared into a massive console. The female's face was strong-boned, likely attractive when full of life, but hanging slack and expressionless now. Drool formed a glistening runnel from the left side of her mouth.

I'd seen faces like this before. Her mind had been damaged, possibly completely erased or at least blocked. This must be the operative Bowman spoke of, the one whose mind-deadener had failed.

A broad expanse of black uniform made a backdrop behind her—Terk, who required special tailoring for his wide shoulders. "Shouldn't your wife be here?" he said. "I thought she was the expert in this—this mental rape." His harsh challenge startled both of us, though Morgan didn't oblige me by looking up to glare. His gaze remained fixed on the female's face.

"I told you when you asked me to help Kareen—this isn't something Sira can do," Morgan replied calmly enough, though I shared his emotions: doubt, concern, a determination to succeed. A perplexing certainty I wouldn't approve any more than Bowman, hence the attempt at secrecy.

Why wouldn't I approve? Bowman might not understand the horrors of being mind-wiped—or have her own reasons for keeping this Kareen from us—but I understood too well. Any hope this female had of regaining her personality rested with my Chosen, not with Human technology. I thought of letting Morgan know, but this was a dream, after all; I didn't control much more than paying attention or not.

. . . Not, it seemed, for I must have lost the moment when Morgan approached Kareen, startled to suddenly be leaning over her, watching his hands running lightly over her forehead.

Could she feel their warmth? I despaired with him.

Morgan made a sound of triumph, having found what he wanted, and pressed his fingers tightly to her skin. He'd tried to explain the process to me more than once, before taking my advice and giving up. Our Talents differed in ways that couldn't be translated into Comspeak or into whatever language our minds shared. My Talent included moving whatever I chose through the M'hir; among his, this bizarre ability to discover some physical reference to a nonphysical attack and use it as a focal point for healing.

He readied his Power. I'm not sure if this severed our dream connection or if I somehow managed to draw myself away, unwilling to risk any potential distraction.

I opened my eyes to darkness, dry-mouthed and troubled. Asleep, Morgan had shown a disconcerting ability to share my dreams, especially—and unfortunately—any emotionally-charged nightmares. This involuntary sharing of his waking presence by my dreaming self was something entirely different, new to my experience. It could be my Joining with a Human telepath. Perhaps Morgan had a name for this, knew more than I.

He might—however, I was reasonably sure the very private Human wouldn't be happy about it. He'd be even less pleased to learn it seemed involuntary. I had a vision of Morgan waking me up every few minutes to be sure I wasn't dreaming him. This seemed one of those memories not worth sharing.

I flipped over my pillow—a childish habit to rid my sleep of dreams, whether of Morgan, lost children and scheming Clan, or evil Huidos and Human heads on platters—put down my head, then unexpectedly quickly found myself drifting back to sleep.

A sleep I wasn't surprised was again disrupted, given this particular night. Frustrated, I hoped it was morning, so I could stop trying to rest, then found Morgan had slipped in with me, a shivering cold lump already asleep, courteously as far as possible to one

side of our bed. I sensed exhausted triumph and relaxed.

Questions and worries could wait.

I wrapped my Chosen in my arms and Power, and
fell into a dream-free sleep at last.

"Aren't you going to ask?

I'd felt Morgan wake. He'd been uncharacteristi-
cally silent to my other sense, having breakfast alone,
spending some time in the control room—presumably
making a call to the pilot of the *Conciliator* to arrange
our mutual uncoupling. I didn't eavesdrop. But I kept
close enough to his glow in the M'hir to know when he
approached the cargo hold, and to his emotions to be
unsurprised by the gruffness of the question.

So I smiled as I looked up from the cargo inventory,
marking my place on the list with one finger. "Good
morning. Ask what?"

Morgan's blue eyes were bruised this morning, almost purple. I could have eased that lingering weari-
ness with a touch of Power, but knew the Human
preferred to recover in his own way and "not waste
my strength." Irrational, as I had plenty to spare, but I
didn't argue. Besides, I grinned to myself, this time he
deserved it. Sneaking away on me!

He felt my amusement and looked vaguely offended, then suspicious. I kept my inner and outer self
as calm as possible. "Ask what?" I repeated. "It's not
as if I haven't done this before." "This," being a search
through our scant inventory to locate anything worth
trading at Plexis. There hadn't been a formal announcement, captain to crew, that we would be head-

ing for the station. There didn't need to be. I knew Morgan wouldn't forget the Rugheran homeworld— but it could wait. Huido could not. I wasn't sure if I was relieved or more unnerved, but settled for ignoring my inner voice.

"I left the *Fox* last night. You know that." As this wasn't a question, I waited courteously for him to continue. Morgan frowned, then snapped: "Aren't you going to ask why?"

Again, I had to smile. I leaned back in my chair and looked up at him. "If you so desperately want to talk about your wanderings, my love, I'm happy to listen," I assured him.

His frown faded, slowly replaced by a look of pure chagrin. "I do, don't I," Morgan admitted, warmth suddenly running between us. He drew a finger along my cheek. "Terk walked me to the air lock after our little lunch with his boss," he began more easily. "He called in a favor. It turns out Bowman's 'operative' was a friend. Their med-techs couldn't help her. He thought we could—but had no luck talking Bowman into it. She didn't want anyone else learning what might be in the operative's memory."

"Anyone else being me," I suggested.

Morgan gave a tired smile and slouched against the nearest crate, testing the webbing with an idle hand as he spoke. "Wouldn't be surprised. Bowman would like to trust us both—as far as she trusts anyone—but it's not in her nature." More seriously. "I didn't think you'd approve of my getting involved."

I raised a brow. "You have Talent. It must be used to hone it to its utmost. Why wouldn't I approve?"

He looked adorably uncomfortable. *You were so afraid, yesterday.*

"Oh. That." My turn to flush, remembering my flamboyant and totally unnecessary 'port to his rescue. I turned my attention to the list, marking another possibility: a crate of Brillian brandy—an acceptable year, but not outstanding. It might cover our first day's docking fee. Plexis wasn't cheap. "So," I asked the list, "you thought it would give me more courage to know you'd act on your own any time I might disagree about the risk. Is this Human logic?" With the question, I looked back up at him and added gently. "Because I don't understand."

Morgan shook his head, not at me, I thought, but at himself. "Put that way, my dear Witchling, it doesn't appear to make any sense," he admitted, a wry note to his voice, then gave a bow. "I stand corrected."

I made a noncommittal noise in my throat, but accepted what was an apology and hoped it was a promise. "How is Terk's friend?"

His blue eyes gleamed. "Back to normal as far as I can tell. Whoever tampered with her—Kareen—performed a deep scan and then blocked her memory of it. If done properly, no one might have even known about it, but the block was too massive. She became comatose—which alerted Bowman to the unpleasant fact her expensive technology is no longer the protection it was. I pried off the block." I smiled at this remarkably mundane description of a process that would have taken time, skill, and a substantial amount of strength. "Unfortunately, as far as Kareen is concerned, she lost consciousness eight standard days ago and doesn't remember her attacker at all."

"Clan?" I asked. For all I'd said to Bowman, it was at least possible one of my more xenophobic cousins had taken it upon themselves to do some reciprocal spying.

"Too clumsy. And wrong—" He fumbled for a word, then shrugged. "Wrong *grist*, as Huido would say. I'd lay a bet on Human. Terk couldn't tell me who or what Kareen had been investigating for Bowman, but we both know she keeps tabs on quite a few who'd prefer not to be watched. It could have been Ren Symon. He knows a few—tricks. This is within his style." Morgan's voice was too casual.

Symon. A name I'd naïvely hoped Morgan never would hear again. Our other enemy, my father, had faced me in Challenge and lost. As was his right, Jarad di Sarc had preferred exile to living among Clan with that shame. The Clan way. I'd known better than to expect Symon to behave as conveniently. Humans were less—predictable.

I didn't share Morgan's Talent to sense impending danger or change as a taste in the M'hir. That he didn't mention such a sensation wasn't completely reassuring, given such warnings usually arrived in time to dodge a blast, not prepare for one. "Know this," I told him, and sent everything I'd learned from Tle, as well as my own guesses.

Morgan couldn't help his Human reaction, an instinctive mix of anger and repugnance at the idea of not only separating children from their mothers for profit, but using pirate ships to do so. To his credit as a Master Trader, well used to alien ways, he tried to keep that reaction to himself. "Are you going to tell Bowman?"

"This is Clan business," I countered. "Not Trade Pact."

My Human nodded slowly, but I could feel him thinking. "She'll know," he decided, "or will find out, where those other six ships went. A trade for that information could be worthwhile."

I tightened my shields to contain my instinctive disagreement. Every so often, my Clan heritage reared, throwing up its barrier of distrust for anyone or anything alien. I'd learned to be as wary of making decisions based on that part of me as I was of making them solely as Sira Morgan. "Risky—exposing so much of us," I temporized. "You know perfectly well Humans would have—difficulty—with this aspect of the Clan. You do."

"No need to reveal secrets, my Lady Witch." Morgan's smile was pure mischief. "I believe we've already supplied our half of the trade. Shall I pay my good friend Russ another visit before we leave?"

A Master Trader indeed. I could almost feel sorry for the other Human.

INTERLUDE

"A terrible waste, Hom Huido. I feel sorry for him, you know. Such a terrible waste—"

The Carasian bent a second eye at Ansel. The two were sharing breakfast in the private dining area of the *Claws & Jaws* while going over accounts and orders, not because this was the most ornately—and expensively—decorated part of the restaurant, but because Huido liked the view. Through the shimmer of a one-way force shield, he could keep several eyes on the rest of the dining area, presently empty. "That fish-faced excretion?" he boomed incredulously. "He probably goaded the transport servo into running over him. I, for one, don't mourn him in the slightest."

Ansel shook his head sadly. " 'Any Sentient's Loss Diminishes Us.' "

Huido rumbled something but didn't bother countering the Human's belief—little as he shared it concerning the Neblokan. Like many of his staff, Ansel had begun attending services at the Turrned Mission on this sublevel, predominantly a wholesalers' district, but one-third spinward being restaurants and other, less enlightened entertainments. The Turrned faith offered the freedom to worship the deity of your choice complete with lunch, as long as you accepted their remarkably expanded definition of intelligent life. Huido had had to insist his staff stop apologizing to the fresh prawlies before tossing them into the pot, as it not only disturbed any customer who happened by, but slowed the cooking process considerably. Otherwise he had no problem with the Turrned religion, even quietly arranging the delivery of excess food and the occasional bottle of wine to the delighted missionaries.

But the Carasian refused to lament the death of his former chef, killed the previous night by a malfunctioning transport. Loss of sentience? Poetic justice, more likely. A boon to the galaxy, even more so.

Ansel wisely changed the subject: "Ruti seems a most satisfactory replacement, Hom Huido. I must confess, her abilities came as quite a surprise. Ah . . ." His voice, faint at the best of times, faded away completely.

Three more eyes joined the two already watching the Human's face. The rest remained fixed on a heaping bowl of cooked grain, half afloat in Feenstra's Patented Hot Sauce—Huido preferring to start his day with something robust. With beer. "Ah?" he prompted, knowing this sudden quiet was Ansel's way of introducing a topic likely to promote considerable noise from his employer.

"The inspectors, Hom Huido."

"What about them?" this around a clawful of soaked grain.

"Plexis will eventually ask to see Ruti's Trade Pact

Certification. The rules are quite strict these days about who can prepare food for a mixed clientele—that unfortunate incident in the Exalted Goddess Tearoom with those poor Skenkrans always comes up. She does have certification, does she not?"

"Not."

"Ah."

A huge handling claw raised and snapped in the air, a challenge as well as a summons for more beer. "I'm sure you'll be able to take care of that—minor—detail before the next inspection, Ansel." Four more eyes swiveled to study the Human's rather ashen face. "As always, I have every faith in your abilities. The certificate's just a piece of plas."

"Just a piece of—"

A pitcher of beer smashing on the floor stopped Ansel's weak protest and caused a horrified realignment of all of Huido's eyestalks. "What do you think you're doing?" the Carasian roared.

"But—but—Hom Huido! How did you get here?" The server, a usually docile Vilix, seemed oblivious to the mess at her feet, almost babbling through the flailing cilia that bearded her lower face. "I left you in the kitchen!" she exclaimed, then collapsed on the floor, wagging her fingers in disbelief.

Huido flicked his upper handling claw once, deliberately, sending bits of grain flying like the first warning flakes of snow from an avalanche. Then he rose slowly, plate sliding over plate with a warning hiss.

The doorway to the kitchen suddenly filled with Huido's mirror image: a huge, gleaming black shape, massive claws held up and out, eyestalks erect, rapier-thin fangs protruding in clear threat.

Ansel grabbed the Vilix's arm and yanked her to safety as the two Carasians exploded into motion, splintering the table between them as they collided. A deep bell-like sound rang from their armor on impact, its echoes lost in the deafening clatter as claws fought for a killing hold.

"It's better if family calls first," Ansel half-shouted to the now-cowering Vilix, her eyes hidden behind a wall of cilia. "These surprise visits never turn out well."

Chapter 6

MORGAN'S final visit to the *Conciliator* was every bit as profitable as we'd hoped, at least in terms of his private conversation with Terk. I reserved my opinion concerning my Human's blithe reassurance that Bowman was done with us. "The *Arakuad, Dashing Boy, Maren's Melody, Silcil 48, Steve's First Pick, Trouder 3,* and *Uriel's Enchantment,*" Morgan recited from memory. "Don't let the names fool you, Sira. These ships belong to the scum of the quadrant—known pirates or pirate wannabes. If it wasn't the Clan dealing with them, I'd say they'd just asked for mass kidnappings."

I snorted. "All they needed were captains who'd dealt with Yihtor in the past." The founder and former ruler of Acranam had had his own ways of ensuring compliance, a seemingly quite effective combination of profit and punishment. "Do the Enforcers know where each ship went?"

Morgan shook his head. "Not all. The *Arakuad* and *'Boy* slipped Bowman's net. The Scat won't be hard to pick up again, but Bennefeld captains the *'Boy*—she's smart and tough. If she wants to keep out of sight, she will."

"Then the Council will have to find those fosterlings. The others?"

"The *'Melody* went to Veres Prime—presumably to deliver the child Tle claimed was found there. The rest? You aren't going to like this." My Human obviously didn't, given the sound of his voice. "The *Silicil 48* and *Troudor 3* stuck together—as you'd expect; Ordnexian ships travel in pairs—and went straight to Ettler's Planet." He hesitated. "Do you think it was because of the Rugherans?"

I shook my head at his worried expression. "You're interested in the Rugherans, because you are so Humanly curious," I reminded him. Other words came to mind, but I kept them private. "The Acranam Clan wouldn't be interested in aliens, especially any they can't manipulate." *Not to mention how they'd react to a Rugheran in the flesh*, I sent, feeling Morgan's relieved amusement. "Ettler's is no more or less than the closest Human system," I continued aloud. "A practical choice—those fosterlings are likely suds. Where did the others go?"

"*'Enchantment* stopped at Omacron, then headed for Auord. The *'Pick*—" Morgan paused and frowned. Busy estimating the nearest M'hir pathway to either system, I almost missed his low-voiced: "Why would Brukman—? Odd."

The fosterling carried by *Uriel's Enchantment* had too many choices for comfort; depending on his or her strength, possibly even one of the wealthy Human Inner Worlds so favored by the Clan in the past.

Acranam was nothing if not ambitious. Then I noticed Morgan's sudden preoccupation. He'd keyed up our course and was studying it intently.

"What is it?"

"The *'Pick* headed through empty space, toward the outer systems. No Human settlements along her path—not so much as a mining colony."

"Where is she now?"

"Impounded on Tact 105 for smuggling oxygen—methane breathers take a dim view of it. But that's hardly a planet the Clan would want linked to Acranam. Too far as well, based on what you've told me."

I began to frown, too. "So where is the fosterling? Stuck on this methane world?"

"I doubt it." Morgan's eyes met mine, his grown ice-cold. "The *'Pick* crossed the path of Plexis Supermarket three and a half weeks ago."

Again.

The black, seething void of the M'hir stretched in all directions but one, where an infusion of warm, golden light marked Morgan's presence. His gold was Joined to my sense of self by glittering threads of power: permanent and deep, yet constantly changing. At this instant, they were thinned, as close to nonexistence as either of us could manage—or bear.

This was Morgan's trial, not mine. I stayed aside as he practiced, striving to relocate his physical self through that other space. The locate was, of course, firmly in his thoughts: the galley of the *Fox*. Steps from the control room, none at all through the M'hir.

For me. Not for the Human. As he threw more and

more of his strength into the effort, I kept track of time. *Enough*, I sent. Though he resisted, I pulled us both back to the control room.

Subjective time was the danger in the M'hir. The longer one stayed within it, kept aware of it, the more power it took to remain whole and remember how to return. I drew up one knee, outwardly at ease on the copilot's couch, and watched Morgan wipe sweat from his face and neck. He grinned at me, eyes sparkling. "Better?"

Since he hadn't accomplished anything, I wasn't exactly sure how to respond. "Do you think so?" I asked cautiously. Our powers differed, that much I knew.

He tossed the sweat-soaked rag at me, but it disappeared before it reached the hands I automatically put out to protect myself. "I'm willing to be an optimist," the Human said lightly. "After all. A month ago, you would have caught that."

"Where is it now?" I started to ask, only to have the rag rematerialize and continue its trajectory to my face, managing to utter a meaningful: "Phwsuhmpf!" as it hit.

Morgan's laughter flooded my mind as well as the control room. I *pushed* the rag into a stowage cupboard, resisting the urge to return it to sender. One thing I'd learned about living with a Human—practical jokes stopped only if one didn't retaliate. And, I thought to myself smugly, there was always later. It would take another two days to intercept Plexis, with constant nursing of the *Fox*'s ailing translight engine.

"It's as though I'm too real," Morgan said abruptly. "I follow your directions: picture the locate—form a mental image of a place I know—then pour Power into it. That works for things. But not for me."

"It's true your mind has an—" I hunted for a word to describe how tightly Morgan's natural shielding wrapped his sense of self, "—an independence from the M'hir that differs from Clan." I considered this. "Part of my thoughts or those of any Clan are always in that place. They mingle with each others' at a level we know exists but can't consciously tap into."

"Just as well," he chuckled.

I grinned. "True. But you've never shown that level of connection to it, only what you've developed since our Joining. It may not be a Human ability," I said, preferring to be honest. "Even among Clan, there are those who must rely on others to 'port any distance."

"But they can all still do it."

Stubborn determination was a Human ability I knew all too well. I shrugged. "That ability defines the M'hiray. We believe none of our ancestors could 'port—likely why those who could left our Homeworld." I sometimes dreamed of that exodus, of how the Power of so many moving through the M'hir in unison must have burned a path in that space.

Morgan snapped his fingers, jarring me from the image. "But don't you see? You're assuming this process is uniquely Clan. What if it's only the way you achieve the result that's unique to your species?"

"I don't follow—"

"You form a locate," he interrupted excitedly. "That might be what works for the Clan—but, as you say, I'm different. I don't see the M'hir as you do. Perhaps

I shouldn't try so hard to be Clan in this. Maybe I need to go at this another way, a Human way."

I didn't like the direction this was taking, but kept my disquiet to myself, saying only: "I thought the point was that there might not be a *Human* way to 'port at all."

Morgan waved dismissively, leaping up to pace around the control room, his growing enthusiasm sizzling along my nerve endings until I had to dampen my sense of him. "I think I'm onto something key here, Sira. Why don't I get into the M'hir, *then* fix on a location to emerge—" I felt his power building as he concentrated and *pushed* . . .

NO!

My instant, utter denial was a blow that not only stopped Morgan's ill-advised attempt to enter the M'hir, but dropped him to his knees, hands pressed to his head. "Gods, Sira—" he growled as he staggered back to his feet, using the nearest console for support. His eyes blazed at me. "It was just an idea—"

I didn't remember standing, but I was, my arms outstretched to their fullest—not to guard Morgan from danger, but to keep myself back. Hair lashed my cheeks, hard enough to leave welts, whipping against my shoulders and back as if frantic to cause more harm. I knew myself out of control, driven by instinct to protect our link, our lives. But how could my Chosen be the threat? The unimaginable, impossible conflict raged within me, a drive confused and misdirected, yet too powerful to ignore.

My Lady Witch, softly, carefully. Morgan, somehow, was calling me back to sanity. *Sira. Chit.*

"Don't . . . try . . . that . . . again . . ." I managed to gasp, afraid of what might happen if I tried to contact him mind-to-mind. Our link, such a precious thing on every level to me, seemed on fire. "It's not . . . safe . . . Dissolve . . . you'll dissolve . . ."

"Not a good plan," I heard him say. "I won't, Sira. I swear. I'm sorry."

My hair responded first, falling flat as if it had never come to life and attacked me. Morgan hurried to my side, cursing under his breath as he examined my face, easing me back to the couch. I wasn't sure if my cheeks were damp with tears or blood. "If you'd succeeded, you'd have killed us," I whispered, in case Morgan made the terrible mistake of believing I'd overreacted and tried again. "Entering the M'hir without a way to leave it—where there are not pathways in place to guide you to safety—it's death, Jason. Traveling there isn't something you learn by trial and error. You won't survive a mistake. We won't—"

He sat beside me, gathering me in his arms, holding me painfully tight. I closed my eyes, listening and feeling his heartbeat, concentrating on the caring flowing between us. Then, ice entered my veins as Morgan spoke, his lips in my hair. "I have to keep trying, Sira. I'll be more careful—I promise you—but I'm so close. Too close. I can't give up now. Can you understand?"

Reluctantly, I nodded, against his chest, muttering under my breath: ". . . cliff dancing . . . cliff dancing . . . cliff dancing . . ."

There was a dubious benefit to listening to Morgan's passionate resolve to master the ability to 'port immediately after having hauled him back from the brink of dissolving in the M'hir. I could no longer feel quite the same level of apprehension for minor matters such as rebellious Acranam, mysterious Rugherans, Symon, or Huido's unfortunate menu.

Which only proved how little I understood of each.

INTERLUDE

"Do they understand?" Rael nodded at the row of silent, watching Drapsk, from both the Makii and Heerii Tribes. They stood in front of a formidable and completely mystifying machine, the sort designed by beings who firmly believed there was no such thing as too many warning lights. The Clanswoman didn't know or care what the machine was; her question addressed something more fundamental. "They aren't to touch me. They are especially not to pinch me. No matter what."

Barac hoped she didn't hear the faint hoot from Copelup. He and the Skeptic waited to one side of the long, low bench the Drapsk had coaxed from the floor for Rael. There were no other Skeptics present—a feat accomplished by the unoriginal ploy of waiting until the middle of the night, when any Drapsk not assigned to a specific task tended to be at home.

If they slept in those homes, Barac had yet to find proof of it. His mildly curious questions in his early weeks on Drapskii only confirmed what Sira had told him: Drapsk answered what they chose to answer, and charmingly deflected what they did not, which included questions about their physiology. The yellow-plumed Skeptics were particularly adept at confusion, a peculiar trait in individuals supposedly beyond tribal affiliations and dedicated to uncovering the truth.

"What if Levertup finds out?" he hissed to his companion, as Rael laid herself down, two Drapsk bustling up to cover her legs and torso with sheets of issa-silk.

Copelup's antenna bent toward the Clanswoman, fluttering ever so slightly as if reading something in the air above her. "He will enjoy himself," the small being said confidently. "If we succeed, he will be gratified, and find some way to make it the glory of the Heerii, whom he favors for some inexplicable reason. If we fail miserably, he'll take immense satisfaction in berating the Makii and yourself."

Barac raised an eyebrow. "But not you?"

Copelup hooted. "Of course not."

"Why—" *When you're ready, Cousin?* Barac winced at Rael's impatient thought, while all the Drapsk raised their antennae with delight. Before Rael noticed, and was more unnerved, Barac sat down on the stool beside Rael's head and placed the fingers of his left hand on her forehead.

"Ready," he lied.

They'd discussed what to do; Rael had decided, over his protest. She'd passed to him Sira's less-than-comforting memories of her own efforts to reconnect Drapskii to the M'hir. His cousin had been trying to repeat Sira's procedure on her own—twice in the last hour—but without success. As Rael described it, the planet had no presence she could detect, while the M'hir stayed its usual, tormented darkness. Yet Drapskii had been manifest to Sira.

Perhaps the M'hir around Drapskii needed, in Rael's terms, a nudge. Sira had been unChosen, a Chooser whose Power was out of balance with the M'hir. She'd been a lodestone for its creatures. Perhaps she'd also attracted the planet itself.

A feather's touch, so light as to be imagined, against one cheek. Barac didn't look at Copelup, but knew the being tried to encourage him. Was he ready? Barac kept his fingers pressed against Rael's cool skin—not the least impressed to be bait simply because he was the only unChosen available—and opened his awareness of the M'hir.

Power. It was everywhere. Dizzying, seductive.

Focused by an Other, as if her greater strength dimpled some unknowable surface into a lens.

Nothing new in that. Hers was the greater Power everywhere, especially here.

Here? Barac abruptly found himself consumed in a darkness different from the rest, a twisted, oily mass tightly rolled on itself, as if moistened string were clenched in a giant's fist. He felt a moment of panic, then *knew* as the Other gave a soundless cry of triumph, reaching insubstantial fingers to pluck the mass. *Drapskii.* As though Her touch was a source of ignition, tiny flamelike flickers followed, expanded. This was *right.* The flickers became a reaching of their own, gathering Power.

A Power that sought outward, as he sought. Even

Barac recognized something kindred, a taste of desire matching his—*something* turned and entered him.

Ecstasy! Self vanished within completion. This was everything he'd been waiting for—to Join with another, to be accepted, made whole. What remained of Barac gladly returned Power for Power. It mattered not that his was insufficient. He was unworthy. But he would give until he had no more. . . .

How perfect to die, if this was death.

Others disagreed.

Barac's awareness returned to his body just as it was pushed off the stool to thump on the floor. He opened his eyes with an incoherent protest, finding himself flat on his back and trying to breathe through an agitated mass of purple-pink, blue-green, and a hint of yellow.

"Mystic One! Mystic One!" The dozen or more soft, worried Drapsk voices were overwhelmed by a single, outraged bellow.

"Barac! What in the Seventeen Hells of Deneb did you think you were doing?"

Joining with a hunk of rock, Barac answered to himself with disgust, and closed his eyes again, weary beyond belief. An alien rock at that.

He'd be embarrassed later.

Chapter 7

IT seemed a firm tenet of Human belief concerning the workings of the universe that whatever could go wrong, would. And always at the worst possible moment. While I preferred a universe that ignored me, even I was tempted to question fate when, within a day of our planned rendezvous with Plexis, the *Silver Fox*'s engine failed and she plunged from translight—to leave us stranded here.

"It could be worse," Morgan had said in that patented "Traders cope" voice of his.

Since "here" was within hobbling distance, in starship terms, of the Kimmcle System and nothing else—said system boasting a garish red sun orbited by three gas giants and a band of airless, icy rocks fondly called the Bonanza Belt by a deranged multispecies group of miners—I didn't share Morgan's view of our situation. Although, should we survive the trip, I knew Huido would appreciate another keg of the local brew. He'd waxed downright poetic over what we'd brought from our previous visit here.

A visit that hadn't, as far as I was concerned, gone well. "They are insane," I'd reminded Morgan.

"Only on weekends," he'd said back.

Which didn't improve my feelings about the entire issue—given we'd be arriving dead center of the Belt's Saturday night.

"Welcome! Time to say welcome! Who are they? Oh, yes. Traders! Morgans! Been before. Coming again. Welcome! Welcome!"

I did my best to look friendly rather than apprehensive. The Human trumpeting this running self-dialogue while approaching at a waddling run appeared happy enough. He also appeared capable of squashing us flat through sheer mass, so I was relieved when he began to slow his charge a few steps away. When I was convinced the Kimmcle had his inertia under control, I stepped out of the air lock to stand beside Morgan.

"Of course we came again," Morgan said in a near shout. Kimmcle miners were typically almost deaf by their second season. There didn't seem to be effective ear protection in their line of work, at least for Humans; Morgan told me most hoped to buy replacement organs when they retired. I'd refrained from comment. "You have such wonderful hospitality, 'Berto! How could we stay away?"

'Berto? I looked closer, trying to find the slim youth who had greeted us seven weeks ago within this behemoth. It didn't seem possible, even if skin and eye color matched.

Morgan sensed my confusion and sent: *It's a tradition. Any one who greets guests is 'Berto.*

So what do they call their mechanics—when they are working? I replied, thinking of the *Fox* in dry dock. A most deserted and unappealing dry dock.

Expensive.

I felt his laugh as we followed 'Berto down the tunnel. My hair wanted to respond and pushed at the netting I'd wrapped over it, yanking at my scalp before settling in a sulky knot. Hopefully, 'Berto hadn't noticed. My hair's self-expression had caused a near riot last time; I didn't intend to give it a second opportunity.

The place probably had its charm—one well hidden from the prying eyes of casual visitors like Traders. I remembered to watch where I put my feet. About a third of the miners were Festors, a species that shouldn't ever drink. The slimy green repercussions were everywhere.

And the night was young.

Just like old times, I sent to Morgan, deep in a shouting match with our guide about repair schedules. It did sound reassuringly as though the Kimmcle actually did have beings who stayed sober and worked over the weekend. I presumed they partied the rest of the week to make up for this lack.

It wasn't that I objected to relaxation—from the way Morgan described the five-day work shift of the miners, locked in small, fragile ships with nothing but the dark of space and rock for company, relaxation was essential— it was just that sobriety didn't seem particularly valued within the hollowed guts of this asteroid the

Kimmcle proudly and mysteriously referred to as "Big Bob." Big Bob had made the fortunes of many who no longer had to live here, while luring their hapless replacements to try their own luck.

Most never left. As far as I could tell, from my necessarily brief and restricted view of their society, those Kimmcle who stayed had evolved a culture that worked for them. It successfully combined claim jumping and mine salting—terms Morgan had made sure I understood before we came—with a distinct camaraderie.

In other words, any Kimmcle would rush to another's rescue without hesitation, and, as a matter of course, pick each other's pockets in the process.

Our destination, sad to say, was the same cavernous expanse—euphemistaclly called Big Bob's Recreation Complex—that Morgan and I had been in before, hopefully this time to be sans argument, sans brawl, and sans time spent confined with three intoxicated Festors.

The Complex was impressive, if you liked overwhelming confusion. To start with, it had been created as drilling followed the veins of various ores. As a result, the walls bent inward and outward at completely unpredictable intervals—granting the dubious sensation of having already lost one's ability to focus, which I supposed could save a few credits when buying drinks. Buying drinks wasn't a problem, of course. Outward curves of any significance housed breweries of various size. Any prominent inward protrusion of the walls hosted a bar. Supply and demand, close enough that some breweries could forget the kegs and run tubing from the vats to the nearest barside spigot.

Between the walls, floor space was also subject to supply and demand—in this instance, the demand for entertainment. Various areas were cordoned off by thick rows of beer-waving spectators, busily cheering on whatever activity was happening within their circle. Morgan had assured me it wasn't worth the effort to push through the crowd just to find out what that might be. Since his sending had been tinged with an amusing mix of embarrassment and discomfort, I'd been reasonably sure he was right.

The Complex's ceiling was high enough to allow Skenkrans, a species not usually associated with enclosed spaces, to hang their teardrop apartments. Those near to a wall were typically clustered over the closest brewery, some hung so low that tubing ran upward to each. Convenient.

Don't forget to watch overhead, Morgan sent, having noticed my attention. By the movement of his lips, he might have spoken aloud as well, but voices were pretty useless in the din. I nodded. While the *Fox*'s tapes on other species claimed Skenkrans to be the most courteous and civilized of beings, those who lived in Big Bob had developed a nasty habit of seeing how many of the throng below they could knock over each time they dropped from their homes. The other Kimmcle species took this as yet another game within the Complex, painting targets on the floor and daring one another to stand in them.

I prided myself on being exceptionally open-minded about aliens and their ways—for a Clan, at least—but this sort of reckless behavior was enough to make me long for the civil hostility of my own kind. In

Big Bob, I had to divide my time between obsessively checking the floor for Festor deposits—or freshly painted targets—and scanning the dark holes that served as Skenkran doorways. Morgan must be doing the same, but somehow managed to make his scrutiny so imperceptible he might have been taking a stroll down a corridor in the *Fox*.

Another of my Human's more arcane skills.

"If it isn't my Little Love Buds!" Another regrettably loud and personal shout, but this time I smiled.

"Hello, Rees!" I bellowed back. Ahead of us, the asteroid's rock wall fingered its way into the floor space, surrounded by the ubiquitous curved metal countertop. I went with Morgan as he and 'Berto cleared standing room along the bar—designated Big Bob's Bar # 46 with Kimmcle efficiency—for us.

Morgan hadn't been sure about Rees' species, and it wasn't polite to ask. It wasn't important—all who called the Bonanza Belt home referred to themselves, sometimes with a profane adjective, as Kimmcles. She poured us beers, grabbed a bowl of the fried sweet I'd liked on our last visit for me, and sent 'Berto off to greet someone else—after stamping the disk he waved at her. Morgan had explained this was to prove he'd done his job, namely ferrying another set of customers from the air lock to her particular establishment. The various bars paid a premium for the service, although I had to wonder how essential it was. How many unsuspecting tourists and traders could possibly be lured to Kimmcle? It wouldn't be my first choice. Or fifteenth.

Still, I thought, sipping a beer disappointingly like

every other I'd had since meeting Morgan and Huido—they claimed I lacked taste buds—I did like Rees. She'd hurried off to other customers after serving us, but waved at me periodically. The friendly being had not only welcomed Morgan and I during our previous visit, making me feel every bit the blushing bride, but had also been responsible for freeing us from jail. Just in time, I remembered; my meager tolerance for alien byproducts having worn off hours before and only Morgan's good sense keeping me from 'porting us both out, locked doors or no.

A gleeful, high-pitched shriek made me turn with everyone else, looking upward for the source. There. A Skenkran launched himself from his home, thankfully safely distant, and began plummeting to the floor. There was barely time for bets to be shouted before the being snapped open his shoulder casings, releasing the shimmering membrane silks that slowed his descent from suicidal to merely dangerous. With impeccable timing—or practice—he was able to suck in his silk before it became tangled in the mass of less-than-swift moving beings who'd unwittingly formed a landing pad.

"Good'un," proclaimed the Human beside me, slapping his companion on the head—the only part of a Festor not likely to ooze on contact.

I could 'port us to Plexis, I reminded Morgan. *We're within range.*

His eyebrows rose. *And leave the* Fox *here?*

Before I could formulate a reply to that, Rees slid to a stop before us, wiping her hands on a cloth slung over one shoulder. Her smile stretched from ear to ear.

Literally. Which wasn't the only remarkable thing about her mouth. It was abundantly populated with large, yellow teeth, each filed into a different shape, several with tiny inset jewels. As often as a Human might blink, the slender black tips of her tongue would run over her teeth, upper and lower, as if it was important to feel this unusual adornment during all conversations. While her loose-fitting dress, a strident orange that showed every stain, didn't reveal much about her body type beyond a couple of inexplicable bulges to the back, Rees did use two humanoid-like arms with five-fingered hands to serve drinks. Above her wide mouth and tiny, plug-shaped nose, her eyes were large, dark, and kind. She'd had price lists applied to her broad eyelids in some fashion since I'd last seen her. I found myself trying to read the items each time she closed her eyes.

Rees might be from any of a hundred systems, Morgan had told me. The root species of her kind, the Hoveny, had spread itself that far and possibly farther before its interstellar empire collapsed—around the same time Humans were four-footed shrews. Study of the Hoveny Concentrix was one of the most highly funded fields of research among Trade Pact cultures, given that newer species were determined not to repeat whatever mistakes the Hoveny had made in their empire building.

Humans were downright paranoid on the subject.

I could see their point. Rees might own distant Hoveny ancestors, but no one living could say if she resembled them or had evolved into something completely new and unique to her homeworld. The

Hoveny hadn't left images of themselves, only records of trade and sophisticated, often baffling technology. It was somehow humbling to think how very different from us a future generation might be. Not that Humans were overly humble, I thought, listening to Morgan's impassioned conversation with the bartender.

"—deal of the decade. Have I ever steered you wrong, Rees? Only snag is the *Fox*—we need an emergency refit and only have a couple of days to make it happen. If we can't catch up to Plexis by then, the buyers will haul out of orbit. You do know everyone worth knowing in Big Bob. What do you say? Can you get us a priority one?"

Rees turned her scintillating smile on me. "Always charming, your Jas-On. Still Love Buds, Si-Ra? See you've tamed your hair. Good'un."

One couldn't help but smile back. I drew my arm through Morgan's and snugged the offending lump of hair against his shoulder. "After last time," I said fervently, "I've no intention of causing a disturbance." I felt him chuckle.

"Dis-Turbance?" Rees laughed, leaning companionably on the bar despite the calls for service on either side. "Live-Liest night in for-Ever, Si-Ra. You had that Hu-Man yelling how your hair would turn ev'ry-Being to rock, the Fes-Tors thinking you had a Min-Kly spider on your head and trying to steal it—as if they need more fer-Tility drugs—then your Jas-On here taking of-Fense at all the attention with ev'ry-One at once. That was a good'un!" she concluded, smacking her painted lips together. "Tho' sor-Ry you wound up in jail rest of the night. Love Buds like you should have pri-Vacy."

"The *Fox?*" Morgan repeated.

Rees' smile became a little fixed. "Can't get pri-Ority on po-Tential deal alone, even for you, Jas-On. The mechs want something sub-Stantial for hurryup." Then her small hand thumped the bar. "You think of selling any o' that hair, Si-Ra?"

"Frequently," I muttered to myself, wincing as it squirmed in protest under the net, then said loudly: "No, Jason likes it, Rees."

She laughed. "Thought so. Love Buds."

Morgan's fingers wrapped around mine, but his attention was on our hostess. "How much will the mechs want?"

She seemed to assess his seriousness before nodding. "I can ask. You Love Buds relax a bit while I do. Not a pro-Mise, Jas-On—"

"We appreciate any help, Rees, to get us on our way as soon as possible," I told her with complete sincerity, having managed to finally pry the skin of my left palm from the noxious puddle that had glued it to the countertop during most of our conversation.

I'd learned, when sitting alone in Big Bob's Recreation Complex, to keep my eyes fixed on my beer and ignore the occasional slobbering sounds from underneath the table. Looking around inevitably provided a view of distended abdomens, Human and Festorian, while taking notice of the exuberant antics of the imported Retian ort-fungi would only brand me as a tourist. Knowing the mobile scavengers as I did, which was too well, I settled for keeping my feet curled up beneath me on the chair.

I wasn't really alone, of course. Under the sights, sounds, and smells of hundreds of strangers lay the presence of my Chosen, a mutual awareness more real than having his physical self within my sight.

It hadn't taken as long as I'd feared for Rees to be back in touch—she'd sent a Festor with a message for Morgan to meet someone within the hour. Alone. Which he wasn't either, I thought smugly, briefly extending my other sense to include Morgan's heartbeat, strong and steady, and the cautious attention he was paying to that someone. His shields were in place, effective against any other being. I backed away, lest I disturb his concentration. He'd let me know if he needed me.

We'd practiced this through trading sessions on— I stopped, amazed to realize the total was now nine different worlds and one way station. We'd found ways to use our inner connection to advantage, or, more precisely, to counter the advantages others had over us. When we ended our contract with Huido—Morgan's other regular clients not having any work available— my Human had done his utmost to select worlds where the *Fox* had a chance to bid for small, profitable cargoes—those unlikely to interest the larger Traders with their generation ships. With the universe's fine irony, on our very first stop we'd docked beside three. Each Trader had sent a representative and runner, coms being forbidden during negotiation, to every table—including those where the deals were for crumbs. To have a chance ourselves, we'd split up, with Morgan offering me advice on my first negotiation through our link.

It wasn't so much that I'd been brilliant, as it was that Morgan was able to share his success with me the moment it happened, letting me confidently outbid a very surprised chit from *Ryan's Venture* based on expectation of profit from Morgan's deal—this well before any *'Venture* runner started moving with the information.

Morgan and I were too careful to let this become a pattern, but we found other ways. Sometimes I would stay at the *Fox's* console, keying up information on prices and quantities to slip into Morgan's mind as needed. When we sat together at bidding tables, I'd watch one dealer while Morgan checked on another— information we could share without speech.

Making two more effective than one. I smiled at my beer. It was still a game to me, one which I could play, watch, or dismiss depending on my mood—though I gauged the importance of each trading session by Morgan's intensity. Some mattered more to him than others; those I made sure to take seriously as well. The others? Suffice it to say, Morgan suspected I knew more than I'd ever admit about how we'd lost the contract to transport those sacks of valuable beetle dung for that Whirtle.

Beetle dung, indeed. In my ship?

A hint of something not-right. I sat up straighter, putting down my feet without thinking, only to step on a heaving disk of fungi. I kicked the thing aside and concentrated.

From Morgan. *Not trouble. Something . . . unexpected.*

I calmed myself, wary of acting on impulse again, and prepared to wait.

Being sure to first lift my feet from the floor and keep my eyes on my beer, as one should on Saturday night.

INTERLUDE

Kimmcle miners of any species were easy to spot—especially on Saturday night, when the garb of choice was whatever came in the brightest colors. Festors, like the one who'd delivered Rees' message and now guided Morgan through the crowd, preferred flamboyant calico bibs which turned a truly disgusting shade of brown with the addition of green ooze. As oozing followed every belch, and Festors belched between every swallow of beer past their limit, the hue was a reliable indicator of how sober a Festor was at a given moment.

Implying this one had either changed bibs recently, Morgan observed, or was atypically pure for a Saturday night. Perhaps a professional messenger, not someone doing Rees a favor.

"Not far," his guide said, as if worrying the Human might decide they'd walked too far already. "Near wall—by Bar # 105—Rees said to take you there, Hom Morgan."

"Thanks." Morgan walked lightly, an eye to the Skenkran divers as well as to those they passed. All seemed harmlessly preoccupied. He'd known to wear something bright himself—a sure way to blend with locals—and had switched from his faded spacer coveralls to a jerkin and pants of vivid red, a fanciful design picked out in gold-and-blue thread. Sira had refused to change, but then she couldn't blend in anywhere in the Trade Pact, the Human thought, smiling to himself.

Sira had only grown more lovely these past months, a beauty as hard to define as it was to ignore. Perhaps it was how she carried herself like a queen, he decided, which to the Clan she essentially was, yet it was an unconscious pride, as though her Power somehow manifested itself in posture and grace. Her face, in turns framed or veiled by that amazing hair, was exquisitely expressive: dark gray eyes dancing or serious, generous lips as quick to smile as purse in thought.

Or to offer a kiss. Morgan drew his thoughts firmly back from that highly distracting direction. He did, however, promise himself to collect such a kiss when this meeting was over.

"Here we are, Hom Morgan."

The Festor had stopped at a more elaborate establishment than most, one that offered booths—improving the odds of holding a conversation without shouting. Morgan flashed a look at the booths to either side of the one the Festor indicated. Their privacy fields were engaged but not opaqued, so one could see quite clearly what was going on inside, but mercifully be spared sound effects. As usual, there was a cluster of spectators and bets being placed—an indication a significant number of Kimmcle were at last drunk enough to enjoy watching anything that moved. However slowly.

Morgan took his seat within the booth, joining the shadowed figure waiting there. The Festor bowed, switching on full privacy as he left them. The rest of Big Bob's Recreational Complex faded from view, leaving several disappointed Kimmcle to use their imaginations.

A small port light brightened above the center of the table, revealing a tray of mournful-looking cooked prawlies imprisoned in jelly, a decanter filled with an amber liquid, and the ubiquitous pitchers of beer.

"Brandy, Captain Morgan?"

"Beer's fine." Morgan studied his host as frankly as he was being examined in turn, seeing a small man in a flowered shirt, his black hair thoroughly peppered with white, with a nose that looked to have been broken several times—assuming his parentage was pure Human. "Hawthorn, isn't it?" he said. "Head of the Miners' Association?" When Hawthorn's eyes widened in surprise, the Trader grinned. "One of your election posters is still inside the main air lock. A little dated, I'd say. Congratulations on your win." Morgan stretched his hand over the table to meet the other's grip. Hawthorn's hand was strong and callused along the base of the palm—sign of a driller.

"You pegged it. Giles Hawthorn," the Kimmcle admitted, grinning back. He poured a glass of beer and pushed it to Morgan, splashing brandy into another for himself. "Rees was right—you're an interesting man, Captain Jason Morgan of the *Silver Fox*, Karolus

Registry. You see, I read the fine print, too. Seems you have a problem with your fine ship."

Morgan took a sip of his beer, savoring the cool rich taste on the back of his throat. Another satisfying brew. They really knew their hops in Big Bob; the only drawback was the difficulty in finding the same brewery in operation two trips in a row. "A problem you can help me with?" he asked.

"Possibly. I do have a—job to be done. From what Rees and others tell me, looks like you might be exactly the being I need."

"Depends on what they said about me. Hope it's good," Morgan replied with a easy smile, on impulse checking the force blade up his left sleeve. He let out a tendril of thought, carefully aimed at the mind nearest him.

Nothing.

The unexpectedness of it skimmed across his link to Sira, who responded with a questioning thought. Morgan reassured her, then focused on his companion.

So, Hawthorn had a mind-shield. Its slightly metallic feel within the M'hir meant it wasn't natural, but rather one of the implanted devices used by Bowman and her elite group of Enforcers. Morgan considered, and dismissed, the possibility that he faced another of Bowman's operatives. Politicians, business tycoons, and crime lords were just as prone to fearing mind invasion—the elected Head of the Kimmcle Miners' Association would be all three.

Hawthorn had continued, oblivious to Morgan's moment of preoccupation: "One of the first duties of my new administration is to host the Ore Meetings.

They begin tomorrow morning and we've got delegations from over fifteen systems and organizations. These meetings are critically important—do you know why?"

Morgan leaned back, a posture not inconsequentially giving him a wider throwing range in case new targets happened to arrive, and nodded. "They're where you find out how high you can jack ore prices before the refineries start going elsewhere."

Hawthorn slapped both palms down on the table and gave a startlingly deep laugh for someone of his body mass. "If everyone at the meetings would admit that, we'd save about thirty standard hours of pointless rhetoric. 'Course there is value to following protocol—"

"You can hope someone falls asleep before noticing what you've slipped in?" Morgan suggested.

Another belly laugh. "Rees was right. You're no one's fool, Captain Morgan. Now, all I'll need is for you to attend the meetings—and stay awake. You just let us know if anyone tries anything—peculiar. We'll deal with them."

"Peculiar?" Morgan frowned. "I'm no expert on ore pricing, Hom Hawthorn."

"Ah, but you are a telepath—of considerable ability—are you not?"

Morgan schooled his face into polite astonishment and nothing more. "I don't know what you've heard, but I'm no—"

Hawthorn picked up his brandy glass and took a deep swallow. "Don't bother," he advised, his tone level, almost somber. "It's not a secret, Captain. Not any longer. Why do you think you've found contracts drying up, old customers becoming hard to reach?"

"My contracts are my own business, Hawthorn," Morgan snapped.

"Seems you don't have much left, then. Word's out on you. Mindcrawler. Telepath. No one's going to trust you again, you know. I'm sure you have your own way to—sense—why I might be the exception."

Morgan took a deep breath, controlling his expression, thinking hard. Unlikely any of the Clan had exposed him—giving secrets to Humans wasn't their style. Besides, they seemed to have, however grudgingly, accepted his status as Sira's Choice. Bowman had known for years, but had sworn she'd told only Terk and 'Whix. Why would she damage his credibility, when she so often wanted him as her spy? The Drapsk? Huido? Neither would betray him. The Retian, Baltir, would have done so with glee—but he was rumored to be a rug in a Makii tavern.

Leaving one possibility. Ren Symon.

Morgan smiled pleasantly. "Let's say, for the sake of discussion, that I have some small—Talent. What would it have to do with your Ore Meetings and getting the *Fox* back in space?"

He drew a spiral on the table with one finger as Hawthorn eagerly explained, wondering not so much about Symon's motives—those were never •obvious and any guess likely wrong—as how to avoid sharing this particular detail with his Chosen.

After all, she was expecting him to return with good news, not proof that their trade had been deliberately sabotaged.

Chapter 8

BEFORE I felt Morgan's return, I had had time to finish my now-warm beer and refuse three separate offers by strangers anxious to remove their clothes while dancing on my table. Since neither table nor would-be dancers looked capable of such a performance—the former being uneven and rickety, and the latter equally unsteady on their varied limbs—I followed Morgan's advice for such situations. I shook my head firmly, then said in a melodramatic tone he'd made me practice: "Go away or I'll take out your knees with this blaster."

It worked whether the species in question had knees or not—even proving effective when both my hands were on the table, making it transparently obvious I had no such weapon or intention. A puzzle Morgan tried to explain by saying it wasn't what I said, but how I said it. I'd argued it would be much more effective to 'port such annoying beings into the nearest sludge pond, but had to admit, the bizarre Human tactic was more discreet.

"All quiet?" Morgan asked, sliding into the other

seat. As he had to lean forward and shout this at me, I had to smile, a smile the Human took as invitation for a brief, surprisingly passionate kiss. Not that I complained. A lock of my hair squirmed free of the netting to reach for him as he moved away again. I tucked it back, regaining my composure with the gesture. Another hopeful dancer stopped his approach and wandered away.

"You could say that," I told him, also shouting. If ever there was an environment for mind-speech, this hall full of bedlam was it, but we both knew better than to fall into a habit of communing silently in public. There was an understandable alarm aroused by knowing a telepath was nearby—one of the few transcending species' and cultural barriers—an alarm that could provoke a violent reaction from those who couldn't, or wouldn't, understand the limitations of this particular "gift." Another reason the Clan preferred to remain anonymous. "Is the *Fox* going to be repaired?"

He nodded. "They'll get on it tonight, but it's going to take a couple of days."

"And how many credits?" I asked, studying his face. When Morgan wore that carefully sincere expression, he'd been devious lately.

"The mechs have a scrap engine to rip up for parts—that's a savings. Part of the delay, of course, but it turned out for the best because I can . . ."

The latest shrieking dive of a Skenkran into the crowd made it impossible to hear him. *You can what?* I sent, mouthing the words and daring him with a look to argue anyone watching could tell the difference.

We haven't enough credits to cover used parts, let alone new, Morgan sent, saying it aloud at the same time—the feel of the sending remarkably sanguine considering its content. *But credits aren't an issue,* he explained, likely sensing my confusion. *The Kimmcle use a barter system—Rees found a way to let me work off the debt.*

Doing what? He was keeping something back. I didn't need my other sense—I could see it in his eyes.

The noise level diminished so I could hear Morgan's answer. It didn't mean I liked it any better.

"Security. They have a series of meetings here over the next two days and want a bit of extra protection for the delegates."

"And that's worth the price of repairing a translight engine?" Used parts or not, this didn't make sense. I studied his too-controlled face. "Protection from what?"

Morgan's smile was angelic—on the surface. Something darker lay underneath. "That's the beauty of it. Probably from nothing. The Kimmcle are panicked by a rumor that a competing mining operation has smuggled in a telepath to spy on their meetings. You and I both know how unlikely that is—"

"Unlikely isn't the same as impossible," I countered without thinking, then stopped to stare at him. "They asked you? Why?"

His shrug was a little too offhand. "I've a reputation. Rees knew it."

"As a lucky pilot," I disagreed. "Not as a telepath." Suddenly the crowd around us seemed threatening. I controlled the urge to 'port. "How many of these Kimmcle know you are more than lucky?"

"Rees and I go a long way," my Human said almost too smoothly. "She knew we needed the favor—and that the Miners' Association was willing to pay. My contact with them is Giles Hawthorn, the newly elected Association Head. He's the only one who'll know why I'm there. Trust me, Sira. It will be two days of standing around, looking attentive and suitably grim. Boring but profitable."

I sensed energy pouring into the M'hir, maintaining a barrier deep within Morgan's mind. It could have been an unconscious secrecy. On one level, my Human believed I kept my distance from his private thoughts— he should, given how often his practical jokes took me by surprise. On another, the Human instinctively guarded parts of his mind and memory. This was as it should be. We were Joined and partners, not blended into a single being.

I was also aware that his Human ideas of our relationship, both as lifemates and crewmates, sometimes differed from mine in ways I couldn't predict—or understand, for that matter. Nothing about our pairing was uncomplicated.

Everything about it was worthwhile. I smiled at Morgan, trusting him with his secrets, and said cheerfully: "Then tonight is ours, Husband."

He captured my right hand and brought it to his lips. "While I'm in complete agreement, Wife, we really must think about Huido." I must have looked— and felt—shocked, because Morgan gave me that low laugh guaranteed to provoke delicious shivers down both sides of my spine. "Believe me, I'd let him stew in his own pot—but now that we know about Acranam?

Neither of us likes that coincidence. And you know as well as I do that Inspector Wallace isn't about to sit back and let the Enforcers take over any case he has his hooks into. Huido may need our help."

"Huido," I echoed wanly. "You want to send him a com signal?" Such a civilized technology—and one we could possibly even afford, thanks to Rees' help.

Morgan shook his head and held my hand in both of his. As another Skenkran targeted the crowd with the requisite assault on everyone's hearing, I felt: *Not a message—you. You said Plexis is within your range. I want you to go and help Huido while I wait for the* Fox.

I'd already made the choice to trust him. He'd known. So I did the only thing I could do.

Nodding, I tugged free a lock of hair. It immediately slid down my arm to wrap itself around our clasped hands. Morgan's eyes turned that impossible blue. With the merest hint of the desire pounding in my blood, I sent: *I'll go. But not tonight.*

INTERLUDE

"Hom—Huido?" Ruti looked from one statue-still Carasian to the other. "We were going to consult on tonight's special?"

The mammoth lower right claw of the being to her left rose slowly.

The mammoth lower right claw of the being to her right rose just as slowly.

Both stopped at precisely the same height.

"This is a ridiculous way to run a restaurant," the young Clanswoman said with disgust.

"I told you it wouldn't be easy." Ansel shook his head. He stooped to add a spoon to the collection of utensils in his apron, its shining metal easy to spot amid the pieces of broken wood. Being from a planet overgrown with trees, Ruti wasn't impressed by wooden furniture, intact or otherwise. She was impressed by the thoroughness with which Huido and his visitor had turned the special dining area of the *Claws & Jaws* into scrap.

"Well, something has to be done, and it's not up to me. I can make all the decisions I want, but you know as well as I do the staff isn't going to listen to me. They barely let me cook as it is."

As Ansel sighed agreement, Ruti put her hands on her hips and surveyed the nearer of the two Carasians. There had to be a way to tell them apart.

They might have been in stasis. Every eyestalk was rigid and erect—and focused on the other. Monstrous bookends, Ruti told herself. Before she lost her nerve, she walked up to the nearest of the two aliens, and stretched out her arm until her fingers brushed the cold hardness of his shoulder.

When he didn't react, she felt bold enough to repeat the process with the second, Ansel watching with a puzzled expression. "That one's bigger," she announced, stepping back from both and pointing.

"Finally—someone with decent manners in this place!" The Carasian so indicated heaved upward, rattling like a entire cupboardful of pots that had come loose and fallen to the floor, his claws snapping in the air. At the same instant, the other compressed himself into an approximation of a lump—eyes peeking from behind the pulsing halves of his head carapace and clawtips tactfully tucked under his body—before saying in an almost falsetto voice: "Hello, Uncle Huido."

"Well, don't just cower, Small One," Huido rumbled. "Tell me which misbegotten spawn of the family you are—then catch me up on the gossip. How's old Noiko doing?" A cymbal sound. "Ansel, what are you waiting for? A new day? Hurry and get some of the best for my nephew here. Ruti?" Three eyestalks peered over the edge of his lower head carapace. "I had no idea you were so versed in Carasian etiquette.

Thank you for your assistance. My little relation here and I might have had to stare at each other for another week—no hardship for him, of course—" This delivered with a laugh that seemed forced.

"My pleasure, Hom Huido," Ruti said, not bothering to make any sense of it beyond being glad the stalemate had ended smoothly. "Do you think you might have some time—later—to discuss tonight's menu? I was thinking perhaps the Denebian lamb?"

"Oh, I like lamb," said Huido's nephew, emerging from his crouch with movements so excruciatingly cautious they sounded like a chain being pulled through a massive eyelet, one rusty link at a time.

"Jake was right, Lara," Ruti whispered. She threw herself backward on her bed, hugging the tiny doll to her chest. "He was right!" Her new friend had been an immense help to her already; even so, she'd been astonished to find he'd known how to free the giant aliens from their irrational standoff. Yet Hom Huido was in the kitchen now, berating those who'd tried to keep her, Ruti di Bowart, from her rightful place as Master Chef.

"Because of my friend." Ruti lifted the doll in both hands, staring into its gleaming brown eyes. They didn't move. Lara wasn't a spooky high-tech toy, but a treasured heirloom who'd been passed at fostering time from mother to child through four generations of Clan, a companion who'd listened to innumerable private dreams and stories, keeping them safe forever.

The doll was no bigger than the palm of Ruti's hand, easily slipped into a pocket or hidden in a sleeve. A little shabby, perhaps. A new dress and ribbons had been due, but Ruti's mother hadn't had much time to prepare for her fostering. Neither of them had, since one hadn't seemed possible—first because Acranam's Clan hid their children from the Council, then because the Council ignored them.

Ruti controlled the burning rage that surged up each time she thought of that day, when First Chosen Wys di Caraat had burst into their kitchen and dared stab her gnarled old finger at her, had dared insist she be one of the seven to be dispersed by Acranam immediately. Not to be fostered, not to be the honored guest of a worthy House—her mother had told Ruti how it used to be—but to be smuggled away on alien scows, dumped at a distance and told to remain hidden as long as their bonds lasted. Sacrificed for the greater glory of Acranam.

Ruti hugged Lara hard, closing her own eyes to better feel the tenuous binding between herself and her mother, Quel di Bowart, the power from both constantly and desperately feeding their only connection. More than love—other than love—it was a drive for survival that used up almost all the energy Ruti had to spare. She found herself constantly tired, constantly hungry . . .

And constantly angry.

At least, thanks to her friend, Jake Caruthers, she had this place. If he hadn't found her, shown her the way to Huido's, kept her safe from the patrols scouring Plexis for Clan? Ruti shuddered. Jake had hinted what happened to young females in the hands of unscrupulous Humans. She'd believed it, after they'd walked through that sublevel.

Ruti opened her eyes and glanced at the wall chrono. She should have time for one call before she was needed in the kitchen. Maybe Jake could meet her after tonight's shift. She had so much to tell him.

"I don't care how you keep him occupied, just keep him away from my apartment, Ansel. Is that clear?"

As the Human nodded vigorously, Huido gave a heavy sigh, echoes rattling from the nearby stove. "It's the price of success, old friend. Scavengers sneak close, full of plots and schemes to take advantage—waiting only for the opportunity to lunge at your *arux* and rip it open." Then dip in your pool to celebrate, he shuddered to himself. "I'd hoped," with a melancholy click of claw to claw, "being so far from home, that those at home would forget about me."

Ansel unwisely offered advice. "If this nephew, Tayno Boormataa'kk, is such a danger, Hom Huido, why not send him away?"

The Carasian surged up, claws snapping so close to Ansel's face the resulting breeze lifted the few hairs left on the smaller being's head. "And refuse this glorious honor! Humans." This with complete disgust.

"Carasians," Ansel muttered to himself as he turned, running a finger along his nose as if checking to make sure it remained intact.

Huido pretended not to hear. The old Human was more confidant than servant; the Carasian could, if he made the effort, twist his brain around to appreciate Ansel's reaction as well-intentioned and protective.

An instinct admirably suited to family groups and herd behavior, if not to a species where males competed from maturity till death for a chance to breed, with only a few judged worthy.

Though cheating was definitely encouraged and cuckolding a refined art.

His "nephew"—an otherwise meaningless word Carasians had found helped avoid tedious explanations of why their species didn't bother specifying biological relatedness, only home surf—was presently occupied taste-testing various brews. But for how long? Huido decided to change the locks on his apartment at the first opportunity.

Which should come once Ruti arrived to take over. Where was she? His eyes searched the kitchen. No sign of her. The prawlies in the big stewpot took advantage of his momentary distraction to leap out, yipping with pain as their ventral paddles contacted the hot stove surface. Huido whirled and tried to grab them, but they danced about, continuing to yip and almost impossible to catch. Finally he resorted to batting them away with his upper handling claw, cooks to either side ducking as half-roasted, yipping prawlies shot past their heads.

"Where's Ruti?" Huido roared.

"I'm here, Hom Huido." Her cheeks were flushed and her eyes glittered, signs of excitement and pleasure, he judged, not a reaction to his temper. She might not have even witnessed it, given she hadn't been in the kitchen a second ago. Fortunately for her supposed Clan desire for secrecy, the rest of the staff had been avoiding flying fish and hadn't noticed their new Master Chef wink into existence. In fact, several were still engaged in hunting prawlies who'd wriggled underneath various cupboards, retrieving indignant culinary delights now covered in dust.

Huido spared a moment to worry about his *grist*— after all, one's pond performance was a delicate matter, easily perturbed by things like this willy-nilly moving through other dimensions by the Clan—then cheered. He could have Ruti take his nephew for a few trips . . . of course, that meant trusting her. Unlikely.

"You wanted me, Hom Huido?" the polite question interrupted his thoughts.

"The lamb needs braising," he rumbled, then waited until she moved out of his way before striding off.

He didn't get farther than the exit before a voice heralded a new problem. "Hom Huido! Wait!" The Carasian clattered to a halt, two eyes longingly on his apartment door, the rest scouring the hallway and kitchen anteroom for ambush. It might be easier for his nephew to hide his bulk among the slick tidal rocks preferred by females on their homeworld—that didn't mean he wouldn't try crouching behind furniture. Huido spared one eye to glare at Ansel.

"If it's not about my nephew, I'm too busy."

"There's someone to see you, Hom Huido."

A claw snapped in midair. "Not another relative!"

Ansel shook his head. "No, sir. It's Plexis security. Hom Huido—it's Inspector Wallace himself, with other officers. They want to talk to you about someone named Naes Fodera."

Huido, in the midst of a shrug, stopped. Six more eyes clustered to look at the smaller Human. "You don't think . . ." he began, then stopped. They'd taken great care to dispose of Neltare's regrettable pâté and ribs: packing them up as a catering special, then marking the container as spoiled by a failed stasis system. It should have been destroyed by the recycling plant immediately. The *Claws & Jaws* paid its taxes. "It can't have anything to do with . . ."

Over the years, he'd learned Ansel's expressions and thought he knew them all. This ferocious scowl was something new. "For all we know," Ansel almost hissed, "that creteng chef ran straight to Wallace. A shame he wasn't run over sooner."

"If he had," Huido said sensibly, refusing to add more paranoia to his day, "they'd have been here within the hour, not days later. No, this is probably about our last inspection. I suspect Wallace is here to scam another case of my brandy." He clicked clawtips together delicately. "Still, make sure Ruti keeps out of sight—send her shopping if you must. Put out some of the cheaper appetizers for our 'guests.' Stall them while I change this lock code."

After all, first things first, the Carasian thought smugly. "Then, Ansel, I'm putting you in charge of watching my nephew."

"Your nephew? But—?" Ansel's face fell. "Yes, Hom Huido."

"Keep him happy. Show him the business. It's important—" Huido stressed the word, "—to convince Tayno the restaurant is very successful. Sell him a franchise, if you can—preferably on the far side of Carasia. And—most of all—keep him away from this door!"

"But it's locked. Even if he got inside, wouldn't your wives—" the Human's voice trailed off suggestively. Ansel, like all the staff, knew about the less-than-delicate nature of Carasian females. The "let's eat what moves" aspect of this nature, combined with an armored and clawed body half again as large as any male's, had proved sufficient to quell even primate curiosity.

Huido raised all four claws, hissing in frustration. "I've no time to explain, Ansel. Just guard the door and don't let Tayno near it." He tilted his head carapace at a bizarre new worry, all eyes riveted on the Human's face. "You can tell us apart, can't you?"

Ansel licked his thin lips. "I know you're bigger, Hom Huido," he said quickly, then hesitated.

"Well?" the Carasian rumbled.

"A password might be wise," the Human admitted weakly.

Chapter 9

MAYBE it was weak of me, but I waited until Morgan slept before starting to pack the few things I wanted to take with me to Plexis. I was finding items by feel in the darkness when suddenly his low voice ordered up the lights, adding: "Don't forget your flute."

"I didn't mean to wake you." I opened the next drawer and pulled out the battered case of my keffle-flute—a Joining gift of sorts from my sister Pella, who'd insisted it not be sold. "I won't have time to practice," I decided, putting it back.

"You might still want to take it."

"Why?"

Morgan chuckled, sitting up so I could meet his eyes in the mirrored tiles. "While the Kimmcle will claim their mechs are beyond reproach, I wouldn't leave anything to tempt them. That—" with a nod to the drawer, "—comes under the heading of very tempting." I scowled but lifted the case out again. He was right about its value. The case might be ordinary; the instrument inside was anything but—having more history in its precious inlays than the M'hiray, including having been played in concert by nineteen master musicians. It had been my most prized possession, once. I alternately cursed and blessed Pella for making me keep it.

"We could lock it in the hold."

"The hold is sealed and under vacuum—we didn't want to pick up any stray fungus from Big Bob, remember?" He blinked sleepily, hair adorably ruffled. "Take it. I'll feel better knowing you have it with you."

I shoved the case into my carryroll. "Fine. Maybe I'll be able to pawn it on Plexis." He didn't rise to the bait, knowing I couldn't part with it.

It wasn't because I still loved the instrument; I hated it. Alone among the joys of the past three months, the keffle-flute was a thorn in my skin, a stubborn symbol of what I'd lost. Ever-helpful Pella had sent recordings with it: brilliant, complex renderings made with a stranger's skill. The fading calluses on my hands lied to me of that music; all I had left were a few halting notes from a tune that slipped into silence whenever I tried to play it.

Proof my mind hadn't recovered from the blockage. Proof I wasn't whole. What else had I lost of Sira di Sarc—of her life before meeting this Human, becoming this new person? My inability to ever truly know chilled me at times like this, certain at any moment I might see something or meet someone I should remember, but wouldn't. Worse, I imagined having lost some skill more crucial than music, a lack waiting to cripple me.

I kept packing, feeling Morgan's silent empathy as

a gentle reminder that no matter what I'd lost of that old life, this and more I'd gained. My 'port to Plexis without him would be our first real distance apart, but not a separation. I understood our Joining would only be strengthened by distance. Intellectually. Sira di Sarc understood.

Sira Morgan didn't.

Suddenly, illogically, any distance between us was too much. I dropped the bag and threw myself violently toward the bed, feeling Morgan's strong arms catch me before I bounced off to the floor. Without a word or sending, he settled me within the curve of his body and drew the blanket over us both, my tool belt with its assorted accoutrements disappearing from around my waist before I noticed the discomfort of lying on it.

Tomorrow wasn't, yet.

"Rise and shine!"

I cracked an eye, unsure why Morgan felt morning on a starship—especially one parked inside an asteroid's repair dome—required hammering as well as this bellow from the doorway. Then I realized the hammering was a vibration coming through the floor plates. "The mechs?" I grumbled.

"Already back to work in the engine room, sleepyhead. Good thing the com woke one of us."

"At least they knocked," I muttered, but the Human was gone again—presumably to hover over his beloved engines until it was time to go to the Ore Meetings.

Which would be my signal to leave as well. We'd worked out a plan to account for my absence over the next two days. After breakfast, I'd accompany Morgan to our temporary quarters on Big Bob—the mechs having considerately requested we clear the *Fox* before they started ripping out potentially explosive components—and stay there. Well, it would seem I stayed there. Morgan would order meals for two, vistapes, whatever seemed reasonable.

After the fiasco of our last visit, it shouldn't be hard to convince anyone who knew me I'd prefer to hide out while Morgan worked and the *Fox* was off-limits.

I made sure the cabin door was locked before stripping out of my coveralls and heading for the fresher stall—taking Morgan's advice about not trusting the Kimmcle to stay beyond reproach.

Foolish, to see this as anything more than a brief good-bye. No matter how sternly I told myself this, I hurried around the small apartment, moving in ridiculous circles as I found inconsequential things to do. Morgan stayed out of my way, leaning beside the door. His eyes were hooded and inscrutable, as though his thoughts were on what lay ahead.

As mine should be. I made myself stand in one place, carryroll in hand, and looked at him. "Everything in order, Captain?" I asked.

He came close, fingers brushing lightly at the red flash of fabric on my left shoulder—a relatively new Trader custom to distinguish a ship owner from mere crew. We'd adopted the practice after trading on Cura Primus, where Morgan noticed those ship owners with flashes received preferential seating at the bid tables. Again, by custom, ours bore the name *Silver Fox* as well as a summary of her cargo rating and engine stats to entice potential clients. "Isn't it straight?" I asked, craning my head to try and see for myself.

"It's straight. But do we want to advertise?" Morgan mused. "It might be better to keep a low profile, this trip."

I glanced at him, surprised. "A low profile? All that'll get us is a shipload of debt when we leave Plexis. If you're worried about what deals I might make—" I endeavored not to sound offended, but my hair began writhing at the ends. "You know I'd contact you before signing us up for anything."

"No, no. You're right," Morgan said almost too quickly. "We can use the business. Just don't be disappointed if no one makes an offer. Plexis is unpredictable—one trip you hardly dock before getting cargo, and the next? The ring will be overflowing with Traders who've off-loaded and are hungry for scraps. Now remember. The main thing is to keep Huido calmed down. He always thinks the louder he says something, the more likely people will agree. It won't work with Plexis security. Not if they have evidence."

I suspected my Human's somewhat rambling speech of having the same cause as my erratic pacing of a moment before. *I'll be fine*, I sent, adding much more beneath the words: caring, assurance, a tinge of concern. *You look after yourself and our ship.*

Morgan took my right hand, bringing it to his lips. I allowed myself to drown in his eyes for an instant, then stepped back, concentrating on the locate I'd selected. Before I could hesitate, I . . . *pushed* . . .

. . . finding myself darkness within darkness, power

within power. It was a long 'port, but well within my ability, if I were careful not to be tempted by this path or that, to lose my way following imagined symmetries. Though I didn't tap Morgan's considerable strength through our lengthening link, I drew focus from it and . . .

. . . became solid again, looking around quickly to be sure no one was nearby who might have witnessed my unusual arrival. I tested my link to Morgan. He was *there*—distant but real—a reassurance I'd badly needed. Here?

I was alone.

Unless you counted servos. I stepped to one side to let a lumbering transport by, resisting the temptation to duck as messengers zoomed past just overhead. I was inside one of the service corridors—tunnels really—that formed the veins and arteries of Plexis. A bewildering machine world, kept pressurized and heated to eliminate the need for air locks at each business entrance, kept well-lit for those servos who used visual sensors for navigation.

A bustling, noisy world that ignored me—the nonfunctional intruder—completely. I took my bearings and headed left, avoiding the row of waste canisters busy chewing their contents. Each let out the occasional belch of methane, immediately sucked into tiny hovering air sweepers that expanded, balloonlike, with every capture.

The rear door to the kitchen of Huido's restaurant was just ahead, but I discovered I wasn't the only intruder in the corridor today. I dodged behind the last canister, hoping I'd moved quickly enough to avoid being seen. Keeping my head close to the floor, I peeked around the hard-working device.

The door was as I'd remembered it, except now it was being studied by four Plexis security personnel, one of whom was running some type of sensor over the doorframe while another made a vid of the entire procedure. They weren't the sort Plexis employed on the shopping concourse—those helpful, approachable beings who offered friendly advice to stray customers while checking for air tags. No, these four had more in common with Enforcers like Terk—armed, serious, and probably annoyingly suspicious, especially of someone on the wrong side of that door.

So much for Bowman's taking over the investigation. Inspector Wallace, a Human I remembered Morgan describing as stubborn and shrewd—as well as always on the lookout for his own best advantage— must have reacted to the Enforcer's interest by an increase in his own. This wasn't good. I considered 'porting right into Huido's kitchen, but there could be more security inside. The safest approach would be to blend into a crowd and walk in the front entrance like every other being.

For that—I rubbed one hand pensively over the smooth skin of my cheek—I'd need an air tag.

Faking an air tag wasn't within my capabilities. I could offer the illusion of one or, more accurately, temporarily confuse someone looking at me into wondering exactly what was on my cheek—but only if that someone's mind was susceptible. It helped if the beings I tried to confuse were already under the influence of some intoxicant, or at least uninterested in my face to begin with—both highly unlikely in those selected to staff Plexis security checkpoints.

The little blue or gold patches—for low budget or noncustomers and high-credit customers respectively—were living things, affixed to one's skin or comparable external covering by Plexis personnel at a tag point. As those were only at normal accesses, I'd have to find a way to appear at one of those. When and where no one would notice.

If I'd been able to make the unobtrusive entrance to Huido's I'd planned, the Carasian would have lent me one of his business patches. Those were blue air tags like the rest, but removable. Every permanent station resident or business owner had one or more of the tags, usually stuck to a wall somewhere for convenience. Employees would peel one off to wear conspicuously on cheek, or appropriate body part, in order to move around on the main concourses. It was simpler than showing residence chits to security every few steps. Plexis took "the air we share" concept very seriously.

Instead of recording the exchange of gases occurring within their wearer, business patches died after a set time. The withered blue corpse was returned to an air tag point where it was recorded, the owner's account charged, and a new patch issued. Replacing a "lost" tag typically required bribes in order to avoid criminal charges.

A tag of my own was definitely my first priority. I might have asked Morgan for advice, but my tentative *reach* across our link encountered a wall of preoccupation. I could intrude, but at the risk of pulling his mind from whatever had its attention. As this could be anything from daydreaming about his next painting to dodging a Skenkran, it wasn't worth the risk.

Besides, I admitted guiltily to myself, part of me had been eager to 'port here alone instead of waiting for the repairs. It wasn't only to help Huido. While a murder was nothing to ignore, and I took Bowman's suspicions about Ren Symon's involvement very seriously, this was my first chance to actually have a good long look around Plexis. Considering this was the most famous supermarket in the Fringe, I owed myself at least that. How was I supposed to be a Trader, I reasoned as I walked, unless I took time to learn what there was to trade? But I'd need that air tag first.

Between the thought and my next step, a heavy weight suddenly rammed against my right shoulder and back, shoving me to the floor. I landed painfully on both knees and an elbow, my carryroll flying off to one side. I tried frantically to see my attacker, presumably a servo with malfunctioning avoidance reflexes, but was crushed flat as the weight distributed itself more evenly across my back. I couldn't breathe . . .

Instinctively, I threw my awareness into the M'hir, preparing to 'port myself away . . .

. . . instead, it was as though a song plunged through me. If music could be swallowed, it would resonate through the body like this, tasting of longing—of needs, dark and primal; of promises, sweet and breathless . . .

Somehow, I remembered myself and the feel of the

floor, the weight on my back, and the importance of air reaching my burning lungs . . .

. . . Then I was back, sitting up and breathing in great tearing gasps. Belatedly, it occurred to me being able to sit up meant I was free of whatever had pushed me to the floor. I paid more attention to my surroundings, expecting to see a servo transport of some other device blinking at me in dismayed apology.

The floor stretched away to the walls on either side, those walls curved and distorted until I blinked to clear my watering eyes. The nearest servo was a tanker parked by a closed door, presumably waiting for a delivery. There was nothing within reach, nothing that could have attacked me.

Attack? I rubbed my sore elbow thoughtfully, checking my link to Morgan. It was calm—undisturbed even though my entire body continued to tingle as if shot through by some current—or as if still resonating a need.

An attack? Or, I suddenly wondered, had it been something else?

INTERLUDE

"We can try something else."

"We tried everything else. This worked. You are being ridiculous."

Barac covered his eyes with a forearm. His cousin might have 'ported into his bedroom and torn open the curtains, spilling revoltingly bright sunshine over his bed, but he didn't have to acknowledge the morning. "Ridiculous or not," he insisted, voice thick from the sleep she'd interrupted. "I won't toss myself back into the M'hir as bait for that—that—"

"It's a planet. A planet with some weird connection to the M'hir. An inanimate rock with some type of Power associated with it. Your dead aunt's ghost! I don't care what it is, Barac, and neither should you." Rael paused for breath, her hair lashing about her face as though continuing her tirade. "We made progress, Cousin. You weren't damaged. In fact," she traced his outline in the air between them as she spoke, "you seem in remarkably fine shape. You know what Copelup and the others said—"

"Their machines showed a 'spike,'" the Clansman

mumbled through his arm. "What's a spike? What does that mean? They don't even know."

"It means they are happier today than yesterday. With any luck, we'll make them happy enough they'll declare our mission here a resounding success and let us go home. You do want to go home, don't you?"

What he wanted was to 'port his cousin away, preferably far away, and resume ignoring the universe. This not being remotely within his power, Barac sighed and pulled down his arm to glare at Rael. "Since I don't have a home at the present time," he told her bluntly, "I'm understandably more concerned about remaining safe than hurrying to what doesn't exist."

Rael frowned. "I thought you owned that repulsive bar on Pocular."

"It's now a warehouse," he corrected, "used to store truffles before they are shipped offworld."

"But still yours."

"Technically." Barac pushed himself up, having to flail his arms to clear a passage through the pillows that seemed to have multiplied overnight. Finally, he tucked a couple behind his back and tossed the rest to join the lopsided piles on the floor. The Drapsk occasionally erred in favor of excess when trying to provide luxury for their guests. The Clansman settled, contemplated Pocular, and shuddered deliberately. "I might own the building, but do I want to live in a fortress, guarding bags of drying fungi, and surrounded by beings convinced I'm one of their witches in disguise? Let's not forget this is a population whose idea of culture is to drink, gamble, or dance naked around fires—preferably at the same time. My future home? I don't think so."

"Then where will you go, once we're done here?" Rael sounded honestly curious. Barac peered through the strong sunlight at the Clanswoman.

She'd climbed into the window seat. The Drapsk had designed everything here to Clan proportions, so there was ample room for Rael to stretch out her long legs. She was studying the view rather than him and the sun's rays played through her hair, teasing fire from its silken, living darkness.

"Janac's a fool," Barac said without thinking.

She faced him, clearly startled. "Why? What's he done?" A brief pause in which Barac could feel her *reaching* through the M'hir. "He's working on his plants again," she said finally. "What made you think of him?"

"Don't you?"

"Which?" Her lips curved in a mocking smile. "Think he's a fool, or think of him at all?"

"Think of him. Think of going to him, instead of back home to Deneb." Barac couldn't explain to himself why he dared to be so curious. He and Rael might have become unusually close for Clan, but she was what she was: *di.* It wasn't merely impolite to question a Chosen about his or her Joined partner—the offense could prompt a quite-justified challenge, one a *sud* couldn't hope to survive. Instinctively, he tightened his mental barriers.

Rael didn't look angry, only weary. "No. Council has never ordered it, if that was your next question. The old Council judged our potential offspring as too likely to be *sud* or worse. Perhaps now, with what's changed on the Council, what we know about our kind—that will change. Why ask me this?"

Barac slid his legs over the side of the bed, rubbing the heels of his hands into his eyes with more force than necessary before looking at her again. *It seems a waste*, he sent, offering his view of her in the sunlight.

"While I thank you, Cousin, for so flattering an image," Rael said, the corners of her mouth turned up in a half smile, "I suspect you've been around Sira and her Human too long. To Join is to be made complete, but not all Joinings are joyous. And," she licked her lips, "not all Joinings become more—intimate—than mind-to-mind, through the M'hir."

He dared more: "Did it ever occur to you to try? To spend time with your Chosen? Don't you feel a need—" Barac shut his mouth, gesturing appeasement with both hands.

The Clanswoman shifted position on the window seat, her face becoming a silhouette, the feel of her Power against his an enigma. "The Joined, my un-Chosen and oh-so-lonely cousin, dream as one. Our needs, as you indelicately put it, are met." Not offended, yet, by her tone. Not pleased either. "I'm only telling you this because of Drapskii and what happened to you yesterday."

His turn to be startled. "What do you mean?"

"You weren't alone, you know." Rael paused, as if reluctant to continue, but did. She spoke slowly, cautiously, as if feeling her way. "What you experienced, what you felt . . . I can't deny there was a similarity to what exists between the Joined. I don't know how that's possible, or what it means—"

"It wasn't real!" Barac leaped up, striding away from her in long, angry steps until he reached the door to his apartment. He stopped, facing the door and its false promise of escape. "It wasn't real," he repeated, hearing defeat in his own voice, feeling it ricochet through the M'hir between them.

"Of course it wasn't," he heard her say, the sound closer. She'd followed him. "But your need for it to be—that's real enough."

Is there nothing more for me? Barac couldn't stop the thought or the flood of despair that rose with it. *Is there nothing more for you than dreams—for any of us? Is Sira right? Are we the last of the M'hiray?*

A sigh he felt on the back of his neck. *We may be,* Rael sent, holding in her emotion so the words came as sharp pieces of truth. *Sira's Trade Pact vows to help us— if they fail, with all their technology and science, where else can we turn? And if they succeed? Do you believe we'd pay their price?*

Barac understood Rael's bitterness all too well. No Clan but Sira—tainted by Human thinking—expected altruism from aliens. No Clan—after generations living in secret on Human worlds, influencing Humans and other species as needed for safety, for gain, for entertainment—would willingly offer their Talent to serve aliens. If the Trade Pact demanded that service in return for the key to Clan survival?

Exodus. The Watchers were prepared. They would gather the Clan, guard and guide the journey from Trade Pact space as they had from the Clan Homeworld. Perhaps, Barac thought wistfully, they'd become a fantastic tale Humans would put on their vids and tell their children: ethereal beings who chose to disappear rather than tempt others with their Power.

A legend? Rael's thoughts wandered with his, Barac having let down his barriers. *I'd prefer a living legacy.*

As would I, he replied, involuntarily reliving that moment when the dream had seemed real, the memory only making the emptiness worse.

Chapter 10

HALLUCINATION—some sort of dream, I decided as I searched for my belongings on my hands and knees, peering under canisters. The carryroll, so long proof against psychotic baggage handlers of several species, had split open when I'd fallen.

Been pushed.

Fallen, I told myself firmly, ignoring the persistent irrationality rattling around in my thoughts. I shook my head, aggravating the ache centered somewhere in the middle of my skull. My probing fingers had found no sore spots, so I hadn't been stuck by some flying servo. The likeliest possibility, a nearby refuse canister, gave an obliging belch—attracting a horde of air cleaners to intercept the gaseous prey. I'd probably been overcome by such fumes and fainted, dreaming I'd been violently pushed to the floor.

And violated.

That certainly hadn't happened. Delusion. Another side effect of the fumes.

I had to get out of here as soon as possible. I stretched my arm to its fullest, rewarded by the feel of something solid yet easily moved, and grabbed it with my fingers to pull it out.

The keffle-flute case. It would have been safer on the *Fox* after all.

I used a belt to tie my ruined carryroll into something approximating a bag, putting the narrow case in first, then surrounding it with the sort of things one didn't want protruding in public. My other pair of coveralls made an excellent outer layer, filling the split area of my new "bag" with only a slight bulge of blue fabric.

Wonderful. I was conspicuous enough already. My hair, as if in complete agreement, chose that moment to wake from its lethargy to whirl in a blinding mass.

Plexis welcomed starships. After all, the station relied on them to transport everything from goods to customers who'd pay extravagant prices for those goods. Liners and private yachts received preferred parking, their air locks opening into well-appointed lounges where uniformed staff discreetly offered air tags and free drinks before politely shooing shoppers directly on to the upper concourses.

Scheduled deliveries had their own access points, efficient and thorough, though lacking free drinks. Traders, tourists, and other visitors who forgot—or couldn't—post a substantial credit rating, competed for the remaining parking spots along Plexis' belly. No free drinks here either. In fact, the station's first act of greeting for such ships was to secure them with grapples, and woe betide any Captain who didn't save enough credits to cover the parking fee.

Fortunately, however, the lack of courtesy granted such ships included forcing their crew and any passengers to navigate a labyrinthlike corridor system to reach the tag points. I possessed a locate, a visual memory, for the portion of this system where the *Fox* had docked in the past. It would mean gambling no one else would be there when I "arrived."

A station night would have helped, but Plexis didn't keep a day/night cycle—claiming, truthfully, that its customers were of such varied species it would be impossible to establish a cycle well-suited to most, let alone all. Instead, Plexis featured night-zones, packed with suitable entertainment. If you wanted dark, you went there. Sleeping wasn't a particularly sought-after option. Stores could keep their own hours, and did, resulting in a lively and frequently exhausting competition to see which could stay open longest. Restaurants, like Huido's, tended to cluster in areas with designated mornings, afternoons, and evenings, making it possible to actually plan a daily menu.

So it wouldn't be dark, or necessarily quiet where I was going. I remembered Morgan's gesture for luck and crossed the first two fingers of my right hand before I *pushed* . . .

. . . and quickly sidestepped into the partial concealment offered by a stack of plas crates on a waiting grav cart. My heart was pounding as I listened for a shout or any other sign my arrival had been noticed. After a couple of deep, steadying breaths, I began to relax, considering how best to join the crowd.

For a crowd it was. I assumed the only way my en-

trance could have been missed by the seething boil of
beings filling the middle of this corridor was their
need to concentrate on their footing or be trampled,
the mass apparently hurrying toward the tag point.
Maybe I'd been wrong about the free drinks. I spotted
Humans in bewildering variety, a Whirtle or two, then
a straggling group of Turrned Missionaries passed me,
each with a small shoulder sack. Without thinking, I
moved to join them.

The Turrneds walked quickly for such tiny beings,
easily keeping pace with those possessed of longer, or
more numerous, legs. On my arrival, however, the
nearest immediately turned their great, disklike brown
eyes up at me instead of looking where we were
going—causing a momentary confusion as they collided with one another and had to stop to hug one another in apology. Before this resulted in impatience or
worse from those behind—a group of Denebian
traders towing grav carts laden with coils of sparkling
marel roots, presumably destined for those shops offering seasonal decoration—the Turrned sorted themselves out and we began marching along again.

However, the beings somehow managed to keep
their eyes fixed on me in a soulful gaze that made one
either melt on the spot or start talking. "First trip to
Plexis?" I asked involuntarily.

"Yes. We go to the Mission." "You are troubled."
"Come with us. We will pray for you."

I couldn't tell who said what—the Turrned kept
their mouths closed and vocalized with their throats.
"Where is the Mission?"

More Turrned began gazing up at me. Having seen

some of Morgan's vids of Human companion animals, I now better understood why he sometimes called the species "evangelical puppies."

I swallowed and shifted my bag under one arm. Ahead, the corridor opened up as we neared the tag point. The crowd was starting to split into faster-moving streams, like water being forced between the rocks of a rapids, as beings hurried to the line they thought would move a microsecond faster.

"Sublevel 384, spinward third?" I persisted. "Is that the one?"

"The Mission." "The Mission." I felt a warm, dry hand take mine, fingers not quite long enough to cross my palm. The skin was rough, but not unpleasantly so. "Come with us." "Come with us." "Come with us."

As that was exactly what I intended to do, I smiled quite happily at my new friends as they took me with them through the tag point—saving me the effort of explaining to anyone official how, despite my spacer coveralls and owner's flash, my ship wouldn't be docking at Plexis for another three standard days.

It was, of course, not the same Mission. As far as I'd deciphered from the Turrneds during our trek to the nearest rampway from the tag point, there could be seven or a thousand Missions on Plexis; they weren't overly clear on the distinction between an individual Mission and a leased room. Luckily, I did know the station well enough to appreciate the difference between a sublevel and one of the exclusive upper ones, so when my new friends wanted to herd me to a rampway populated by gold-patched customers, I politely—

and with some guilt—disengaged. I watched them stare adoringly up at a pair of suddenly uncomfortable-looking Humans and grinned to myself before heading in the other direction.

Plexis, I supposed, was ideal for the Turrneds' purpose: an admirable, if at times overly-enthusiastic, attempt to spread their belief that all life should be treated with the same courtesy civilized beings paid one another. This seemed relatively harmless—involving a ritualistic apology before slicing into supper and a sensible discouragement of rude behavior in general—but I could only wonder what species like the Scat thought, whose intraspecies courtesy contained a basic "kill-you-first" aspect.

Not that the Turrned would encounter any Scats on Plexis. The station discouraged their presence. Not overtly. Plexis was well aware any attempt to ban a particular species would bring down the wrath of the Trade Pact and an unwelcome, likely permanent, Enforcer presence. Instead, they'd simply and quite legally banned the Scat's main food item as undesirable pests, requiring proof of ship sterilization from any Scat ship asking to park.

The Scats hadn't protested. Those interested in Plexis brought their ships near enough to do business but not so close as to alarm the station. As Morgan put it, they were like predators: homing in on the scent of prey, then waiting in the dark for the chance to ambush in safety. He shared, I'd noticed, Plexis' low opinion of the species.

I had mixed feelings. Compared to Humans, I'd found Scats predictable, reliable, and—though I hated to admit it—more like Clan. The days when I'd been more affected by a species' appearance than its true nature were, thankfully, long gone.

Smell, however, I still noticed. Sharing air on Plexis, particularly in the less-than-exclusive sublevels, meant doing everything possible to avoid sharing with one's olfactory organ. I'd have worn a respirator, except it was considered snobbery unless mandated by biology. Even then, you'd get dirty looks.

Sublevel 384 was, as I'd expected from the mass coming on-station where I'd met the Turrneds, packed with beings, all sporting blue patches like the one slapped on my left cheek, but there any similarities ended. I was surrounded by a blend of local residents, tourists, shoppers, and spacers—of every species imaginable, each with its unique way of mixing with others.

The Humans weren't bad. This time and place, few would be intoxicated—yet—and most had likely bathed within the week. We were similar enough in size and motion that I didn't find them a navigation problem. Well, not the solitary ones slipping and dodging through traffic. I did know to avoid Humans in groups, such being prone to stopping for no apparent reason and without warning, oblivious to how this impacted on any other beings in their vicinity.

Lemmicks, however, were much worse. I kept careful watch for their greatly elongated skulls, which towered over all but the tallest servos, and knew I wasn't the only one on guard. Granted, they were inoffensive, pleasant beings—graceful, in a way, with their long faces and delicate limbs. Snappy dressers, too, always sporting the latest colors and fabrics and eager to see the newest styles Plexis could offer. Perfect customers—who, to put it tactfully, made sharing air a brutal challenge to any humanoid-type sinus.

Stores who regularly catered to Lemmicks either invested in air scrubbers, potpourri, or incense. Or all three. It wasn't that the beings smelled bad. It was more that the unseen component of a Lemmick could bring tears to the eyes and make one want to crawl away into a dark, quiet place—preferrably inside a well-used space suit. They could have felt the same about being near humanoids. On Plexis, one coped to shop.

I held onto my bag, and my stomach, and mutely endured the barrage on my senses, ducking the odd elbow and other body part aimed—accidentally, of course—at me. My hair, for a change, hung as hair should. I finally passed into a portion of the crowd where those around me were relatively shorter, permitting me to get my bearings. From this perspective, the heads of shoppers and visitors might have floated on a restless ocean, their voices surf breaking in the distance. At least I could now see the walls, where the stores would be. Without my making a conscious decision to detour out of my way to Huido's, I found myself taking advantage of an eddy within the foot traffic that promised to take me closer to the nearest wall. Wholesalers only, on this level, but still . . .

My half-formed thoughts about fine gemstones and other profitable merchandise vanished as I found myself abruptly free of the press of beings. I was puzzled, until the reason burned my nostrils and I looked around rather frantically to see where the Lemmick might be.

I couldn't see any of the shapely beings, just others evacuating the vicinity. As I did the same, I noticed a pair of Humans—an older male who towered over his companion, a younger female—both looking more nauseated than I felt.

I don't know what made me suddenly careful, to give no more than a glance before slipping behind a foursome of Ordnexian spacers. My Talent didn't include precognition. Instinct, perhaps, something more fundamental to survival.

Because in that glance I saw enough. I knew one of those Humans. I kept walking, hoping I hadn't been recognized in turn, my inner self so tightly controlled I should be all but invisible. Should be, but this was a being who'd surprised me before. I didn't use my Power to confirm his identity; I'd never forget that face: older than Morgan's, harsher, with cold, dead eyes and a passionate mouth.

Ren Symon.

Had he seen me? Unlikely, but I paused to put more distance between us, tucking myself beside a convenient bit of greenery , one of the plant clumps Plexis was prone to put anywhere people might be tempted to walk in a straight line and I supposed forced the traffic to zigzag closer to the various stores. I wasn't worried about losing my quarry. Symon was distinctive enough even in this crowd. I wouldn't need my inner sense to track him.

I was more concerned with my own growing visibility. The press of beings was thinning once more, split like an opening braid to file between the tables and fountains marking the entertainment and refreshment area of this level, as well as to avoid the less than steady clusters of celebrants returning to their ships. Typical of Plexis, the area ahead was a night-zone, the better to entice shop-weary travelers to the clubs and bars lining her walls. Once I was sure Symon was safely ahead, I would follow him through it, trusting the raucous and overlapping music, combined with the dimmer lighting, to keep him from spotting me in turn.

The thought of hesitating to follow, even into this less than savory part of the station, didn't occur to me. I wasn't going to lose the Human—not until I knew exactly why he was here and what threat he might pose to Morgan.

INTERLUDE

By the halfway point of the second round of the Kimmcle System's 72nd Annual Bonanza Belt Ore Meetings, Morgan had begun to hope the improbable threat Hawthorn feared would materialize. Or a pipe would burst. Anything would be an improvement over listening as nineteen supposedly mature individuals verbally disemboweled one another.

He was quite sure that was what they were doing, despite the smiles, nods, and free-flowing beverages. Mutual destruction, all in the truly obscure dialects of ore refining and profit margins.

The Human shifted his weight from his right to his left foot, keeping his shoulders pressed against the wall, and stifled a yawn. The Kimmcle weren't big on formality, so there'd been no nonsense about a uniform. The Head of the Miners' Association had greeted him with a short, sharp nod, without introducing him to the others filing into the room. It would have been a waste of time, given that every non-Kimmcle delegate had arrived with one or more security personnel who had immediately, and with professional grimness, stood at attention behind their client. Morgan had amused himself by guessing which of the stalwart figures would be first to join him in slouching against the wall. So far, no takers.

As he'd done every few minutes, Morgan opened his awareness, that way of looking through another, nonphysical eye he'd had all his life, gingerly extending it to include those in the room. It was like opening a curtain to find the sun too close, providing so much light, so much information, it blinded rather than illuminated. With a practiced mental slip to one side, Morgan withdrew himself enough to begin sorting what he felt.

There were two ways to pick out a telepathic mind from the confused mayhem of the nontelepathic. The untrained, or those with little Power, were pitifully transparent to his other sense, their deepest thoughts spilling into his unless he guarded himself. Those trained or powerful enough to possess natural shielding were as easily detected by what didn't show. A shield mimicked emptiness, placing a void where there should be a mind. Among those in this room? It would be like a warning shout: Over here!

Nothing. The only telepath at the Ore Meetings—and probably in this system—crossed his arms and stifled another yawn.

Hawthorn had chosen better than he knew, Morgan thought, assessing himself with cold detachment. Symon, for all his betrayals and lies, had taught him the importance of knowing his own Power, of being able to clearly see his abilities and rank them against others'. Joining with Sira had enhanced many of those abilities a hundredfold or more; her training continued to add completely new capabilities to his mind. Despite this—or because of it—Morgan found it reassuring each time they encountered seemingly unsurmountable differences in their powers, to know himself still more Human than Clan. There were things Morgan drew upon his Human Power to do, such as detect and heal damage within a mind, things as mysterious to Sira as her ability to move herself through the M'hir remained to him.

Not that he denied he'd been changed by their Joining. Morgan judged himself, in an interesting irony, perhaps the only non-Clan who could actually do what Hawthorn feared—enter a susceptible nontelepathic mind, rip loose its secrets, and, in the process, destroy it.

As for other Human telepaths?

Morgan shied from the thought, standing straight and paying attention to the meeting now breaking for supper. He gave Hawthorn the single nod they'd agreed on as a signal that all was well. A glance at the wall chrono showed he'd have time to check on the *Fox* before rejoining the Kimmcles' guests for tonight's banquet.

As Morgan left the room behind Hawthorn, the thought circled back on itself like a snake—the truth, he knew, no matter how much he'd rather not admit it even to himself.

Human telepaths? As Morgan was now, with the Power and abilities Sira had granted him, it would be all too easy. He hadn't met one who could hide from his seeking thought. Not one who could protect themselves from his assault.

Not even Symon.

"Tomorrow's when . . . it gets down to the tough . . . the tough *and* dirty, my friend," Hawthorn asserted, eyes owl-wide, pupils dilated. The Head of the Miners' Association, Morgan decided, was well past hammered and not the least concerned about it. Since the other delegates appeared in a similar state—having imbibed the stimulant of their species preference "on the house"—Morgan presumed this was an expected consequence of the Ore Meetings.

The other security on hand hovered about, expressions ranging from noncommittal to bored, obviously more interested in how soon their clients would need help to return to their suites than protecting them from harm. However, Morgan felt a twinge of responsibility for the Human now sprawled on the table across from him. The repairs on the *Fox* were going well, due to Hawthorn's faith in what he couldn't see.

What he couldn't see. Morgan smiled to himself and *reached* into the M'hir for Sira, still amazed the binding between them could disregard space and distance.

She was there. He could feel her presence, but nothing more. It was as if her mind was locked away. *Why?* Morgan refused to let his imagination run wild. Sira kept her shields tight around everyone but him, and now she was on Plexis, a popular stop for the Clan. She was being careful; it didn't mean she was at risk.

He could *reach* deeper—deep enough to regain her

attention and have the warm feel of her thoughts slipping through his. And disturb her concentration, Morgan chided himself.

Hawthorn gave a happy little mutter, pushing his arms outward to knock over his almost empty glass. Morgan intercepted it as it rolled to the table edge, then froze, glass in hand.

There was something wrong.

Not with Sira. *Here.* He put down the glass and loosened his force blades, holding them hidden in both hands, ready to throw.

"There he is!"

Morgan casually looked for the source of that shout. The private room used for the Ore Meetings presently contained over thirty individuals who might qualify as the "he" being found, if one included the quartet of androgynous security personnel lurking by the bar and the multisexed Nrophrae. But the Human believed his own warning.

Trouble, indeed. The dozen—no, make that two dozen—squat, round beings now bursting through the doors might look harmless, their white eyeless faces surmounted by blue-green frondlike antennae seem inoffensive and mild, but hardened security guards and their drunken charges scrambled out of their way as quickly as they could.

Even on Big Bob, a motivated Tribe of Drapsk commanded respect.

Morgan replaced his force blades in their sheaths as the first Heerii Drapsk reached his table, talking too quickly to make any sense at all. The Human held up his hands to stop the excited being. "Just a minute," he said. It was a reasonable guess that things were about to change. Morgan reached over to pat the comatose Hawthorn on one shoulder. "Thanks for the job."

Then he looked at the Drapsk. Privacy wasn't an issue—the small beings had already supplanted any guest who'd remained conscious, those guests having vacated the room as rapidly as they could stagger out the door. The Drapsk formed a ring around his table, an anxious, very quiet ring with antennae pointed slightly in his direction. Several members of that ring were sucking their tentacles.

"So," Morgan began, more curious than dismayed— he hadn't been too excited about another day of Ore Meetings, especially with all the delegates bound to be hungover. "What brings you to Kimmcle?"

Chapter 11

WHAT had brought Symon to Plexis? I asked myself as I continued to follow the pair. He had to know the Enforcers were hunting him, despite Bowman's discretion. And who was with him? Frustratingly, I hadn't caught more than a few glimpses of the young female, enough to guess she might be a child. Symon's?

Or his latest protégée, I thought grimly. I knew from Morgan's own past how Symon enjoyed finding young telepaths, how he'd steal their strength while he taught them, how that training twisted each young mind until they either learned to enjoy pain, as he did, or provided it for him.

I took advantage of a dawdling group of Humans, using their argument as cover to sneak closer. At last, a good look. The female was no one I'd met and not as young as I'd first thought. I frowned, tempted to use my Power to learn more about her, but reluctant to risk discovery. I didn't know Symon's full capabilities, except that he'd proved more than elusive. He'd successfully hidden not just from Bowman but from me.

Morgan didn't know I'd had Clan Scouts hunting for Symon, though it had been almost my first order as Speaker for the Council. My Human had thirsted for revenge against Symon too long. That desire had almost consumed him once already. I'd been proud when Morgan conquered his inner darkness and was able to put Symon out of his thoughts; I'd been grateful to know he'd found such peace.

Because it left me free, in the eloquence of the Scat, to eat our enemy's heart.

So who was Symon's female? They'd moved quickly through the night-zone, more quickly than I'd expected. It was as if she'd hurried to avoid it. I could understand why. The music from the various halls vibrated through the floor plates; the dimmer light turned every being into a silhouette who might or might not be drunk enough to grab at random; and even the beauty of the tiny port lights, floating high above to mimic a starry sky, couldn't disguise the fact that several beings had recently ejected the contents of their digestive tracts.

Add a few Skenkrans overhead, move some dubious entertainment into the main area, and a Plexis night-zone would be astonishingly like Big Bob's Recreation Complex, I concluded, unsure whether to attribute the similarity to the Human tendency to keep building what worked, or if this was some socio-economic trend that crossed species' barriers. Spacers, loud music, and bars.

The night-zone ended as abruptly as it had begun, delineated by bright full-spectrum lighting and businesses whose windows didn't contain flashing signs advertising: "No matter what your taste, we have the species for you!"

Perversely, now that it was easier to see and be seen, I lost sight of my quarry. I ran up one of the side ramps to a balcony overlooking the main concourse. Most levels were taller than a single floor—a result of retrofitting a refinery designed to munch asteroids—and Plexis took full advantage by hosting stores and other businesses up its walls as well as along the floor.

The concourse wasn't busy. From the finer clothing and lazy movements of the beings below me, I guessed it was late evening in this section. I put my bag on the floor and stepped closer to the rail, looking for Symon. He should be easy to spot—taller than most Humans, big through shoulders and chest, his coarse brown hair unfashionably short and sprinkled with gray.

There. The two of them were almost out of sight, heading in the direction of the *Claws & Jaws*. Another threat to Morgan's giant blood brother, this time coming in the front door? I snatched up my bag and, taking the chance, *pushed* myself into the M'hir . . .

. . . to stand within the shelter of one of the arched entranceways to the vast Skenkran-operated cafeteria. The cafeteria might be Huido's neighbor, but it hardly afforded him competition as it was closed more often than it was open. I wasn't surprised to find the door behind me locked, its surface plastered with several lurid "unsafe for any species" signs. More likely, they hadn't paid their taxes. Huido had told me Plexis forgave poisoned patrons before bad credit.

The tall entranceway—one of five—was set deeply into the wall, with lumpy inlaid tile and plas plants competing for attention. Intended to make one feel as though entering a true Skenkran dome, it succeeded in being an ideal place for ambush.

Of course, I'd planned to be the one doing the ambushing, my plan to crouch in wait until Symon and his companion walked by. What I'd expected to do next was unclear even to me, but I had no chance to try.

Within a heartbeat of my arrival, I knew I wasn't alone.

Before I could turn my head, everything went dark. I began to drown beneath a swell of unheard music, its wild notes flooding my bones, singing of need . . . desire . . . an urgent, restless heat . . .

"Fancy meeting you here."

The shock of that intrusion was visceral. I gasped as if struck, fought to regain vision, any sense of what had happened, what was happening—losing that sense even as I was able, barely, to clamp down my connection to Morgan, to keep him safely unaware. Otherwise he'd hear that voice through my ears. *Symon*. My Chosen would try to come to me—to 'port. I knew it—

"What's wrong with her, Jake?" I heard, higher-pitched, softer—no less cruel. *Jake?*

"I don't know." *Neither do I*, I thought, still blind, feeling rough hands grab my arms and pull me against a hard body, too numb to protest or act in my own defense. "Too much to drink, probably. You go home, Ruti, dear. I'll look after her."

"Why don't you just leave her here?" Petulant, as though the child begrudged me Symon's care.

Care? I tried to struggle, but he'd wrapped his arm

painfully tight around my shoulders, supporting me in a parody of kindness.

"I look after my friends, don't I?" Symon didn't wait for an answer. "Now go. Remember what I told you about the Carasians. And watch for my friend Jase Morgan at the restaurant. I want you to tell him how very much I need to see him."

"I know, Jake. I keep watching for him, but are you sure he's coming?"

Morgan? My attempted sending was too late; I was too close to losing consciousness. Desperately I set my inner defenses as Symon dipped to put his other arm behind my knees, then lifted me against his chest.

"I'm quite sure," I heard the renegade telepath say, a sickening note of triumph in his voice.

INTERLUDE

Ruti scowled as she walked up to the *Claws & Jaws*, bypassing the main entrance in favor of a smaller door set inconspicuously at the juncture between the restaurant and the upscale hostel beside it. She keyed the code for the doorlock, tapping her foot as she waited for it to accept and admit her. Why the Carasian didn't use a more conventional palmlock was beyond her. . . .

As was the behavior of her friend. This was supposed to be their time together, she fumed, time hard enough to come by without his wasting it on some drunken spacer!

The door unlocked. Ruti pushed it aside rather than waiting for it to open. She peeled the air tag from her cheek, slapping the cold, grotesque thing to join the line of its cousins on the wall, then hurried down the hallway to the kitchen. Since graduating to chef, she'd succeeded in avoiding cleanup—a situation that wouldn't last if Ansel or Chee, the head dishwasher, spotted her without something to do. She could 'port to her room, but Huido seemed to know whenever she entered the M'hir. Tonight wasn't a time to make the

Carasian irritable, not if she wanted to be able to leave early again tomorrow night.

Surely Jake would rid himself of that—that female by then. No matter that she'd been . . . Ruti swallowed, then admitted the truth to herself. Regardless of her shabby spacer clothing, Jake's "friend" had been stunningly beautiful, with red-gold hair hanging in great, heavy waves down her back and huge, unfocused gray eyes. And Ruti wasn't completely naïve—you couldn't be after working nights shoulder-to-hip in a kitchen with beings who chatted about every physical aspect of life in obscene detail. Ruti had seen Jake take pleasure in the feel of that body against his.

When Ruti Commenced, she would be more beautiful. Far more beautiful than any Human spacer dreg. Jake would see her and forget anyone else existed.

Ruti might forgive him by then.

A few more steps. Ruti took an involuntary glance into the kitchen, then stopped to stare. It was full of beings, but no one was cleaning. Staff, looking miserable, angry, and, in one case, sound asleep, stood or sat near the back. For the first time since she'd arrived, the mammoth stove was silent, grease congealing on its cold surface. The giant steam table no longer boiled. Cupboards hung open, drawers were pulled into the aisles—even the doors to the undercounter stasis units were ajar, vegetables sprouting as they made up for lost time.

And Plexis security was everywhere.

"There must be another way."

Huido swiveled three eyes to examine Ansel's anxious face. "I'm all ears," he said without humor, continuing to reach for various sidearms and other weapons, securing each to a clip embedded in his chitonous plating. The two of them were in the outer room of his apartment, the Carasian having reluctantly decided this wasn't an opportune moment to be distracted by his lovely wives—no matter how they savored stress and excitement. "Inspector Wallace has asked me to come quietly to the station brig in five minutes. You know how many beings don't leave there on their own limbs?"

Ansel wrung his hands together. "Then you must leave the restaurant now, tonight. Get off the station."

"That's what I intend to do, old friend. Make sure you stay in here. With security at every door, it's not going to be a quiet exit." Huido hummed contentedly as he dropped a set of blast globes in a mesh bag.

"You can't mean to fight your way out!" The Human looked appalled. "Maybe you should go with them after all, Hom Huido. It's only an inquest—" he pleaded.

More eyes swiveled to gaze at the Human. "Wallace has that misbegotten pâté and ribs—which have to be pretty ripe by now—and claims I killed the Neblokan, too. A wonderful notion. I wish we'd thought of it."

"You've done nothing wrong—the Enforcers will believe you! The Sector Chief knows you personally." Ansel, who measured influence as carefully as he kept the restaurant accounts, had been overjoyed to find Bowman's name near the top of the restaurant's list for an annual truffle gift box.

"Plexis security doesn't like me much, Ansel, especially since they know I've kept track of 'special fees' they've requested over the years for certain less-than-legal services," Huido rumbled. "Plexis likes Bowman and her Enforcers even less. You think Wallace wants an inquest? Hah! He wants to toss me out an air lock before anyone else asks questions. So if you don't mind—" Huido pulled a particularly nasty and highly illegal biodisrupter from its hiding place, "—I like my plan. Blast my way out and take what opportunities arise."

"Wait!" Ansel came to stand directly in front of the larger being. "The Inspector . . . his people . . . they haven't seen your nephew—he's been in his quarters the last couple of hours going over the accounts. We can use him as a diversion. He can pretend to be you—trust me, that would work." At Huido's menacing claw snap, the Human added quickly: "As long as you aren't together. Then they'd notice immediately how much bigger you are."

Appeased, the huge alien subsided, continuing to gently snick one claw together as if it helped him think. "I'm not saying I agree to this—but then what?"

"Then?" Ansel was breaking into a sweat. Huido suspected he was nervous around armaments that could take out the side of the station. A wise fear, though the Carasian had no intention of making such a mess—at least not in his own apartment. Suddenly, Ansel's face brightened. "Then—you go through the service corridor to the Mission. The Turrneds will help—I know they will. They can get you offstation until all this is resolved."

"Which leaves my nephew here to either be dumped out an air lock or to try and explain to Inspector Wallace," Huido's eyestalks began to dance. "I like your approach, Ansel. I definitely do." He slipped his carefully padded vest over his weaponry, not so much to conceal anything as to prevent the metal-on-plate sound. The Carasian stood statute-still for a moment, then said: "Fine. Go tell Ruti to pack. She's coming with me."

"Sir?" Ansel, who'd started for the door, looked around with a frown. "Why take the child?"

"She has no records," Huido reminded him mildly enough. "Any digging by Plexis could reveal her origins—something I doubt Sira would want. I'll take care of her. Now hurry. Wallace must be finished ruining my kitchen by now. Which reminds me—don't forget to make a full accounting of spoilage—including whatever they slipped into their pockets. We'll send Wallace a bill. A big one."

"Yes, sir." Ansel seemed on the verge of saying something else, then stopped, nodding as if to himself. "And taking Ruti is a very good idea, Hom Huido. I'll make sure she's ready."

Once Ansel was gone, Huido went to the amber-colored sideboard he used to store important items such as crystal decanters of Brillian brandy and the hideously expensive translight com system Morgan had insisted he install. Well, it would have been hideously expensive, but Sira hadn't been the only one to make friends on Drapskii. The Makii had given him a very generous discount.

Yes, Huido thought as he prepared his message. He'd take good care of Ruti. Especially since the child had set him up so perfectly.

Carasians didn't forget.

Chapter 12

I HADN'T been set up, as Morgan might put it. I couldn't remember everything leading to my present less-than-desirable situation, but I did recognize the hand of fate.

And the folly of overconfidence.

I ran one hand over the smoothness of a wall that was more than it seemed. Since awakening here, in this peculiar little room, I'd had plenty of time to puzzle over its unique properties.

No furniture. What was left of my carryroll and its contents lay piled in one corner, where they'd obviously been tossed without care. My keffle-flute was still in its case, none the worse for rough handling. I couldn't seem to get rid of the thing. Nearby, like an afterthought, was a belt of C-cubes and a container of water. What light there was came from a globe I'd found on the floor after fumbling in the absolute dark.

The memory of that darkness raised gooseflesh along my arms, and I wrapped them tightly around my waist. I'd mistaken it for the M'hir at first, believing utterly I'd become lost in that otherness. My desperate, futile efforts to *reach* for Morgan had seemed proof of death.

With the globe and its light had come reason. This was a prison, built specifically for me, or those like me. And there was something all too familiar about the prickly, unseen barrier keeping me here, locking me from the M'hir—and Morgan. The Drapsk had vowed to stop selling their devices when I'd become their Mystic One, admitting they'd less-than-openly made some of their technology available to "interested parties." The Makii Tribe, I corrected to myself, had vowed to stop. They were my tribe, and in ascendance over the rest on Drapskii. But did they really speak for all? I'd avoided learning Drapsk politics—now I wondered if that had been wise. If they'd sell this technology to Symon, who else might have it?

Still, it wasn't a perfect prison. I could sense the M'hir's restless boil, but at an unreachable distance. My link to Morgan? It was there, however untouchable. It had to be. I couldn't send thoughts outward along our link, couldn't sense Morgan in return, but took cold comfort from my continued existence. If I lived, so did Morgan. That was likely all I'd have of our living bond so long as Symon kept me in his box.

The emptiness where Morgan belonged had a distinct structure within my mind, as if my thoughts were a weave and his had been the threads adding color and strength. Without his presence, I was no longer whole.

Symon would die for this, I decided, coldly and calmly.

Unless I died first, of course. I'd developed a spacers'

sensitivity to air and what I was drawing into my lungs now was considerably less fresh than when I'd awakened. Perhaps that was his intent—there wasn't a door; the structure might have been built around me. If I didn't exert myself, I probably had another hour or so before I'd notice the first symptoms of asphyxiation.

Of course, that assumed I didn't freeze in the meantime. The temperature had been dropping steadily. I'd attributed my soon-continuous shivering to dread, until I went to take a drink and found ice floating in the container. My breath now left clouds in the air.

As a rule, the Clan weren't fond of technology. I'd learned most of what I knew as crew on the *Fox*, but the true nature of my prison remained a mystery until it was too late.

A Human might have noticed this room looked a great deal like the inside of a stasis box, only larger.

That resemblance only occurred to me when a sickly sweet smell heralded a rush of dark green gas, and my next involuntary, shivering breath was the last thing I remembered.

INTERLUDE

Morgan shivered involuntarily, unsure why he suddenly felt cold. The Drapsk ship, the *Heerama*, was pleasantly warm inside, his hosts adept at hospitality. This meeting lounge could be modified to suit a customer of any species, including—he'd heard—non-oxy breathers. "Forgive my inattention," he said quickly. "You were saying, Captain Heeroki? Captain Heerouka? Captain Heeru?"

Not that any of three beings sitting with him was likely the captain, but Morgan preferred to be polite. Unlike the Makii, the Heerii didn't correct his assumption—implying they either all had that rank, or couldn't be bothered explaining who was who to a being unable to tell them apart without assistance. "I was saying, Oh, Mystic One," this from the left-most, Heerouka, "that the Makii have been most unwise. We need your assistance."

"I was under a contract—"

The Drapsk farthest to Morgan's right, Heeru, waved one stubby-fingered hand in the air. Dismissal. "We have dealt with Hom Hawthorn in the past. A being who tends to—obsess—on certain issues. I assure you, Mystic One, your contract will be resolved to his complete satisfaction and your benefit. We have already taken care of the remainder of the repairs to your fine ship. With excellent new parts. She'll be ready to lift this time tomorrow."

"Really." Morgan let the noncommittal word sit between them, watching as the Drapsk, one by one, sucked in a tentacle to chew. Before they became too distracted, he said: "If you don't mind, I'd like to contact Hawthorn myself—in the morning," he added, thinking of the poor Human's likely condition at this hour. "You do realize I'm scheduled to head straight to Plexis—"

"With the Makii's Mystic One," Heeroki interjected quickly, a note of reverence in his voice. "When may we meet her, Captain Morgan?"

"Sira took herself to Plexis already." Morgan grinned and waited for a reaction.

It wasn't what he expected. Heerouka immediately curled into a tidy white ball of distress, while the other two stood up, antennae fully erect and tentacles fanned in a shocked circle around their tiny mouths.

While Drapsk were overly dramatic at the best of times, Morgan felt uneasy. Full *eopari* seemed a drastic response to missing the chance to meet Sira in person. "What's wrong?"

"Oh, Mystic One," Heeroki blurted, hands working in the air as if to fan some urgent message toward him. "She shouldn't have traveled the Scented Way. Not now. She's in danger. Great, grave danger. It's all the fault of the Makii—and their ill-advised Mystic Ones—"

Morgan surged to his feet, ignoring whatever else the Drapsk said as he drove his thoughts outward, *reaching* with all his strength.

There. She was there. But not. This wasn't the familiar sense of preoccupation—it was if he hammered against a transparent wall, seeing Sira from behind but unable to attract her attention and make her turn her head to see him. Morgan kept trying, expending power until it felt as if he left bloody handprints on that wall. Still he fought to *reach* her.

"Mystic One! Mystic One! Cease, before you call danger to her! Please!"

The frantic tone, more than the words, penetrated Morgan's consciousness. He drew back into himself, staggering once before standing firm, feet slightly apart. "What danger? Who did this?" he demanded in a voice that made both Drapsk start to back away.

"We don't know *who*. We only know something has her scent. Something in the Scented Way. Something is—interested. Our enemies. We came to warn you—"

"Something—?" Morgan stared at the small white beings, but saw another, darker shape, glistening as if wet, its fibrous arms stretched toward their cabin door. *Toward Sira?* "Who? What? Is it the Rugherans? Tell me!"

The Drapsk sucked their tentacles, then Heeroki suddenly rolled to join his shipmate in abstaining from further conversation.

Morgan took a deep breath, rearranging his features into a mask of polite attention. He, a Master Trader, surely knew better than to lose his self-control in front of another species; scaring the remaining Drapsk into an incommunicative ball wasn't going to help Sira.

Mollifying his tone to something almost normal-sounding, the Human continued: "Your pardon. I experienced an—intense—emotional reaction to a threat to my mate." Understatement wasn't a lie, he thought grimly.

The Drapsk's antennae stopped quivering. "Is the Mystic One all right?"

Drapsk, but not Makii, Morgan reminded himself, abruptly wary as he recalled that it had been the Heerii who had found the Rugheran homeworld and brought one of those beings to be their candidate for Mystic One. A candidate defeated by Sira, in Human terms, though not necessarily in Drapsk. The interface between any two thinking species was never a perfect match; even basic understandings could prove dangerously skewed the moment you relied on them.

Yet this warning had been brought by these Heerii, not the Makii. Trust had its place in negotiation, if only temporarily. "She's trapped, somehow," Morgan admitted reluctantly. "I can't communicate with her. I'm not sure she's conscious—or even on Plexis. But she's alive."

"Oh, my." For an instant, Morgan worried this Drapsk would desert him as well, but Heeru was made of sterner stuff than his shipmates and merely trembled. "We had no idea the situation had deteriorated so quickly, Mystic One. Our ship was dispatched to find you when it became clear to our Skeptics that they'd lost control of the Clan Mystic Ones—"

"Rael and Barac? But they went to Drapskii to help you."

"Their help," Heeru said grimly, "may destroy us

all. We hoped you and the Makii Mystic One could be persuaded to return to Drapskii with us, to stop them before they disturbed That Better Left Alone. Now—"

"Now," Morgan interrupted brusquely, "I must find Sira."

Instead of arguing, the Drapsk coaxed a stool from the deck and sat. "Of course. My ship is at your disposal, Mystic One. But where do we start?"

Captain Heeru, was it? Morgan didn't comment, taking the hint and sitting, reluctantly. Adrenaline might be roaring through him— the urge to do something, even if it were just to kick balls of Drapsk around the room, nigh overpowering—but he knew there wasn't anything he could do—yet—alone. Not without knowing more. "What can you tell me about the Rugherans?" he asked.

Two tentacles disappeared within Heeru's mouth. The Drapsk chose to speak around them, turning his words into a moist and barely comprehensible mumble: "The Rugherans? They can't be involved." The tentacles popped out again. "They are quiet, peaceful beings. Quite planetbound, Mystic One. Ours was the first starship they'd ever seen. They have none of their own—"

"They travel the M'hir—the Scented Way, do they not?" Morgan posed the question, then leaned forward, forearms on his thighs, to study that blank globe of a face. Not that he expected it would help. None of his research into the Drapsk helped him reliably read meaning in the ensuing wriggle of a rosy tentacle or pursing of a lip. Those feathery antennae, presently flicking upward along one third their length? Beyond his Human comprehension. Unfortunately, the opposite wasn't true. The Drapsk sensitivity to scent and sound likely gave Heeru all manner of information about his, Morgan's, emotions. As well, he told himself wryly, try to hide his state of mind from Sira.

Still, he thought the Drapsk was surprised. Not outright shock—more as if he'd given the Captain of the *Heerama* something new to consider. "You sound sure of this, Mystic One," Heeru said slowly. "Why? We have not observed the Rugherans controlling their entry into the Scented Way, as do the Clan. Our Skeptics believe their contact is limited."

Reasonable question—reasonable trust, Morgan thought, and no more. "Because," he said smoothly, sitting up straight. "I've seen one do it."

Chapter 13

AT first, I wasn't sure how to do it, how to move in this place. I floated, or did I soar? The sensation was of both water and air. Or neither. My mind lacked words for the medium in which I rode—or which moved past me—as well as for how I traveled here.

Why I wanted to move? That, I understood. I was being drawn, but not against my will—by my will. The pounding of what had been blood, the unbearable burning in what had been a body, pulled me onward. I sought—release.

As if summoned, the Singer came toward me, his song a rush of power through my being, his need my own. I fought to reach him.

I failed.

Something was between us: an obstacle, cold and harsh, entropy made tangible. It kept us apart in spite of our passion. I writhed with desire that couldn't be fulfilled. Under the strain, my mind *ripped* . . .

* * *

"Welcome, Sira di Sarc. What do you think of your new home?"

I thought I'd rather live anywhere than in this hovel perched on a mountain. This wasn't an answer which would be received at all well by the First Chosen of sud Friesnen, obviously proud of her home, so I waited in silence for her next question, my mind politely still and calm, as I'd been taught. A small, very private rebellion.

The rooms set aside for me were pleasant and well-furnished; bare of anything personal, though someone must have been displaced on my behalf. The wide stone balcony hanging out over the cliff face wasn't a novelty to someone raised on a planet blanketed with glittering, cloud-kissed towers. Being used to heights I supposed, with time, I could grow used to staring out at an emptiness of sky, ice, and rock.

Adia sud Friesnen, First Chosen, wasn't so easily ignored. "Are you hungry, little one?"

I'd have stayed silent to this, too, offended by the familiarity from someone so inferior in Power, but my stomach answered for me with an embarrassingly loud rumble. My mother, Mirim sud Teerac, had warned my appetite would increase once I left her. I hadn't realized it would be immediately.

My hostess tactfully didn't smile. "Do you have any favorite foods? I'd be happy to have our cook make them for you."

"I will join your House at its next meal, First Chosen," I said, making the gesture of gratitude, but with the twist of my wrist that indicated superiority. "I'm sure whatever is served will be satisfactory."

"You are most gracious, Sira," Adia said with a bow. There was a suspicious twinkle in her eye, as though she found my pride amusing. I allowed it, all too aware I would be in this House, under the rule of this Clanswoman, for at least the next few months of my life. And the First Chosen of any House, even sud or weaker, held authority in everyday matters over both kin and guest.

Any other authority was established by Power. My mother, sud to my father's di, had not been asked her opinion as to where I would be fostered. I, more powerful than either of my parents, had. They'd brought in a chair suited to my child's lack of height at that Council meeting, but made no other accommodation to my age. The meeting blurred in my mind; understandably, since they had held it well after my bedtime in a strange, M'hir-encased room, speaking in terms that alternately confused or bored, until they began telling me what they wanted.

The Council wished to move to a new Human world, called Camos; they claimed it was a better, more central location now that our kind had begun to expand beyond the Inner Worlds. They said other things I didn't understand, about concealment and how Stonerim III was no longer secure from prying eyes. But first, Camos would need to be connected through the M'hir to wherever Clan had chosen to live, with pathways any Clan could travel at will.

Other fosterings were being arranged to produce those pathways to neighboring systems, or to those already linked in a chain to Camos. Their need of me? They wanted to take advantage of my unusual strength to forge a single, direct pathway from Stonerim III to Camos, for the Council's convenience and safety. This pathway would be shared with other Clan once the Council had moved and reestablished itself.

I was more bewildered witness than participant. The Clan Council voted unanimously that I should 'port myself within the day from Stonerim III, my home, to Camos. An unheard-of distance and a threefold risk since, should I fail and be lost in the M'hir, I could pull my mother with me. Her loss, in turn, would doom the mind of her Chosen, Jarad di Sarc, newest member of the Council.

My father seemed willing to take the risk. I accepted his confidence as a reassuring belief in my untried abilities, too young to appreciate it as a sign of ruthlessness, that Jarad would do anything to rise within the Council. Those senior to my father believed the most direct pathways were begun by fosterlings who 'ported themselves through the M'hir. My father knew it wasn't true, that what mattered most was the Power ebbing and flowing across the mother-offspring link. The greater the difference, the stronger and subjectively shorter the path produced. And he knew my mother was weak . . .

. . . I struggled to seal the tear before it set this of all memories free . . .

Adia's smile was determined, the feel of her Power soothing and kind. "Would you like to meet your cousins, Sira?"

Having already scanned my surroundings and detected the Power of nine individuals—two tasting young enough to qualify as "cousins" and none approaching my strength—I stayed seated, my hands on my knees, my back perfectly straight. "I would prefer some time to rest, First Chosen," I told her.

A shiver of awe in the M'hir between us—a reaction I would come to expect. Adia and the others of my new home understood better than I, perhaps better than the Council who'd sent me, what I'd accomplished coming here. I'd changed forever the limits the Clan had thought existed. Now, some would dare the unthinkable, forbidden distances; measuring themselves against a prodigy. I hoped, with the callous pride of youth, that they'd fail.

To her credit, Adia saw more than my fame and Power. The Clanswoman, all elegance and grace, sank to her knees on the floor before me, her hands reaching to cover mine. I felt her concern against my shields; her hair, like cool weighted silk, slid over my arms. "It's so far. Do you still feel her?"

I nodded, mute. The link between my mother and I held, filled with warmth and support, a living connection I couldn't imagine being without.

It was a link I maintained with my own Power, for as I'd 'ported to Stonerim III, I'd felt my mother slipping away as I passed beyond her ability to *reach* me.

I'd felt . . .

. . . *No. I wouldn't relive this* . . .

A different room; another world. Our right hands rising to touch, palm to palm. My mother's was larger, warmer, and dry; mine trembled until I felt hers press firm against it.

Unusual for Clan, Mirim's face wasn't a study in

fine-boned symmetry. Her gray eyes were smaller than average and closer set than most. Her hair was a lovely red-gold but unfashionably restless; she kept it caged within a net of spun green-toned metal, a pre-Stratification relic from her grandmother. Her mouth was her best feature, wide and ready to smile whenever she saw me.

Except today. Today, everything and everyone was serious. I was tempted to laugh—it was less shameful than tears. I felt her thoughts in mine: *steady, little one; you can do this.*

Having been able to do anything I'd tried, best any challenge from my age-peers and thoroughly intimidate my elders, I didn't need confidence. But this was somehow different. Through our bond, I could feel my mother's anger, an anger she sent openly along her link to my father and tried unsuccessfully to keep from me.

He showed no outward sign, standing in a row with the others from Council—powerful guests to witness my fostering. Mother insisted it was an honor. I watched them out of the corners of my eyes.

The locate I was to use rested in my mother's thoughts, given to her by a visitor from the House of sud Friesnen, where I would stay. As our palms met, she put it in my mind: a bright, spare room with walls that appeared to be of stone. The sense of *place* was intense and rich. The locate must have come from someone who'd lived in this room, not just wandered through to collect this mental reference for me.

Go forth, little one, she sent. *I will stay with you.*

With the courage of inexperience, I nodded, then

looked deep into my mother's glistening eyes, and *pushed* . . .

The M'hir had been my playground until now, safely defined by the lines of Power etched into the space encompassing Stonerim III and those neighboring worlds with Clan. For the first time, I threw myself past it all, the locate drawing me like a lodestone, my mother's link like her hand in mine . . .

Within an instant, I found myself in a room I *knew*, though never having seen it for myself before this instant. I wasn't alone. A tall Clanswoman stood making the gesture of welcome.

. . . Lies . . . Lies . . . my mind ripping farther apart as belief and memory went to war . . .

Our hands, palm to palm . . . The locate in my mind . . . Her calm: *Go forth, little one . . . I will stay with you . . . I pushed*, my mother's link like her hand in mine . . .

Our link . . . began to fail almost at once, as if her fingers were being wrenched from mine to leave only the cold of fear behind. My mother was too weak to hold me. Desperately, I poured more and more of my own Power to support that weakening thread between us. I couldn't exist alone!

I felt myself thinning within the dispassionate confusion of the M'hir, the only locate still clear in my thoughts that room on Camos—a safety I could reach if I drew my Power away from my mother. If I let go of her hand in the darkness.

A child shouldn't be asked to make such a choice.

I could sense my mother becoming frantic, putting

herself at risk to stay with me; I shared her growing
hatred of this place that threatened to tear us apart.

A blinding snarl of images, no single one comprehensible, together a horrifying mirage of *things* forming from seething patches of energy; unseen shapes
molding me into theirs; what weren't hands grabbing
for whatever Power lay within reach: mine, my
mother's, *others*; like a flash of light, all perspective
shifting as I became the one taking what I needed to
survive, tearing it free to add to my sense of self
until . . .

Mine was the greater Power.

. . . a floor appeared beneath my feet. Air thrust itself up my nostrils and slammed against the back of
my mouth. I found myself in a room I *knew*, though
never having seen it for myself before this instant. I
wasn't alone. A tall Clanswoman stood making the
gesture of welcome.

I couldn't move, blink, or breathe on my own until
I felt my mother still in my thoughts, despite distance
and fear, our link steady, strong—and mine to keep.

. . . *Not right . . . another link . . .* I fought to leave the
past.

"Welcome, Sira di Sarc. What do you think of your
new home?"

. . . *What was happening to me? . . .*

INTERLUDE

Of the many things that had happened to him lately, Barac sud Sarc, former First Scout and Mystic One, thought with permissible self-pity, this was the first he could honestly say he'd done to himself.

And was proud of it. It took work for a Clansman of his experience to reach this stage of inebriation. He peered owlishly at the low table, whistling soundlessly to himself as he counted eleven empty bottles of Drapsk beer and noted he hadn't quite finished the glass of Denebian wine that promised to put him nicely over the edge of . . .

. . . of what? Unconsciousness? Nowhere near that point yet. Barac sighed, a deep, heaving breath that shuddered through his entire lean frame and sent him staggering back against the wall. He grinned. Clever shortcut, sitting on the floor.

"Mystic One?"

Barac's head lolled to one side as he attempted to see who'd said his name. Either his vision had finally blurred, or there were two identical Makii Drapsk standing beside him. An unfair advantage. Couldn't they see he was occupied? "Call me Barac," he said very clearly and distinctly. "I resigned, you know. Didn't Cop-up tell you? So go away."

"Don't worry, Mystic One," one said. "We'll help you. Maka?"

Before Barac could point out that he'd done just fine without any help whatsoever, he felt a sharp pain in his side. "Ouch! What was that?"

Maka, finished stabbing him with a needle easily as long as Barac's hand, didn't back away as the Clansman tried, unsuccessfully, to stand. Instead, the Drapsk brushed his antennae very lightly over Barac's mouth. As the Clansman coughed and sputtered, the Drapsk announced proudly: "There. It's working already."

"What's working?" Barac closed his moth, suddenly and drastically aware what the being meant. The Drapsk thoughtfully got out of his way as he lurched to his feet and ran for the fresher.

An appallingly uncomfortable few moments later, and totally sober, Barac returned. "That was—" Words failed him as he glared at the two obviously delighted Drapsk. "Effective," he finished, giving up the struggle and sinking into the soft comfort of a chair. "May I ask why you felt it important to—interrupt—my evening?"

"You have a call."

He rubbed his aching head, impressed despite himself how the pain was already fading. Resourceful, these friends of Sira's, if the word "friend" applied. The Makii had continued the practice of wearing their names on small ribbons attached to their work belts—

the only adornment Barac had seen on a member of the species. By those ribbons, his "helpers" were Maka and Makoori, the former having been Captain of the *Makmora* and the latter, as far as he knew, presently holding that post. The Clansman had seen enough *gripstsa* around Rael to know the uniquely Drapsk means of switching roles under excitement, stress, or tedium included each participant somehow learning all he needed to know about the other's job.

Interesting, but hardly helpful in understanding what these two were doing off their ship and in his apartment, nor why they'd taken it on themselves to induce all the symptoms of a hangover before he'd finished enjoying being oblivious.

"A call." The words finally penetrated, but made no sense. "You came because I've had a call. What are you talking about?"

"It came to the *Makmora*—in the shipcity. Addressed to you, Mystic One, and in strictest confidence," Captain Makoori informed him. "We must hurry. Can you—take us there?"

"'Port?" Barac blinked, now unsure their potion had sobered him up after all. While Drapsk seemed to relish being near the use of Power, most seemed vehemently opposed to becoming involved in that use. Almost as bad as that Carasian, forever moaning about his pool.

"It was an urgent message. Translight. From Plexis. We worry there has already been—a delay—in bringing this news to your attention."

A typically-tactful Drapsk way to put it. Barac stood, offering a hand to each of his guests. "You've breathable air in your ship's lounge?" he said, gathering his Power with a certain sense of vengeance. They took his hands, in Maka's case with a momentary hesitation and an inhalation of the last of his six tentacles.

"There should be—" Makoori began. Barac half smiled and *pushed* . . .

. . . materializing, with the Drapsk, in a part of the *Makmora* he remembered very well. The air was acceptable, if you didn't mind the ever-present draft going by your ears. The long benchlike table was gone—replaced by a set of three chairs with humps where the seats should be. They must have been bargaining with something distinctly nonhumanoid recently.

Barac shrugged fatalistically. Furniture on a Drapsk ship was no more permanent than its Captain. Fortunately, a locate's specificity within the M'hir involved more than details of visual memory. For no particular reason, he remembered the Clan fable about two Choosers who had favored the same unChosen. Each gave him the locate of her Joining Chambers, waiting eagerly to see him appear. When he didn't do so immediately, they spied on one another and, unbeknownst to either, came up with the same plan. Each made an exact copy of the other's Joining Chamber, intending to trick the unChosen into 'porting to hers. But when he finally appeared in the Chamber of one, eager to offer himself for her Choice, she couldn't be sure if he'd meant to come to her or to her rival, and sent him away.

The fable taught the absolute uniqueness of a locate, since the story was always followed by the revelation that the Chooser had been wrong. The unChosen could only have 'ported to *her* Joining Chamber, no matter how she'd tried to made it appear similar to her rival's. Just as well, Barac thought, or the Clan would never be able to 'port to changeable locations, let alone to moving objects, such as starships and planets. An old and totally implausible tale for children, misleading and cruel.

For Choosers no longer courted the unChosen, having become too deadly for games.

Like many Clan, Barac never worried about how his Power worked—only how it compared to that of others. Given Rael was his superior on Drapskii, he hoped this so-urgent translight message came from someone superior to her. Sira, for starters. She'd understand better than anyone how he felt about getting too personal with that planet in the M'hir again.

While he'd been busy with his thoughts, the Drapsk continued to hurry him through their ship to the bridge, Makoori in front, Maka behind. They moved quickly, though every Drapsk they passed in the organically curved corridors immediately left what he was doing to join what soon became a procession. Barac did his best to ignore them, although it was difficult once it began to sound as though a hundred or more pairs of feet moved behind him.

The extra Drapsk didn't follow him on to the bridge, stopping short and dipping their antennae his way in farewell. Barac curbed the impulse to wave back. They might appreciate the gesture, but not the breeze it would produce. He had no idea how Drapsk "saw" without eyes, though he'd learned to take this

ability—or result—for granted, but he did know causing an uncontrolled draft indoors was considered impolite.

There was no door. Drapsk appeared to tolerate
them only where essential to separate atmosphere
from vacuum, or to keep things from falling out of lifts
on the wrong level. Barac followed Makoori to the com
without bothering to glance at the confusion of other
consoles tended by beings who hopefully knew what
they were for—he valued such expertise, if didn't care
to gain it himself.

The com was ringed by five more Drapsk all sucking their tentacles in confusion or consideration. They
patted him in greeting, moving aside but not far
enough.

"You said this was a confidential message, Captain?" Barac asked pointedly.

Makoori made little shooing motions with his
hands, emphasized by flutters of his antennae. Or was
it the other way around? The Clansman grinned to
himself. The crew dispersed, all but one. Barac read
the ribbon on his belt. "Makeest," he greeted. "You're
the com-tech?"

"What else would I be, Mystic One?" the being said,
sounding slightly offended.

It probably wasn't done to refer to pre-*gripstsa* oc-
cupations, although Barac was reasonably sure this
com-tech had been both a tailor and engineer's assis-
tant within the last year. He only hoped to get off the
ship without setting them off again—it had been a
while for this crew. A good thing Rael wasn't here.

"Don't keep the Mystic One waiting!" ordered

Makoori impatiently. "He brought us here using the Scented Way." This announcement caused three nearby Drapsk to fold into balls of distress, rolling away gently until they wound up under a console.

Makeest, perhaps apprehensive he'd be dragged into the M'hir next, rushed to the console, waving for Barac to join him. His quick stubby fingers worked over the board for a moment, then he indicated one button, winking green. "It's audio only," he told the Clansman, backing away with the Captain to a discreet distance.

It was an apology. Barac nodded politely, reaching for the button. While there wasn't a vid to allow visual messages, this system was able to transfer an incoming signal into appropriate chemical signals for true Drapsk communication. Makeest doubtless felt anything less was incomplete.

Barac listened, frowned, then asked without turning: "How do I replay this?"

"Press the button again. Is something wrong, Mystic One?"

Barac ignored the question as he replayed the message twice more. Finally, he straightened and turned to look around the bridge. All the Drapsk were silent, intently watching him for a cue.

"It's from Huido." No need to ask if they knew the name. Every set of antennae stood at attention—except for the three still performing *eopari* under the console. "He needs my help—he asks me to meet him on Ettler's Planet—the coordinates are in the message."

"Can you travel so far in the Scented Way, Mystic

One?" This worried question from Makeest provoked a shiver up more than one pair of antennae.

"No. I'd need a ship—" Barac raised his eyebrows suggestively. "Do you have one to recommend?"

"The *Makmora*, of course, Mystic One," Makoori said quickly. "We are yours to command. Anything to help Hom Huido and yourself."

Maka, silent until now, other than the occasional slurp as he anxiously chewed a tentacle, spoke up. "We must find a Skeptic. We cannot transport a Mystic One without a Skeptic."

"You did," Makoori countered testily.

The Clansman held out his hands, dropping them again when he felt a current of air. "The Skeptics are working with my cousin, the other Mystic One," he told them. "There's no need to take them away from their work."

"And from your work?" Maka asked, obviously still unhappy about his trip through the Scented Way.

"I resigned, remember?"

"That's true. He did," Makoori said firmly.

"So—when you're ready, Captain Makoori? Best speed to Ettler's Planet, please. And, Captain?" Barac added as the bridge crew exploded into action at some unseen command from the Drapsk, except for the three under the console. "Huido wanted us to keep this confidential. He's in a delicate situation—if you don't mind?"

Makoori understood immediately. "Makeest? Call up a docking tug. If anyone asks our course, tell them we have a private cargo run and aren't at liberty to say.

Port Authority won't argue. They know those Heerii are forever trying to listen to our com signals."

"I thought Drapsk didn't compete," Barac ventured.

There were subdued hoots from the entire bridge.

"We don't compete within a Tribe, Mystic One," Makoori said, after a few hoots of his own. "Between Tribes? We don't compete. The Makii win!"

Chapter 14

PAST and present continued to compete for my attention, both *wrong* in a way I couldn't endure. If I'd had any control over this journey, if that's what it was and not the comfort of insanity, I would have stopped it by any means possible.

. . . *Nothing and everything was possible here* . . .

"Must you practice all day, Sira?"

I licked my swollen, numb lips, resting the keffle-flute on my lap with a sigh of resignation, my palms vibrating with the memory of music. I'd had the piece close to perfection, before Crisac di Friesnen decided to interrupt. My voice was mild as I explained, again: "I enjoy practicing." He was a child, the newest guest of the sud Friesnen House, and powerful enough to treat politely—however annoying he might be.

I knew why he was here, even if he likely didn't. Any Clan visiting this House brought their young un-Chosen to meet me. Adia was not a Clanswoman to keep secrets, not from those in her care and certainly not when she disapproved. She'd explained that other

Houses hoped I would look with favor on their young males and now imposed—her word—on sud Friesnen's hospitality at every opportunity. I was too young to fully grasp what she meant—and too carefully watched to be able to slip out and join the illicit games in the gardens that might have taught me something more.

So I put up with a stream of fidgety visitors who would much rather be playing 'port and seek than listening to my music, and couldn't understand why I would rather not play in that darkness.

. . . Memory spun me around and around, helpless to escape its whirlpool . . .

If I let go of her hand in the darkness . . . A child shouldn't be asked to make such a choice . . . my mother becoming frantic, putting herself at risk to stay with me . . .

/attention/interest/

Suddenly, in the midst of everything that was pulling at me, I felt a presence. There was something here. Something *watching*.

My mother's mind denied it, grew hysterical with fear, tried to flee. I grabbed and held her. She mustn't leave me alone here!

/curiosity/

A blinding snarl of images that faded . . . Time slowed in the M'hir, or was it that a mind trapped there could experience more than one sequence of time, live multiple events that had to be squeezed into a consciousness built to remember everything as linear, maddened by what was concurrent? For a brief instant, or many at once, I saw my past as it had happened, and happened, and happened, and happened . . . fragmenting into those selves:

One self: passing through the M'hir without incident, arriving at Camos safe and unchanged.

One self: using my strength to keep connected with my mother, somehow finding enough to arrive at Camos safe and unchanged—but with an awareness of what might have been lost, a desperate need to protect our link.

One self: aware of other life, frightened, but more afraid of losing the precious link. Fighting my mother's fear and hatred of the M'hir, of its life, doing anything to keep her with me. Robbing that life for the strength to arrive at Camos safe and unchanged—but with the guilt of having forced my mother into that fear, and the dreadful knowledge I'd killed to survive.

One self: aware of something watching, something that sang into my soul, tasted my heart, invaded my dreams . . . */disappointment/* . . . I wasn't ready . . . it released its grip, sending me to Camos safe and unchanged—but unfulfilled.

. . . a floor appeared beneath my feet and that me, that child, knew only that I'd made it to my new home, feeling shy and hungry.

. . . *How had I lost all this? What else lay buried in my past? . . .*

INTERLUDE

Ruti's past hadn't prepared her for any of this: a kitchen under siege by scowling security, drunken spacers, and a friend different than anyone she'd imagined. And now, here was Ansel telling her—just as her mother had—that she had to pack and leave?

"I'm not going. Tell Hom Huido I'll be fine—"

The old Human shook his head, his face pale but determined. "He knows best, young Ruti. You can come back soon. Well," he qualified, tossing a second bag to her, "as soon as this is straightened out. Hom Huido has friends—powerful friends—and once they learn what's happened, they'll come in a hurry. Then you'll see Plexis singing a different tune. Not to mention I'm planning to file grievances. Serious grievances. Did you see what they were doing with the cooking wine?"

As Ruti had kept herself as far from the kitchen as possible, she could only shake her head. Unwillingly, she started putting her few things into the first bag, tucking Lara surreptitiously into a pocket. "I don't see why we have to go offstation, if he has these friends. Why can't we just—hide out?"

Ansel blinked at her. "Hide Huido?"

Ruti couldn't help it. Her lips quirked and she almost laughed. "I see your point. Okay. Okay." Maybe this could work to her advantage, she thought, packing more carefully. Acranam wanted her here, on Plexis; more accurately, what must stay here was one end of the link to her mother. While Ruti didn't care about that, she did care to keep her link intact—and that meant not risking it by trips that might take her too far away. But if she took an air tag and abandoned the Carasian at the first opportunity, Jake would have no option but to take her in. He had to have quarters on the station. He cared about her. She knew he did—

"Did you hear me?" Ansel must have been talking to her. Ruti blushed and shook her head. "Thought not. Well, you'd better pay attention to everything Hom Huido says to you. I want you to take good care of him."

"Take care of *him?*" A new concept. She arched a brow at Ansel. "I thought he was taking care of me."

Ansel looked embarrassed and glanced around as if to be sure no Carasian had snuck up on them. "I worry about him all the time," he said in a conspiratorial whisper. "He gets himself into trouble so easily. You'll have to watch out. Don't let him get into fights, especially with weapons in a confined space. That's never good. And don't let him near any Scats."

"He's going to listen to me?" Ruti questioned doubtfully.

A quick smile. "He listens to you in the kitchen.

Haven't you noticed? You're a good girl, Ruti, with a level head. That's what he needs. Someone with a level head."

Ruti tucked this interesting view of herself away, not sure what to make of it, but returned Ansel's smile. For a Human, he was a worthy being. "I'll do my best," she promised, ducking her head to search in a drawer, adding to herself: *while we're together, anyway.* "Do I have time to make a quick call? I was supposed to meet a friend tonight. I should let—her know."

"Him, you mean."

She looked up to find Ansel's thin face as grim as she'd ever seen it, his washed-blue eyes sharp on hers. "Don't look so surprised," he said. "It's my job to watch after Hom Huido. That includes seeing who comes and goes by the service doors—and who is waiting outside."

"You spied on me." She held in her Power, knowing there was nothing to be gained by lashing out at him. "I trusted you—"

"And we trusted you," Ansel interrupted, unrepentant. "Do you know who this friend of yours is?"

"Do you?" she countered, half afraid of the answer.

The Human took a deep breath, then let it out slowly. "No. Not by name. But there are two things I don't like about your 'friend,' Ruti—and before you start to huff and puff at me, I want you to listen to them—"

"He's too old?" she challenged. Jake wasn't. He was strong, vibrant—more alive than any younger males of Ruti's acquaintance. His maturity gave him experience, confidence, the skill she felt from his Power. A considerable skill and strength, for a Human. Enticing.

"No," Ansel corrected. "I don't mean his age. I don't like the fact that he doesn't come here to see you. That you sneak out to meet him. Why?"

"He—"

"Don't try to find an excuse. I know why," he snapped. "Because he knows we'd recognize him. And that's the second thing I don't like about him. The kitchen staff and I all saw this friend of yours come out of the freezer."

"The freezer." Ruti began wondering about Ansel and the cooking wine.

"Some months back, while Huido was away from the station, there was an incident. Sedly—our old chef—heard banging inside the freezer and called me. We unlocked it together. There'd been some—problems—in the freezer already and no one wanted to take chances. Your friend was standing inside, looking furious, and pushed by us all without a word of explanation. How did he get in there? Hmm? By putting himself there, that's how. Teleporting, or whatever your people call it."

"You think he's Clan?" If Ruti hadn't been so flustered by all this, she would have found this ironic. "Don't you think I'd know? Ja—he's just a nice Human who's been kind to me. Why is that so hard to imagine? As for how he ended up in the freezer—sounds like a Clan played a trick on him , and not a very safe one. Maybe it was Sira di Sarc herself. She has that kind of Power, doesn't she?"

"If it was Fem Morgan," Ansel said firmly, "she

would have had a good reason. She doesn't play tricks."

Ruti closed her bag. "It doesn't matter, does it? I'm leaving with Hom Huido. Just give me a minute to call my friend so that he doesn't worry about me while I'm gone. You did say we had to hurry."

"Give me his name, and I'll put the call through for you. I'm only trying to protect you, Ruti. Believe me." Angry brown eyes met determined blue ones. Blue won.

Besides, Ruti decided, she had nothing to hide. Neither did Jake. "His name is Jake," she said proudly. "Jake Caruthers. You won't need to connect through Plexis. He's coded into my com already."

Ansel didn't react to the name, merely nodded as though memorizing it. He activated the com while Ruti stayed sitting on her bed, bags to either side. The com hissed and popped to itself, then: *This code has been disconnected. There is no forwarding code. This code has been disconnected. There is no—* Ansel drew his hand from the shutoff. "Do you have another code?" he asked gently.

Ruti was already trying in her own way, concentrating on the feel of Jake's mind and throwing all her Power into a sending. *Jake!* Nothing.

"He left with her," she wailed, uncaring that Ansel had no idea what she was talking about, that he saw the tears spilling down her cheeks. "He left with her!"

The *Claws & Jaws* had been carefully designed to allow its larger-than-most owner access to every room. Access didn't mean extra space. For instance, a

Carasian's carapace came close to scraping both walls of the corridors leading to the private apartments and staff quarters, as well as those leading discreetly outside.

Huido rumbled to himself. He would have doubled that width, despite the cost, if he'd known this would happen. Ansel had outdone himself in orchestrating his and Ruti's exit without Wallace's security being the wiser. Until this critical point.

The two Carasians stood, a meter apart, eyes to eyes, without any room to pass one another. The nearest doorway where one could let the other pass was behind Huido. Which was out of the question. Not only were security personnel relaxing in that room, Huido certainly wasn't about to back up from his nephew.

"Why doesn't Huido climb over him?" an impatient voice hissed from behind. Ruti, finally speaking. She'd looked dreadful, eyes and nose red, her bags clutched in both hands. There hadn't been time for explanations. Perhaps she missed the kitchen.

"That's just—not done," Ansel said quickly.

"We can't stay here like this!"

Huido was open to suggestions.

What he got was a nasty reminder of how the Clan acted for themselves. Before he more than registered the light brush of fingers on his back, Huido found himself staring down an unimpressed exit door instead of an abject and confused Tayno.

Ruti had 'ported them both to the far end of the hallway.

Huido decided, under the circumstances, he

wouldn't worry about his *grist*. He'd be lucky to ever see his pool and mates again as it was.

Not that he planned to thank Ruti for the experience anytime soon.

Plexis security, with a Carasian—a bad-tempered Carasian at that—to bring to justice, hadn't taken any chances. A broad area in front of the *Claws & Jaws* had been cordoned off to allow space for servo-deployed metal barriers and not one but three grav sleds were parked inside that clearing, carrying such useful equipment as auto-grapples and string-steel nets of the sort more typically found in freighters. Wallace knew who and what he was dealing with.

Or thought he did. Ruti almost grinned as she stood beside the real Huido, surveying the scene on the Turr-neds' news monitor. Their exit out the back of the restaurant had been easy enough. Wallace, having believed he knew where his quarry was, had called all the guards from the kitchen to help him. Perhaps he'd suspected Huido wouldn't come quietly.

"What will your nephew do?" Ruti asked curiously. "If they try to take him away, that is?"

A slither of plate over plate as Huido chuckled to himself. "Resist, I hope. But he's likely too soft-shelled for that. Besides, it shouldn't take long for even Wallace to realize his mistake. My nephew is a poor substitute."

Ruti didn't argue the point. She couldn't tell the two Carasian males apart and sincerely doubted any other humanoid could—unless it was Huido's infamous blood brother, Captain Morgan, who hadn't appeared before they'd left, despite Jake's confident prediction. So, if Tayno did as promised and didn't answer any questions—Carasians apparently didn't lie well—they might have a considerable period of grace before Wallace figured out he had the right species but the wrong problem.

While she had a problem with another species. Ruti stole a look around, shuddering inwardly as she confirmed all seventeen Turrneds were looking back. Didn't they blink? Their attentive courtesy bordered on horrifying. She wasn't the least convinced they weren't planning to sacrifice her and Huido—after a suitable and heartfelt apology, of course.

She and Huido had made their way here with a minimum of fuss—well, at least until they'd broached the back entrance of the Mission. Getting inside where servos off-loaded was one thing; getting both of them through the tiny door into the Mission itself had taken another use of her Power. The Carasian seemed resigned to accepting the inevitable, if not to being gracious about it.

"We're in luck, Ruti," Huido rumbled quietly, as if sensing her thoughts. He turned and crouched in an awkward position, probably finding it hard to sit properly while festooned with heavy artillery. "Plexis happens to be making its closest approach to Ettler's Planet this standard year. While I'd hoped to go elsewhere—anywhere else, in fact—this will do. A friend of mine keeps property there; a secure place for—unexpected emergencies."

"And how are you planning to get there? I can't 'port us without a locate, even if it's within my range."

A shudder rattled more than the huge black being's natural armor. "That won't be necessary, Ruti. These fine beings—" Huido waved one of his larger claws in a gesture that sent the nearest Turrneds scampering to hide behind those farther back, slowly peeking out to shine their eyes on Ruti. The Carasian seemed not to notice, continuing: "—are willing to send more representatives to their Mission on Ettler's. I reminded them it's a system full of vile and violent individuals. Luck again," he repeated. "They'll gladly take us along."

Ruti sagged with relief, sitting on a nearby bench. She pulled her two bags on the bench with her, keeping hold of both. The one under her right hand contained what she'd brought to the station: clothing and her doll, Lara. It was safer than her pocket. The bag under the left held belongings she'd earned working at the *Claws & Jaws;* those, and gifts from Jake. The only other possession she could claim lay within, the reassuring warmth of her mother's mind touching hers. She didn't care if leaving Plexis ruined First Chosen di Caraat's plans for a pathway to the station; she did care about taking any risk with her link.

But Ettler's Planet was in the nearest inhabited system to Acranam's, Ruti thought with a deep sense of rightness. It was as though the station had brought her home these past weeks, instead of taking her farther away.

Ruti leaned her head back against the cushions and closed her eyes as Huido began talking over final arrangements with the purring Turrneds, feigning disinterest. In truth, she was concentrating, sending her thoughts questing through the M'hir. Perhaps Jake had to shield himself. He could be in danger. Ruti couldn't believe she'd so quickly assumed her friend had abandoned her. Jake Caruthers wasn't like that, she knew. He cared about her. Didn't he want the best for her? Hadn't he protected her when she'd arrived on Plexis?

If Jake let down his shields, Ruti would find him. Then she'd leave Huido for her true destiny.

Chapter 15

WHAT happens after destiny? Does a story come to an end, absolute and final? Or is it metamorphosed into the next struggle—cycling over and over, as life and death cycle through populations of living things?

Does memory hold the future as well as the past?

It wasn't idle speculation. I'd been here—wherever this "here" was—before. At intervals, I could recognize I was experiencing what was past, not the present. It was as if my life was being replayed to ready me for something to come.

. . . *That which tried to think fractured from that which couldn't* . . .

"And do you still feel her? Your mother?"

Adia found the question difficult to ask. I sensed her embarrassment as easily as I could the tightly-forged connection between my mother's mind and mine. "You ask it as if I shouldn't," I said, rather rudely. The question felt threatening, although I couldn't say why. I had no complaints of Adia's care these past five years: she'd been kind to me and justly unkind to those who'd sought to trouble my peace. Why did I now sense she was unhappy with me?

"She asks because we're proud of you, Sira. It's highly unusual for a link between mother and offspring to last more than a few months—a year at best. You've done a fine job of building a pathway between Stonerim III and Camos."

I smiled at my father. Jarad had materialized during supper, without warning to the sud Friesnens as was his right as Councillor and di Sarc. I'd been permitted to join the adults in Adia's burgundy-and-gold sitting room—heart of the sud Friesen House—as well as to sip on a very small amount of brandy. It tasted vile, but I knew it was meant as a compliment.

And a warning. Something was brewing, in this civil exchange of spoken and unspoken thought. If I extended my other sense into the M'hir, I knew I'd feel it hiss and boil around each of the others here: Jarad, Adia, her father—Nanka sud Friesnen, a quiet, venerable Clansman whose claim to fame among our kind was in fathering an unheard of four offspring, three of whom were *di*. Those had left his House to set up their own, while Adia had returned after her fostering and Choice, to rule here as First Chosen. Her mother had the discourtesy to protest, despite her inferior Power, and now lived with one of her sons.

"Isn't it a good thing that my link to Mirim sud Teerac remains?" I asked.

"Of course," my father said quickly.

His shields were impenetrable, so I had to rely on

his expression for clues. Most frustrating. "But . . . ?" I began, raising my eyebrows.

"The pathway has been established, Sira," Nanka told me, offering me a second brandy which I refused hastily. "There's no point having you and Mirim continue to pour your strength into it."

"And every benefit," Jarad said smoothly, "in using your strength elsewhere. Even as we speak, Mirim is getting ready to leave Stonerim III."

I leaped to my feet, almost tipping over the tray beside my adult-sized chair. "And come here?" I asked eagerly. The link was central to my peace, but it was a poor substitute for my mother's physical presence.

They looked to one another rather than at me, granting me time, I realized, to collect myself and behave more appropriately. "Forgive me, Father," I said, dry-mouthed, making the gesture of appeasement. I sat back down. "Where is my mother going?"

He didn't spare me; I supposed it didn't occur to him. "To Deneb. The distance will test your link, but I'm sure you will succeed—to the enhancement of the M'hir for us all."

When? I remembered my manners even as he frowned at my sending in this group of adults. "When?"

Jarad's expression became withdrawn. I let out my other sense more cautiously this time, and felt his focus turn inward, to the Joining between himself and Mirim. More than focused. His gaze suddenly sharpened on mine. "I've told her to go—now."

. . . not this . . .

Even as he spoke, I felt my mother leave Stonerim

III, her home since before my birth. She had pushed herself through the M'hir at his command, an immediate distancing that stretched the link between us past the breaking point.

Somehow I held it.

The link between mother and child attenuates by nature, a weaning process that frees the parent to become pregnant once more, while the child goes on to seek a new, more permanent connection through the M'hir to replace it. Natural, but there was nothing natural in this severing. Jarad risked all of us again. I knew it—this time understanding it was his ruthlessness, but seeing nothing he could gain.

For no reason, I thought of the parade of unChosen visiting sud Friesnen, interrupting my music.

I held and held. The effort drew my consciousness deep into the M'hir. I'd never regained the easy confidence of a child here, not since my terrifying journey to Camos, and did my best to feel my body, to cling to reality as I struggled to keep my mother.

Mirim was wiser. She knew it was time for us to part, even if this was a brutal uncoupling. She resisted my effort to pull us together with a strength that distance matched to mine. Our link weakened . . . I cried out in the darkness . . . it broke . . .

I was incomplete . . . I must have more . . . The M'hir heaved its reaction in stygian waves, directionless and violent, frothing with rejected power. Terrified, I fought to find myself within the chaos . . .

. . . opening my eyes to find my father leaning toward me, his hand outstretched as he felt the air around my face, his mouth widening in a smile as he said to me: "Welcome, Chooser."

Jarad had known he couldn't lose, part of me comprehended. Had the link held, my mother and I would have built another valuable pathway for the Clan, increasing our family's prestige. Since it failed, the House of di Sarc gained—me. As the most powerful female of my generation, I was a bargaining chip of inestimable value. My aching emptiness meant I was ready to be offered candidates for my Choice, candidates who would be selected by the Council and screened by my father to find the most worthy of Joining with di Sarc. His dynasty would continue.

Part of me refused to comprehend I'd been ripped from my mother to further his scheming. How had he made her agree? What did she think? Was she feeling this agony as well? I couldn't know. I couldn't feel her thoughts any longer.

. . . *memory had a pallid underbelly, hidden from the light until forced to turn over* . . .

. . . my father's voice . . . my mother pushing herself into the M'hir at his command . . . leaving me behind . . . I fought to hold her. It was only natural . . .

. . . but nothing about my link to Mirim was natural. I'd maintained it past time, strengthened it, insisted on it, despite what had grown to be her horror of the M'hir, despite her every struggle, waking and sleeping, to be rid of me. When I might have known, I'd convinced myself it was the M'hir itself trying to tear us apart. I swore to her—to myself—I hadn't known.

It didn't matter. Mirim freed herself with a snap of rejected Power that burned without fire. I glowed in the M'hir, dazed and alone, reaching for . . . what? I didn't know.

But it knew me. From the unimaginable depths, it came. A Singer, ghostly familiar yet utterly strange. Where were the Watchers to protect me? I tried to flee, screamed without sound for my mother's aid, for anything to save me.

My scream was answered by a touch in the utter dark, a hot, moist exploration that dismissed my shields, my identity, and sought what it needed. What was me reeled in horror . . . in pleasure beyond bearing. I became trapped in ecstasy that wasn't mine but was, imprisoned by a rising urgency for completion that threatened everything about me and yet . . . had I been older, had I a way to relate what was being done to me to anything real, I might have succumbed. I might have followed the Singer . . .

But the strangeness drove me back. The M'hir heaved its reaction in stygian waves, directionless and violent, frothing with spurned power. Terrified, I fought to find myself within the chaos . . .

. . . opening my eyes to find my father leaning toward me, his hand outstretched as he felt the air around my face, his mouth widening in a smile he said to me: "Welcome, Chooser."

INTERLUDE

"Welcome to Plexis, Captain Morgan. Do you accept responsibility for the air you share while onstation?" The busy official didn't wait for an answer before deftly applying the blue air tag to Morgan's cheek. "Next."

Morgan stayed within the line heading to the rampways, but seized any opportunity to surreptitiously lengthen his stride and ease around slower beings. Gray-uniformed security was always on the lookout for those in a hurry. Mind you, they'd pull aside those moving unusually slowly as well, on the reasonable basis that customers couldn't be parted from their credits if delayed in transit.

The Human knew he was good—damned good—at controlling his outward appearance, at blending into any crowd. He should be, given the years of practice he'd had. This time? The only reason he could continue to govern himself was his awareness of Sira. The barrier stayed between them—she didn't or couldn't acknowledge his strongest sendings—but she did exist. They were still one, in a fashion.

Or perhaps, he thought dispassionately, coldly, he could function without their full link because he wasn't Clan and didn't have part of his conscious self existing within the M'hir.

Morgan was willing to take any advantage he could.

He'd taken advantage of the *Fox*'s speed, waiting impatiently for the Kimmcle to complete their repairs, then easily overtaking the *Heerama* to reach Plexis before the Heerii Drapsk. Not long before, he estimated. They should dock within hours. But sufficient to let him avoid their well-intentioned but always conspicuous help.

Was it well-intentioned? Morgan sidestepped a Whirtle with a tangle of grav sleds in tow, finally out of the main press of beings and into the concourse. He couldn't forget the warning he'd felt before the Heerii arrived, a warning just like those he'd learned meant imminent and very personal danger. He had no idea why the Drapsk might be a threat to him—it didn't mean they weren't.

First stop? The *Claws & Jaws*—to find the only being he trusted as much as his Sira.

The Human seemed to vanish among the throng of spacers and customers.

Early evening, a busy crowd, even for Plexis, and the restaurant was closed. Morgan studied it from his vantage point across the concourse, considering his next move. If he'd mastered the ability to 'port, he could have put himself on the other side of those strangely locked doors. If he could—

As well wish for the ability to see through walls, the Human chided himself. There were other ways. He inserted himself within a passing group of Human spacers, accompanying them as they walked near enough to the restaurant to allow him to dodge into the shadow of the adjacent doorway. Morgan keyed in the override code Huido had given him and held his breath.

The door accepted the code. Morgan eased inside the instant the opening was wide enough to admit him, ordering the door closed and locked again.

Silence. That in itself was unusual enough to put Morgan on alert, testing his surroundings with his mind as well as his other senses. He immediately touched the painfully reassuring maelstrom Huido used as a brain. No, more than one—the wives.

Possibly an indelicate—and dangerous—moment to interrupt his friend, Morgan suspected, withdrawing his Power with a wince. He'd do it from a distance.

Quickly and quietly, Morgan walked down the service corridor to the kitchen, noticing most of the air tags were missing from the wall—implying Huido had sent away even those members of staff with apartments attached to the restaurant.

Maybe Plexis had closed the *Claws & Jaws* on some trumped-up health violation. Inspector Wallace wasn't above that sort of not-so-petty revenge if his investigation into Fodera's murder had been stymied by the Enforcers.

Morgan turned the corner leading to Huido's private apartments, only to stop short.

There was an adult male Carasian collapsed outside

the door—but he wasn't Huido. This sorry-looking individual looked exhausted, the black of his claws
streaked with white plas, eyestalks hanging limply
over the lower rim of his head shield. No wonder,
Morgan thought, cautiously moving closer. From all
appearances, the being had been trying to pound his
way through the door, doorframe, and neighboring
wall for hours. Unsuccessfully, which was understandable given the outrageous reinforcements Huido
had insisted be built around his future pool. Morgan
grinned to himself. Apparently his blood brother had
had good reason.

"Excuse me," the Human said. "I'm looking for
Hom Huido." His voice didn't seem to startle the
huge, comatose being, but the name definitely gained
a reaction.

The Carasian flung himself away from the door
with an astonishing leap that sent him sliding into the
far wall, impacting with a thud and vibration Morgan
felt through the carpeted floor. Once against the wall,
the being immediately crouched in as small and inoffensive a posture as was possible for an organism built
like an antipersonnel servotank and uttered in a
ridiculously high-pitched squeal: "I wasn't trying to
get in! I found the door like that!" His eyestalks were
swinging in every direction so wildly, Morgan was
reasonably sure the distraught creature hadn't actually
seen him yet.

"I'm Captain Morgan of the *Silver Fox*," he intro-
duced himself, keeping the nearer of the two exits
from this antechamber in sight, somewhat unnerved
by a whimpering Carasian. It could have been the

combination of lethal claws, a body mass five times his own, and the distinct impression this being had misplaced an important part of his mental capacity. "Please calm yourself, Hom. You're in no danger." Well, if Huido was on the other side of the apartment door, this smaller male was probably right to cower, but Morgan couldn't believe his friend would sit inside and listen to an attempted invasion, no matter how futile.

Eyestalks began clustering in Morgan's direction, two, a dozen, then all. "The door was like that," the Carasian insisted rather weakly. "I was worried about my uncle. Hom Huido."

Having heard innumerable stories of Carasian courtship, Morgan somehow kept a straight face at this. "When was the last time you saw Huido, Hom?"

A shifting of plates as the being raised itself into a more normal position. "My name is Tayno Boormataa'kk, Captain Morgan. Hom Huido's nephew. I am honored to meet you at last." A dip of his head carapace to each shoulder in turn—a shrug. "As for the last time I was privileged to gaze upon the awe-inspiring massiveness of my uncle?" Tayno paused. "I was told not to answer questions." This more firmly, as if the Carasian had finally found himself on some higher moral ground.

"From anyone? Or from someone in particular?"

"From Inspector Wallace and Plexis sec—" His eager answer trailed away. "You are trying to trick me, Captain Morgan. I must not answer questions. I promised."

Morgan narrowed his eyes in consideration, then

walked over to the abused door. He rested his fingers on the keypad. "A shame, Hom Tayno. Did you know I have the emergency override codes to this door?"

The Carasian lurched erect, eyestalks whirling in a frenzy, claws out and snicking together in anticipation, then quickly withdrawn as if he feared this display of enthusiasm could be misconstrued. "How—remarkable," he ventured. "Obviously my uncle, the magnificent Hom Huido, places a vast amount of trust in you. How can I not do the same, Captain Morgan?"

"When did you last see him?"

"Seven hours ago, standard time. We met in the hallway that leads to the back—the one to the service corridor used by the machines. Do you know it? He went into it while I went to sit in a room with that impolite Human, Wallace. He mistook us, you know. We are very similar in size, my uncle and I. It's quite understandable—"

"Do you know why he was leaving?"

"Perhaps we should discuss such sensitive topics inside the apartment?" Tayno suggested coyly, taking a noisy step toward the door.

Morgan lifted his hand from the keypad. "Huido has over twenty wives, you know," he drawled. "He tells me they are—incredible. I'd hate to see you distracted before you could tell me everything I need to know."

One huge claw snapped in threat, plas dust falling from its interior. Over half of Tayno's eyestalks were now riveted on the door.

Morgan merely smiled and leaned against the wall. Another snap, but Tayno didn't argue. "If you insist, Human," he rumbled. "The accountant, Ansel, arranged for me to impersonate his master long enough for Huido and some female from the kitchen to evade security. She had the oddest *grist*—I'd heard about Clan before but—"

"What was her name? Was it Sira?" Morgan interrupted, coming alert.

"How should I know her name? All you humanoids look the same. It's very confusing," the Carasian complained. More of his eyestalks slid to stare at the door.

Mogan controlled himself with an effort. "Where did they go?"

"You'll have to ask Ansel—they didn't tell me. Now, please hurry and let me inside." Tayno was almost prancing on his spongy feet. "Hom Huido—my uncle—won't mind at all, Captain. He meant to give me the code; I'm to protect his wives from danger. He had to leave too quickly—a mistake I'm sure he'd want you to correct. Let me in."

The Human's smile didn't reach his blue eyes. "And I think Huido would be overjoyed to know you are standing guard on this side of the door, Hom Tayno."

"But—?" Tayno sagged, claws dropping to rest on the floor. "You were never going to open it, were you?" he concluded sorrowfully.

"I am Huido's blood brother," Morgan reminded the miserable being. "But cheer up. You look after the place and Huido might not help you molt before your time. You are planning to stay, aren't you?"

All of Tayno's eyestalks pointed wistfully at the forbidden door. "How can I leave?" he confessed. "This is the closest I've come to a pool in my entire life."

Morgan left the now-melancholy Carasian, heading quickly down the corridor in the direction of the staff apartments, choosing to take a shortcut through the too-quiet kitchen. He didn't slow down even when he saw the destruction inside, though he had to step more carefully to avoid the worst of the spilled and melted food on the floor. Plexis security had been somewhat obsessive in their search. Morgan shook his head in disgust at how they'd treated the chefs' knives. Dropping those treasured and very personal tools in the sink? Most would be ruined. Heads, or some appropriately essential body part, would roll once Huido was back.

Back in the hallway, Morgan moved quickly along, passing the doors to the staff apartments. Ansel's was the farthest—quieter and larger than the rest. Morgan's quick mental scan gave him nothing conclusive. The apartments were close together and shared walls with the hostel next door. Without probing deeper than was wise, he couldn't be sure who or what he felt.

Ansel's door wasn't closed. Suddenly uneasy, Morgan slowed to edge along the near wall, moving soundlessly. Ansel was a very private person—living in so public a place, his door was always closed. Morgan shifted one of the force blades into his right hand, triggering it on. He paused beside the door to listen.

Breathing. Broken, ragged. In another time, under an open sky, Morgan had learned to interpret such sounds: one person, in pain. A victim.

Morgan hurried inside, shutting off his knife and putting it away. He dropped to his knees beside the crumpled shape on the floor. "Ansel. What happened?"

The elderly Human, never sturdy, felt little more than bones and air in his hands. Morgan turned him over gently, supporting Ansel's head on one arm, his eyes and free hand searching for a wound, any clue. Ansel moaned, but remained unconscious, his face was soaked with sweat and twisted in remembered agony. Morgan carefully lifted the lid of one eye, only to drop it with a curse. The cornea was suffused with blood.

Morgan steadied himself. He placed his hand on Ansel's forehead—a light contact, no more, searching, searching. *There.* He pressed his fingers more firmly into the chilled skin. Through the touch, he sent his mind *reaching* into Ansel's, to find—nothing.

He jerked his hand away as if burned, staring down at the helpless Human, unable to stop shaking. The constable, Kareen, had suffered from a similar assault, but she'd been Terk's friend, not his. This was different. This was Ansel! Morgan had known Ansel as long as he'd known Huido. With his gentle, persistent efficiency and shy wit, the Human had been a point of stability for them both. *Who had dared* . . .

Morgan deliberately dampened his feelings, sought self-control. Sira had taught him that, to rule his Power, not be led by it. He could help Ansel.

He would.

He returned his fingers to that spot his other sense told him mattered. His initial impression had been of a void where Ansel's thoughts should have been. Morgan refused to accept that, sending his Power deeper.

Ansel wasn't a telepath, but his mind had some of those characteristics. He'd possessed enough ability to instinctively resist his attacker—ironically, it was likely that resistance had caused some of the damage Morgan found everywhere he looked. But not all. Someone had torn through Ansel's mind as Plexis security had torn through the kitchen, with as little care for the result. Thoughts were littered like broken dishes on a floor . . . incomplete images, nightmare shapes. Syllables of Comspeak that weren't words mingled with words that weren't Comspeak but the singsong language of Ansel's youth, on Imesh 27. Emotions like shards of glass, incomplete and irrational, painful and distracting . . .

Small steps, Morgan reminded himself, ignoring the drain on his strength as he sought whatever remained whole within Ansel's mind and drew that together, as a med might knit the ragged edges of a wound closed. He didn't worry about what made sense to him, only what seemed to belong, one to the other. Over and over again. Some areas were too damaged and he bypassed them. Others came together almost of their own accord.

Morgan was breathing in great, heaving gasps by the time he withdrew, slowly, carefully, continuing to heal Ansel even as he pulled free. Done at last, he hung his head, eyes closed, and strained to recover, knowing he had no time to waste on weakness. On that realization, Morgan dared remove his mind from the here-and-now, despite the danger of being surprised while so distracted. He *reached* into the M'hir, replenishing his strength from the Power Sira had given him in that place, feeling its strange, inhuman glow surging through him.

It seemed endless, that other source of Power, but wasn't—not really. Vast, but exhaustible, should he expend it too quickly. It burned too hot, like a barely-controlled explosion, Morgan judged, even as it restored him. His own Human Power obeyed him, reliable and steady, like a well-stoked furnace.

Drawing on what surrounded him in the M'hir cost more than lowering his guard for an instant in the real world. His Human mind didn't belong here; to remain open to the M'hir to access that Power meant a constant battle against disorientation and confusion, a fight against the illusion of being somewhere else.

Somewhere else. To Morgan's inner sense, the M'hir was gray on gray, as if he walked in dense fog beside an unseeable ocean, the crashing of nearby surf the only guide to avoiding a plunge into its deadly depths. Without Sira there, her presence like a sun whose rays pierced the mists around him, he was always that one step from losing his way. A risk Morgan took now, to regain his strength in time to help Ansel.

"Ja-son . . . ?" The voice was almost too quiet to hear, with a note of disbelief.

The faint voice drew Morgan back, his eyes flashing open. "Ansel! Yes, it's me. What do you remember?" he asked, hoping against hope there was sense behind the red-rimmed gaze meeting his. "Do you know who did this to you?"

There was too much sense. Ansel's face crumpled with shame. "I couldn't stop him, Jason. I couldn't stop him. He was in my mind . . . he took everything—"

"Easy. I know." Morgan said, stopping the outburst. He found Ansel's hand and gripped it tightly. "You did your best. Tell me who it was, Ansel."

"Ruti's friend . . . it was Ruti's friend. *Imde la zic v cronis. Imde la!*" this outburst in another language, then quieter: "Ruti's with Huido. Find them before he does, Jason. Find them."

So it hadn't been Sira, Morgan thought. He wasn't sure if he was relieved or not. "Who—" he began.

"He took his name. He took it back." Ansel's other hand came up to grip Morgan's arm, fingers tight and desperate. "But I saw him in the freezer," he wheezed, lips having trouble forming the words. "*Imde la! Cronis imla de!* Jason. Ruti's friend—in the freezer. Ruti said— Sira put him in the freezer."

Morgan's muscles locked. He'd done his utmost to forget, but he'd known. The style of attack had been too familiar; the needless carnage within the centers of memory, the emotional rape, were markers he knew too well. "Symon," he said in a voice that wasn't his own.

"Symon?" echoed Ansel, his face contorted with stress. Words kept pouring out of him. "*Imde la!* He wants the child. Huido *makesdi la* Ruti. *V! Amasdin ef v lavde!* Your safe place. He knows! I couldn't keep him out. I couldn't keep him out. He knows!" With that final shout, Ansel's body convulsed, eyes rolling upward so only the blood-red showed. Morgan wrapped his arms around the shuddering form, doing his best to hold and protect his old friend.

Until it no longer mattered.

*   *   *

"Morgan. Morgan, wait!"

"Later, Terk," Morgan snapped, somehow not surprised to find the Enforcer lurking beside the *Fox*'s air lock, but in no mood for conversation.

Something of his lethal frame of mind must have showed, because Terk put up both hands. "Hey, I'm not the enemy here," he said quickly.

"Time is." Morgan began punching in the codes on the station side of the air lock, transferring the outrageous penalty for early undocking to Plexis admin. When it squawked a complaint about a lack of credits in his account, Morgan didn't bother arguing. After a quick glance to either side to confirm they were alone, he slipped out his force blade and sliced the panel open, reaching into the gap to pull out carefully selected wiring. The station air lock obediently cycled green, *unlocked*.

"Interesting trick," Terk commented.

Morgan whirled, the force blade still humming in his hand, his eyes wild. Terk didn't flinch. They stood like that, both tense, for a long moment. "What's wrong?" the Enforcer asked, his rough voice unusually gentle. "Has something happened to Sira?"

The Trader straightened from his half-crouch, running a self-conscious hand through his hair to disguise hiding his knife with the other. "You're late," he accused.

"Is that all? We came as soon as we heard Plexis had tried to arrest the Carasian. Chief Bowman's reaming out Inspector Wallace even now." From Terk's voice, that was a conversation he'd hoped to enjoy in person. "'Whix has gone to check in with your friend. When we saw the *Fox* listed, I came here." He looked abruptly embarrassed but resolute, running one hand through his pale, wispy hair before saying: "I wanted to tell you in person that Kareen's doing well. Very well. The med-techs can't get over it."

"Good," Morgan said, taking a second breath, feeling anxiety and grief competing for attention now that he was no longer in full attack mode. "Good. But tell 'Whix—" He changed his mind mid-sentence. No point confusing the Tolian; there was a Carasian in the restaurant. It just wasn't the Carasian they expected. "Tell 'Whix there's a body in one of the apartments. Ansel Delacor. He—worked at the restaurant."

Terk swore. "This isn't going to help Huido's case, Morgan."

The Human lifted one hand; Terk subsided. "It's nothing to do with Huido," Morgan said tonelessly. "Ansel was attacked by Ren Symon. I did my best to help him, but the damage—the strain—was too much for him. He died in my arms."

Terk scowled. "You wouldn't have left with your engines at translight if you didn't have a lead on Symon. Don't try and go after him alone, Morgan. We can—"

"Can what, Russ?" Morgan demanded, eyes intent. "I've had another taste of his Power. Enough to tell me that Symon, or one of his disciples, was responsible for the attack on Kareen's mind, too—likely for the same reason: information. He's got some new device of his own, some new trick, but what matters is nothing will protect you from him. Not your body armor and ship—and not your implants. Are you hearing me?"

"And you're so safe?" Terk protested. "He hates your guts, Morgan. It's no accident Fodera's body was dumped the one place it would bring you running."

"Am I safe?" Morgan repeated, then gave a short grim laugh. "Not in any sense, my friend. As Symon will find out."

Chapter 16

I HAD to find out what was happening to me or go mad. *Was I already?* Surely it wasn't normal to be three at once. At least three: a Self existing solely within the M'hir—an obvious sign of insanity, to imagine that; a Self reliving her own memories, peeling away layer after layer of untruth—more proof; and a Self barely able to whisper to the others, a self whose softest questioning could lure . . .

The Singer.

. . . my seducer . . .

I recognized the choice, if not how I made it: *. . . the song or my past . . .*

"There."

Adia's voice was full of pride. I stared at myself in the mirror and wondered dully what she possibly saw that I could not. The white robe—which was ridiculously hard to put on without help, even had this one been my size—made my body into some grotesque thing, like a pole supporting a sail. My thin hair had ignored all of Adia's valiant efforts to glorify or even tidy it, while my eyes—

I turned away, unwilling to admit seeing my own fear. This was the next stage in my life, when I'd go from an overprotected and indulged Chooser, virtually captive in this House, to Chosen—free to go where I wished, when I wished. That longed-for freedom was minutes away.

"What's his name?"

Adia, busy cleaning up the bath area, shook her head at me. "Sira, you know his name. Your father announced it last night."

I was tempted to stick my tongue out at her, but the heavy ceremonial robe seemed to inhibit such spontaneity. "Somewhere during the names of those candidates Jarad hadn't approved, I stopped listening to him," I confessed.

The First Chosen was too well-mannered to reply to this, but I felt a warmth in her Power against my shields. "Coryl di Parth, my dear Chooser," she informed me. "Firstborn and the most powerful of all the candidates available. Having him selected for your Choice is quite an accomplishment for the House of di Parth. When Coryl becomes di Sarc—as all predict, given your Power—they may yet gain a member on Council." She came close, trying to affix a flower to my hair, something tiny and fragrant. I held still, hoping it would stay, but it slid free the moment Adia took her hand away.

I tried to dredge up the memory of a face to match the name, but failed. "Have I met him?" I asked. "This Coryl?"

"No," Adia said, giving a light sigh of frustration as she absently tucked the remaining flower into her own thickly cooperative hair. She stood back and inspected me. "Ah, but you are fine as you are, Sira. It's your Power-of-Choice that will draw him to you. And when you've Commenced, we will have more luck with flowers, won't we?"

Commenced. Choice. I felt a shiver of apprehension down my back that turned into something quite different: a dark warmth that moved within me, awakening places I'd never known could feel before. Awakening a need deeper than appetite.

For the first time since losing my link to my mother, I began to believe I'd be complete again.

My father and members of the Council, representatives from the House of di Parth—conspicuous in the triumphant, if unmannerly, taste of their Power—and other witnesses lined the Joining Chamber of sud Friesnen. I couldn't have named any of them. The moment Adia led me through the door, my attention was locked on the Clansman kneeling in the red circle on the floor before the Speaker.

"The Chooser has appeared," the Speaker intoned. "Bring forth the *duras*, so that all may witness."

My candidate. His eyes flashed up to mine, then modestly down again. Dark, uncertain eyes.

"Witness the blending of Power . . . Joining lasts forever . . ."

There was something wrong with the air, I thought, finding my breath coming deeper and faster as Adia brought me to kneel within the red circle, the stone floor cold on my bare feet.

Kneeling, my candidate—I remembered his name, Coryl di Parth—was taller than I by head and shoulders—slender, with fine elegant bones. The expression on his otherwise pleasant face, now that he looked at me, seemed an uncomfortable mixture of anxiety and some other feeling I couldn't name, but shared. Perhaps it was anticipation.

He reached his right hand toward me and, as I laid mine in it, I was pleased to note he had long, supple fingers, the type needed for the keffle-flute. It had taken me years to work out a technique allowing my shorter fingers to reach the uppermost . . . his hand was hot to the touch, I realized, losing my train of thought as that heat seemed to spread to every part of me.

"Power seeks Power through the M'hir . . ."

A *duras* cup was pressed into my free hand. Coryl didn't look away from me as he brought his to his lips. I mirrored his actions, taking a deep swallow of the *somgelt*. Within a heartbeat, the age-old spice worked its magic, showing me Coryl as he'd appear in the M'hir itself. As Power.

Power. The Power-of-Choice, my legacy as Chooser, boiled up through me, an irresistible force whirling us both into the M'hir . . .

I was the center of all things. The source and the goal. I was . . . There was an Other! I reached out with all my strength but couldn't touch his distant glow. I tried and tried, but the more I stretched toward that brightness, the farther it seemed to be, as if the Power-of-Choice refused to let us combine.

There was nothing else I could do. *I pushed . . .*

. . . and opened my eyes to see Coryl, shaking his head, disappointment plain to read on his face and in his Power. He dropped my hand as if its touch burned him. I felt him concentrate and watched him disappear—leaving me more alone than I'd ever been before.

I'd failed.

. . . the lie parted, the truth protruding from beneath like the white splintered ends of a fractured bone through flesh . . .

Power. The Power-of-Choice, my legacy as Chooser, boiled up through me, an irresistible force whirling us both into the M'hir . . .

I was the center of all things. The source and the goal. I was . . . searching for something. Ah. With a shudder, I remembered that urgent ecstasy and stretched arms of Power to seek it again . . .

One arm touched an Other! An Invader! This was my domain. Mine and . . . The Power-of-Choice smashed into the dim, futile glow that dared approach my glory, that dared pretend to be my equal—snuffing it out completely . . .

Finding nothing else to hold my attention, *I pushed . . .*

. . . and opened my eyes to see Coryl sprawled loose-limbed on the floor, his jaw slack, eyes rolled back so only the whites showed. Someone—Adia—pried my hand free and pulled me to my feet; someone else was screaming, in my mind as well as in my ears, until Coryl's body disappeared.

I tasted the Power exerted to *push* Coryl di Parth's empty husk into the M'hir. I could have done it, I supposed, a final courtesy for my brave candidate.

I wasn't sure what to do. This wasn't supposed to happen.

No one died during Choice.

My mind, my Power, felt bruised but not drained. I leaned against Adia, feigning weakness, so she fussed and insisted on taking me out of that chamber of death.

I couldn't tell her part of me was sickeningly triumphant, that my Power-of-Choice surged with desire to defend my emptiness again.

I could only hope Council wouldn't find another candidate.

INTERLUDE

"I only hope Barac knows what he's doing. He won't listen to reason—just keeps telling me I'll be fine without him! As if I would ever need the help of a *sud!*"

Copelup gestured something peacefully noncommittal, tentacles holding a container firmly against his mouth as he reclined comfortably on the couch in Rael's suite. The Clanswoman started to glare at him, but gave up. There was nothing satisfying in glaring at someone who was not only eyeless but was, to all intents and purposes, more interested in lunch than in her predicament.

She should have taken Barac more seriously. He'd obviously overreacted to their last experiment with Drapskii. Typical of the unChosen to scamper away at the slightest hint of danger.

Which wasn't true of Barac, Rael reminded herself, picking up her own wineglass and sitting down slowly. He'd proved himself long before now. If he'd left her to be the only Mystic One on Drapskii, it wasn't abandonment—hers was the greater Power, and it was only fitting Barac should leave if his was unequal to their task.

Which wasn't true either, Rael suddenly realized.

Barac was weaker than she, of course, but he'd learned to use everything he possessed to its utmost. But something had changed in him following their latest encounter with Drapskii, almost as if he'd been unable to pull completely free of the planet's presence, as if it still clung to him in the M'hir. If that were so, and Barac believed it dangerous, it might be why he left.

"Perhaps he has a point," she conceded, talking more to herself than the Drapsk. "Huido is a being we both hold in high regard. If Barac's power is better used assisting him—for whatever reason—"

The container, now empty, popped free. Copelup caught it deftly in one hand, putting it with others on the table. "A splendid representative of an admirable species," he agreed.

He meant the Carasian, of course. Copelup had been fairly blunt in his assessment of the Clan and its, in his words, arrogant presumptions about the M'hir. The Scented Way, Rael corrected to herself, aware she'd held all of these presumptions and her own share of arrogance before coming here.

"Barac would come back if I—" she asserted, then stopped, feeling: *a sending.* Copelup's antennae flopped in her direction as he sensed it, too. "There. I told you." Rael started to smile as she opened her mind, then she locked down her shields to keep in all emotion. This confident, powerful contact wasn't her runaway cousin.

To what do I owe this honor, Councillor di Parth? Rael sent, as they tested each other's Power in formal reacquaintance.

Tle was powerful, but younger, with the too-easily aroused passions of a Chooser frustrated by a lack of candidates for her Choice. Rael was impressed she'd been able to keep those passions from alienating her fellow Councillors. So far. She could feel the tumult of conflicting emotions within Tle now, barely under control. Not a social call.

Greetings, Rael di Sarc. I have information for the Speaker.

Then why not contact Sira yourself? Rael allowed Tle to feel her amused scorn, well aware other Clan were afraid of Sira's greater Power—not to mention her Human Chosen. Rael highly approved of that respect, even if she had little patience for cowards.

If that were possible, I would have done so, with a snap of unease rather than temper. *She has—withdrawn.*

Explain. Rael didn't notice how she sat straighter, glass forgotten in her hand. Copelup did, and chewed a tentacle thoughtfully.

She exists—as does her Chosen. The Watchers confirm it. But her mind is . . . Tle's sending faded, as if she needed to concentrate elsewhere for a moment.

Her mind is what? Rael demanded with snap of impatience to the sending, anxious to try reaching for her sister herself.

We don't know. There's something wrong. It's not retreat or our form of stasis. It's as if Sira has become spread within the M'hir—

Not dissolved? Rael's fierce denial of that possibility caused Tle pain. She didn't care. Sira was appallingly vulnerable through Morgan—a being with too colorful a past for Rael's comfort, however admirable his personal qualities.

Tle didn't protest—a sign she was truly concerned. *There's no diminishing of Sira's Power. But she's become—*

fragmented. There isn't enough of her in any one place to form a locate. I'd hoped this was part of your experiments with those aliens, that she was there with you. Obviously I was wrong.

The link was draining Rael's Power as well as Tle's, Power she would need to find Sira for herself. But she needed to know more. *What does Morgan say?*

The Human? Hesitation.

Ossirus, save her from xenophobic fools. *Her Chosen—who should know better than anyone where Sira is now!* If he didn't, Rael realized with a sinking feeling, he'd be doing anything to find her. She'd seen firsthand the extent of Morgan's attachment—his love—for Sira. There were risks to searching the M'hir. Morgan might be uniquely powerful for his species, but he was alien to that other space.

Tle surprised her. *None of us are sufficiently familiar with the taste of Morgan's Power to try a sending, and he isn't answering his com. We believe he isn't on his ship,* she sent almost primly. *Perhaps you would have better luck.*

I'll let you know. Rael promised grimly. As she prepared to pull away from their link, she felt Tle's power holding them together. *What is it?*

The information Sira wanted. She was right. Acranam's fosterlings were dispersed using starships. Under threat of deep scan, the First Chosen of sud Eathem admitted the involvement of Wys di Caraat. She didn't know the destinations of the others.

Rael knew Yihtor's mother, First Chosen di Caraat, better than she cared to: a thoroughly unpleasant, powerful Clanswoman unlikely to forget or forgive Sira's rejection of her son and its result, but someone she'd considered harmless while on Acranam. As for fosterlings? Rael quelled her envy. *I don't see how this matters now—*

A dark, painful flare of emotions: anger, grief. *It matters. We've located another of the fosterlings: Nylis sud Annk. The Scat ship took him too far from his mother, destroying their link. The Watchers warned Council, but not in time. Nylis must have tried to use his Power in front of the aliens, and they killed him for it. He was alone, Rael. Abandoned by his own House. How can such a thing be?*

Acranam, Rael sent numbly, as if that could explain it, but it couldn't. Nothing could. To send a fosterling away from safety instead of to it? Insanity. To lose one like this? To have him killed even as he struggled—without help or comfort from his kind—to comprehend the shock of his new state, of suddenly becoming an un-Chosen? Rael couldn't imagine it. Tears welled up in her eyes, tumbling like something cold, hard, and foreign over her cheeks.

Sira must know about this. I'll do what I can to find her and tell her, she vowed to Tle and herself, ending their connection.

She opened her eyes, having closed them to better concentrate on the sending, to find Copelup standing in front of her, his chubby hand patting her knee. "What's wrong?" the Drapsk asked. "Has something happened to Hom Huido?"

"Huido?" Rael choked on the word. "No, Copelup. No. But there's been a death. A tragic one. And we seem to have—lost—my sister. When I regain my strength—"

The Skeptic seemed to compress into himself. For an instant, Rael feared he'd continue shrinking into a useless ball of uncommunicative alien, but he stayed with her.

"Don't tell me she's—" All six tentacles popped into his tiny mouth, as though to stop the next word.

"Oh, no, Copelup," Rael assured him quickly, putting her hands over his. "No, Sira isn't dead. I'd know. I'm sure I would. I just need time to recover before I can search for her myself. There's something going on—" She stopped herself in time. Clan business, this business, wasn't for aliens, not even the Drapsk. "Sira could simply be trying to have some privacy."

Tentacles popped free with a fine spray of moisture that thankfully missed Rael's face. A feather's touch against her ear. "You don't believe that. You're worried." His voice became firm and determined. "What can we do to help, Mystic One?"

Rael blinked. She hadn't considered the Drapsk and their technology. "We must try to reach Jason Morgan. Otherwise? I don't know, Copelup," she said slowly. "But as it seems beyond the experience of our Council, perhaps it's more within your understanding of the Scented Way."

Somehow, the Drapsk managed to look smug.

Rael finally admitted—to herself—that she missed Barac, a *sud*—something she judged a consequence of their atypical friendship and a mark of personal weakness. Right now, however, surrounded by what could be mistaken for a riotously blooming garden, but was actually the varicolored plumes sprouting from the heads of far too many Drapsk crammed into a single room? She'd give a great deal to see her cousin trying to make his way through to her.

The *Silver Fox* had responded to their hail with an automated message about cargo holds and speed, but Copelup had responded to his new mission with gusto. He must have invited every Drapsk scientist even remotely connected with research into the M'hir—and they'd brought assistants. While the room where they gathered was large—a multileveled open space, with machines lining two walls—Rael worried if it held enough air for them all.

There was one good thing about a crowd of Drapsk. They were so quiet Rael could hear her own breathing. Most didn't speak at all, seeming to prefer to convey information, especially more technical details, chemically. Given the intensity of discussion now underway, with antennae flipping first one way, then the other in hilarious unity as different unheard ideas attracted attention and debate, Rael decided she might as well be in a garden tossed by winds from every direction. She tried her best not to sniff.

Rael tried her best to be patient, too, but after half an hour of soundless debate, she was finished waiting. The Clanswoman closed her eyes, assessing her reserves. Adequate for a heart-search. She couldn't *reach* for the Human—she'd never bothered to learn the taste of his Power. But she knew Sira's. Rael drew an image in her thoughts of her older sister, focusing her Power, concentrating on how Sira had looked last time they'd seen one another: the spacer coveralls, faded and patched, the familiar face that tended toward solemn until you looked into those gray eyes and saw the joy brimming within, her . . .

Sira!

Contact. Or was it? It was as if the two of them hung

suspended in the M'hir. Rael could "see" her sister—more correctly, sense the brilliant, almost blinding sphere of power that distinguished Sira in this place—but couldn't touch her thoughts. It was as if Sira had become oblivious to anything outside herself. It wasn't retreat, that defensive technique where a telepath drew on life's own energy to build an impenetrable shield, a shield that could only be opened by another. No, this was something Rael had never encountered before. As she strained harder, the sphere of Power that was Sira seemed to become two, then three, then an infinity of repeating globes before coalescing into one again so quickly its fragmentation might have been an illusion. The M'hir crackled and seethed—clear warning.

To her as well. Rael pulled herself free, reluctantly. She opened her eyes, expecting, and finding, the Drapsk to have reacted to her use of Power. Sure enough, those remaining on their feet were oriented toward her and statue-still. There were remarkably few balls of effectively-absent scientists, but she did spot a pair performing *gripstsa* toward the back. It seemed polite to ignore them.

"Were you able to reach her with your Power, Mystic One?" Copelup asked, predictably the least impressed.

Rael took her time before answering, aware Drapsk tended to add their own interpretations to whatever was said. She didn't want a misunderstanding to affect how they used their incomprehensible machines. "The technique I used," she said carefully, "what we call the heart-search, is very specific. It cannot be fooled. It took me where I could sense Sira in the M'hir, the Scented Way, but—"

"But?"

"She wasn't there. Not *there* as in a location. Assht," Rael hissed in frustration. "There's nothing I can describe for you—"

"Did you sense Drapskii? Was Drapskii there?" The eager questions came from another Skeptic squirming his way past the others to her. Levertup, Rael guessed, although he could have been any of the dozen or so yellow-plumed Drapsk dotted among the scientists. Still, Levertup seemed unique among the polite Drapsk in treating all around him, including Mystic Ones, with an odd mix of benign contempt and exasperation. Of course, Copelup was just as easy to identify; Rael need only find a Skeptic who blithely assumed he knew more than anyone else about everything.

Now, Copelup turned to his fellow Skeptic and their antennae whisked past one another in a feathery blur.

"What?" Rael demanded. There was only so much of this voiceless whispering she could tolerate.

"There's a reason, a good one, for Skeptic Levertup's question," Copelup told her evasively. So she'd been right. "Before I explain, Mystic One, please tell us: were you able to communicate with your sister?"

Rael shook her head out of habit, though they couldn't see the gesture. At least not in a way she understood. "No," she said aloud. "She didn't seem aware of anything outside herself. And there's something else. Tle—Councillor di Parth—described Sira's mind as fragmented. I saw that for myself. Sira seemed to be in more than one place at once for an instant—or there was more than one Sira." Rael heard the note of wonder in her own voice and coughed lightly. "It might have been an artifact of the Scented Way. The longer one's consciousness lies within its boundaries, the harder it becomes to sort reality from imagination."

"You say that other Clan also observed this, however, so we can—"

"But what about Drapskii!" Levertup, usually a very dignified being whose idea of dinner conversation involved pompous dictionary references, was hopping from one foot to the other in front of Rael. "Did you sense it?" He pressed closer, and the rest of the Drapsk took this as their cue to do the same, the entire roomful moving closer while hopping madly in unison. Only Copelup stood still, his back to the Clanswoman. He held up his small hands, his antennae fluttering wildly at the rest of them. *Saying what?*

Not since that utterly loathsome night on Ret 7— when she'd had to deal not only with a city's worth of Retians copulating in the streets but that Carasian—had Rael felt so near to being overcome by the alienness of other beings. She stood to gain height, backing hurriedly around the benchlike seat they'd made for her to find some shelter. She took shallow breaths to help control the instinct to 'port. Her hair, so well-behaved since her Choice, squirmed on her shoulders and threatened to lash into her face. "Stop this," Rael ground out. "Stop this now!"

If the Drapsk were capable of anything, it was of acting together in a way that defied reason in any more independent organisms. The words hardly left Rael's lips before every Drapsk in the room assumed an identical posture: antennae drooping behind their backs, hands held together, and tentacles within their mouths—which began chewing rapidly, producing a peculiarly soothing sound.

Except Copelup, who uttered a satisfied: "At last," and turned to Rael. "My colleagues' enthusiasm cannot excuse their behavior, Mystic One, but does explain it," he said reasonably. "We have been so very encouraged by what you and Hom Barac accomplished. Frankly, looking at the data, I concur with my fellow Skeptics: we've never been closer to success. You must understand that's most exciting. Most exciting."

Funny how a Drapsk being reasonable was always more confusing, particularly this Drapsk. Rael had no doubt Copelup knew exactly what he was—and wasn't—telling her. Something had changed—she grasped that much—something that warranted the passionate interest of so many Drapsk. But it wasn't Sira's plight, as she'd thought at first. Rael didn't doubt they cared about Sira, particularly the Makii, but right now? Her sister was incidental.

If they'd been Clan or even Human, Rael would have been furious. As it was, she lifted one brow and said quite calmly: "Make sense or I'm leaving." Copelup opened his tiny mouth immediately, but Rael interrupted him before he could utter a sound. "Five, Skeptic. Five words to convince me any of this is worth time I could use to help my heart-kin."

"Drapskii could lead you to Sira," Copelup pronounced confidently. "Oh. Was that six? My apologies, Mystic One."

She ignored the sarcasm, knowing this Drapsk, and sat on the bench seat. "Go on."

Copelup beckoned one of the other Skeptics to approach, a gesture that raised hopeful antennae in a wave starting at Rael and moving outward to the far walls. Where, Rael was disturbed to note, several additional pairs of Drapsk immediately leaped into *gripstsa* with one another. At this rate, she'd be dealing with a group of scientists who'd all been assistants moments ago. Hardly reassuring, no matter what Sira claimed about the interchangeability of Drapsk. "Netanup will explain," Copelup stated, then added rather firmly, "with haste."

"During your last glorious efforts on our behalf, Mystic One," the new Skeptic began quickly, rocking back and forth, "*su-gripstsa* occurred between Drapskii and the Mystic One who left us, Hom Barac. We measured it—quite remarkable. Would the Mystic One care to see the data?" Copelup's antennae shuddered warningly. "Of course not," the Skeptic hurried, the words now tumbling out so fast that the tentacles around his mouth jiggled. "How foolish of me. What matters in this instance, the instance of the Mystic One who also left us— much earlier than Hom Barac left us—that would be Fem Sira . . ." The Drapsk threw up his hands as if in self-defense. "We weren't expecting to ever have more than one Mystic One, Skeptic Copelup. It is leading to a great deal of confusion and could cause inaccuracies. But we don't want to debate semantics now. Of course not." He paused for breath. "Where was I?"

"Sira?" Rael reminded Netanup gently. So poor Barac's embarrassing moment of unreal bliss had not only been recorded by their devices, but had a name in their language? *Su-gripstsa*. She wouldn't tell him; an unChosen's ego was fragile enough.

"Part of that junction—for lack of precisely translatable terminology in Comspeak—remains intact, Mystic One," Netanup proceeded, a proud lift to his antennae. "We have been able to use it to follow Hom Barac's movements—insofar as those correspond his presence in the Scented Way." His voice rose in triumph as he reached the conclusion: "I see no reason why we can't—"

"—use the same technique to help find your magnificent sister, Mystic One," Copelup broke in heartlessly. The other Skeptic didn't appear offended by this interruption, bobbing his head in agreement. "After all, Fem Sira was the first Mystic One to touch Drapskii. There could still be a similar junction between them. Netanup," the Drapsk conceded generously, if late, "is to be commended for his efforts."

Netanup's tentacles spread in a ring of happiness, then one snuck into his mouth. "There's no guarantee," he admitted. "Hom Barac's *su-gripstsa* was intense and recent. And we don't know if Fem Sira engaged in such a junction with Drapskii. Did she mention this to you, Mystic One?"

Rael searched the memories Sira had shared of her encounter with the Drapsk's planet in the M'hir. Sira had been a Chooser at the time, subject to the same cravings as any unChosen. She hadn't, Rael was somewhat relieved to remember, been able to satisfy those cravings with a rock. "No," the Clanswoman concluded aloud. "But we can still try, can't we?"

"Of course," Copelup and Netanup said at once. Nods of agreement were followed by a drift of color throughout the room as groups of Drapsk headed to the machines lining the walls. The rest turned from her, their attention now on their devices and those using them.

"So will I," Rael said under her breath. She swung her legs around, and laid back on the bench.

Copelup hadn't left her. He patted her arm. "Be careful, Mystic One," he advised, adding, before she had to ask: "I promise. No pinching."

Rael closed her eyes, finding it oddly reassuring to know the little being watched over her, though he couldn't follow. She opened her awareness to the M'hir, ready for the strange feel of Drapskii . . .

. . . and was shocked to find it changed. The bundle of tangled energy that had meant Drapskii to her before was gone. In its place was a tight coil, some areas so dark as to seem outside the M'hir, others too bright for her to examine directly. Size had no meaning; Drapskii might have been the largest object in the M'hir or the smallest. Regardless, it impacted that space more intensely than anything Rael had ever experienced. She could feel how the M'hir itself was distorted around the coil, forbidding passage closer. Even as Rael absorbed this, the whole seemed to turn, presenting a new curled edge.

Along that edge, the coil extended arms of lightning, jagged eruptions of outward-flowing energy that licked at the M'hir, as if tasting it. She couldn't tell how far they stretched—the existence of any one was too fleeting, seen more as a burn left along her other sense than substance. They were unpredictable and breathtakingly beautiful, as if Power had danced to unheard music.

Rael held herself together and, curious, *reached* for one of the bolts. Seeming to sense her intention, the nearest turned aside and sped toward her, glowing brighter and brighter until she tried to flee instead. But it caught her, held her fast, began to drain Power from her, began to feed . . . while another bolt strengthened, using her energy, sought outward again . . . She struggled, trying to free herself . . .

. . . *Pain!*

"Enough," Rael whispered, pulling her hand out of what felt like Copelup's mouth. Good thing he had flat teeth. The Drapsk had an interesting way of keeping promises. She kept her eyes closed a moment longer, not so much to avoid telling him what had happened, but because lightning still flashed behind her eyelids—too glorious to abandon, no matter how deadly.

Barac had noticed that Drapsk with bad news tended to arrive in large groups; perhaps they felt safer. Judging by the number assembled outside his cabin—which didn't have a door—the Clansman was reasonably sure they brought very bad news indeed. The way they were all sucking tentacles didn't help. "What's wrong?" he said, leaning back in the bowlike chair they'd provided. It leaned back with him, which would have been more alarming had it not grown out of the floor and remained firmly attached. Quite comfortable, in fact, he thought. A lot more comfortable than these Drapsk looked, especially Captain Makoori, who stood in the midst of the others as if seeking shelter. "We did land properly. This is Ettler's Planet."

"Of course, Mystic One," Makoori spat out a tentacle to deliver a shocked protest. "Any vibration you may have felt was due to the poorly maintained docking tug

Port Authority sent to bring the *Makmora* to the Rosietown shipcity. We ve lodged a complaint."

"So—?"

"We can't stay, Mystic One. The inferior docking tug is coming to reattach within the hour. Our profound, humblest, most abject apologies—but if you wish to stay on Ettler's Planet and help Hom Huido, you will have to leave the *Makmora*—now."

The Drapsk's distress was obvious. Barac shared it. Having a shipload of Drapsk watching his back was one thing, being marooned on this marginal Fringe world— a Human colony too poor for any Clan to consider for a home and too far for him to 'port anywhere? "Why?" he demanded. "I was counting on your support."

Makoori wrung his hands. "Mystic One, I can't tell you how sorry we are. The Makii are shamed. We will leave you one of our atmosphere vehicles. A substantial deposit has been made for your convenience at the Rosietown credit bureau. You can—"

"Why?" Barac repeated.

Another Drapsk, Maku by his tag and the *Makmora's* tactical officer, took a step forward. "It is my fault, Mystic One," he said miserably. "I checked existing tribal trade agreements with respect to this system and its worlds before we left Drapskii. There were none, I promise you. This is too small a system to interest any Tribe. But in the time it took us to travel here, it seems the Heerii have claimed ascendance."

"Worse," Makoori snapped, "there is a Heerii ship already docked: the *Heerama*. Her Captain does not welcome our presence, even though I stressed we were not looking to trade. It is his prerogative to insist we leave immediately—and he does. We must obey."

Another Drapsk ship? Barac let out a long breath, relieved to know he wouldn't be without allies after all. He knew more individuals from the Makii than the Heerii Tribe, but they were all dependable, polite beings. Who carried weapons, large ones, if need be. Their internal politics wasn't his concern. "Who is the *Heerama*'s Captain?" he asked. "Should I introduce myself or is he expecting me?"

Before Barac's horrified eyes, all thirteen Drapsk in his door performed *eopari* and curled into balls, a few gently bumping into one another, then rolling away.

"What did I say" he asked the quiet, pink-walled corridor.

Chapter 17

WHAT did I do to deserve this? demanded the parts of me. Surely this was too severe a punishment for any crime: to be split into a growing number of fragments, each suffering its own torment, each unable to comprehend a purpose, let alone see an end.

As if the longing to understand had been a summons, the Singer reappeared. Those selves which were me were thrust farther apart, as some responded with dread and others eagerly echoed desire . . . an urgent, restless heat . . .

Closer. Closer. Suddenly, I was one again and the barrier between us seemed to disappear—or had the Singer become more powerful than ever? Its music entered me. I shuddered under its sweet, unfelt touch, fought to deny its Power even as I opened myself more and more, ready to . . . ready to . . .

No. Something of who I had been pushed through, forcing me away, back into the relative safety of memory . . .

. . . *until that safety crumbled . . .*

*   *   *

"Excuse me, Sira, for this intrusion. The First Chosen asked me to remind you about tonight," young Enora said very properly, then added in a passionate rush: "It's my fostering party. You have to come!"

I'd restyled my rooms several times over the past years; the present look was dark, with heavy draperies and shadowed corners. One such corner held my favorite chair; tonight, it held me as well. "I don't have to come if I don't wish to, youngling," I said less than gently.

Enora had come lately into my life, born several years after Council had realized there were no candidates for my Choice. While I waited for the next generation, my body's aging and maturation halted by the Power-of-Choice, I was permitted to live in peace, as long as I kept away from any unChosen. I had asked to remain here, with Adia, in her mountain fortress.

But it hadn't been home, until Enora was born— the last child in the House of sud Friesnen, a bright spark of personality and affection with almost no Power of her own, save over our hearts. With her arrival, my hermitage became filled with giggles and toys, secrets and learning. Adia, busy with the affairs of her House, was happy to leave Enora in my care. I . . . was simply happy. And tonight it would end.

"You are coming, aren't you?"

I curled myself tighter in the chair, knowing she couldn't see my face in the dim light. "I don't feel well. Give the First Chosen my apologies. Now go. You'll be late."

She stepped closer, eyes dilated, her small hand reaching toward me. Enora's Talent lay in her empathy and, even this young, it was impossible to hide feelings from her. She didn't confuse my sorrow as illness. "Sira? Why are you so sad? Fostering is a happy time. Mother says so. She'll be with me. And you and I can still talk mind-to-mind. Please come."

Come? Be there when she used what strength she had to 'port away from her mother, from me? "I can't, Enora," I confessed, feeling tears spill down my face. "I'd disgrace you. I can't stand there and pretend to be happy you are leaving."

Fostering was only Enora 's first step away from me. I looked at her, seeing the lovely lines of the Clanswoman she would be, one day. There would be no lack of candidates for Enora sud Friesnen. She would foster, become a Chooser, Join, and move to a House of her own. I knew the pattern too well, having watched my entire generation move on and leave me behind.

Even my mother. I couldn't leave the Cloisters, as the sud Friesnens now called their home, without risking the unChosen. Mirim had never come to me. Now, she was preoccupied with caring for my newborn sister, Rael di Sarc. In time, Jarad claimed, Rael might be fostered with me, so that the passage from Camos to Deneb might be strengthened. He was always planning for the future.

I couldn't imagine one.

Enora climbed into my lap, a familiarity I permitted, and tucked her tiny head under my chin. She smelled of flowers and soap. "I can't go very far," the child said without shame. "I'll still be on Camos. You could visit me."

"Camos has become too full of Clan, little one," I

sighed, hugging her close. "It would be too dangerous for any un—" She was too young for details. "It
wouldn't be wise for me to travel away from home,
right now," I temporized.

She pulled back to look into my eyes. I could feel
her determination. "Then I'll come back here. I swear
it. After—after—whatever lies ahead, I'll come back
here to live with you. Unless you've gone . . ." This
last was said with a tremble, as though she'd suddenly considered I might change after all, and no
longer be waiting to play in my gray stone tower.

I gave Enora a gentle shake. "I'll either be here, or
I'll be visiting you. How's that, little one? Now, why
don't you help me choose something suitable out of
my closet? I think I do feel well enough to come to
your party."

*. . . years could be an instant, as easily as an instant
take years . . .*

"I wish you could attend, Sira," Rael didn't quite
pout, but the intention was there.

I raised a brow rather than laugh at my heart-kin.
"No, you don't."

She was radiant. That was the only word I could
find for my sister as a Chooser. Rael was strong in her
own right and Talented, but now, augmented and encased by her Power-of-Choice? If I slipped into the
M'hir, she was dazzling; to my ordinary vision, her fair
skin glowed and her eyes sparkled with excitement.

And why not? Joined, Rael would be free to leave
the Cloisters, a home she'd shared with me happily,
but which had never been enough for her spirit. Rael,
like many Choosers her age, was powerful enough to

be lethal to a weaker candidate. Council fluctuated between joy and dismay at this change in our kind: joy, because the surge of ability within this generation benefitted all Clan; dismay, because mine hadn't been the only disastrous attempt and Houses were becoming less willing to risk their unChosen sons.

I had no fear for Rael's candidate, confident she would successfully Choose Janac di Paniccia. I should be; I'd selected him. Our father hadn't argued—not because he agreed with me, but because he judged Janac too weak and likely to fail. What he called, privately, "the weeding out of the inferior among us" didn't bother Jarad at all.

It bothered me. I'd spent the last three years delving into family records, researching, hunting for the best possible match for Rael, a candidate whose Power complemented hers in more subtle ways than mere strength. I had never met Janac in person, of course, nor contacted his mind—for the same reason I wouldn't be in attendance at my own sister's Choice. The unChosen couldn't help but seek the more powerful Chooser, as insects to flame. So Rael would 'port to Deneb for her Joining to avoid me. Our mother and new sister, Pella, would be at her side.

My remaining role in Rael's life? To help her pack.

"They say the firstborn of di Caraat has exceptional Power," Rael said suddenly. "What's his name?"

I slipped a gift into her last bag. The servants had taken the rest. "Yihtor," I told her, though she knew perfectly well. "Council rejected him."

"Or you did." Her eyes flashed in sudden anger.

"You have to take a chance, Sira, or you'll be here forever—"

"If that's what it takes to make sure no one else dies, then so be it!" I fired back, but gestured appeasement immediately. "Forgive me, heart-kin."

"Always," she said quickly, but shook her head. "Understand you? Never."

"Maybe Pella will do better, then. She starts her fostering with me very soon."

"Will you try and teach her, too?" My sister picked up my keffle-flute and tossed it at me.

I put it to my lips and trilled a laugh. "Someone else in the family must be able to carry a tune," I said optimistically. Rael hadn't the patience to master the flute, though she'd worked diligently to perfect her Talents.

We both felt the summons. "Time to go, Rael," I told her. "Janac's waiting. Be well. And come back to visit as soon as you can."

Her eyes glistened with tears. "I will. I promise."

I watched Rael disappear, leaving me alone, again.

. . . was I safer skipping through memory or was that safety a lie, too . . .

The explosion may have been minor, but it took us unawares. In the hall, I caught the sleeve of one of the servants, an older Human named Persio. The air was choked with dust. "Are you all right? Was anyone hurt?"

"I'm fine, Fem di Sarc. So is everyone else. But you shouldn't stay down here. There could be another explosion."

"There shouldn't have been a first," I said dryly,

letting him dash away on whatever errand was required. Cleaning, that was certain.

After Adia's death, I'd taken the sud Friesnens' home as my own. I was the only Clan who lived in the old stone building these days, with the exception of the brief and usually tumultuous intervals when my fosterling, Pella, deigned too return. She took advantage of my preoccupation with my studies, 'porting around Camos with a fine disregard for her age and responsibilities as fosterling. Her link with our mother would probably last less time than Rael's, even with the solid pathway already in place between Camos and Deneb. At least Pella enjoyed the keffle-flute, somehow attaining a reasonable proficiency despite having the attention span of a water drop under the midsummer sun.

For once, I was pleased by Pella's absence, since it meant she'd missed the mysterious blast which had taken out part of the lowermost floor of the Cloisters. Only one room and an entrance, both hardly used, had been damaged. The building was as solid as the cliff that hosted it, and only the most precariously perched crystal had broken. The puzzle remained: why? Technology wasn't an interest of mine, but taking on the duties, if not rights, of First Chosen meant paying attention to the household. So I knew the room had contained nothing that could explode—just some old exterior storm panels. They'd become unnecessary once Camos established complete weather control. It made, I grumbled to myself, no sense.

Until I 'ported back to my rooms and immediately found all the explanation necessary. The harmless explosion had been deliberate—a diversion that allowed an intruder to land his aircar on my balcony without notice. I would have felt any Clan 'porting into my home, but not this.

So now, a handsome stranger confronted me in my own bedroom, one who dared to smile and greet me, as if his Human-like subterfuge would please me. "Chooser."

"Fool," I replied. This had to be Yihtor di Caraat. An unChosen. I could feel his need inflaming the M'hir between us—the dark eagerness inside me responding no matter how I tried to ignore it. "Is this how you wish to die?" I demanded harshly. "There are other Choosers, suited to your Power."

"I will offer you Choice," he said thickly, as if he hadn't heard or didn't care to hear. I thought the latter. "You, the jewel of them all."

I should have 'ported away the moment I saw him, but it was already too late. I wasn't immune to instinct. Compared to my emptiness, his longing to be fulfilled was a grain of sand to my desert. I stared at the hand Yihtor held out to me, feeling reason slip away as mine lifted to meet it.

Suddenly, my father was in the room, and others from Council. Yihtor's handsome face turned into this desperate, ugly thing, screaming defiance even as the other Clan 'ported him out of reach. I would have followed, but for a second, my 'port was blocked.

It was long enough for sanity. I found myself again, shuddering inwardly how close I'd come to—I stopped the thought and bowed with an unusually fervent gesture of gratitude to those lesser in Power to both the Councillors and my father. "How did you know?" I asked Jarad, then shook my head in wonder. "You expected Yihtor to try something like this. You had him followed. Why didn't you stop him sooner?"

"He wouldn't take no for an answer. Or listen to Council dictates."

We'd never become affectionate, but knew each other well enough after all these years. Jarad had aged impressively, gaining presence and poise. I hadn't aged, outwardly, but at times like this I felt even older. I'd changed; he had not. Jarad performed the occasional courtesy for me, such as reserving every table at a restaurant in the nearby city so I could leave the Cloisters for a meal with him. He would listen to my music or my studies, finding both agreeable pastimes if not extended too long. I judged each of these encounters by what he wanted to gain—at times no more than to remind himself of my Power, as if he gauged me against some candidate he investigated.

At others, we discussed Council matters. I was older than most on Council, more powerful than any, and, as Jarad was fond of telling me, I should be on it. I wasn't so sure he'd relish our debates when a vote depended on our agreement—because we rarely did.

So now, I glared at him, understanding the exquisite timing of Jarad's arrival with Yihtor's. "You wanted to prove to me how far he'd go. What he'd dare to reach me."

Jarad's eyes gleamed. *Just so, Daughter.*

"Now will you listen to our advice, Sira?" Councillor Sawnda'at asked.

I scowled. "You want to fortify my home because of one fool you've already caught."

"Because of the others to come, Daughter. Unless you've changed your mind and wish to receive unqualified candidates for your Choice?" Jarad said with false compassion.

"Install your fortifications," I told Sawnda'at, looking at Jarad. "But before you lock me away, I want the Council records I've been using for my research transferred here."

Crisac di Friesnen, older than when we'd first met, but not much wiser, objected immediately. "Ridiculous! Krea di Mendolar, our late Speaker, was right to refuse you any access within the Council Chamber. It was only after his untimely death that your father swayed Council into humoring this absurd pursuit. Now, you'd ask us to risk sending such irreplaceable—"

I stopped him with a pulse of Power—rude, but effective. "If you want me to stay here, Councillors, to await your needs, it will be on my terms, not yours," I said evenly, including my father as I gazed at them all in turn. "You cannot keep me here. You cannot force me to Choose. And do not pretend you can guarantee I will ever have Choice or be free of this prison you'll make for me. The records that I want. By tomorrow."

As one, they disappeared, leaving the M'hir tasting of capitulation and respect, with a touch of triumph I knew was Jarad's. Their emotional response didn't concern me. I would have what I wanted, those records and my privacy to research their secrets. To find out how to stop all of this . . .

I picked up the keffle-flute and went out to my balcony. With a disdainful flick of power, I *pushed* Yihtor's aircar out of my way, sending it to join the rest of the destruction he'd caused in my home.

The cliff dancers came out slowly, used to me, if not to disappearing machines. This time of year, the tiny creatures dared gravity to prance and perform for their mates. Much like Yihtor, I thought with a sigh. The music I chose to send over the cliff was filled with melancholy and despair, an outlet for my impossible longing. I played for hours, through the sun's setting. I played until my fingers grew too cold to hold the flute, then, comforted and calmed, I sought my bed.

. . . sought the truth, fought to remember . . .

The cliff dancers . . . I lifted my flute to my lips and began to play notes of loneliness and aching need. It was as if the sound came from inside me, not the instrument.

I couldn't stop playing as the Power-of-Choice struck at my consciousness: demanding, craving, wanting. It had been aroused once and wouldn't be ignored . . . or satisfied. So I played louder, with more and more passion, as if the music could lift the pain from me and carry it off the cliff.

It bought the Singer instead.

The portion of my mind touching the M'hir heard him first, underscore and thunder roll of percussion, adding depth and resonance beneath the flute. Each beat pushed my heart harder and faster, sent blood pounding in answer. I kept playing even as my body burned, wanting more.

Because part of me finally understood. This wasn't an attack or invasion. It was a seduction, begun when I'd fought to hold my mother in the M'hir, continued throughout my life to this moment. Seduction by an unChosen, of a kind, who cared nothing for Sira di Sarc or the Clan, but who lusted for what I had to give: the Power-of-Choice, perhaps Choice itself. Seduction by a master, whose fingers of Power stroked and tormented my inner self with rising crescendos of unheard music, until I could hardly remember who or what I was, knew only a desperate need to be filled, a need that seemed suddenly attainable.

Yet I held at that brink, somehow finding the strength to see the truth through the heaving darkness, to know this wouldn't be my completion, but the Singer's, that our Joining would consume and destroy all I was. I couldn't deny the temptation to submit, to leave my life behind in one orgasmic moment, if this was all there could ever be. But I refused to believe that. I demanded more. I demanded hope. The Singer's spell over me faltered, weakened for a single beat. I could pull free . . .

. . . to find myself lying half over the balcony wall, staring down into the confusion of rock, shadow, and twisted shrub that dropped straight to the valley floor. A disgruntled cliff dancer squeaked its annoyance before scurrying impossibly down the vertical stonework to disappear beneath the overhang.

My keffle-flute almost fell from my sweat-soaked hand. I almost let it, afraid of what the music had brought to me.

Afraid I wouldn't be able to resist next time.

INTERLUDE

The next time Barac relied on Drapsk transport, if ever, he'd pick a better destination—just in case they marooned him again. He presumed Huido would have transport already arranged to get them both off Ettler's Planet. The name was rumored to have started as "Settler's Paradise." If so, thought Barac, it was more perverse Human wit, since no world could seem less attractive from orbit. Ettler's was almost completely arid and owed its wealth to a happy concentration of minerals rare in neighboring systems.

Well, at least the Makii had taken him away from Drapskii. The Clansman sighed, pulling his cloak tighter around his neck. The bite of the morning's wind advised raising the hood as well, but it seemed too long since he'd felt fresh air moving of its own accord. Besides, there was no harm in showing Humans his face—Barac knew his looks were considered attractive by most of that species and exceptionally handsome by some. Why waste Power to obtain cooperation, when a smile would do?

Not that a smile would have helped obtain more

from the Makii. Barac wasn't sure the *Makmora* would be able to lift before her crew was convulsed in *gripstsa*. He'd never seen Drapsk so upset. They hadn't been able to explain their aversion to his contacting the Heerii with any clarity, babbling about ascendance, danger, and some nonsense about a risk to Drapskii.

Barak had found himself wishing for Copelup. The Skeptic only made sense when he wanted to, but it was more often than this. He'd been tempted to contact Rael, to pass along the question to the Drapsk, then changed his mind. She'd been abundantly clear in her opinion of his leaving Drapskii in the first place. This?

She'd gloat at his being marooned. He knew she would.

There was no doubt, however, that the Makii believed the Heerii posed a danger. What that could be, beyond more alien confusion, Barac couldn't imagine, but he wasn't about to ignore anything that made four hundred Drapsk roll up into balls. A good thing the docking tug alarm jarred most awake.

They'd been generous, if hysterical. Barac had willingly used their credits to park the *Makmora*'s aircar at the edge of the shipcity, feeling more comfortable traveling on foot in a new city. City? The Clansman surveyed his surroundings with an experienced eye. Rosietown wasn't quite that, but he was pleasantly surprised to find any sophistication out on the Fringe, especially on such an uncomfortable-seeming world.

The shipcity itself was standard: an ever-changing conglomeration of ships and the shipways between them. It sprawled over most of a huge salt flat, which donated an acrid dust to be raised by anything that moved, from feet to docking tugs, stinging eyes or whatever exposed tissue might be sensitive. A fickle wind took any dust inclined to settle and stood it in columns between the ships, while the intensity of the rising sun promised a glare from every reflective surface by noon.

Rosietown was separated from the shipcity by the usual All Sapient's District of spacers' bars, hostels, and trading markets. An eroded mountain leaned along the far edge of the town, presumably sheltering it from some of the worst winds. The streets boasted actual greenery, albeit protected from the elements by force fields, and various substantial buildings Barac decided wouldn't look out of place on an Inner System world. It took wealth, agreeably permanent wealth, to produce structures that were also art forms. The Clan might want to investigate the possibilities of the place after all.

Perhaps being without the Drapsk was just as well, Barac concluded, feeling his training as a Clan Scout renewed as he chose a path that wove between Rosietown and the All Sapient's District, heading toward Embassy Row. The town and its less-planned neighbor blurred into an upscale market area that produced such unintentional quaintness as a Whirtle-run Human used-clothing outlet beside a Human restaurant claiming to serve authentic Whirtle haute cuisine. Advertising 'bots hovered in wait above their respective businesses, ready to bob helpfully in front of any passersby who looked their way, displaying the day's specials and other enticements.

This early, nothing appeared to be looking except himself and a host of servos, sweeping dull yellow sand and streaks of glittering salt from the pavement. The wind was no more than a gentle stirring now, but Barac had no doubt it was the reason the local architecture featured attractive curves and an abundant use of stone.

Barac kept his senses, all of them, alert as he walked. He didn't expect trouble, but he'd prefer a bit of healthy paranoia to an unpleasant surprise. Huido had given him an address, along with the cryptic information that he'd either be met or there would be a message telling Barac where to go next. That was all, nothing about why he wanted Barac, in person, as quickly as possible, out in the Fringe. Not that it mattered. Any reason to leave Drapskii, the Clansman shuddered, was a good one. He did his best not to remember the feel of it in his mind.

Besides, if there had been anything seriously wrong, Huido would have contacted Morgan. No, Barac decided, more than likely the Carasian had come up with another scheme to corner the market in whatever unique consumable this place might produce, a scheme needing someone with more charm than crust to make the deal. Barac had done the same for Huido twice before: once negotiating over translight com, the second time hosting a meeting on Drapskii. The old shellfish paid well and, Barac shrugged as he walked, there were worse ways to make a living. He'd known there wouldn't be much of a long-term future on Drapskii even then.

At least with Huido, there should be breakfast. The

Makii had hurried him out on an empty stomach, probably, he estimated, a good two standard hours before anything resembling a restaurant would open. *Aliens.* He spent more time with them than his own kind. Sira's fault, Barac thought, but fondly. After this business was over, he really should make the effort to get in touch with his illustrious cousin and her Chosen. Sira, he knew, would be far more sympathetic to what he'd been enduring than her sister Rael.

Ruti woke from a nightmare and instinctively reached for her mother. There were no words in return, just that comforting sense of presence. Reassured, she ordered on the port light.

Nothing happened. Ruti shook her head with disgust and fumbled at the side of the cot for the portable lantern Huido had given her. No outside power supply, he'd explained. As if that was a surprise in this hovel.

She didn't know why she'd stayed with the Carasian during their flight from Plexis to this place—wherever it was. Habit, probably. Obey those older and supposedly wiser. She shook her head. Not that there'd been much opportunity. The Turrneds had kept staring at her every minute on Plexis. And she must have dozed through most of the trip by starship—so much for the so-called restorative tea Huido had insisted she drink.

Ruti yawned, stretching until her sholders creaked. Breakfast and then she'd insist on some answers—including where they were and what was going to happen next.

Huido had brought them to the All Sapient's District of whatever town this was. Ruti hadn't seen much of it yet. Their lumbering, smelly escort had effectively blocked any view of her first shipcity and, within town, a chill, sand-laden wind kept her head inside the huge, shapeless robe Huido had insisted she wear. She'd been warm enough, at least. The Carasian might have gone to great lengths to keep them inconspicuous, but Ruti doubted it had worked. Each time sand had slithered over his tent-sized robe, Huido had expressed his misery with such loud mutters and clanks, it was hard to imagine any being capable of hearing sleeping through the din.

He'd known where to go, at least. The right doorway had been at the end of a blind alley, inhabited by scaled vermin that hissed alarmingly before scurrying up walls, hopefully to avoid them and not launch an attack. Huido had opened the door with an antique key before hustling Ruti inside. He'd almost run her down in his hurry to get out of the wind and shed his sandy robe with disgust.

The place had no power, but was clean enough, with furniture that suited both Clan and Carasian anatomy. There was a tiny kitchen Ruti had inspected with a tired eye before Huido showed her to this cupboard of a room where she would sleep.

Tiny or not, the kitchen had looked functional and this morning she was starving. Ruti padded on bare feet down the short hall, only to stop in her tracks. *Voices.*

A stranger's—male, possibly humanoid, deep—answered by Huido's; the Carasian's tone matter-of-fact enough to ease her mind, if not make Ruti any more inclined to announce herself. She tightened her shields, crept as close as she dared, and listened.

The stranger: "—glad to find you, safe and sound."

A proud claw snap. "Why would I not be? Did you think that minuscule nephew of mine would prove a challenge?"

"Never, my giant friend. The virtue of your wives remains quite intact." The voice sobered. "Huido. This young Clanswoman you've brought with you—Ruti. What's her connection to Ren Symon?"

"Symon?" a slithering sound, as though Huido had come to attention. "Where did that—? You don't mean that scrap of molted shell was behind all this? Why—?" Then, the Carasian answered his own question, his voice a dangerously low growl. "To bring you to Plexis. Much becomes clear. But how do you know about Ruti? And how would she know Symon?"

"Ansel—" the name bitten off, as though the speaker almost said more but changed his mind. He continued: "Ansel told me your Ruti claimed Symon was her friend. And warned me Symon was after her—would follow her here. You've seen no sign of him?"

Ruti leaned closer, eyes wide with astonishment. Symon? Ansel knew her friend's name was Jake Caruthers.

"If I'd seen anything of Ren Symon—or smelled the stench of his *grist*," Huido replied with complete conviction, "he'd have been on the menu. But what aren't you telling me, my friend? Your *grist* isn't right—"

A grim laugh. "I'm not surprised. But bear with me—I need to know more before I tell you my—news.

This Ruti—who is she? I can feel her. Clan. Young. Why did you bring her here?"

"Who is Ruti? From Acranam, arrogant, makes an acceptable omelette. Ansel found her on my doorstep—he's forever complicating my life with his strays. I let her stay because her *grist* was like yours had been: full of rage and betrayal. I don't know any more than that about her. But why did I bring her here?" A pause during which Ruti barely breathed. "She maneuvered her way into being my chef with Clan tricks. You know I'd never leave a potential enemy near my pool." Ruti's shocked dismay vanished as Huido went on: "But at the risk of having you and Ansel believe I've gone soft before my next molt, I don't believe there's any harm in the little one. She's done what she had to, to survive a hard situation. I brought her with me for her own safety. We can't have Plexis security finding her—you know Wallace has ties to those who'd pay well for a vulnerable being of Ruti's potential."

"Including Symon," the voice said thoughtfully. "Who wanted her enough to be seen on Plexis—where Bowman has a reward for his head."

"So we hunt?" a satisfied clattering, as though Huido rummaged through the weapons hanging from his chest to select a favorite.

"I do. There's no easy way to tell you this, Huido." The voice lowered, slowed, as if the speaker hated what he had to say next, but pushed on regardless. "Ansel's dead. Murdered. Symon ripped apart his mind after you left. I tried to repair what I could, but it wasn't enough." A pause. All Ruti heard was her heart pounding. Then, "Symon did it to find Ruti. Ansel died trying to protect you both, my brother. Grieve and know I will honor the debt between us." It was said as if a vow.

Ruti covered her mouth with both hands and reeled back against the wall. She squeezed her eyes shut and reached for her mother. *Nothing!* She reached again and again. *Nothing!* Desperately, she poured her Power into their link. Finally, a whisper of recognition and warmth.

It didn't help. Ruti ran back to her room and threw herself on the cot.

Jake—no, this Symon—had killed fussy, harmless Ansel? To find *her?* She couldn't doubt the voice; there had been too much pain in it. Ruti sobbed into the dusty robe that had been her blanket last night, her hand gripping tiny Lara until the precious doll bent in half. Poor, poor Huido. There wasn't a sound from the kitchen: no roar of anger, no ringing snap of a claw that could cut through a Clansman's waist. The silence was infinitely more sorrowful.

"You must be Ruti," said a quiet voice. "I'm sorry you had to find out about Ansel that way."

She turned her face to stare up at the silhouette of a Human in the doorway, shorter and less broad than Symon. Seeing her look, he took a step so his face caught some of the poor light thrown by the lantern. She stared into impossibly blue eyes, eyes that seemed to contain all the sadness and kindness in the universe at once. "You're Morgan," Ruti said with wonder, her voice breaking in a hiccup. She remembered this face

—who of the Clan could forget what Sira had shared about Her Chosen?

Without thinking, she did as she would when meeting any Clan and opened herself to the M'hir, testing his Power with hers.

So much the same, yet so different. Morgan shone in the M'hir, the link to his Chosen burning to infinity through that other space, like a beacon in the night. But— Her eyes widened, and the sob trying to climb her throat stopped in amazement. Where a Clan would hide behind shields, using those to proclaim his or her Power, where Symon had done the same, claiming the need to protect her, this Human left his thoughts and emotions exposed—an offering, she realized.

Go ahead, child, he sent, his mind voice inexpressibly gentle. *I know you're one of Acranam's fosterlings and belong in a Clan House with your kind, not hiding here with Huido. I swear we'll keep you safe and get you home. Ren Symon betrayed you, and I understand how that feels, better than you can know. But I need your trust in order to help you, Ruti. You don't know if I deserve it. So scan me and make your own decision. Please.*

Ruti hesitated. Offers of such intimacy were rare among Clan; the only other mind she'd explored had been her mother's. Morgan waited, unmoving, his face tired and grave. His shoulders seemed bowed under the weight of his coat, or his grief. At last, Ruti swallowed her fear and let her awareness move into his mind, at first tentatively, then more confidently.

Clear thoughts, like crystals she could pick up and examine one at a time, the emotions coloring each dimmed for her protection. Ruti followed the trail they led through Morgan's mind, seeing his starship; his learning about the ships launched from Acranam; talking to bizarre aliens; his trip to Plexis; the terrible discovery—

Ruti flung herself away from his memory of Ansel's crumpled form and found herself led to Morgan's concern for her, for Huido, a place where she rested a moment, safe and protected. Reassured, she reached deeper, to find herself confronting a barrier. Was this where he hid thoughts of his Chosen? It wasn't completely solid. Curious, she tried to slip through, only to be struck by wave after wave of incredible desperation, a sense of loss and dread to intense she couldn't believe she hadn't detected it before. She tried to flee but found herself caught instead by rage, black and deadly, a rage focused on a face she'd thought she'd known, changing it into something horrific. It was too much. Ruti began to gasp for breath.

Morgan blocked her from his mind, gently but firmly. "I'm sorry," he said so calmly Ruti might have imagined the storm inside him. "I didn't mean you to feel that."

Ruti sat up and rubbed one sleeve over her face, then gestured appeasement. "I intruded," she confessed. "But I don't understand, Hom Morgan. Any of this. Oh, I believe you—" when he began to look worried. "How could I not? But Jake—Symon—said he was my friend. He treated me as if I was important to him. Why would he do that? Why would he—harm Ansel? What does he want from me?"

Morgan knelt by the side of her cot, a spare, graceful movement that reminded Ruti of the professional fighters she'd seen on Plexis, demonstrating their art. "Nothing good, Ruti, for you or any of us," he said, the hint of emotion underlying the words dark and utterly convincing. "I know Ren Symon better than anyone should. He thirsts for Power," he paused to study her face before adding, "and he enjoys causing pain. Ansel isn't the only one he's killed."

"Who else?" she asked reluctantly.

"A Human telepath named Naes Fodera, on Plexis. The one who ended up in Huido's kitchen. Symon put him there and tipped Plexis security, knowing I'd come."

Ruti put out her hand and traced the air in front of his face. One of her Talents was the assessment of strength and she frowned at what she felt. "Yours is by far the greater Power, Hom Morgan," she assured him. "Why would Symon risk angering you?"

His lips twisted. "Because he knew I wouldn't come alone. He's after Sira. He tried before and failed."

Ruti shook her head in disbelief. "No Human would dare—" Then she froze, staring at Morgan, a terrible surmise filling her thoughts. She raised her hand again, this time pressing two fingers to Morgan's forehead. Without hesitation, she lowered her own shields and found a memory, sending it into his mind: that face, stunningly beautiful . . . red-gold hair hanging in great, heavy waves . . . huge, unfocused gray eyes . . . that body, cradled in Symon's arms . . .

Sira! The impact of Morgan's recognition and horror threw Ruti from his mind, a reaction he dampened immediately, sending a flicker of power to soothe away the sting.

"I didn't know," Ruti breathed, trembling. "When the Watchers summoned me to Camos, I was too small, too far back in the crowd to see her—I didn't know it was her—"

Morgan was already on his feet, standing in the doorway with his back to her and one hand on the frame as though needing the support—or something to hold him in place, Ruti decided, seeing how the knuckles of that hand whitened as he gripped the edge, the only part of Morgan within reach of her pitiful light.

"I'm so sorry," Ruti whispered.

With dreadful compassion. *It's not your fault, child. None of it.*

Somehow, through her own anguish, Ruti understood what trapped Morgan in her doorway, when the M'hir wailed with his urgency to leave, to hunt for Sira. It was his concern for Huido—and for her. She'd never met anyone who could do this, who was capable of restraining his most primal instincts to think of others first. She couldn't imagine the willpower it took him to stay.

No wonder Sira had Chosen as she had.

Ruti stood, her hands shaking until she clenched them together. She'd watched Symon mistreat the most powerful Clan of them all, and thought only of her jealousy. He'd killed Huido's friend. Her friend. She felt sick and worthless, but there was one thing she could still do. "Go. Find her," she ordered Morgan. His head moved from side to side. *No.* "I'll look after

Huido," Ruti persisted. "We'll head for your place in the dunes, as he planned, and wait for you there. We'll be safe. Find her, please." Ruti couldn't help adding: "And kill Symon."

Morgan's head tilted as if he listened to more than her words. Then, like some force unleashed, he was gone, his footsteps thudding down the hall. She waited, but heard nothing from the kitchen. An instant later, the exterior door opened and closed.

Ruti took a deep breath. Easy words: look after Huido. Resolutely, she grabbed her lantern and walked down the hallway.

The Carasian had never looked so inorganic. A discarded servo might have crumbled in a heap like this, its power source removed, parts scavenged over the years. The various armaments festooning his shoulder and chest plates increased the illusion that this was a pile of leftover, unwanted machinery—not a living being. Ruti hadn't known a Carasian could close the two halves of its head carapace, but now, not one eyestalk showed.

There was a Clan-sized—Human-sized, Ruti corrected—chair by the table. Morgan must have sat there, to tell Huido about their friend's fate. Still hungry, no matter the situation, she grabbed the riper-looking of two nicnics from a bowl on the tiny counter, then sat in the chair to contemplate the immense mass of misery filling the rest of the room.

Her mother always seemed to know what to say when there was loss or sorrow, but Ruti suspected even Quel would be at a loss facing a grief-stricken Carasian. She sighed and peeled the fruit, deciding on the truth. "Ansel asked a favor of me, before we left," Ruti began, keeping her eyes on her hands. "I didn't understand then—but I do now. He told me that he always looked after . . ." Her voice threatened to crack, and she paused to swallow, ". . . looked after you. He wanted me to do that, while we were away from Plexis. I couldn't imagine anyone as big and smart as you could need looking after, but Ansel insisted. He told me he kept watch, all the time, so no one would take advantage of you. That's how he found out— found out I'd been seeing someone secretly. I'd been seeing a Human named Jake Caruthers—but that wasn't his real name. I saw his face through Morgan's memory. It was Ren Symon."

When there was no sound, Ruti risked a glance. As far as she could tell, Huido hadn't moved. She could see the hearing organs on his massive arms, so he should hear her; that was no guarantee he was listening to a single word she said.

"I believed Symon was my friend. My only friend." This time her voice did crack, shamefully. Ruti bit some of the nicnic, glad it was too tart and stung the roof of her mouth. "He met me when I 'ported on the station—he found me right away; he never said how. Symon told me how dangerous Plexis was, how I'd need a safe place to stay. He took me to you, but said it should be our secret, that you'd accept me only if you thought I was alone. I believed that, too."

Still no reaction.

Ruti plunged onward, oddly relieved to be confessing at last, even if it was to a grieving alien—who might be unconscious, for all signs to the contrary.

"Symon taught me things, gave me presents. Hom Morgan showed me what Symon's really like—I understand now he was trying to manipulate and control me. And it worked," she said bitterly. "Symon flattered me; told me lies to make me believe I was special. He suggested I take over as chef—that he'd make sure Neltare lost his job. I scanned the Neblokan to learn what to do—he had a weak, susceptible mind. But I swear, Hom Huido, I didn't know Symon planned to influence Neltare, to make him take a dead body and—and cook it!"

Still no reaction. A pair of flying insects landed on Huido's bulbous back, ambling across its shiny surface to investigate the various scratches and dents in his plating.

She couldn't stop now. "Chee told me Neltare died in an accident." Ruti shuddered. "If it was an accident and not Symon covering his own tracks. But the worst thing I did, Hom Huido, the very worst—" She fought back tears. "Please don't hate me. Morgan doesn't. I felt he doesn't. I don't know why not. Because I watched Symon take Sira away. I was there. I didn't know what she looked like. I swear I didn't. But it shouldn't have mattered. I knew there was something wrong, and I kept quiet because I was angry. I was jealous! Symon was supposed to be my friend, and now he's not . . . he never was . . . and Ansel's dead because of me . . . Sira's lost . . . and, and you must think I'm as brainless as your wives!" she sobbed, close to hysteria.

There was a sickening crash as a mountain of plated flesh blurred into motion, motion that ended with

Huido staring down at her with every eyestalk. His claw encircled her waist, but didn't close. Then, as Ruti held her breath, the eyestalks parted to let two needle-sharp fangs protrude. They stopped short of her face. Fascinated and appalled, she watched a drop of something shiny and green glisten as it slid down one fang, then pause at the tip before falling free.

"Your *grist* has changed," the Carasian announced quite calmly.

Ruti blinked. "My what?"

"Never mind. It smells much better." With that mystifying compliment, Huido retracted his fangs and claws, settling down on his haunches at a more polite distance. His eyestalks whirled a moment, then he informed Ruti, as if this was the single most important thing to tell her: "My wives are not brainless. Did they not pick me and my pool?"

Perhaps, Ruti decided, inane conversation was how Carasians dealt with death. "They picked you?" she echoed in a weak voice, deciding to cooperate. "But the kitchen staff said you have new ones shipped to Plexis as often as you can afford it. You keep them locked in your apartment. I was told they can't even talk."

"Of course they can talk. But why would they?" Huido's eyes danced in every direction, as if looking for anyone else in the room. "They're too busy," he said obscurely, most of those eyes back on Ruti. "You should know, being female."

"I'm not a female Carasian," Ruti pointed out. She wasn't sure she wanted too many details about Carasians and their pools of wives, but Huido being coy was a vast improvement over being a miserable heap—or attacking her. "But if I were," she asserted, "I wouldn't let you lock me away and keep me 'too busy' to talk."

Something she said surprised a laugh from the barrel-shaped chest. "Ah, you'd make a fine and exhausting wife," he claimed, shocking her speechless—probably his intention, since Ruti knew Huido found the humanoid ability to blush vastly entertaining. "I must explain myself, or you will take my compliment as insult. It's not something we spread around to other species, you understand. They might get the wrong ideas. Even my blood brother does not know the truth." Another rather unnerving scan of the room.

"But you? I will tell you, young Ruti. It will be our secret, but you mustn't ever tell anyone—especiallly my wives." He waited for her puzzled nod. "You see, our females prefer aliens think of them as, shall we say, less than intelligent. That way, no non-Carasian disturbs the sanctity of their pools and it makes their occasional dietary—adventures—more easily forgiven."

"They do it so they can get away with eating other sapients?" Ruti demanded in horror. She'd heard all about the dangers of wandering in Huido's apartment.

"Only if those sapients invade their pool," Huido said defensively. "And, of course, are safely edible in the first place."

Ruti suddenly wondered if the Carasian was teasing her. "That doesn't prove they're smart," she accused. "Why would they stay locked up in your apartment by choice? Especially on Plexis!"

"They are not locked—" Huido stopped and

calmed his voice. "Our females, in your terms, are not smart. They are more than smart. They are our species' scholars and scientists, our inventors and artists. We males run businesses and compete to be worthy of providing the luxury these glorious creatures deserve once they retire."

"Retire?" Ruti was reasonably sure the word in Comspeak couldn't possibly mean the same thing to Huido as it did to her.

"Yes. Once any Carasian female feels she has reached the pinnacle of her field of study, achieved everything she can, she retires. She removes herself from the distractions of the outside world, and moves to a pool where she can synergize with other retired females. They exchange information, debate, and philosophize until satisfied they have added their accomplishments to our culture. I don't claim to understand all they do—if I did, I'd be female!" Another laugh. "Synergy can take years, especially for a female with strong or unusual ideas, so she picks the pool of the male she judges will be the best and most stimulating provider. And the largest. Size always matters to those delightful creatures. After all, so much concentrated thinking makes them, well," his eyestalks began spinning about "completely insatiable. They seek pleasure and procreation constantly during this important and admirable stage of their lives."

"They think in the pool," Ruti repeated, to be sure she grasped the concept. "And this makes them—"

"Hungry!" Huido made a happy bell-like sound with his smaller handling claw. "For everything. You can see why Carasian males place such a high value on thinking in their females." The Carasian rose to his feet, weapons swinging from their clips. "And you, young Ruti. I want you to practice a great deal of thinking while I'm gone."

"Gone?" Ruti didn't like the sound of this. "Gone? Where? I thought we were going together. I promised Morgan—"

"And Morgan is what matters, now. We can only hope his poor *grist* recovers. He needs me to protect his back while he hunts for Sira. I will not fail him!"

Ruti stood as well, feeling insignificant next to the massive being. She gathered her determination. Ansel had believed she could do this. "Not alone, Hom Huido. I promised Morgan—and Ansel—I'd take care of you. I'm going with you."

All of his eyestalks formed an intimidating stare. "You will wait here. Barac is coming, and the two of you will go to Morgan's secure house—out on those revolting dunes."

"Barac?" Ruti waved her arms in the air, suddenly furious. "Who's this Barac? Some dreg from the ship-city you've hired to watch me? I will not wait here, in this, this powerless hovel, while you wander around looking for a fight!"

"And I will lose no one else from my heart!" Huido's bellow was far more effective than hers, its volume bringing dust from the ceiling. Ruti sank back into her chair, realizing the banter of a moment ago had been Huido's attempt to ease her feelings, not his own. "I have lost Ansel, my first alien friend," the Carasian said, his voice dropping to a desperate, unhappy rumble. "Morgan and Sira are at terrible risk.

Know that my heart and soul are yours as well, Ruti from Acranam. You must take care."

"After all I've done?" she whispered. "Trusting Symon? Lying to you?"

"You're young," Huido reminded her. "Spawn are supposed to make mistakes. It's up to you to survive them—or not. Keep yourself safe and wait for Barac. Promise me."

Ruti walked up to the Carasian and pressed herself against his hard, chill exterior, carefully avoiding a biodisrupter and a netful of blast globes. Her arms couldn't stretch around enough of him to call it a hug, but she did her best. She wanted to admit her fear, to keep her last protector with her. Even arriving on Plexis, she hadn't felt as alone as this. Ruti doubted she could reach her mother or any other Clan with a sending, should anything happen to Huido or Morgan. And only those two—and Symon—knew where she was.

But Ruti discovered herself less a child this morning than she'd been yesterday, able to push back from Huido and safety to say: "I promise. Look after Morgan."

"I always do," the Carasian boasted, then unhooked one of the smaller weapons from his chest to offer her. "Take this. You must avoid using your Power, Ruti, even to contact Morgan. Symon may be able to detect it—either with some device or his own abilities. Did he not find you when you arrived on Plexis? Did he not find Sira?"

She stared at the ugly thing, then took it in her hand: some type of projectile weapon, with a handle that molded itself to a perfect fit within her palm before surprise could make her drop it. "How do I—?"

The delicate tip of a handling claw indicated an area on the handle. "Point it at someone you don't like, then press here." Huido paused thoughtfully. "Make sure there isn't anyone you do like nearby. You have the coordinates for Morgan's house in the dunes?"

Ruti nodded, patting the pocket that held the slip of plas Huido had insisted she keep with her at all times.

"Good." The Carasian headed for the door. Three eyestalks rose over his back to look at her. "Don't forget to do the dishes. There's no recycler, and you don't want to attract any more wildlife."

Involuntarily, Ruti shuddered and glanced around before recognizing the Carasian was trying to deflect her thoughts again. "Ansel didn't deserve what happened, Hom Huido," she said solemnly, because it had to be said. "He was a good person."

"And a pest. And overcautious. And inclined to treat the universe as a giant accounting problem instead of a joy to be experienced." Huido snapped his lower right claw against his body in a way she'd never seen before, creating a low, heavy tone that Ruti could feel in her jaw as well as hear. "But Ansel always understood the great truth, young Ruti: that our worth is measured by what we are willing to give of ourselves."

Huido opened the door and bent a few eyestalks forward to inspect the alleyway. Grunting with satisfaction, he clanked around to focus on Ruti. "Lock the door behind me," was the last thing he said before leaving.

*   *   *

Ruti obediently locked the door, then leaned her back against it and surveyed her surroundings. She deliberately turned her mind to what needed to be done. After all, the powerless hovel was hers now, complete with lanterns in three of four rooms and a very nice portable cook stove with a stasis unit underneath. There was plumbing, if no built-in power features. If she was to meet this mysterious Barac— hopefully soon—she'd better wash off yesterday's dust and today's tears.

She scrubbed her face and hands with what little cold water dribbled into the sink and ran her fingers through her hair in a hopeless attempt to bring some order to chaos. Her clothes somehow smelled of sand and salt, in spite of a vigorous shaking. She put them back on anyway, tucking Lara in a pocket, and found her sandals, or what was left of them. Her wardrobe was suited to Plexis, not marching through a miniature sandstorm. Had these people no control over their climate?

Acranam didn't, but it wasn't necessary, Ruti remembered with longing. The air around Caraat Town was moist and fragrant, carrying the light sweetness of elosia blossoms in spring and the rich spice of ripening sarlas in early fall. No need to argue with rainfall. Showers fell with convenient predictability, washing heat from the air twice a day, and creating interesting new ponds for tiny fleets of sarlas shells for those young enough to have time for such things. Mind you, she, Olea, and Nylis could usually draw the others into mock naval battles between chores.

Ruti shook off the memory. She was as clean as she could manage. Time to eat. Huido's weapon slipped into the inner pocket of her cloak. There was nothing else to pack or carry; Huido had ordered everything left behind on the starship that had brought them, to be returned to Plexis. He would, he informed her, take no chances that their things had been bugged by security. Ruti had no idea why security would contaminate her belongings or Huido's, but he'd been implacable.

Perhaps there would be spare clothing at this place of Morgan's, this house hidden in the desert. Ruti read over the coordinates and directions for the fifth time. The numbers made no sense to her, but she supposed they would to this Barac.

Breakfast. She rummaged in the stasis unit and found eggs her stolen knowledge told her would make a fine, if rich, omelette. Ruti pulled out what she needed, then doubled it, in case this Barac would be hungry as well. The familiar motions of cooking soothed her, even under these circumstances, and she was aghast to catch herself humming as she broke eggs.

What kind of person was she to hum when Ansel had been killed, when others were at risk?

Ruti poured sombay into a self-warming cup. She was, she told herself firmly, a person who wouldn't make any more mistakes. She hurried to turn the omelette before it browned too much on one side.

An hour later, stuffed with Barac's breakfast as well as her own, Ruti sat in the kitchen and studied the door. She knew perfectly well what lay outside: a messy, vermin-infested alleyway. Whatever lay beyond that wasn't her concern. She wasn't about to commit the mistake of leaving. Huido had told her to wait and she would. It was a simple, clear task. Wait.

She wasn't good at waiting.

The dishes and cookware were clean, as best she could with the pathetic dribble of water offered by the kitchen sink. Perhaps water on this world was in such short supply the pipes were smaller than normal. She'd moved the table to several locations within the room, each offering Ruti a slightly different view of the door. Which led to a messy, vermin-infested alleyway. And an entire world she'd never seen.

She'd promised. But it was hard. Especially when she didn't dare play with her Talents. Her mother had always praised Ruti's ability to 'port, her sure knowledge of the strength of others, but Ruti's favorite Talent was unusual among Clan. She could move things with a nudge of Power—not through the M'hir but through ordinary space. Not far, but far enough to be fun. Like the lantern—Ruti stopped herself just in time. No more mistakes. Huido had sounded certain Symon could somehow know, a possibility Ruti now found terrifying.

A window might have helped, or would one simply allow danger easier access?

Why had she thought about danger?

There was a strange taste in her mouth. Ruti swallowed, but it didn't change. Not the eggs. Not in her mouth at all. The taste was of something dangerous. Something . . . *coming.*

Ruti stood, pushing the chair back, and lunged for her cloak where it lay draped over Huido's low seat.

Her hands shook as she fumbled for the pocket and the weapon hidden there.

She'd never tasted a warning through the M'hir before.

That didn't mean she doubted it was real.

Chapter 18

WARNINGS. Hull breach alarms. The too-short shriek in the night as one of the herd is taken. I heard them all and knew they weren't real.

My mind, what remained of Sira Morgan, played games to keep itself alert and alive, pretending emergencies and imagining rescue. Rescue from what? The question splintered away another part of me, spinning into the abyss until something swooped upward to meet and consume it . . .

The Singer. Waiting, ready, hungry.

. . . But I was ready too, and dove into the safer pain of memory . . .

"These—numbers." Distaste twisted Jarad's lips, but I gave him credit. He'd listened. "You claim they prove this assertion of yours?"

"That we're doomed?" I drawled, putting my feet up on the table and grinning at my father. "Oh, there's no doubt at all."

He sank into a chair. We were in my bedroom, which was more a library and office these days. My computing needs had dictated the elaborate interface discreetly built into an otherwise unremarkable table, but there was no hiding stacks of plas sheets or the pre-Stratification era chests bursting with the rolled, permanent parches used by the M'hiray before they'd met Humans and taken to newer technology. Even my bed was piled high with research notes. Enora, bless her, had brought in a cot. She knew me too well to suppose it worthwhile clearing the bed itself.

There was no time, I fumed to myself, even as I pretended to wait at ease for my father's questions. There was very little hope either, but that I was prepared to challenge. If he let me. If Council let me. Our people didn't have to keep dying.

I didn't have to stay here forever.

I told him the bitter truth. "My own existence, a Chooser without a suitable candidate for her Choice? That's the warning—the alarm we must heed, Jarad. There are already others like me. It's no secret young Tle di Parth won't find a match. Probably both daughters in the House of di Mendolar. If the Council continues pairing only the most powerful? There will be more and more Choosers who cannot be mated, until the M'hiray are a memory." I waved at the old parches. "And these."

Jarad's eyes were hooded; his formidable Power hidden from me as well. Signs I had his complete attention. "Suppose," he said, "—just suppose—I believe all this. I respect your zeal, my daughter, though I've no idea how you found anything useful in these antiquities." He dismissed the parches with a glance.

"You realize I can't go to the Clan Council with a pronouncement of doom and nothing more."

I dropped my feet to the floor and leaned forward, but otherwise controlled my excitement. "You know I've studied the Power-of-Choice, how it differs from the Power Clan usually use within the M'hir. I've also been collecting data on other species." I ignored his sudden frown, expecting that and worse before I was through. "Human telepathy proved the most—interesting."

"Human . . . telepaths." It was as if Jarad's mouth was deciding which word offended it most.

"You've listened to me this far, Father," I challenged. He frowned, but waved a hand for me to continue. "What I've been looking for is a way to control the Power-of-Choice, the way any Clan controls his or her Power. With such control, a Chooser could influence or completely bypass the Testing of a Candidate entirely during Joining, and Commence. We'd be free of the drive that is killing our species."

I hadn't thought it was possible to render Jarad di Sarc speechless. I took advantage of it, and called up a display to hover over the table between us. "Look at this," I said, more for myself than my father. I doubted he would try to follow the elegant graphical analysis I'd prepared, but it helped me focus my thoughts, my hopes. "While it's true Human telepaths have much less Power than any Clan, they appear to be free of the Power-of-Choice. In fact, the M'hiray seem uniquely cursed among telepathic species in having this need to test the Power of potential mates. So," I took a steadying breath and cleared the display. "I believe we should move in a new direction. We've been bred for Power by the Council. I think we should breed to eliminate the Power-of-Choice."

"How? Every female M'hiray possesses it." A painful swelling of his Power in the M'hir between us. I ignored it. "You can't be suggesting—"

"Yes. I am. I believe we should attempt to hybridize with a compatible humanoid species that doesn't possess the Power-of-Choice. At best, the result will be a new race, with our ability to use the M'hir but freed of the deadly consequences to the unChosen. At worst—" I owed him this, "—at worst, it could prove a way to bring Choosers to Commencement without wasting the lives of any more of our unChosen."

Jarad loathed every word I was saying, his outrage simmering in the M'hir between us, but he was still listening, his nostrils flaring every once in a while. When I stopped for his reaction, he said frigidly, but calmly enough: "Offer Choice to a Human. That's what you're proposing, for all this talk of hybridization and compatibility. Would you offer yourself to one of those— aliens?"

In answer, I keyed a request and a list hung in the air between us. "I've identified twenty-one individuals for closer study," I told him. "All match parameters I established for a potential—" even I stumbled over the word, so fraught with meaning to my kind, "—Choice for myself. I would never propose, Father, risking any one else in an experiment to prove or disprove my own work."

"And if the Human's lack of Power in the M'hir

destroys your mind, but leaves your body ripe and ready? What then, Daughter?"

I felt like ice as I looked at him. "An empty mind can't heed the dictates of Choice. If that happens, the Council can use my body as it wishes."

"What Clansman would—" He stopped, then went on incredulously, "—you know that. You know no Clansman would be able to touch a mindless body. Choice and the Joining affect both."

"Yes, Father, I know. We will have to buy technology—knowledge. There is a Retian by the name of Baltir who apparently has considerable expertise in assisted fertilizations and interspecies hybridizations. He's willing to offer his services, discreetly, for a price." My research hadn't been confined to what lay in this room.

He stood and took a step back. "I don't know you," Jarad said in a strangled voice. "I don't know you at all."

"You should." I raised an eyebrow. "I am what living as a Chooser these seventy years has made me, Father. Desperate, pragmatic, and determined to solve this problem—not just for our kind, but for myself." I stood as well. "We will die out and be forgotten. There will be no di Sarc dynasty—no proud Houses—nothing. The Power-of-Choice will ensure I and the other barren Choosers will live to see it, Father, even if you and your fellow Councillors won't. Believe this: I am not willing to be the last of our kind. You can help me now—or by the Seventeen Hells of Deneb I'll swear I'll wait for you all to die and seek help from the next Council."

. . . memory skipped ahead, following a path of its own . . .

"Your father's back. He asks admittance."

Courtesy, between those of great personal Power—the Clan had become fond of such play-acting. Enora's face, always easy to read, showed concern. She didn't know about my research, or my impassioned threat to Jarad those weeks ago, but her Talent read my emotional state—and his. Obviously, both di Sarcs were raising a storm in the house. "How courteous of him," I replied, making a greater effort to keep my temper from troubling the M'hir. "I'll see him on the balcony." She bowed slightly and turned to go. "Wait, Enora."

She stopped and looked at me. She'd matured into the Clanswoman I'd expected: capable and warm, with the beauty granted by fine bones and a life of laughter. When her two sons left her household, Enora had left as well, returning to live with me, as she'd promised so long ago. A gift, to have her with me.

A stark reminder of how all of those I loved now would grow old and leave me behind. The Council had to agree, I told myself.

"Yes, Sira?"

I had nothing to say that would cause her anything but pain. "My keffle-flute," I said instead, looking around as if it would magically reappear from wherever I'd buried it this time. "I thought I might play for my father, if he plans to stay for lunch. Do you know where I left it?"

Enora looked surprised, but went straight to a cupboard and brought out the case, before leaving to bring my father. She knew I hadn't played since the last time Pella had visited and insisted we play together. My sister's foolish habit. She kept hoping her skill would surpass mine.

It never would. I opened the case and took the flute into my hands. The inlays of precious stone caught the light as it fit perfectly, as always, into calluses seemingly too deep to fade. It wasn't because I practiced; I rarely touched the instrument anymore. Since that day Yihtor invaded my home, when I'd played with the Singer and almost lost myself, something in that experience had forever changed my music. Now, part of it thrilled within the M'hir each time I played—though no one else seemed to realize they were hearing with more than ears alone.

But I knew the difference, and how easily it could summon what I might not be able to resist again.

Thank Ossirus, Pella always asked for the liveliest of dance songs, where she could show off her impeccable technique. Those were bad enough. I dared not play anything with passion or sorrow. Or alone.

I laid the instrument back in its case, putting that safely under the nearest pillow.

"Daughter."

Jarad might have waited to be admitted—he hadn't waited to change from his Council robes. I nodded a dismissal to Enora, who looked as though she might refuse to leave me. Somehow I produced a smile and nodded again. She left, but not without giving my father a doubtful glance.

"Father," I greeted, making the gesture of welcome to one lesser in Power. "I take it you have news for me."

Damn them.

Like that, was it? I didn't bother sending the

thought. "Probably," I replied aloud. "Please. Sit. We might as well enjoy the sunshine while you tell me the worst."

The table was set with fruits and a choice of chilled drinks suited to the summer warmth. Jarad took the nearest goblet and drank as if he couldn't taste it, staring out at the view. Pretty, with clouds chasing one another over the mountaintops, but hardly worth such attention.

I knew my father. Part of his agitation was theatrical: a show for me or the leftover drama from his actions before coming here. The remainder was most likely fury. He didn't care to be opposed.

We shared that.

"The Council rejected the proposal," I concluded.

"Heresy was the mildest word used. I warned you—"

I smiled without humor. "—that the Council would never consider interbreeding with another species? Several times. I am," I added honestly, "surprised you tried."

Jarad shook his head. "I wasn't going to, at first. But your predictions scared them—badly. The ideas that began sending around? Yours, frankly, wasn't the worst. I proposed it to try and gain some sanity back, but it was hopeless, Sira. Hopeless."

"What do you mean?"

He showed me his open, empty palm. "They will summon you as soon as the candidates arrive on Camos. By this afternoon, at the latest."

"What candidates?" I held up my own hand to stop his answer, knowing well enough. "The fools," I hissed. "There's no one close to my strength. I'll kill any unChosen they bring near me. They must know that."

"Of course. But Sawnda'at's conservatives are willing to pay that price if there's a chance you might reach Commencement as a result."

"Impossible. The Power-of-Choice grows stronger with each failed Choice—that's what bars my body from Commencing! But even if it somehow worked, what then? They can't want a Chooser who has Commenced—I'd be no less deadly! And I still couldn't mate—"

"You said it yourself, Daughter. 'An empty mind can't heed the dictates of Choice.' They'll tame the Power-of-Choice by erasing your mind. Then, I believe Council will suddenly find the concept of using reproductive technology to be—acceptable."

"They wouldn't dare," I protested through numb lips. "No Clan would stand for it. The Watchers—"

"No Clan outside the Council will know," Jarad said grimly. "And the Watchers appear neutral. The Council is afraid of now, not the future, Sira. They are afraid of losing your Power, Sira. And that of your progeny."

"So are you."

A raised brow. "Of course," he said, as if surprised I had to say it. "Rael is powerful, but her Chosen is unlikely to father anything more than *sud*. Pella? A disappointment. But you, my most puissant firstborn? You must not only survive, you must bring your Power into the M'hiray." Jarad brought his fist down on the table, rattling the glassware and Enora's favorite metal tray. The M'hir between us rang with equal fury. "I utterly reject this Council of fools and their mad scurrying into any hole that looks like safety. I told them so. This is the last time I will wear this robe."

More dramatics, or sincerity this time? It didn't matter. I needed to believe I had an ally, however unexpected. "If you mean that," I told my father bluntly, "I have a plan."

. . . I'd died once already; it wasn't enough . . .

Jason Morgan of Karolus. A Human of little wealth beyond ownership of an antique starship and a reputation for being lucky. I scrolled past that entry, paused, then went back to it. He was the right age, comparatively, and had Power. An undetermined amount of Power, since he apparently possessed a substantial natural shielding. That might help. Or hinder. I couldn't know ahead of time.

"No one will miss that one," my father offered helpfully, studying my selection. "You have to watch for affiliations within the species. Humans keep closer ties than we do. Some on your list have families that might become a nuisance."

"This Morgan might not have family," I argued, "but he's a Trader and probably has to keep some kind of schedule. That could be awkward. What do you think of Fodera?"

We discussed one or two more, then I found myself back at the entry for Jason Morgan. I wasn't sure why. Perhaps it was simply that he'd been in contact with Clan before, seeming to have a business relationship with Enora's sons, Kurr and Barac. Familiar names, from a trusted House. If he'd deal fairly with them, perhaps he would do the same with me.

Not that fairness entered into any of this. I forced down any doubts. I was taking as much of a chance with my life as with Morgan's. I'd only need to worry about the consequences of Choice with a Human if I succeeded. If I failed, neither of us might know it. No matter how confident I was to my father, I knew this was all guesswork and conjecture. Human Power might be totally incompatible with Clan. Morgan might shoot me on sight. Humans could be violent and unpredictable in groups. I didn't have much information on what individuals were like. My servants were gentle, polite beings. I had no guarantees a Trader would be.

But the only thing that would save my mind from being erased by the Council was to produce a Commenced and Chosen Sira di Sarc—to prove there was an alternative to what they planned.

"Just hurry and pick one, Sira," my father urged. "Council could summon you at any minute."

"Has Cenebar agreed?"

"After all that arguing? He'd better. I'll bring him. If you're ready."

I ran my fingers over the name, Jason Morgan, and nodded once. As my father concentrated to summon Cenebar, I tried to convince myself what I was feeling was hope and not dread.

. . . the lies had lost; the final betrayal was my own . . .

"I'm a healer of minds, not a butcher." Cenebar di Teerac might have agreed to help me, but he wasn't about to do it without a final protest. "We can't take so much—you'll be damaged."

Trust me, I sent to him, with overtones of affections for a true heart-kin. A Clansman who would never willingly cause harm to another, as well as a trusted friend. I wondered if Cenebar remembered being among those male children paraded for my favor, so many years ago.

"There's no time to debate further. She must be in stasis, to protect any unChosen she meets."

"Stasis isn't the problem, Jarad. It's this blockage she plans to impose on her own mind, the extent of it—are you sure it's necessary, Sira?"

I examined my hands, studying their calluses. "I know myself, Healer. It's well and good for me to propose attempting Choice with a Human, here, in this room. Out there? Will I be able to offer this—" I held out my right hand as if for Choice, "—to an alien? There's too much training, too much prejudice—too much Clan in me—to guarantee I won't run the other way. And I will not fail. Besides," I added almost lightly, "you'll implant the trigger mechanism to restore my full memory once Choice has been consummated and I have—Joined."

"With this Human. If you both aren't hauled into the M'hir first. Or—I can think of a dozen ways this could go wrong."

"I've thought of a thousand," I said flatly. "None of which matters. The Council will murder me if I don't try this. At least this way, I'll prove something—either that this will work, or that it won't."

I felt him acquiesce, however reluctantly. Before he

could change his mind, I lay down on my bed, miraculously clear of debris. I'd asked Enora to pack away all of my things while I was gone. She didn't know where, only that there was a mysterious candidate and I was hopeful, at last, of completing my Choice. She'd been so happy for me, I'd felt a pang of guilt. But she couldn't know the truth, not until I'd succeeded or died.

Cenebar and Jarad came to stand to either side of me. The healer would impose mental stasis, the binding to help restrain my Power-of-Choice until, hopefully, it was freed by the presence of Morgan's power. Jarad would layer my mind with guides, compulsions that would pull me to Morgan and his ship, make me avoid Trade Pact authority. There were those among Humans with an interest in the Clan, despite all our care to remain aloof and uninteresting. Such mustn't interfere with my purpose.

I would need these compulsions because, when we were done, they would be all I knew until Choice freed my mind again.

My role? I began to ruthlessly block my own memories. Cenebar had shown me the forbidden technique— another Prime Law I would flaunt today, after a lifetime of obedience. He and Jarad would complete the process, once so much was blocked that I no longer knew what to do or why I was doing it.

I worked methodically, having planned exactly what I wanted buried. Cenebar worried that I'd be damaged. To his knowledge, no one had ever blocked so much of their conscious mind without permanently losing portions of their memory.

I hoped so.

I began to seal away what I must forget in order to look a Human in the eyes without revulsion.

And, memory by memory, I sealed away what I wanted to forget forever.

Forcing my mother through the M'hir.

Refusing her freedom until we were torn apart.

Fleeing from the M'hir's other life.

Destroying the first candidate for my Choice.

Lusting for my seducer's touch.

At this, I flinched and hesitated. The Singer was my private nightmare: something I'd tried to believe couldn't exist, though part of me knew it did, aware it waited in the M'hir for its next opportunity to tempt me. But nightmare or real, I wouldn't keep anything in my memory that might interfere with my attempt to Join with the Human.

Which meant I couldn't keep anything that might leave me vulnerable to the Singer.

My music.

So be it. I sought out every memory that held my keffle-flute, blocking each away as deeply as I could, no matter where I found it. I tore apart my past, fragmenting what I'd been into jagged shards.

Still I continued, until I began to lose track of where I was, who I was, why I was. I felt my father's mind, soothing away the beginnings of fear, of *not right!*

Then I ended, so another might begin.

. . . fragments drew closer, touched, knit one to the other as though the compulsion to be complete was all-powerful . . . the Singer surged forward, grasping, reaching,

but too late, too late . . . blood began to warm . . . conscious-
ness reassembled itself from nightmare and pulled free of
the past . . .

My mouth tasted like something had died, then rot-
ted in it. I sputtered and spat, desperately wiping at
my lips. They felt wet. So did my face, as my fingers
rediscovered it in the absolute dark. Nothing mattered
but finding Morgan. I sent Power flying along our link,
seeking my love's mind.

I reeled under the impact of Power rebounding
from that too-familiar wall, wide-awake and furious at
the misbegotten Drapsk who'd invented this technology in the first place. There would be a need for some
intense *gripstsa* once I was free.

Symon had had a reason for putting me into this
stasis unit. I sat up, slowly, exploring by hand what I
couldn't see. My hair shivered itself dry, but my sod-
den coveralls didn't have that ability, the fabric cling-
ing and cold. The floor was slick with moisture as well,
implying the entire box had been filled with preserving fluid. I lay where I'd first fallen, but wasn't stiff.
Drugs in the fluid or gas must have kept my body pli-
able, or I'd only been unconscious for a moment—
something I didn't believe.

I crawled, or rather slithered, along the floor, hunting the bottle of water I remembered had been put in
here with me; my first priority was to stop the torment
in my mouth. I found the globe, but its light no longer
functioned. I tossed it aside and reached again. There.
I fumbled it open and rinsed, then spat. The effort became a retch as I heaved up what felt like most of my
insides.

Somehow I moved myself away from the mess until my outstretched fingers encountered something hard and smooth. My keffle-flute case. I picked it up and hugged it close.

I knew how to play it.

I forgot the taste in my mouth. I forgot the ache where Morgan belonged. Astonishment filled me as I *remembered*.

The life of Sira di Sarc was once more full and complete within my mind, as my past self had hoped it would never be.

I wasn't at all surprised to begin to heave again.

INTERLUDE

The warning struck again. Morgan shook his head to clear it, grimly hopeful this latest premonition meant he was on the right track. Of course, any All Sapient's District had its share of risks, and Rosietown's was no exception—from recruiters hunting unwilling skilled labor to a Scat on the prowl for a meal that would fight back. Unlikely such would be up so early in the day, he knew, or would bother him if they were. In Morgan's experience, predators avoided prey that looked as if it was on the hunt itself.

Not that he'd been obvious in his preparations. A blaster rode his hip, but hidden under the flap of his dune-skimmer. The heavy, dull-yellow coat was common in Rosietown, at least among those who appreciated the triple threat of sand, sun, and wind. Morgan's was no tourist's fancy, fresh from a store. The shoulders and back showed darker, shinier patches where storm-driven sand had polished away the soft roughness of the rowlahide; there were very useful hidden pockets in several locations; and the inner lining had been replaced—at a cost—with flexible strips of body armor.

Morgan hadn't taken chances before going to Huido's hideaway either, using a roundabout route from the shipcity and leaving the *Fox* rigged to send an alert if certain individuals left com messages—or if an uninvited guest attempted to enter. He'd deliberately docked her in the Trader's Enclave, the constantly-changing community of owner-captained starships, traders and short-haul freighters that formed in every shipcity. Togetherness for mutual self-protection, on worlds where Port Authority existed to gouge Traders for more than docking fees. In more civilized surroundings, such as Ettler's Planet, the enclave served as a convenient gathering point to scout the competition, exchange crew and gossip, or find life-partners. Most were family-run; the children running free around ramps and fins knew who belonged near their ships. They'd play under the *Fox* today for a few credits, a common service if not the most reliable.

When he'd bought the *Silver Fox* and started this life, Morgan had kept his distance from other Traders—dealing fairly and politely with those he met, but resisting any temptation to form closer ties. He'd told himself it was more comfortable to stay away from the disturbing awareness of other minds on his, but Huido had known better. Over a few beers, and with typical bluntness, the Carasian had told Morgan it was high time the Human climbed out of the battle-scarred valleys of Karolus and joined the rest of the universe, which included trusting other beings besides his handsome self. Not blindly, of course—Huido digressing into a few entertainingly incredible tales about males who trusted others with the location of their tidal pools—but without fearing that everyone Morgan trusted would die, leave, or worse, betray him as had Symon.

Huido might not have remembered that conversation the next morning, or tactfully pretended not to, but Morgan had never forgotten it. The Carasian had been right. More, his words echoed those of Morgan's uncles and parents, buried so long ago under the grief of their loss. Hadn't they raised him to think of others first, to honor their trust by never failing his responsibility to the whole? How had he let Symon taint their memory?

Morgan would never trust easily or shed the inner wariness forged by his past. Still, over the years, he built friendships, as well as friendly rivalries, among his fellow Traders, Humans and aliens alike. These days, a quick walk down any Trader Enclave shipway, a glance over the starships docked there, told Morgan exactly who he could call upon for help. For a price. Traders stuck together against a threat to all, but getting such free spirits interested in a more personal entanglement usually involved a debt owed or about to be incurred. Even among friends.

Two such friends of his and Huido's were insystem on Ettler's Planet: *Ryan's Venture* and *Gamer's Gold*. Both were larger and newer than the *Fox*, but not as fast, putting Morgan's relationship with their respective captains more in the friendly rival category. Regardless, he started his inquiries there, striking it lucky with the second ship. In fact, Captain Aleksander of

Gamer's Gold had not only transported the Carasian to Ettler's, he had a terse and biologically impractical message for Morgan to convey to his former passenger.

It turned out Aleksander had agreed to take Huido's friends as well, which, Morgan was amused to learn, included not just Ruti but a group of Turrned Missionaries. This in itself wasn't a problem. It was a short haul, given Plexis' current location, and the *'Gold* had been enroute anyway. Payment was in advance, and the Turrneds had, in Aleksander's words, kept their eyes away from his business.

What had Aleksander considering steamed Carasian as his dish of choice was the steaming mess around his beautiful ship. Morgan had been grateful not to have a vid on his com as the *'Gold'*s captain explained, in great detail, that while he understood Huido had only been trying to leave his ship without being noticed, he didn't appreciate the end result. It seemed Huido's new companions, the Turrneds, operated their Mission from a rowla ranch on the outskirts of the shipcity. Rowlas were an indigenous domesticated beast easily half again the size of any Carasian. Drovers found the larger shipways convenient shortcuts to the wells on the other side of Rosietown, so they regularly incensed Port Authority by driving their herds between the starships—halting docking tugs and leaving reeking towers of rowla droppings behind. The Turrneds had simply arranged for their herd to arrive at the base of the *'Gold'*s ramp, so Huido and Ruti could walk away from the ship, hidden from sight among the larger animals.

Which had, naturally, left unfortunately large some-things for Captain Aleksander.

Good to know Huido was safe. Morgan hadn't ex-pected a com signal—Huido wouldn't risk it, not with Plexis security likely sending hysterical warnings to the nearest systems about murderous Carasians. They were probably trying to blame Huido for poor Ansel's death, too. At least Terk knew the truth of that, Mor-gan thought, although the Enforcers were a potential complication he'd face sooner or later. Hopefully later, because Bowman wouldn't hesitate if she thought Symon was within her reach; she knew too well the potential danger of allowing telepaths to use their abilities for interspecies crime.

There was also the specter of not knowing who Symon might have bribed or influenced. He'd never worked alone in the past, Morgan recalled. Just think-ing about Symon brought back that appalling image from Ruti's memory: *Symon's big, scarred hands gripping Sira, his ams around her.* Morgan groaned to himself, forced to see *Symon pressing Sira's helpless body against his. The look on Symon's face . . .*

Enough! Morgan stopped dead in the street, fortu-nately still empty of witnesses, and rubbed one hand violently over his face. His heart was hammering in his chest; there was the taste of bile in the back of his throat. Not jealousy—fear. How could Sira be helpless? Had she been drugged? What was happen-ing to her?

And if Symon touched her—harmed her—Morgan vowed to prove to his former mentor he was more than an apt pupil. Ansel had suffered. Symon would scream.

Huido hadn't known Symon was behind his troubles until Morgan's arrival; Plexis security had driven him here, a haven despite the Carasian's utter loathing of sand. Which was why Morgan had known to look in his old apartment first—trusting Huido to find any excuse to delay actually traveling over the free-moving sand of the Singing Dunes north of Rosietown.

Now it was up to Ruti to get him moving. Morgan shook his head as he walked, unsure he'd done the right thing listening to her. She'd only urged him to do what every fiber of his being demanded—find Sira. But he'd learned from bitter experience to mistrust such impulses. Should he have waited? Made sure Huido unfolded from his prayers for Ansel before the poor child assumed the alien was in a coma? He should have at least confirmed their arrangements. She was so young.

Or was she? Morgan wondered. Sira had looked similar to Ruti's age when they met—in Human terms, a girl barely old enough for puberty, only her eyes hinting at the years she'd lived before his birth. No, Ruti was younger. Morgan had felt some kind of link, silk-thin, between Ruti and someone else. Nothing like the one binding him to Sira, yet steady and undeniable, clear proof Ruti was a fosterling, connected to her distant mother. And he'd seen the doll she'd held in her hand. A child.

Of all things alien about the Clan and their ways, this remained the hardest for Morgan to accept. He understood, intellectually, it was because the Clan seemed so outwardly Human. It was too easy to fall into the trap of judging them by his standards. A Master Trader should know better. Ruti might be a child, but she wasn't a Human one.

Kill Symon. Certainly that cold, vengeful exhortation hadn't been from a child of any species. She'd known exactly what she'd asked.

He had to trust them both, Huido and Ruti, to look after themselves. There was only one way to make them all safe—and that was to find Symon. And Sira. Morgan kept walking. He was going back to the ship-city, intending to speak to Captain Ivali of the *Venture*. Ivali had heard rumors of telepaths offering their services to the highest bidder; she'd sent a runner to find more information.

Danger! The warning was annoyingly persistent, if nonspecific. There were safer routes than this labyrinth of narrow streets, connected by even narrower alleyways. Every intersection was licked at the corners by tongues of yellow sand from the last storm, and the rising sun created dark shadows. Fine. He wasn't interested in avoiding trouble. In fact, Morgan decided grimly, stepping over another tongue of sand, he was looking for it.

He wasn't looking for Drapsk. So when a group of small beings suddenly rounded the next corner in front of him, Morgan ducked into the nearest alley's mouth to watch them from hiding. These were Heerii, not surprising of itself. Several systems within this loop of the Fringe were apparently claimed by that Tribe, who seemed to enjoy trading at the edges of known space. There was no reason, the Human told himself thoughtfully, to believe these beings were from the *Heerama*. Why would that ship have detoured here, when Captain Heeru had been so set on joining Morgan on Plexis, to help search for Sira?

This group consisted of twenty-one individuals, three across, seven deep, moving quickly and in Drapsk-like unison. They might have looked like servo dusters in search of a street to clean, if it hadn't been for the crossed bandoliers supporting a pair of biodisruptors at each waistless middle. Armed and intent Drapsk. They escorted a servo transport, low-slung and open to the air, its cargo a nondescript pallet of the type used to convey large, bulky cargo from the warehouse to a waiting ship.

Morgan held in his breath, knowing the sensitivity of those restless blue-green plumes and hoping to hide his presence. There was nothing he could do about any scent trail he'd left. He didn't try to fathom his instinctive caution, even though until now he'd considered the Drapsk inconveniently helpful at worse. There was no doubt they adored Sira and seemed to extend that admiration to him as well—now that his *grist* had improved, according to Huido.

Morgan slipped back into the street, content to be careful. He stepped up his pace and, when the chance came, doubled back along a series of parallel streets. The advantage of knowing his way around, he smiled without humor. He'd lived here—in that hideaway where Huido and Ruti had waited—most of a planet year, earning credits to get the *Silver Fox* her first major refit.

He knew the surrounding desert, too, with its shifting dunes and endless starry sky. He'd planned to bring Sira to the secret home he'd made there, imagining how her hair would lift into the wind as her arms reached for him. Morgan lost himself in a bittersweet daydream.

Danger! Attackers boiled out of a doorway—closed, like all the others lining the street, until Morgan walked by it. His inner warning had the Human already in a crouching spin, one hand reaching for his blaster, the other blocking a blow from the first of the three. He abandoned the attempt to draw his weapon; they were too close. Instead, Morgan continued his spin, moving up under the arms of the second assailant to drive his force blade into an exposed torso. The blade slid through clothing and bone as if through air. Two to one.

A sharp blow over his kidneys sent Morgan to his knees. A stab, foiled by his body armor. He rolled away, feeling hands grab and miss the shoulders of his coat. He kicked without looking and heard a satisfying grunt.

The Human changed his attack. Closing his eyes, he *reached* outward with his power. Two minds left. One shielded—a telepath. One vulnerable. He concentrated on the weaker, shutting down the centers of motor control, withdrawing as he felt that mind lose consciousness. Now. One to one. The other.

Morgan's eyes snapped open, and he stared into the thin, bearded face of the Human standing over him. "Put that down," he said, backing the order with a warning flare of Power, seeing the other's eyes widen as he realized his shields were intact only because

Morgan hadn't bothered to breach them. There was a thud as the blaster dropped from a limp hand. "Move." The telepath stepped back, holding his hands away from his sides. His eyes roved the deserted street as though looking for help.

Morgan stood and dusted off his coat. "Who sent you?" he asked.

"Is Agger dead, too?" the other Human glanced nervously at the tidier of the two bodies.

"I'll ask the questions," Morgan countered. "Who sent you?"

"He'll kill me."

Morgan's eyes were like ice. "I'll do worse."

The telepath looked as though he'd argue the point, then something in Morgan's expression changed his mind. "He said you'd know."

"Ah." Morgan shrugged, outwardly casual. "Games. Symon always liked them. You do realize he expected me to kill all three of you—that he'd waste your lives to slow me down. A few minutes. That's all you're worth to him."

"Mebbeso," the telepath agreed shakily. "But I'm not going to spill either. Symon's no enemy I want."

"Do you prefer having me for one?" With that, Morgan stripped the shielding from the other's mind and waited, doing no more than show some of his Power. He estimated they had no more than a quarter of an hour before shops started to open and this would no longer be a private street.

"What are you?" Honest naked fear. "You aren't Human!"

Morgan's lips twitched. "Twenty generations pure

stock," he stated, letting his Power swell until he saw the other wince. "Now. I'm willing to let you go, you and Agger here, if you let me scan your memories of Symon. It won't hurt a bit. But if you resist? I'll still find what I want, but you won't enjoy the process. Your choice."

Choice. Morgan ran, his heart pounding, hoping he was making the right one. The telepath, Serge Tosnulla, had cooperated—though the filth in his mind had made Morgan almost wish he'd been given an excuse to rip out what he wanted instead. He'd knocked Tosnulla unconscious, leaving the two to explain the gutted corpse of their companion when the local authorities checked the streets, leaving himself the task of deciding between the impossible.

Symon had brought all his lackeys with him from Plexis. He'd never had trouble attracting followers, Morgan remembered bitterly, though the technique varied. Symon could be warm and charismatic, as he had with Ruti, until you believed every word he uttered. Where or when he'd learned that skill, Morgan couldn't begin to guess; certainly before coming to Karolus. More commonly, though, Symon relied on sheer intimidation—sometimes physical, as if to prove he didn't need his mental abilities to control others.

Regardless of why his lackeys obeyed him, they'd already intercepted and kidnapped the two fosterlings brought to Ettler's Planet by the Ordnexians. Now they were on the hunt for Ruti. They'd had a tip on the Carasian's whereabouts. It was never easy to hide Huido for long.

A gang of renegade telepaths wasn't all Symon had brought from Plexis. Tosnulla had seen a stasis chamber, locked, that Symon had kept in a sealed compartment of the ship's hold. It had been transported to Symon's own quarters, in a secret location in Rosietown.

Stasis—the Human version, not the Clan's. If Sira was inside such a chamber, it would explain why Morgan couldn't reach her mind. She was in suspended animation, and would stay that way until released.

Final unpleasant surprise? Symon and his renegades were using Drapsk technology. Rasmullum hadn't recognized the devices and machines he'd helped carry and set up, but Morgan did. He'd have to talk to the Heerii Drapsk. But later.

Choices. Morgan had gone from too few to too many. But there wasn't really a choice. He had to make sure Ruti and Huido were safe, first of all.

He ran faster.

Chapter 19

TIME, I decided, must move faster outside my box. It didn't move at all inside, where I sat in one corner, reassured by the pressure of two walls on my shoulders, and waited—and waited—for someone to remember to turn on the lights. Or feed me. Or offer me access to other conveniences that were becoming quite important to my comfort. Not to mention clean the floor.

On the other hand, I was reasonably sure the box itself was moving—or there'd been a particularly prolonged series of station tremors. Not that I had any reason to believe my box and I were still on Plexis. The Drapsk barrier was my true prison. This box? I pulled my knees to my chest and rested my forehead on them, trying to think like Symon. His motives seemed clear enough. Clan-like, he valued Power. Human-like, he wanted it for himself. He must still believe I could somehow enhance his abilities, as Joining with me had so multiplied Morgan's.

There were, of course, fools in both our species. At least Jarad di Sarc had had the dignity to choose exile;

a state reinforced by the aversion of my self-centered kind to disgrace and the Watchers.

Symon's motive, however, didn't explain why he'd put me in this box. If he hadn't trusted the Drapsk technology, he could have simply drugged me to unconsciousness—but he would have had to care for me, which meant people and the risk of exposure. Had that been it? Putting me into stasis would make it easy to move me without notice. It would also make it easy to keep me somewhere for a prolonged period of time.

Time that would have moved faster outside this box. I raised my head and stared at the dark, refusing to believe years might have passed. Symon wasn't that patient.

Secrecy. That made sense, especially since Symon knew Morgan. My Chosen was more than capable of tracking him down and freeing me, I thought proudly. Mind you, I wasn't sure exactly how Morgan would manage these feats. Symon must be days ahead of his pursuit, since no amount of impatience could change what it took to get the *Fox* through her repairs on Big Bob. But if I knew anything about my Chosen, he was coming for me. It was only a matter of time.

Time. The past. I lowered my hand, finding my keffle-flute case by touch, owning its music again as I owned all my memories. So much made sense now. I understood what had so terrified that other me, an understanding based in the strength of the person I'd become, Sira Morgan, and what I'd learned. There was life in the M'hir. Strange, wild, incomprehensibly alien life that interacted with my kind, with me, throughout our existence. This Singer? I didn't doubt its existence anymore or that it was still seeking me. I could pity it, a M'hir beast that seemed like our unChosen, desperately seeking completion, somehow becoming aware of me—drawn to me—instead of its proper kind. I understood its Power and the danger it posed.

The Singer shouldn't be able to seduce my conscious self, now that Morgan and I were Joined. I was complete. But it was waiting, eager, as if time was nothing in the M'hir, or as if there was no way to stop itself. And, reluctantly, I had to admit a terrible truth: a part of me now remembered the thrill of the Singer's touch through the M'hir and still longed for it, craved it as if addicted to a drug. The mere thought and my heart treacherously pounded faster, my body warming as only Morgan had warmed it. What would happen if I opened the case, cold to my fingers, and played? If I released my music into the M'hir? The Singer would come—even through the Drapsk's mechanical wall. He had already, and only my flight inside my own mind had saved me.

Symon couldn't have known what would happen to me in this chamber, that I'd be assaulted and have to do battle, bursting through the final blocks in my memory to do so. I leaned my head back and smiled in the dark, doubting the rogue telepath would care that he'd done me a great service. Sira di Sarc had hated those moments of fear and failure enough to try and eradicate them forever. I didn't enjoy them, but how wonderful to recover what she'd sacrificed at the same time. My music. Joyous times with Enora, Rael, and even Pella. The love I'd shared with my mother, Mirim, as a child.

I couldn't wait to tell Morgan.

Although it appeared I'd have to—at least, and my smile turned wolfish, until someone made the mistake of opening this box.

If I'd hoped the thought would be a signal, I was wrong. It was another long weary time before light smacked into my eyes and I heard the sound of something mechanical sliding in its track. I covered my face and sent out an urgent seeking thought—but the Drapsk barrier was still in place.

When I was finally able to squint through my weeping eyes, I knew why.

I was surrounded by dear little Drapsk.

"Would the Mystic One care for sombay?"

"I'd care for an explanation," I said without hope of an answer. If Makii were good at being evasive, the Heerii were masters. Despite what seemed hours spent yelling, coaxing, cajoling, and engaging in meaningless pleasantries, all I'd been able to get out of the six I'd met so far was hospitality.

Unusual hospitality. I'd been led from the stasis chamber—a torment for the olfactorily-inclined beings, from the way they'd kept their antennae folded and the haste with which it was removed through the freight door—into what appeared to be a converted cargo hold. My powers were confined here as well, implying the Drapsk had put another of their barriers in place before opening the box. Why? And why was I on a Drapsk ship? I had a list of questions, but no one interested in answering them. I had one need—to reach Morgan—and they were not in the least interested in helping me do that either. Why? I was back to questions.

They'd provided a fresher stall, as well as an assortment of clothing in my size. There was a table covered with an assortment of food and drink—all carefully selected to my preference. The Heerii, like all Drapsk, researched their customers thoroughly. And, it seemed, their prisoners.

Hard as it was to believe, that's what I appeared to be.

There were six identical Heerii in the room with me. They hadn't left, having all the supplies they'd offered me already here. I'd presumed, cleverly, they couldn't open the hold's door without releasing my Power. So when that door finally opened, I hurried to test that presumption. Beyond causing all of them to orient toward me, antennae aquiver with excitement, there was no result. I was still trapped.

And now a new Drapsk walked into the cargo hold. "I want to know what's going on!" I demanded of this one, rising to my feet but making the effort not to shout. I'd tried that. They'd sucked tentacles and waited for me to stop, then offered a tranquilizer.

The new, seventh Drapsk was obviously someone of authority. At last! He coaxed a stool from the floor and gestured to me to sit down. "Our apologies, Mystic One. I am Captain Heeru, of the *Heerama*."

I sat. "I've had enough apologies to last a lifetime, Captain," I told him. "It's time for some answers, don't you think?"

They could have been my Drapsk, as I thought of the Makii, were it not for the blue-green shimmering up their antennae. That color could be changed, during *lar-gripstsa*, if another Tribe came into ascendance. Odd how the color was enough to make me uneasy, as if I was dealing with an unknown species again.

"You are most correct, Mysic One," Heeru said amiably. As this was exactly the sort of courtesy a Drapsk used before disagreeing, I braced myself to argue, only to stop as one of the other attendant Drapsk stepped up with a plate in his hands. On it were two bright red tentacles, each the length of my thumb. Both, I assumed, those missing from the ring around his smiling mouth. He offered the plate, and its contents, to me.

I recognized the ceremony. *Ipstsa*. By taking those pieces of Drapsk-flesh into one's mouth and chewing them—then spitting them out—the taste of that Tribe was incorporated into one's body. I'd performed it with Makairi, of the Makii, and would bear their taste forever, according to Copelup. This "taste" wasn't anything a Clan or Human could detect, but the end result mattered to the Drapsk a great deal.

Too much to take *ipstsa* lightly, now that I understood more abut these beings. "I am Makii," I said, pointing out what had to be obvious to them.

"The Makii are not in ascendance here, Mystic One. You must become Heerii."

I blinked, wondering if I'd just been given the closest thing to an ultimatum I'd ever heard from a Drapsk. "I am Clan," I reminded Heeru.

"You are Makii. There can be no Makii here. I do not permit it."

As ultimatums went, Heeru's didn't impress me, having known a Scat or two. "Then I suggest you overlook whatever makes you consider me as Makii," I informed him with an edge to my voice, "and get on with answering my questions—or let me leave, now." When he began to sputter a protest, I snapped: "I've no interest in *ipstsa* with the Heerii—a Tribe keeping me prisoner and making me exceedingly angry. If you want me to taste that?" I pointed to the plate. "You'll have to force them down my throat."

The Drapsk dropped the plate and its rejected tentacles as it performed *eopari* right in front of me. Captain Heeru kicked the ball of misery out of his way with unDrapsk-like roughness. "Prisoner?" he questioned in a suddenly calm voice. "We have rescued you, Mystic One. We are keeping you safe from harm. How can you be angry with us? How can you not be pleased to perform *ipstsa* and join your rescuers?"

I'd found the best approach to dealing with Drapsk—or the one that caused me the fewest moments of complete confusion—was to ignore anything they said that didn't make sense and focus on what might. "Safe from what?"

"That Human. Hom Symon. He was trying to—" a tentacle disappeared into Heeru's mouth, then popped out again, "—offer you in trade, Mystic One. We were able to intervene and bring you to the *Heerama*. Where you are being kept safe." This with familiar Drapsk smugness.

It was possible. Ossirus knew, I'd had experience with the obsessive protectiveness of Drapsk before now. I narrowed my eyes and studied the captain as he waited for my response. Copelup had told me most Drapsk lied extremely well, something I believed; he'd also mentioned that some Drapsk moved their hands nervously while lying. Heeru's were rock-steady. "Then I must thank you, Captain, and your brave crew," I made myself say. Morgan would have been proud of my self-control. "How long do you think I'll continue to need your protection?"

The six still-conscious Drapsk appeared to consult with one another, antennae fluttering in various directions. As a delaying tactic, I couldn't dispute its effectiveness. One wasn't inclined to interrupt.

Done, Heeru turned his body to face me, tentacles wide in an expression that usually, I'd found, meant an exceedingly happy Drapsk. "Not long at all, Mystic One. We have every reason to believe that Hom Symon will no longer be a threat to you very soon. If you will please indulge our wish for your absolute safety a little longer? A few days at most."

There was, I decided, no such think as a Drapsk whose sense of time included the urgency mine did. "I must contact Captain Morgan," I insisted, "before we discuss anything else. If you won't let me do it my way—give me have access to your com system. Now."

"Of course. We'll send a message on your behalf immediately."

My self-control was having to struggle. "That's not what I said."

"Mystic One. Mystic One," Heeru said soothingly, as if talking to a child. "First you refuse *ipstsa*, then you insist on putting yourself at risk. What if someone was eavesdropping and heard your lovely voice? They would know you are here. The Makii are known for such behavior. You do not seem to be making wise decisions. Perhaps you are not fully recovered from your ordeal."

I wasn't sure what made the word "ordeal" echo in my thoughts, but it did—with a very uncomfortable resonance. "You knew," I accused, feeling my mouth go dry. I stood and backed away, until I faced a semicircle of faceless Drapsk. "You knew what was happening to me while I was in stasis. You knew I was being attacked by something in the M'hir—the Scented Way."

"Attacked?" There was another flutter of consultation. Then, shockingly: "Were you not experiencing pleasure, Mystic One?"

My hand crept to my throat and I felt my hair lifting from my neck. "What's going on?" I demanded in a whisper. "What are you doing to me?"

Another Drapsk spoke. "You have a destiny, Mystic One, tied to ours. It is our honor and duty to see you fulfill it. We regret you have been unwilling to cooperate—until now. We hope to change your mind."

Another: "We have concluded that you require compensation. You are a Trader by profession. We have selected an item we believe you will find worthwhile: information."

Master Traders, with an interest in the M'hir. These weren't the Makii, I realized, dropping my hand self-consciously, but feeling my hair stubbornly—and wisely—refusing to relax. "How can I talk about a trade when I don't know what you want in return?" I asked reasonably. I was willing to bet they couldn't know exactly what I'd experienced with the Singer.

Gauges and monitors were their only way to observe the M'hir.

"You must accept your destiny," Heeru said again, this time impatiently. Another Drapsk trait seemed a sincere belief that repeating something they understood would help an alien grasp the concept.

I went at it from the other direction. "What information are you offering me?"

This pleased them. One bustled over to the cart used to convey the meal—presently cooling on the table—rummaging in a cupboard before bringing out a small carved box. He handed it to the Captain, who opened the lid to show me the contents. An ordinary data cube. I tensed, aware it was unlikely to contain anything I'd want the Drapsk to have.

"In here, Mystic One," Captain Heeru proclaimed proudly, "are the results from the Baltir—the results of their experiments with you."

I was right. This was something I didn't want the Drapsk—or anyone—to have. My hands slipped protectively over my abdomen. The scars were gone, a medical erasing of my past I'd found disturbingly easy, given the cost. The Retian experiments? Simple enough. They'd planted alien tissue samples inside me, in an attempt to see which, if any, of certain "interested" species could hybridize with mine. I'd almost died.

The results had been conveniently destroyed, according to Bowman, furious to have been thwarted in her investigation. But I didn't doubt the Drapsk. "I'm not interested," I told them.

"It states who supplied the Human tissue implanted in your body. I can tell you. A sample of the quality of the information."

Another experiment—the first. "Why should I care?" I said roughly. "It died."

"Not so," another Heerii corrected. "It was killed. We have checked quite thoroughly, knowing your interest. The Makii med on the *Makmora* mistakenly healed you of the Human tissue within your body. It might have survived, otherwise. Did you know the Baltir repeated the experiment with more of the same tissue? Do you want the true result?"

Had it been Morgan's? The thought had haunted me, that the Retian had taken advantage of my Human's unconscious state to steal some of his flesh to implant in mine. If Morgan's, had it survived? These Drapsk dangled that knowledge in front of me. Master Traders, indeed.

"You are the ones who are mistaken," I said flatly. "I'm not interested." I tried not to look at the data cube, to feel this shock of hope. I didn't want offspring, not those cursed with my disastrous, deadly Power. But Morgan's? To give him that legacy, a new life from our union? The joy of that unlooked-for chance was more painful than hope alone.

And what if our two species could be fertile—was my original dream actually possible, of a new race free of the deadly Power-of-Choice?

I hadn't fooled them. "The Human tissue," Captain Heeru announced as if I hadn't denied interest at all, "came from Hom Symon. He had paid to be included in any such experiment, had the opportunity presented itself. As it did."

What had begun to seem almost worthwhile turned back into disgust. I gripped the fabric over my abdomen, as if to rip out even the memory of that invasion. "Keep your data," I snarled. "Let me go, now. I've no intention of letting that—that 'thing' in the M'hir near me ever again. I don't care about your Heerii destiny. Give it up, and I won't report this to the other Tribes."

"I'm disappointed you feel this way, Mystic One. But not surprised." Captain Heeru rose to his feet, putting the box with its cube of stolen data on the table. He gestured to the other Drapsk. Two of them approached me, halting just out of reach. As I eyed them warily, a third went to the cart and brought out what looked like a necklace of some dull, silvery metal. He passed it to Heeru, then reached back to the cart for something else—a stunner he then aimed at me.

Suffice it to say this was not behavior I associated with Drapsk.

The Captain walked up to stand before me, the necklace in both hands, then held it as high as he could reach—about my shoulder-height. "Put this on, Mystic One. Or we will regretfully use force to obtain your co-operation."

I contemplated twisting his antennae into a knot, but didn't care for the likely consequence: a stunner headache, not to mention being helpless while unconscious. So I took what Heeru offered.

The necklace wasn't jewelry, which I'd already suspected. Warm to the touch, what had appeared to be a fine metal chain was a highly complex and flexible device of some kind, filled with tiny mechanisms and almost undetectable lights that blinked as if already at work. There was a simple-looking clasp.

"Put it on."

Having no option, I obeyed, draping it around my neck and bringing the two ends together in front so I could see how to fasten it. Instead, the two ends almost jumped from my fingers as the simple clasp turned out to be some sort of automated junction that fused seamlessly into the rest. I let go, feeling the metal settle like a warm fluid against my skin.

"What does it do?" I asked fatalistically, having ideas about that as well.

"The 94RD-*stsa*-5 is an interdimensional harmonizer that—" Something in my blank look must have informed the suddenly too-helpful Drapsk that I needed a more literal answer. "This is a portable, more sophisticated version of what keeps you from the Scented Way while inside this room, Mystic One. It cannot be opened without the appropriate codes, nor can you use your Power to move it from this space to any other."

"You will, however," Captain Heeru said with a note of complete satisfaction, "continue to receive pleasure whenever you choose to sense the Scented Way. The collar will allow you to rejoin your destiny. I highly recommend you do so as soon as possible."

"I will not," I promised him coldly. "And I suggest you consider what it means to keep me here against my will. The Heerii might be in ascendance on this scow of yours—but are you prepared to face the Makii, the Clan, and the Trade Pact Enforcers?"

A chorus of amused hoots. "Mystic One. Once you

have completed your destiny," Heeru said with that utterly Drapsk air of confidence in the face of complete and total disagreement—mine, "the Makii above all will be grateful. There is no reason to be so concerned—"

My hands formed into fists, and if it hadn't been for the stunner, I might have tried my luck with his antennae. I settled for a warning. "Morgan will find me."

"Again, you have no reason to worry, Mystic One. Please remain calm and in a receptive state of mind. We promised to send a message to Captain Morgan. And we will."

This from a member of a species I belatedly remembered was never, ever targeted by the self-preserving Scats.

INTERLUDE

It was a significant part of self-preservation to know where one was going at all times—especially on an unfamiliar planet. Even more when one seemed habitually at risk on unfamiliar planets. Barac knew this perfectly well.

But a Carasian obviously had a different idea of what constituted clear and understandable directions than a Clan.

Mind you, Barac wouldn't be this lost if the Drapsk hadn't kicked him out so early. By the time there was anyone else moving on the street, he'd wandered so far from where he was supposed to be that the first Human Barac approached for assistance had laughed. Embarrassing as that was, it was less demeaning than staying lost. Unfortunately, that Human had proved—unhelpful.

However, the Clansman had, by this point, been up long enough that restaurants were opening, including a charming café beckoning early risers with an irresistible combination of fresh brewed sombay and baking. It wasn't, he decided more cheerfully, as if he had an appointment with Huido, beyond this being the day they were to meet.

Over breakfast, Barac found himself considering that he might have jumped a little too quickly at the Carasian's mysterious call. Granted, he'd left Drapskii, but he really didn't know for what. Hopefully, the Clansman sighed, something safe and profitable. It would be a nice change.

There was only one way to know for sure. Suddenly impatient to learn exactly what he'd gotten himself into—in case he'd need to get out of it again quickly— Barac didn't delay after breakfast. He found a second, more helpful Human, and obtained much better directions.

Directions to what turned out to be, Barac discovered after a half an hour's steady walk, probably the worst part of Rosietown's All Sapient's District.

He sniffed. There was something dead and not buried in the alley in front of him—the supposedly correct address. What was Huido up to? The now-noisy traffic of servos, groundcars, and varied beings behind him only emphasized the silence ahead.

Barac wasn't fond of alleys, having had his share of unfortunate experiences in them. And this was a particularly dark one. He hesitated.

Danger! As if to confirm his caution, his inner warning flared. Instinctively, Barac formed the locate of an unobtrusive corner of the breakfast café, in case he needed to make a quick exit, then sent out a seeking thought.

A seething mass of minds impacted on his other sense. Barac was running into the alley before he had sorted them all, knowing first and foremost that those ahead were telepaths, Human, and bent on harm to Huido and—

Ruti di Bowart?

The name and awareness of another Clan in danger slammed into his mind even as Barac spotted those trying to break into the door at the alley's end. One more step and he had his force blade out, humming for blood. The next, and he was in their midst.

Two strokes and two fell, in several pieces. Three left. One backed away, trying to use his feeble Human Talent. Barac pinned him—wide-eyed and gasping— with part of his Power, using the rest to maintain his shields.

The other two were inclined to be trouble. Barac danced back, keeping his blade raised in front as they moved apart to approach him from two sides at once. With his mind trapping the third, Barac couldn't 'port out of harm's way. Not that he planned to—this was the most satisfaction he'd had in a long time.

The door opened.

Ruti couldn't wait any longer—not with that hint of a touch against her shields, those sounds from outside. There'd been someone, several someones, trying to break in the door; she didn't need her other sense to tell her they meant harm. Then screams and now nothing? The vermin hadn't been that big. She unlocked the door, then pushed it open cautiously, Huido's weapon in her hand.

There was a body at her feet. Two, her mind quali- fied, somehow putting together the macabre bits she saw floating in what appeared to be an ocean of red blood. A grunt of effort made her look up. Another figure—alive—stood as if paralyzed. Close enough to touch, not that she would. His yellow coat had been sprayed with blood, and his eyes almost jutted out of his skull as he stared.

Ruti, feeling as though she moved in slow motion, turned her head to follow where the paralyzed—no, *pinned*, she realized—humanoid looked.

Three more. She felt the weapon in her hand slip and gripped it more tightly. Her palms were sweating. Two more yellow coats—like Morgan's, she thought. Their attention was on the last figure as they moved to attack him. Even as they did, he glanced past them and saw her.

Barac sud Sarc. A sending, clear and powerful. Identification followed by a warning: *Stay inside*.

Good advice, but Ruti couldn't move, unable to take her eyes from the battle or him. Clan? Barac was taller than the others, more slender at waist and hips, broader at the shoulders. He was dressed in clothing too elegant for an alleyway war and carried a weapon like a sword. Its blade was insubstantial—a force blade, she realized, having watched her share of entertainment vids.

The others had some type of clublike weapon in their hands that didn't appear dangerous until one aimed it at Barac and a blinding bolt of energy shot out, just missing his shoulder. Another scorched the edge of his cloak. That was all the Clansman left in range as he leaped sideways and up, bringing down his blade in a graceful back sweep to remove one attacker's arm and most of his side, blood spraying everywhere.

Ruti heard herself scream.

Another bolt of energy, then another. She threw her arm over her eyes, cowering in the doorway. Heavy thuds. A gurgling sound that stopped.

Then all was shadows and quiet. Ruti heard footsteps over her ragged breathing and lowered her arm to look for the source, tense until she saw it was Barac, walking between what was left of his foes, seeming to examine their faces. His cloak smoldered in a couple of places and he paused to pull it off, favoring one side.

A figure shot by her—the pinned attacker had broken free! Without thinking, Ruti raised her hand and pressed the handle of the weapon in it. Only after the searing flash and concussion sent her hurtling back inside the apartment, did she remember what Huido had said about making sure no one but enemy was in range.

Barac climbed to his feet, giving his head a shake to see if it might ease the ringing in his ears. The ringing became a hammering, so he stopped. There was already a fair amount of consternation and shouting coming from the street behind the alley, so he estimated they had no more than a minute before what passed for authority in Rosietown showed up—with inconvenient questions.

And the first order of business for a Clan Scout? Avoid questions.

He found Ruti lying in the doorway to what had to be the address Huido had provided. She was barely conscious and splattered with gore, but seemed more winded than harmed. Whatever she'd fired could have killed them all. Barac was reasonably sure that meant it was something Huido had left her.

The Carasian wasn't within a hasty scan; Barac was uncomfortably familiar with the result of touching that brain. Well, they'd have to find each other somewhere else. He leaned over to grasp the child's arm, concentrating . . .

"No! We mustn't 'port! Huido warned me—"

Barac rolled his eyes and groaned to himself, but bent down and swept her up. "He'd better have a good reason," he said, adjusting her weight in his arms. She was more substantial than she looked.

"I can walk—"

"Hush, and look unconscious. The only way out of here is through that crowd. Unless we can 'port?" This hopefully. Ruti shook her head firmly, then closed her eyes, going so limp Barac thought she might have fainted. But her lips moved soundlessly: Go!

It worked, as he'd confidently expected it would. Both of them were liberally blood-soaked—though all of it was Human—making it obvious they were victims stumbling away from the explosion. Barac kept his head up and fixed his face into a determined expression, letting anyone in his way, or who thought to help, know he had a destination in mind and was in a hurry to reach it.

The siren-heralded arrival of several emergency vehicles provided the last bit of cover he needed to get them both out of sight down the next alleyway. Barac dumped Ruti to the ground and hurried to the first of the three doors lining the near wall. He started to send out a questing thought.

"No!" she protested again, coming to him. "Huido said we couldn't use—couldn't use Power. Is Huido all right? Who were those—"

Warned by the sudden catch in Ruti's voice, Barac caught her as she began to sag. He pulled them both farther into the shadows, then held her close, feeling her body shaking. "I didn't sense Huido nearby," he told her quietly. "But the old shellfish is probably fine. It would take more than a handful of shipcity dregs to bother him. He gave me the address—I thought he'd be there. Do you know where he went? What's this all about?"

"I've never—" She hiccuped into his chest. "I've never seen anyone die. I've never killed anyone."

Barac took her shoulders and pushed her far enough away that he could look into her eyes. They were, he noticed irrelevantly, quite lovely eyes, if a bit red at the moment. "While I'd like to give you time to deal with the grim realities of fighting for your life, Fem di Bowart," he made his voice harsh, "we don't have any to spare. They're going to be looking for us— the authorities as well as whomever sent those Humans after you. I need you to answer me. Why can't we use our Power?"

She sniffed once but stood up straight under his grip. "Huido was sure Symon had a way to detect it. That he could find me if I used any power at all."

"Ren Symon?" Barac's shock must have troubled the M'hir; he saw it in her eyes. "Where's Morgan—" he started to ask, then stopped. He pulled Ruti close again, moving them both deeper into the shadows. He bent his head so his cheek brushed her hair and his lips touched her ear. "Someone's coming," Barac warned her. "Stay still."

Footsteps, unsteady, as if one of the alley's inhabitants had been roused by all the commotion in the street. Then a knowing chuckle as the footsteps passed them.

Barac waited until he was sure they were alone again before releasing her. "Are you hurt?" he asked belatedly.

"No."

He peered at her doubtfully. The word was too breathless to be very reassuring. Still, she was standing. "Wait here."

There was a faint mechanical ticking from the first door, but when Barac pressed his ear to the second door, he didn't hear a sound. With quick look down the still-empty alley and a cautioning nod to Ruti, he used the tip of his force blade to sever the lockpad from the door. Crude and obvious, but they were in a hurry. He ducked inside, checked there was no one home, then waved Ruti to join him.

Ruti couldn't believe she was washing her hair. She couldn't believe what she was washing out of her hair. She swallowed, hard, bile climbing into her mouth whenever she thought about what she'd seen—what she'd done. But she kept scrubbing. Barac had told her to clean up, and he was waiting for his turn in the fresher. She didn't know how he'd found this place so quickly, an apartment twin to Huido's but with power and water pressure, not to mention signs of being lived in by at least two Humans, possibly three. A pile of clothing was on the floor outside the stall. He'd already taken hers to throw in the recycler.

Barac sud Sarc. Ruti wasn't sure what to think of him. No Clansman on Acranam would be foolhardy enough to take on five Humans armed only with a force blade—for a Carasian and a stranger, no less. But he'd not only done it—he'd succeeded. Ruti was also sure no one she knew would have thought of a way to escape that scene without having to 'port, let alone find the resources they needed.

He'd held her in his arms.

She shivered under the spray. He had held her, she reminded herself firmly, so she wouldn't fall on her own face.

Barac's sending hadn't felt like that of a *sud*. It had felt different. Ruti had wanted to test his Power with hers—but there hadn't been a safe moment for that Clan courtesy. Now, she assumed it would be a foolish exposure of her Power to Symon—if Huido was to be believed.

"Are you done?"

His voice shocked herself back to herself. "Almost!" she called, hurriedly turning the spray to dry, then stepping out with her hair still damp. It was so thin it dried by itself anyway. Ruti went through the pile of clothing Barac had found for her—just as glad she hadn't been the one to go through the personal effects of whomever lived here. They weren't Clan, of course, but this was their home, not hers.

Pants, a shirt that pulled over her head. A short coat of the same yellow hide as Morgan's, too short in the arms, though not, she hoped, noticeably. Coarser fabrics than she was used to, but warm and clean. She'd have to keep her sandals. Ruti had done her best to wipe as much blood from them as she could, hoping the sand outside would do the rest. They weren't too—

Ruti paused, a sandal in one hand, horrified to suddenly realize she'd lost Lara—her mother's gift. The tiny doll must have dropped from her pocket in the alley. It might even have been destroyed in the blast.

It was only a doll, she told herself fiercely. Only a doll.

An impatient knock. "I'm finished," she said, gathering up what she hadn't worn to take with her out of the small room and turning to leave.

Barac had taken this as invitation to enter. It was her first look at her rescuer in good light, without the adrenaline of danger pounding in her head, or tears in her eyes. He was startlingly handsome, after weeks of seeing only aliens, with that Clan grace of feature few Humans seemed to achieve. Thick black hair above a broad forehead. High cheekbones under dark, sparkling eyes; the aura of Power trained and tightly controlled. He was carrying a handful of stolen clothing, too, and must have already recycled his shirt, which had been bloodstained and scorched.

Ruti found herself blushing at the sight of more male flesh than Clan convention permitted, at least on Acranam. Still, she didn't quite mind what she saw, until she noticed the angry bruising along his ribs. "You're hurt," she exclaimed.

Barac seemed to find something about this amusing, or it might have been her blush. She couldn't tell without reaching through the M'hir. "I'll live," he assured her, smiling. "I won't be long. Stay where you can keep watch on the door. If anyone comes, call me. And Ruti?"

She'd headed for the door, stepping past him carefully. "Yes?"

His eyes were suddenly serious. "At the first sign of trouble, I don't care what Huido told you. 'Port out of here. Don't wait for me, just do it."

"No!"

Barac looked surprised by her immediate protest. "Be sensible," he ordered. "Even if Symon can somehow track our Power, it's better than being trapped. Do you understand?"

Ruti scowled up at him and decided not to argue the point. She wasn't helpless and she wasn't going to run away. Hadn't she proved that? Besides, she thought, this Barac didn't know everything. "Huido told me you and I were to go to Morgan's house, in the desert. I have—" she dug in a pocket and pulled out the very crumpled piece of plas she'd retrieved from her original clothes, "—the coordinates. But I don't have a locate to 'port there. Do you?"

"No." Barac dropped his bundle of clothes on the countertop, then touched her forehead lightly with one finger. "What more should I know, Ruti di Bowart?" Between two Clan, his was a courteous request for a lowering of her shields and a sharing of vital information in the fastest way possible.

"That we shouldn't waste time here. Hurry and get clean," Ruti said, keeping her shields firmly in place as she backed away then stepped out the door, pulling it closed behind her.

She leaned against the wall outside, her head back and eyes closed, knowing she hadn't refused to open to Barac because she feared Symon. She'd refused so he wouldn't learn about her and what she'd done. Not yet.

"Not much farther," Barac told his companion, pleased to recognize the Whirtle's used clothing store. Not that he'd expected to get lost twice in the same day—but one never knew.

Ruti di Bowart. He knew the House, or of it. Barac glanced down. She was keeping up, without complaint, despite his longer strides. He slowed a bit, making sure it wasn't obvious. Proud little thing. And brave. He was impressed, despite his abiding distrust for anything and anyone associated with Acranam. Their former leader and founder, Yihtor di Caraat, had murdered his brother, Kurr. Even now, Barac knew the Acranam Clan resisted the Council and Sira at every turn, insisting they could survive alone. They continued to risk their unChosen, he thought, feeling that familiar mix of horror and reckless longing.

As they moved through the now-busy streets, packed with locals in the omnipresent yellow coats and spacers in blue, the Clansman deliberately kept any conversation to the inane sorts of things a tourist might say, indicating the occasional noteworthy site or talking about the weather. Morgan had taught Barac a healthy respect for the power of Human technology, especially as it concerned the invasion of privacy.

Barac saw no reason to believe this Symon wouldn't be just as aware as Morgan of that potential, meaning any of the buildings they passed could have listening devices. One could become quite thoroughly paranoid around Humans.

Although, as a Scout, he usually laughed away the most preposterous of those ideas. Today? Barac looked down at Ruti again. He wasn't taking any chances. It had been a close thing, in that alley. Too close.

Who was she? He opened his awareness to the M'hir the tiniest possible amount, less worried about Huido's caution than his own ignorance.

Good strong shields. Quite an imposing presence for such a tiny thing. Ahh. Barac saw what he'd half-expected and withdrew.

Fosterling.

"Did you come with Huido from Plexis?" Barac asked Ruti casually.

A sidelong look. "Yes. I was working in his restaurant."

Barac put that unlikely information aside to examine later, along with the disturbing confirmation that Acranam had dispersed one of her priceless offspring where no Clan should. "Did you like the station?"

"No." Quick and emphatic. A taste of distress in the M'hir. Barac decided to leave further questions for later.

It seemed to take too long to reach the edge of the shipcity and the parking area where he'd left the Makii's gift. Barac found himself listening for sirens or running feet as he led Ruti down the line of waiting aircars. The Makii's was twice the size of any others in the lot, and gaudy. He'd liked it before he knew he'd be on the run. The Clansman frowned, wondering about a quick trade for something less conspicuous. But Ruti ran to it, running her hands over the glossy sides with delight. So much for pretending it wasn't his.

Speed was the alternative to being inconspicuous. "Get in," he ordered, and followed suit, noting Ruti fit into the Drapsk-sized seat better than he did. The aircar, suited to transporting royalty, could well have some armaments and a force shield, as well as the requisite exterior armor. Barac stared at the curved and elaborate Drapsk control panel, regretting, too late, he hadn't asked the little beings about more than the most basic operation of their machine. Now seemed a poor time to experiment.

"Where to?" he asked his companion.

"I have the coordinates," she said with a doubtful look at the panels. "Do you know how to work this?"

No gain in spreading his own anxieties on that subject to the child, Barak decided, "Of course," he said confidently. "I was a First Scout. Alien technology is my specialty."

"What's a scout?"

Her immediate puzzlement surprised Barac into a self-depreciating laugh. So much for his one claim to fame. "My pardon, young Ruti. Let's say I've more experience with aliens than most Clan. Read me the coordinates, please."

Whatever else you could say about the Drapsk, Barak decided a short while later as he lifted his hands from the controls, they designed admirable machines.

The aircar had digested the coordinates, and now smoothly assumed their flight, Barac having flown manually from the shipcity. He'd done a lazy circuit or two before engaging the autopilot, hoping to see if any other aircars lifted in pursuit.

What traffic joined them in the sky appeared more interested in heading into the town—Traders, more than likely. Huido's coordinates had taken them in the opposite direction, into a cloudless sky and over the beginnings of a march of horizon-spanning dunes. Barac shuddered to himself. There was a lot to be said for skulking in alleyways.

"Are we safe now?"

He turned to look at Ruti. She was pale, with eyes huge in her small face, but her expression was stern rather than frightened. "We should be," he judged. "Who'd look for us in this forsaken place?"

That made her eyes slide to the viewports, then back. Her lips twitched. "I see what you mean. No wonder Huido didn't come with us. He hates sand, you know."

Time for overdue answers, Barac thought. Before he could open his mouth, Ruti continued: "You asked about Hom Morgan. Are you—his friend?"

A very unusual question from one Clan to another, especially concerning a Human—unless Ruti had met the potent Morgan, with his unsettling ability to inspire loyalty from the most unexpected beings. Barac kept his understanding to himself. "Yes," he said, nodding. "We're friends. Why?"

Her face darkened. A rush of emotion-charged words tumbled out: "Morgan's in trouble."

"What do you mean?"

"It's my fault. Now Huido's gone to help him—"

Barac stopped her with a raised hand and a frown. "There's no more time for words," he told her grimly. "Open to me, now." He lowered his own shields, *reaching* outward to find Ruti's gone, but an involuntary barrier of intense guilt and grief in his way. She wasn't used to sharing, he realized, and eased back a bit, letting her control herself. After an instant, her emotions subsided. Relieved, Barac sent his mind into her surface thoughts and memories.

But his relief lasted no longer than the heartbeat it took for him to reach Ruti's memory of Sira.

With Symon.

Chapter 20

REN Symon. Jason Morgan. I sat in my Drapsk prison, finding those two faces intruding on my thoughts like flashes of night and day, dark and light, hate and love. An odd species, Human, to produce two beings who were mirror images of one another, down to their Power. The hate had been love, once. I'd shared Morgan's memories of Symon, perhaps more fully than he'd realized, and knew how Symon had treated him as a son, how Morgan had worshiped the other Human, granting him full access to his mind and heart.

A dangerous vulnerability even now. I understood—as I feared Morgan did not—how difficult it was to defend against anyone, or anything, who'd been given, or taken, that intimacy. Symon had a key to Morgan's innermost self. I had no doubt he planned to use it. Another reason I'd taken it as my personal quest to remove Symon as a threat to us. If I'd known how right I was, I wouldn't have left it to others.

If I'd known more about the Drapsk, I wouldn't be sitting here, helpless, with this ridiculous collar around my neck. I'd passed from fury to panic to a familiar sense of resigned frustration. I could be misjudging the Heerii, as I had the Makii at first; there might be a comprehensible reason for my confinement.

Or they were in league with my seducer, whatever it was, and planned a consummation which would destroy me and my Chosen—to a gain I certainly wouldn't be around to appreciate.

I shied from that thought, and the mouth-drying fear threatening to return with it. No, I couldn't believe the Drapsk expected me to be harmed. They'd offered me *ipstsa*. By making me a member of their Tribe, they'd all assume responsibility for my safety. One thing was sure about Drapsk: any member of a Tribe was defended by the entire Tribe—it was why the helpless-looking beings wandered with impunity through the most deadly spacer dives and hellholes.

The Heerii had known that, better than I, and offered me *ipstsa* anyway. Even if their motive had been to simply remove the scent of an opposing Tribe, they'd been willing to enter into that level of mutual self-interest. So they thought whatever I was to do would be safe.

They were wrong. I sighed at the unlikelihood of conveying that novel concept to the Drapsk. It might have helped if Captain Heeru had seen fit to put a com panel on this side of that locked door. No need to wonder why they'd set up my "guest quarters" in the *Heerama*'s hold. It was the only door they could lock, unless they modified their ship.

I didn't want to talk to Heeru anyway. I wanted to

talk to Morgan. Wanted. The laugh that broke out of me was so hurtful I closed my lips over it. If I'd ever thought the need of a Chooser was powerful and all-consuming, I'd been a fool. Had any other Joined pair been severed apart like this and lived to tell of it?

No wonder the mind of one would follow the other into madness and death. There was no other choice possible but to stay together. Forced into the impossible, I pulled at the collar again, having already cut my neck several places trying to tear it off.

It wasn't only my mind's need for that link through the M'hir. I loved Morgan, in all the ways I knew existed. I needed to know he was safe. Symon threatened him; I could trust my Human to be wary, if not invincible to that foe. But the Drapsk? How could he know to expect lies or worse from them?

I couldn't know how the Drapsk's device might affect Morgan. Did he feel the same anguish and emptiness? I hoped less, but for all I knew it could be worse for Morgan—so much of his new Power drew from mine in that other space. What if he grew desperate enough to—

No. I'd warned him against 'porting. If it was Morgan's last resort, and there was any mercy in the universe, the act would pull us together for one final moment.

In the meantime, I was going to try my own version.

I closed my eyes, fighting an inner battle with a weapon relearned from my past. That other, older Sira had been more disciplined; she'd relied more on her Talents and the Power she could bring to each. She'd also been more afraid of the M'hir, for good reason. It had become a fear that slipped into the real world, making it harder for her to fall asleep in the dark.

That Sira had learned to quiet her fear, to call up sleep when she willed it. To her technique, I added my need for Morgan, my concern for him, and hoped to dream.

Slowly, as though related to how deeply I sank into dreams, my awareness of Morgan grew, saturating my dreaming mind until I almost woke myself with relief.

As before, it was as if I looked out Morgan's eyes. Disorienting, as he was looking rapidly from side-to-side, while what was around him passed so quickly I realized he must be running.

I felt what Morgan felt, saved from being buried beneath an avalanche of dark emotions—grief, fear, rage—only by the distancing of the dream. His feelings echoed mine, but with more urgency, as though his actions fed them. I saw the backs of various beings as he dodged artfully through those on the sidewalk, mostly humanoid—probably Human. Outside, a city, daytime . . .

I'd expected Plexis. Or Kimmcle. Not this dusty, too-bright world. Dull yellow coats, curved buildings, air so dry it stole the moisture from his mouth as he took deep rhythmic breaths . . . these were clues I grasped and tried frantically to combine into a sense of location, but failed. I'd never been here. Morgan either hadn't shared memories of this place with me, or it was new to him as well.

I could make an educated guess. If Morgan and I

were ever separated and in danger, we'd planned to meet on a desert world called Ettler's Planet. Morgan had promised me a visit there soon, saying only it was better seen in person than shared memory. While what I saw didn't appear attractive in the slightest, I was willing to believe that impression had more to do with sharing Morgan's desperation than anything I was seeing through his eyes.

Minutes missed me. Morgan was now walking, no less upset, but quieter, more resolved. And he was no longer alone.

A voice like rocks rolling in a drum: "Well, at least we know Barac was there. He's the only being I know who'd use a toy like that in battle."

Huido! Morgan was looking ahead, not at his friend, but I could feel his relief. I shared it. "And we both know who'd use short-range artillery," my Human said almost lightly, his voice echoing in my dream. "Someone fired a round in that alley."

A proud-sounding rattle. "I left one of those miniature antitank guns with Ruti—for her protection—"

A feeling of incredulity accompanied Morgan's glance left. I could see Huido, ambling alongside the Human. Some of him, anyway. The Carasian was almost completely encased in fabric, looking more like a walking piece of upholstered furniture than a living thing. Furniture that clanked and muttered under its breath something that sounded like: "Did you try to find the route with the most sand?"

"Protection?" Morgan repeated dryly, ignoring what was probably a running complaint. "She might have killed herself and Barac with that thing."

"Psssahht. I didn't smell any Clan blood." Two eyestalks stretched farther out and craned to stare at Morgan. "But you—" a pause, "you smell—suddenly different."

Could the Carasian sense me? Filled with sudden hope, I stared out the windows of Morgan's eyes and tried to convey a message. *I'm here . . . See me, Sira! Tell Morgan!*

"I'm not surprised." There was a heaviness to Morgan's voice, reflected in his emotions. "I am different—without Sira—"

"Not that." More eyestalks folded in Morgan's direction. "Someting . . . else."

I'm here!!!

I felt Morgan shrug impatiently and look ahead. I could see the tips of starships over the next buildings; they must be heading for the shipcity. "What matters, my brother, is looking after those who need us—and finding Sira. Barac appears to be with Ruti. Until they contact us, all we can do is trust him to look after her. You've got the address where Symon is holding the other fosterlings. Hire help from Ivali—not the *Gamer's Gold*—call in Port Authority. Do whatever it takes to get them out."

"I shall be triumphant!"

A warmth from Morgan. "Just be careful, you lummox. They might not be able to penetrate that braincase of yours, but they still have weapons."

"What will you be doing?"

"Me?" Rage resurfaced until I thought I was looking through a haze. "Whatever it takes to find Sira—

including finding out why our featherheaded friends have been trading with Symon."

More minutes lost. Too many. Huido was abruptly distant; Morgan watched him walk away. Some children—Human-appearing—waved at Morgan before running off to another ship. He turned, and I was looking at an unusually slender starship, her surface dark with age. The *Silver Fox.* The sensation of homecoming was doubled, mine overlapping Morgan's, yet filled with loss. We both felt the emptiness of that home.

Morgan climbed the steep ramp, activating codes, stepping into the air lock and through. If I dreamed this, it was a welcome dream, to walk back inside this ship and breathe metal-flavored air; to brush my fingers along walls that held out vacuum and cradled our plans for the future, our laughter and love. I'd had a grander home; it had been cold and barren by comparison.

I knew exactly where Morgan was taking us—the control room. Once there, he sat on my couch, not his. He looked down, so I must, and began hunting for something along the armrest. I was mystified until I saw the red-gold hair he pulled free, a hair that curled itself around one of his fingers as if alive, forming a ring. I remembered how my hair had caught itself in that armrest, one memorable evening; this must have stayed behind.

My vision dimmed. Morgan blinked and cleared it. It dimmed again, and he stopped blinking, letting the tears fill his eyes and drop as they wished, unmoving.

I threw myself at the barrier between us, hammered

at it with all my Power and will until I felt the threads of the dream begin to unravel. *Morgan.*

I was awake, but I wasn't alone.

The glistening darkness of my new roommate had flattened the Drapsk's table—or the table had retreated into the floor rather than contest its space. I didn't blame it. The Rugheran's fibrous arms seemed more like exposed roots this time, stretching in lumpy irregular lines toward me. None, I was glad to see, were close enough to touch.

I sat up, making no sudden moves as I put my feet on the floor, then rose to stand. I didn't bother wiping the tears from my face, too busy speculating. Was this an ally, an enemy, or a curious visitor? I might have only a moment to find out before the Drapsk noticed they had a new passenger.

"Hello," I said, feeling foolish but determined. I remembered Morgan's advice: establish the desire to communicate—without screaming. It would have helped if I'd understood how a Rugheran talked. Or heard. Or if one even knew how to communicate with words. I'd felt something like thought, musical and strange, when I'd met a Rugheran on Drapskii—but that individual had been near death. This being, and the one on the *Fox*, seemed more in control and hidden from me.

Then, I felt: /*curiosity*/

Memory obediently rolled over, showing its belly. "You—" I breathed, staring at the being. "You were there, or something like you, when I was trapped in the M'hir—when I was trying to . . . hold my mother. I've felt you before."

/joy/satisfaction/~!~/impatience/

It could be a response. Or I could be imagining all of this—something entirely likely. Still. "Can you help me leave this place?"

/impatience/

My emotion or the Rugheran's? I brought the memory of my first encounter with one of these beings—or this one—to the surface of my thoughts, concentrating on the moment when I'd felt its need to be with others of its kind. "I want to leave," I said.

Nothing. It was like talking to a mass of uncooked protoplasm. I walked around the being. It didn't move. It simply sat there . . . or laid . . . or perched. I wasn't sure what to call it. Part of the being seemed to penetrate the deck, as though it wasn't wholly in this space.

I put my hand on the collar around my neck, as I sat back down on the bed. "I really don't want to risk this," I told my silent guest. "But if you can help me—" I *reached* into the M'hir, hoping to touch Rugheran's mind, or equivalent.

The prickly sensation I'd expected was there, but not everywhere. True to their word, the Heerii had left me a way into M'hir, if only part. I opened my awareness of it the tiniest bit more.

A song thrust into me, hot and imperative, dark and impatient. The Singer, too-long denied.

I recoiled from that instant of contact, finding myself safely back inside the *Heerama*.

And alone.

INTERLUDE

Alone. Morgan took a long, shuddering breath. He'd been alone before; it hadn't felt like this. Suddenly, coming back to the *Fox*, it hit him harder than ever: the possibility that Sira might be gone. They'd only had months of what should have been a lifetime. Better that much, he knew, than nothing at all.

Which didn't help ease the emptiness; only finding Sira could accomplish that. Morgan checked the com panel again. He'd left on the automessage to screen out chatter—there was enough of that at any port—but set it to alert him to incoming messages from specific sources. None. Too soon, perhaps. Huido wouldn't be calling until the fosterlings were safely in his care. If anyone could be trusted to take care of a group of telepathic malcontents, it was the Carasian with his total contempt for personal risk and his practical "Why knock? It gives them time to load" approach. Morgan had no worries there.

The Drapsk com-tech of the unnamed ship, reached through Port Authority, had been predictably polite; the Drapsk captain had been predictably unavailable for his call. Could the Captain call him back shortly? Morgan had no choice but to agree, although he doubted the Drapsk would be prompt if he suspected a confrontation. It was a species characteristic to delay unpleasantness, as if complaints would fade away if ignored long enough.

Morgan hoped for something quicker from Ivali or Aleksander, both hunting information about incoming shipments containing a sapient-type stasis chamber. Impatience wasn't likely to help—there were fifty-three ships listed as incoming to Ettler's Planet within the last four days, twenty-seven of those from Plexis—taking advantage of the closeness of their approach. Of that number, several were the sort of trader who offered highly personal service to those moving cargo and passengers they didn't want noticed. Getting details from them would be near to impossible. He'd left a timed message for Bowman, so she could act if all else failed. Her ability to track the finest details never ceased to amaze him.

Having set in motion so many others, Morgan felt useless. There had to be more he could do besides waiting here. Sira was lying in a stasis chamber somewhere in Rosietown. Yet, short of knocking on every door, he knew there was nothing to be done but to try and trace that shipment.

Or was there? Morgan rested his head on the back of the copilot's couch and opened his mind to the M'hir, taking a moment to reframe his thoughts in the terms of how he interpreted that space. The great, unseen but heard ocean, the impression of warm sand beneath his feet, the feel of what was colder or warmer air against his face and hands. Only analogies, he realized, his Human mind rationalizing the utterly strange into something it could interpret. Sira had been surprised by his descriptions, so different from hers. But it was how he interpreted the sensations, however presented, that mattered.

She was the Sun, here. That much Morgan knew. Now, her light and warmth was so dim, it was as if clouds blocked her radiance. The connection between them was still so tenuous he had to remember its direction to be sure it existed. So much for trying to find Sira through the M'hir.

He'd seen M'hir-life on the screens of the Drapsk. Never here, for himself, not that he could believe—unless the distant cries over the surf marked their passage through the M'hir. The surf itself expressed any disturbances—now, it pounded with almost deafening force at Morgan's perceptions, making it a challenge to concentrate. The energy contained in those waves was what he could touch and use—as long as he remembered to keep his feet on the sand.

Morgan withdrew, opening eyes he'd closed for no particular reason but habit. He could, he thought without false modesty, stretch across that surf to reach Barac's mind—or even Rael's, so much farther. An unknowable risk. Symon or his followers might have the technology to detect any use of Power in the M'hir, follow it, and find Barac. Logically, if they had traded with the Drapsk for that technology, the Drapsk had it as well—making it unlikely he could communicate mentally with Rael without letting them know.

There was the com system. Ironic how quickly he'd

come to consider that a secondary option. Another move closer to Clan and further from Human, Morgan thought, a grim smile twisting his lips. He didn't regret anything that helped him better understand Sira, though he remained aware, as always, of the peril of widening the gap between himself and others of his own kind. Humans accepted the alien when it wore a different face—not if it wore a familiar one.

Should he send a message to Rael? Morgan shook his head. There was nothing to gain and perhaps everything to lose if the Drapsk eavesdropped. He stood, planning to head to the galley and grab some C-cubes. He had no appetite, but didn't dare neglect his body when he might need all his strength.

A flash on the console. Incoming call. He was across the small bridge in two strides, punching the button to accept. "Morgan."

"Greetings, Captain Morgan. This is the *Heerama*. The Captain wishes to know if you are well."

The *Heerama*. Morgan's eyes narrowed. He queried the *Fox*. The call was originating locally, within the shipcity. His Drapsk friends were supposed to be on Plexis. They might, he thought, have simply followed him here. He'd filed a destination with Plexis authorities—the sort of bureaucratic information Drapsk were exceptionally good at obtaining. "I am very well, thank you," he said pleasantly. "May I ask what brings you here?"

"Your business, of course, Captain Morgan. The Heerii have made every effort possible to locate the Mystic One and her abductor. We are delighted to say we have met with success. We have obtained the stasis chamber purchased by Hom Symon—"

He gripped the side of the console. "Where is it?" Morgan demanded. "Is Sira inside?"

"The chamber is intact and we have arranged its delivery to your ship. It should have arrived by now—"

Morgan ignored whatever else the Drapsk was saying, running for the lift.

The Drapsk hadn't lied. There was a pallet sitting outside the *Fox*'s hold door, sitting on a servo delivery transport. A too-familiar pallet. His warning hadn't lied, Morgan realized with a groan. He'd walked away from Sira in the street, unaware she was inside—this box!

He couldn't open it out here. Burning with impatience, Morgan keyed his ship's code into the servo, accepting delivery. Then he opened the hold doors and brought out the handling arms to gently lift the pallet into the hold itself.

Only after the hold was sealed shut and Morgan was sure it was safe, did he rush to the pallet and open it.

The pallet—a typical cargo crate shaped to fit the racks of most holds—was dented and scraped along one side, as though dropped a few times. The opening mechanism showed some of the same ill use, but worked smoothly enough. The walls and roof folded back and down with a slight protest, revealing the smooth metal exterior of a stasis chamber. An unusually large one.

Morgan might be in a hurry, but he was also wary. This had all the signs of being too easy. Feeding his natural caution was a simple question: why had the Drapsk delivered this to him? It would have been safer for all concerned, including Sira, to call him over to their ship. The *Heerama* had meds, equipment, expertise. Not to mention it was completely atypical for any Drapsk to give up something they already had, especially the Mystic One. So Morgan unlocked a cabinet in the forward section of the hold and came back to the stasis chamber with two things: a sensor and a force drill.

The sensor was an antique but reliable. It was designed to detect biological pests in the cargo, including those hidden inside sealed containers. Morgan ran it over the sides of the stasis chamber.

One biological entity. Large enough to be Sira. Alive—although the sensor wasn't overly dependable at making that determination. There'd been the case of the mole flies Sira had detected in a shipment of Ummit porcelains. Very dead and odorous mole flies, as she'd discovered upon opening the case.

Sira. Morgan swallowed his excitement and walked around to the back of the stasis chamber, hunting the control mechanism. Ah. Sealed, but that wasn't a problem. He crouched down and began drilling at the lower right corner of the panel. If this was a trap, Morgan reasoned grimly, those setting it would logically expect him to open the chamber from the front, using the keypad beside the door.

Ten minutes later, Morgan had drilled through all four corners, allowing him to pry free the access panel and reach the hardware within the stasis chamber wall.

It wasn't operating. The system was cold and quiet.

Did that make this a trap for him—or for whomever was inside? Morgan knew there couldn't be enough air in the chamber to sustain an adult humanoid for more than an hour at best. Would the Drapsk make that mistake? Or had Symon planned this, to deliver Sira to Morgan, but dead? He was capable of it.

Even as the terrible thought raced through his mind, Morgan was running to the front of the chamber to key the door open, one hand on the blaster still holstered to his thigh. It seemed to take forever to cycle through. Then a whiff of stale, too-warm air marked the door unsealing itself. No stasis fluid poured out. Whoever was inside had to be conscious. Had to be! Morgan forced his fingers into the opening as soon as they'd fit, pulling frantically. "Sira! Sira!"

The door swung wide and the *Fox*'s hold light splashed over a figure lying hunched in the middle of the chamber floor, a figure who looked up at Morgan and laughed. "Jase, my boy. I thought you'd never get me out of here."

"Symon!" Like a being possessed, Morgan was inside the chamber before the word left his lips, his hands clenched around the other Human's throat.

A knee thudded into his stomach as two powerful arms easily broke his grip. *Jase. Jase.* Morgan rolled, then gathered himself before launching himself at his enemy again, forgetting his weapon, forgetting everything but the need to inflict as much damage as possible. *Jase.* His fists pounded Symon's face and body, even as he took blows from the larger Human that threatened to crack ribs. They clenched again, rolling over and over one another until they struck the chamber wall.

Jase. Symon's despised—familiar—mind voice kept slithering into Morgan's thoughts, passing his shields with just the word. He grabbed something that felt like an ear, using it to guide his next punch, hearing the pained grunt as it connected.

It didn't silence the voice. *Jase, we were friends; we were a pair, you and I. Remember?*

A flood of memories, paralyzing, confusing. A sunny day, free for once of fighting. Time to learn more, to investigate the Power of their minds to reach one another, to share the beauty around them. A windswept night, filled with death and despair. The comfort of the one mind able to reach into his, the complete joy of belonging, of being understood.

Jase. I've missed you.

Morgan hammered at the body under him—anything to be rid of that voice in his head—only to be heaved upward and back, landing out in the hold. Before he could stand up, the heavier Human was on him, driving his fists and his thoughts into Morgan until Morgan got one hand under his chin and pressed upward.

They broke free of each other for an instant. Both were on hands and knees, blood dripping from cuts on their faces and spraying out with each gasping breath. Symon spat out a tooth and smiled. "Enjoying yourself?" he asked. *Just like I taught you, Jase,* echoed in Morgan's mind.

Morgan sat up on his haunches, drawing his blaster with one smooth motion when Symon tensed to attack again. "No," he said. "And I can keep you out of my head, mindcrawler." With that, Morgan stiffened his shields, adding the layers Sira had taught him, amazed he'd so let himself slip that this—thing had crawled around his thoughts again.

Symon eased back, carefully, but kept smiling that sickening smile. *Jase, you can't keep me out. It doesn't work that way between old friends. Remember?*

Morgan flinched, then, without thinking, he sent wave after wave of searing pain into that evil mind, remembering the way through Symon's shields as if it had been yesterday—or did Symon let him through? No matter. The pain was as real as any physical assault. Morgan could see the impact in Symon's eyes, feel the agony rebounding like surge of pure energy.

And there need be no end to it. He could destroy Symon's mind, but why bother? He would keep him intact, enjoy this satisfaction, this ecstasy of retribution over and over and over . . . *You're right, Jase,* a dark whisper that almost sounded like his own voice. *Don't stop. Don't ever stop.*

Morgan stopped. Symon fell to the floor, as if the pain had held him upright. His mind voice was almost shrill: *Why? Why?*

"I won't become you," he told Symon calmly, triumphantly.

I need—you must—I—

"No. It's over, Symon."

"Never! By now my followers have killed your friend Huido," Symon said in a thick voice, his eyes filled with hate. "What do you think of that?"

Morgan shook his head. "Your followers are dead or captured."

"I traded your Sira to the Drapsk for their technology—"

"The Drapsk betrayed us both," Morgan replied, wiping the blood from one eyebrow that was blurring his vision. "You've lost, Symon. I'll turn you over to the Enforcers, then I'll find out what the Heerii are up to—"

Symon lurched to his feet like some dying warrior rising for one last charge, swaying back and forth. "I had her to myself, you know. All this time. I touched her. I—" He stopped, not because he didn't have more to say, but because Morgan had pinned him, freezing every voluntary muscle in his body.

Morgan sheathed his blaster and walked up to his old foe, feeling nothing but pity. This rambling, blustering shell couldn't be the Symon of his nightmares. "You did nothing to Sira," he hissed into the other Human's ear, his voice soft and cold. "It doesn't matter that you wanted to . . . that you dreamed of it. You wouldn't have dared." Symon's near eye rolled wildly. "I know you. Too well. It's the helpless and the innocent you pick for your prey, old friend." He made the last word sound like a curse. "And that has to stop."

Morgan summoned his remaining Power even as his hand lifted to Symon's forehead, fingers smearing blood and sweat alike as he sought the point of contact he needed. *There!* His fingers pressed in, even as his Power entered Symon's mind.

Deep. Deeper. Deeper still. Morgan didn't question the impulse. It felt right to be doing this, as if he finally took fate into his own hands. He explored every thought, every memory—searching. Deeper, into thoughts so twisted they threatened him with contamination, like some disease. Morgan fought to keep his own separate, then realized he couldn't. Not now. Not if this was to work.

Their bodies became unimportant as both minds ebbed and flowed around each other. Morgan was aware they'd dropped to their knees, facing one another, that his right hand remained on Symon's forehead, his left now on the bigger Human's shoulder. He wasn't holding Symon pinned, not anymore, and his blaster was a finger's reach from his deadliest enemy. It didn't matter.

This battle could only be won here, within their minds. Everything from the moment they'd met on Karolus had been leading to this, Morgan understood at last, even if Symon didn't. There'd been a reason the other telepath had continued to seek him out, to risk Morgan's rage; a reason Symon had been compelled to chase the one being able to destroy him.

It was hope.

Morgan found what he was looking for: a chasm of darkness within Symon's mind, a source of poison, fed by poison. He studied the malignance for a timeless moment, feeling something of Symon's personality studying it with him. They might have stood, side-by-side, along a cliff to admire the view. Two old friends, two old enemies, in conversation.

You can't stay here, Jase.

I must. This isn't right.

I will drag you into it with me. It will become you. You can't stay here. You are better than I ever was, Jase. Go.

Not alone.

With that, Morgan shut out the voice, focusing on the chasm. Where Ansel's torn mind had needed to be reknit, this needed to be destroyed. No. Filled, he thought, sensing an almost familiar void.

He drew Power from other parts of Symon's mind, pouring it into the chasm. In his imagining, that Power became a raging river, washing away the darkness, smoothing the jagged edges, but the chasm seemed bottomless, taking all and demanding more.

Then more it would have. Morgan gathered his own Power then threw himself into the dark pit.

The absence of sound, of any sensation. Even the M'hir was beyond reach here, had he wanted to use it. Morgan waited, somehow sure this wasn't oblivion.

Slowly, steadily, another presence formed. An unfamiliar, hesitant one. An older—or was it younger?—Symon. A Symon remembering—or was it reliving?—his mind reaching out, sensing those around him. A being of Power, surrounded by—

Madness.

But not his. Others'. They were minds Symon healed, slowly, carefully, with skill Morgan recognized with a shock as like his own. Then, one day, the touch of a mind that was different—a mind that hunted the healer. He was repairing damage done to a purpose, restoring memories sealed to protect an alien secret. That must stop! With its inHuman power, this mind *reached* into Symon's, distorting his healing skill into something else, something obscene. And what had been Ren Symon was sundered in two, half fleeing what he'd been forced to become, half rejoicing in the ability to cause pain.

Not madness. The Clan, meddling with a Human mind, uncaring as to the result as long as they kept their existence hidden and Humans conveniently unwitting hosts. It would have been kinder—and safer—to have killed Ren Symon that day. But the Clan, Morgan knew, prided themselves on subtlety. He felt a wave of grief.

The other presence responded. *Jason? What are you doing here?* Disbelief.

I came for you, Ren.

Fool stunt. Gruff concern.

Only if it doesn't work. You are ready, aren't you?

There was a growing pressure on Morgan's mind. He resisted. *Come with me, Ren.*

I've forgotten the way out. Anxious wonder.

Just follow me, Morgan sent gently, and concentrated.

"Gods, boy, that was a fool stunt."

Morgan smiled to himself. "More sombay?"

Ren nodded, then winced as the motion jarred the wounds on his face. They could both use time in the *Fox's* med cocoon, but that was a luxury Morgan, for one, couldn't afford. On the whole, they'd come out even.

I won.

Morgan tried to raise one eyebrow at this, but it was too swollen. "Let's call it a tie and promise not to go for best two of three, okay? I've a wife who likes my face as it is." The words were light, but with purpose. He studied Ren's face, seeing changes beneath the bruises: age instead of energy, a hint of peace instead of intensity. Pain, but this time good, honest pain that didn't cause pleasure.

"You'll get Sira back," Ren replied. "The Drapsk—I don't now why they wanted her so badly, but it wasn't to harm her. They were angry at me for—" As he hesitated, Morgan began to speak. Ren stopped him with a shake of his head. "It's okay. There's lot in my memory I wish you'd lost for me, Healer, but not that. You were right, you know. I didn't hurt her. I couldn't. Sira . . . when I held her in my arms, sensed her Power, smelled her hair . . ." He smiled despite the split lip. "I'd never imagined anything or anyone so glorious. Even as I was, I could never have harmed her. Can you believe me?"

This was the Ren Symon who'd stepped into the firelight, so long ago, where a young, frightened Jason Morgan had sat, helpless to keep away the violence, grief, and fear in the minds around him, worn by his own grief and loneliness, unable to put a name to what made him different. This was the Ren Symon he'd appeared to be, and now, Morgan thought with a deep sense of rightness, this was the Ren Symon he had been once before.

"I believe you," Morgan said a bit unsteadily. "She has that effect on people."

"We'll get her back."

"Which will require a visit to the *Heerama*."

Symon chuckled, a warm sound that invited Morgan to share a joke. "Just don't drink anything. That was my mistake. One sip and I was in that box." A shadow seemed to fall across his scarred face. "Jason, they might have thought they were offering me to you in trade, or as a delaying tactic. The Drapsk are capable of either. But they could just as well have hoped I'd dispose of you. I'd planned—well, let say many things have changed for the better, shall we? Though not your left hook," this with a pensive, thick-fingered hand probing his jaw.

"I don't get much call for it," Morgan said apologetically, showing Symon his force blades.

"Nasty. I suppose I should be grateful you were mad enough to prefer a more traditional pummeling."

Morgan shrugged, a painful movement. His blue eyes became dark and troubled. "Be grateful I wasn't. It was close, Ren. You know it was."

"Never," Ren Symon assured him. "Believe me, I'd have known. You were never going to be the monster I was, Jason. No matter what I did, no matter what anyone else did. That's why Sira picked you. Not for the Power and tricks—for what you are. What other fool would risk his life—and hers—to heal his worst enemy? Don't shake your head, Jason. I was there and I—I know that's what you did. And I'll never forget it."

Blue eyes met brown in a moment of complete understanding. Then, Morgan stood. "I have to go," he said. "Will you be all right here?" He might have healed the damage the Clan had done to Symon's mind, but at a cost. He could feel the other's weakness, the effort Symon maintained to keep sitting upright. "I still wish you'd go in the med cocoon for a day at least."

"While you have all the fun?" A pause. "Remember what I said and be careful around the featherheads. There's something going on that's too important to them."

"Which is why I've called in reinforcements," Morgan explained with satisfaction. Hard to delay when all he wanted was to rush over and demand Sira's return, but the Drapsk were unlikely to open their ports simply because he asked. "Bowman's *Conciliator* will be finsdown within the hour. The *Makmora* is on her way back. I'm expecting their calls any minute."

"Ah. A man with friends." Another fleeting shadow. Given Symon's past, Morgan decided, there were bound to be many of those. There was nothing Morgan could do about that without erasing those memories—which would erase Symon as well. "Friends who have every right to kill me."

"Friends who will believe me when I say you aren't the same person, Ren. Not anymore."

Symon laughed. "As long as you stand in front of me next time Huido drops by."

The galley com sounded an alert, silencing them both. Morgan gave Symon a wild-eyed look of hope before running out the door and down the corridor. Symon watched him leave, then slowly dropped his face into his hands, shoulders hunched, and began to shake.

"I didn't call you, Rael, because I don't trust your hosts." Morgan had been surprised to find the

Clanswoman the second caller waiting on the *Fox*'s com—not so much because he didn't think she'd find out about Sira, but because he didn't think she'd be inclined to use the technology. "Is Copelup there?"

Her voice was low and exasperated. "Of course he's here. He's the one who was able to arrange this call—after I've been trying to get access to the com for hours. You now what they're like." A sudden urgency. "Morgan—Acranam's sent out her fosterlings—one's been killed already. What's happened to Sira—?"

"Mystic One!" Morgan could just picture Rael's expression at being interrupted by the Drapsk. "It is I who had to contact you. You are insisting the Makii return where the Heerii are in ascendance. Why?"

There was no point in secrecy now, Morgan decided. "The Heerii have kidnapped Sira and are holding her against her will," he countered angrily. "Why?"

There was a confused thumping from the other end. Morgan had an image of Copelup turning into a ball and Rael throwing him against the nearest wall. "Why are you still on the *Fox*?" Rael demanded. "Go and take her away from them!"

"That's the idea, Rael," he said expressionlessly, thinking of the previous message, the one that meant he'd made the wrong choices all along. "There's one problem," Morgan told her. "The *Heerama* left Ettler's Planet, no destination filed. They could be anywhere."

A quiet voice intruded into the shocked silence. "I put a tracker beacon in Sira's flute case."

"Who is that?" Rael asked suspiciously. Morgan looked at Symon, standing in the entrance to the bridge. The other shook his head slowly, a wistful expression on his face.

"An old friend who's been helping out," Morgan told her.

"Such a beacon will tell us how far ahead they are," Copelup's voice quivered with strain—or was it a very uncharacteristic rage? Morgan wondered suddenly. "But I already know where they must be taking the Mystic One. Oh, that Drapsk could be such fools!" almost a wail. "The Heerii have believed the Lie. They—"

Morgan gripped the armrests and leaned forward. "Where?!" he shouted.

Copelup had been reduced to babbling: "To the Dark One. They take Sira as a peace offering to the Dark One. He will consume her and so doing will consume us all. The Heerii are wrong, and Drapskii is doomed; we are all—" An ominous silence.

Rael's voice: "Morgan? Copelup's rolled up. Do you want me to find another Drapsk?"

Morgan felt a comforting hand on his shoulder and braced himself. "See what you can get out of them, Rael," he ordered quietly. "I'll do the same here. The *Makmora* is on her way—they may be more forthcoming about one of their own Tribe.

"Meanwhile," he added, "the *Fox* is going to follow that beacon."

The com light went dead and Morgan looked a question at Symon. The other Human flushed under the strips of medplas, but answered it. "Did you really think I'd trade Sira to the Drapsk without a way to get her back?"

"You'd doublecross a Tribe of Drapsk?"

"Crazy even for me?" Symon lifted his hand from Morgan's shoulder, going to sit on the copilot's couch. "I couldn't stop myself. All that Power," he mused, looking down at his outstretched hands. "I could feel it. I had to have it. The Clan children had the potential—I could sense it in Ruti—but Sira—she was, is, one of a kind. And—" His look promised nothing but the truth, however bleak, "—she was yours. I wanted whatever you had. I wanted you. Jason. I didn't know why, then. Somehow, through all of it, I must have known you were my only chance at salvation." A gruff sound, not quite a laugh. "Listen to me. I sound like a Turrned."

Morgan couldn't speak, so he stood and went over to the panel in front of Symon, rapidly punching out a series of buttons before standing, his hands steepled together, to concentrate. The mindlock responded to his thought, activating the control that flipped the panel and brought up an array of sensors and tracking equipment that should have been removed when the former Patrol ship was transformed into a freighter. Symon grunted approval and came to stand beside him, selecting a frequency.

The panel hummed happily as it displayed an acquired signal. "There she is," Symon told Morgan huskily.

"Then that's where we're going," Morgan replied, eyes locked on the display.

Chapter 21

THE *Heerama* went translight without her Captain or crew informing their passenger—me—where we were going.

I didn't need to be told. Given my recent visitor, it was a safe bet we were heading for the Rugheran homeworld. A short trip, as translight sliced space, from Ettler's Planet. Had we been there? Had my dream of Morgan been possible because he'd been so close? If I wrote this into an entertainment vid, no one would believe it.

I couldn't believe I was still stuck in the *Heerama*'s cargo hold. The stasis chamber at least offered distraction—not that I was inclined to enter the M'hir to be entertained by my seducer. Hammering on the door had only tired my arms, since Drapsk liked a lot of padding—of the soft, pink kind—in their ships. I'd tried tossing the furniture, but it simply sank into the floor to avoid me. A few bouts of primal screaming had provided a moment or two of satisfaction, and a sore throat.

Time, I'd decided, for something sure to attract their attention.

One of the mundane truths of interstellar commerce was that transporting goods required a certain inevitable standardization of technology across species' lines. First, there was the principle that what worked for one species was likely to be what worked for another. So some technologies, such as antigrav units, tended to be common to most spacefarers from the onset. Or they were hot trade items during first contact.

Second, was bureaucracy. Port Authorities loved it. Cross-species safety regulations were simply wonderful things: those who complied made the authorities happy; those who failed to comply paid fines, again creating joy.

The upshot of this was a multitude of technological congruencies, including that every ship's hold— Drapsk, Human, Scat, Whirtle, Ordnexian, Retian, regardless—must have simple manual controls to vent the hold to hard vacuum, in case of emergency. By that, Port Authorities meant the presence of unexpected biological guests in ships entering their particular system. The Drapsk had concealed theirs under more of the soft pink lining to their curved walls, either deliberately or not, but I'd more than enough time on my hands—and motivation—to locate it.

And I could be considered an unexpected biological guest. Feeling quite proud of myself, I activated the venting sequence by the nonspecies' specific and highly practical means of pulling down the lever.

Then, I sat down to wait for my hosts to remember my existence and storm through the door.

After a few minutes, I began to contemplate such unforeseen factors as whether the Drapsk were engaged in *gripstsa* or some other preoccupation which might keep them from immediately noticing their hold was venting its air.

A few minutes after that, I began to calculate how much time I had before such notice became rather critical to my survival.

And shortly after that, breathing more rapidly and feeling a growing chill in what air remained, I developed a pretty good idea of what Morgan would have to say about this terrific plan of mine.

Fortunately, that was when a roar of fresh, warm air came blasting in from newly opened grates overhead and the door opened, revealing a mass of agitated Drapsk, three of whom dashed to the venting controls. The rest came hurrying over to me, touching me with their antennae as if frantic to know I was all right.

Dear, demented, Drapsk. Now that I had their attention, it was up to me to accomplish something by it.

Access to the bridge was a start. I doubted Captain Heeru was gullible enough to completely believe my fervent gratitude for his timely rescue, or that the venting lever had dropped to the "on" position by itself. But he did seem to appreciate that I was going to be more trouble in the hold than roaming around.

I found the *Heerama*'s bridge familiar. If it weren't for the blue-green antennae instead of the purple-pink of the Makii, I'd have sworn I was on the *Makmora*. I supposed duplication was the best approach, since this crew could be Makii after they returned to Drapskii. It would be, if I had any say about it. I wondered, but didn't ask, if the ship's name would be changed.

Heeru had assigned a member of his crew, Heeroki, to be my constant companion. As I'd been told in no uncertain terms to stay on this stool on the upper level of the bridge, and no other Drapsk approached me, Heeroki was my only source of information.

Unfortunately, he seemed in training to become a Skeptic.

"Don't you think it might be helpful if I understood more of what the Heerii need from me?" I asked. It was the latest incarnation of the question and I had little hope for it.

Sure enough, Heeroki—droll even for a Drapsk—sucked a tentacle thoughtfully, for a very long moment, and then said: "No."

I contained my temper, but my hair was never tactful. I could feel it rising and an agitated lock or two whipped the air beside my cheek. "My dear Heeroki," I said as calmly as possible. "Do you know who I am?"

"You are the Mystic One. You are Clan. You are Sira di Sarc and Sira Morgan. You are the life and business partner of Captain Jason Morgan, Human. You are—"

"Fine," I interrupted. "Do you know what I did for Drapskii? Were you there?"

"You helped reconnect Dapskii to the Scented Way," he said, antennae becoming still for the first time, as if Heeroki suddenly paid more attention to me than the Drapsk com traffic flowing overhead. "I was there." Just as I began to feel I'd made progress, his voice turned stern. "You put the Makii in ascendance on Drapskii."

"Everyone seemed to be celebrating, Heerii as well as Makii," I countered. "Why?" Morgan had frequently cautioned me about leaping to misunderstandings about alien cultures. At this point, well beyond potential misunderstanding and probably into its consequences, I required information more than tact.

"Drapskii is all Drapsk," Heeroki stated, as if obvious. "What you did benefitted us all—but it wasn't finished."

"That's why I sent Rael and Barac, the other Mystic Ones, to Drapskii. To complete what I started."

"They arouse Drapskii," he nodded, plumes waving gracefully. One tip tickled my nose, and I forced back a sneeze. "This is essential and we are grateful. But only you can offer completion."

A careful rephrasing. I had no doubt I'd just been told something important, something significant. Unfortunately, one probably had to be Drapsk to understand what it was. Still, I filed the information away. "So you are taking me back to Drapskii," I deduced, feeling better already.

Three tentacles slipped into his mouth. Then a fourth. No reply. I lost a bit of my confidence. "You are taking me to Drapskii, aren't you?"

"You have many questions, Mystic One," Captain Heeru stepped up beside Heeroki. He summoned a stool and sat down. "I don't understand. Why do you not simply seek the pleasure offered and be done?"

I lost patience. "Because, Captain, the pleasure you

speak of—in total ignorance, I might add—will kill me. Do you wish that?"

He raised his small, chubby hands in protest. "Not so! Our friends assure us you will be safe."

"Your friends." I wished I had a tentacle to consult. "The Rugherans."

"Of course. You are to be their long-sought Mystic One."

The Heerii had been the first beings to find the Rugherans. I wondered, abruptly, who had found whom. Had the Rugheran I'd encountered on Drapskii been the Heerii's Contestant—or had it come for reasons of its own? Disturbing thoughts. Morgan had told me a Human fable, about someone who foolishly grabbed what they thought was a small snake, only to find they had the tail of a dangerous predator.

Did the Drapsk know what they held?

"What do you know about the Rugherans, Captain?"

"Simple, yet good-hearted creatures," he replied promptly. "Eager to help Drapskii return to the Scented Way."

Captain Heeru might have been an excellent liar, but he made the mistake of doing so in front of other Drapsk. Something in what he said sent three crewmembers into *eopari*—clear warning.

"Why, Captain?" I asked. "Have you given any thought to that? I'm a suspicious creature—Ossirus only knows how I became that way—and I find myself very curious. These Rugherans are much closer to the Scented Way than your species or even mine. I wouldn't be surprised to learn they exist more in that other space than they do here. So doesn't it seem logical that their interest in Drapskii is based in that other space? What will they gain if Drapskii is reconnected?"

The bridge was completely silent. Then, Heeru and Heeroki turned to face one another, both moving together until they could touch. Their antennae fell over their backs while their tentacles disappeared into each other's mouths . . .

"No!" I protested. "Not now!"

But the two Drapsk weren't listening, well into *gripstsa*. If I opened my awareness to the M'hir, I'd likely feel it. When they were done, I would be dealing with the much less informative Captain Heeroki.

That wasn't all. I looked around the bridge.

Every Drapsk was locked to a partner.

My search for information might be temporarily frustrated, but I wasn't about to waste the opportunity. I went over to the Drapsk com station, easing past the two mutually occupied Drapsk in front of it, and began to hunt for familiar controls. *There*. A sob rose my chest as I keyed in the *Fox*'s ident and waited.

And waited. It shouldn't be taking so long. Then I saw what I should have noticed immediately. Drapsk put indicator lights on pretty well everything— another oddity for a species without obvious eyes. None of those lights were blinking. None of the systems on the bridge were active—or accessible.

It seemed the *Heerama* was waiting for her crew to finish *gripstsa*.

INTERLUDE

Subtle," Bowman pronounced, inspecting the crater that marked Ren Symon's alleged hideout. Former hideout. "Saves a lot of waiting around, negotiating, that sort of thing."

"The children are safe," Terk offered. He wasn't about to approve Huido's methods; he did admire their efficiency. So much less administration.

"There's that," she agreed. "Where's the Carasian— and are we sure this one is Huido Maarmatoo'kk?"

'Whix panted unhappily. "I wish you would accept my resignation, Sector Chief Bowman. It's unconscionable that I would make such a misidentification."

She waved one hand dismissively. "If I lost constables for every mistake, 'Whix, your partner here would be long gone. I know I can rely on you from now on." It wasn't a question. Those assigned to Bowman learned from their mistakes, or found themselves transferred.

The Carasian was waiting for her beside the *Conciliator*'s aircar. Rosietown's Port Authority had been remarkably cooperative, moving to clear the streets and generally keeping out of the way. It had helped, Bowman knew, that Drapsk were involved. The Human majority of Ettler's Planet had reacted with predictable alarm when she'd informed them that there was the potential for inter-Tribe strife to spill over on their world.

Mind you, no one in the Trade Pact had known there was any strife among Drapsk. They were always so—polite.

Few in Rosietown had realized that Drapsk came in any color but blue-green. Now, Makii were everywhere underfoot, those who weren't taking their turn to climb over Huido with small moist sponges, hunting—she'd been told—for grains of sand.

Bowman had seen the Drapsk react to Huido before this, and did her best to ignore the ongoing grooming and patting. "Hom Huido. I'm so pleased to catch up with you at last."

A dozen eyestalks rolled lazily in her direction. "You missed the fun," he said calmly.

"That's probably just as well, don't you think? Besides," Bowman added with a wicked gleam in her eye Terk recognized. "I had my hands full with Plexis security. Really, Huido. First bodies everywhere—then those explosions in the restaurant?"

Every eyestalk shot her way, and the Carasian rose to his feet, dwarfing the smaller Human. Three Drapsk fell off his back, but didn't seem otherwise upset. "What explosions!?"

Terk took a quick step to insert himself in front of his chief. She frowned at the wall of his back and pushed him aside with one finger. "No one was hurt, and the damage was confined to your kitchen and staff quarters. Your apartment walls are unusually robust."

Huido laughed. "My poor nephew. He wasn't too badly scorched, I hope."

"Intact when we left—and intent on watching your place for you. Such," Bowman hesitated, "devotion."

"Exactly. I knew I could count on him!" Huido sank back down. He was reasonably "scorched" himself and close to exhaustion—not that he'd admit it. The Drapsk kept up their fussing over him.

Bowman was quite sure they were also listening to the conversation. Fine. It saved her an extra briefing. "We've contacted Acranam. They refuse to admit the children are theirs. The pair won't talk to any of us— an understandable reaction to what's happened to them at the hands of Humans. Are there any Clan in Rosietown?"

"Barac sud Sarc," Huido said, several of his eyestalks careening about as if expecting the Clansman to magically appear. Not, Bowman thought, a totally unlikely expectation. "He took another of the Acranam fosterlings, a child named Ruti di Bowart, away for safekeeping."

"Good. Let's contact him. I don't want to leave the two youngsters in the hands of Port Authority any longer than necessary."

A claw snap. "We've tried," Huido admitted. "Barac went off in a Drapsk aircar that wasn't modified for humanoid use. Scent-based com system. A small oversight by our friends here." Huido shook his head carapace absently, apparently to dislodge a Drapsk who'd boldly climbed on it. "There isn't one where he went either. But Morgan knows the coordinates. He can go and get them when all this is wrapped up. Where is Morgan, anyway?"

Bowman pursed her lips unhappily. "My next question for you, Hom Huido, was exactly that."

The eyestalks resumed their unnerving focus. "He was waiting on the *Fox* for information about Ren Symon."

Terk came to attention. "Then Symon wasn't in there?" he waved at the smoking ruin across the street.

"Of course not. Symon has another hiding place—one where he has taken Sira. You do know about Sira being kidnapped on Plexis?"

"Yes," Bowman snapped. "Believe me, we're looking into that as well. Plexis has a great deal to explain. But Morgan? He left a message for me, claiming the Heerii had taken Sira offplanet." She never let anything slip without a reason, Terk thought smugly, gazing around at a tableau of now-motionless Makii Drapsk, every antennae oriented toward Bowman, even the ones perched on the Carasian. "The *Fox* lifted shortly before we and the *Makmora* arrived insystem."

"Meaning Symon is still here," Terk said hungrily.

"Does it?" Bowman looked thoughtful.

"We are going to hunt for him, aren't we?" Huido rumbled. 'Whix shifted from foot to foot, expressing his own agreement.

Bowman eyed the Drapsk. "Be my guest," she said casually. "Meanwhile, I'd like to talk to the *Makmora*'s Captain . . ."

She wasn't surprised when the Drapsk who'd been standing nearest to her spoke up: "Captain Makyra at your service, Sector Chief Bowman. However, I don't have much time for conversation. The *Makmora* must return to Drapskii immediately, in case the Heerii succeed."

There couldn't be anything as frustrating as a ball of Drapsk, Rael decided, pacing around Copelup. They'd been left alone in the com room since the Skeptic committed *eopari*. The others refused to move him. The Clanswoman stopped and lifted her foot, then put it down again. Sira had kicked Copelup awake; Rael couldn't bring herself to do it.

Sira. Morgan would find her. Rael had heard the determination in his voice. A relief to know he was so close and an even greater relief, she confessed to herself, that it was only Drapsk involved. They were the most obstinate, annoying, difficult aliens in the universe—but she couldn't believe them a danger. Rael bent down and ran her fingers along the curve of Copelup's back, feeling its soft warmness. Not fur, not quite skin . . .

And suddenly very awake. She jumped back as the Drapsk unrolled, his antennae the last to extend to full height, his mouth wide open and emitting a horrible shriek that turned into a furious series of questions. "AHHHH! Who am I today? What's happened? How is time? Where is this? And who are you!?" he stopped to take a breath.

"Rael di Sarc," Rael told him, knowing this confusion was temporary. "Did I—wake you?"

"Thank goodness! This is no time to contemplate the curvature of the universe. We must . . . we must . . ." three tentacles disappeared for a moment, then shot out violently, "get busy!"

"Doing what?"

Copelup rubbed his hands together, his white globe of a face oriented toward her. "Stopping the Heerii, of course. They are misguided, Mystic One. They have listened to the Enemy and believed its lies."

Rael sank into the nearest chair, bringing her closer to his level. "Copelup. I know you've only just awakened, but you aren't making any sense. Listen to me. Morgan is following the Heerii—he'll settle whatever's happening—"

"I'm making perfect sense," the Drapsk exclaimed. "What happens will be within the Scented Way, not aboard a starship. The Enemy is the same that I told you about—the species that has stopped Drapskii from being reconnected to her rightful place within the Scented Way. The Dark One—the terms are not so melodramatic in our language, you realize, it's this Comspeak muddle—"

"Go on."

"The Dark One is—there's actually no suitable word for him in any of our languages. He exists in the Scented Way. Is he controlled by our Enemy or do they worship him? Do they even know he exists? We don't know those answers. He is like a consequence of their actions in the Scented Way. Or its cause. I'm not sure which—but they occur together. And he's very powerful. Am I clear?"

Rael relaxed her hands. They'd gripped one another until the knuckles were white. "No. I understand, with my head, that there is M'hir-life. I understand—with my head—that this life might somehow affect those of us who live here." She tapped the floor with her toe. "What are you talking about—do you mean there is intelligent life in the M'hir?" Rael shuddered. It would have to be insane, or so alien they could never hope to understand one another.

Copelup shook his head violently. "As far as we've ever found, what life is able to think is like your species, able to exist there and here. But some exist more in the Scented Way. Those are—strange. One is our Enemy, responsible for the exile of Drapskii all those years ago. Others might be allies. The Heerii think they have found such a species—the Rugherans. But the Rugherans are aware of the Enemy's Dark One. They approached the Heerii, found means to communicate. They convinced the Heerii that our approach to reconnecting Drapskii—what Sira, you, and Barac have done—is not enough." He came closer to Rael and patted her knee. "They are wrong. You've begun to succeed beyond our greatest hopes. But the Heerii believe the Dark One requires a more, a more—" He paused and sucked a tentacle. Rael held her breath, hoping Copelup would keep talking long enough for her to grab something reasonable out of it all.

"You realize this is all conjecture," Copelup went on. "We have no physical proof, as Levertup would say. Regardless, the Heerii had wanted our Mystic One—Sira—to be delivered to the Rugherans. They insisted this would be the means to reattach Drapskii to the Scented Way, through some 'union' the Rugherans would arrange between our Mystic One and the Dark

One, and its result. The Heerii are not in ascendance on Drapskii, however, and their idea was dismissed. Really, it was the most utter nonsense, without any scientific backing whatsoever."

"Why did they kidnap Sira, then?"

The knee patting increased in frequency, as if the Skeptic sought to reassure himself as well. "You and Barac were very successful. The *su-gripstsa* in particular was most promising. Many of us feel one or two more efforts could finish what you've begun and Drapskii will be whole again. Perhaps the Heerii's alternative requires Drapskii to remain disconnected until they have tried their approach."

"So they don't want us to succeed?"

His answer confounded her perceptions. "Of course they want us to succeed. We all want Drapskii reconnected to the Scented Way. But it is not uncommon for competing Tribes to try differing methods to resolve a common problem. The Tribe which is successful becomes in ascendance over all others."

"So the Heerii stand to gain if their method works."

"If it works before any other Tribe's." Copelup's antennae drooped. "But they won't. It won't work. And enlisting aid from something we can't understand, like the Dark One? From the Rugherans? I fear the Enemy might be the only one to win if the Heerii go ahead."

Rael trapped Copelup's hands in hers. "You told Morgan this Dark One will consume Sira—what does that mean?"

"We can't be sure—I can't be sure. But my research was one of the reasons we rejected the Heerii's idea. I have found a balance to the energies that move within the Scented Way. There are connections along which this energy flows, nodes where it collects, voids where it is altered into other forms—consumed, if you will. The Heerii's Dark One is said to act like such a void. They proposed a connection to our Mystic One, whose energy spans both this space and the Scented Way— surely such a connection would suck the energy, and probably life, from the Mystic One! As for Drapskii? How could it do other than harm to our world as well? No, the Heerii must be stopped."

"Which means I must help Drapskii. It's becoming dangerous there, Copelup. Things are changing."

His antennae fluttered in alarm. "I would never ask you to risk yourself—"

Glad to finally have a goal, Rael smiled as she stood. "As long as you stand by me, dear Skeptic, I will feel safe. Let's go."

They took the moving walkway to reach the Skeptics' Hall, rather than use any of Rael's strength. Still unsure of the technology, the Clanswoman held Copelup's hand, feeling the breeze of their deceptively slow passage lift her hair. The surface of the walkway was too much like her impression of the M'hir to feel solid, yet too solid to reconcile with her inner knowledge of that other space. The contradiction made her queasy.

But it was fast. In short order, they entered the Hall and made their way up to the chamber where the Drapsk scientists waited with their instruments, bowing as one at her arrival. Rael nodded acknowledgment, then headed straight to the bench to lie down.

"Remember, Mystic One. Use caution. A second effort may be safer than spending too much—"

"I know, Copelup," she said, closing her eyes as she laid down, fired with impatience.

And anticipation. What Rael had seen and experienced last time had been frightening, to be sure, but exhilarating at the same time. Now that she knew to avoid the bolts shooting out from Drapskii, Rael was confident she could protect herself. And Sira.

She was wrong. She knew it the moment she opened her other sense and saw Drapskii waiting for her, its lightning arms grabbing her even as she tried to flee.

The M'hir itself became quicksand, trapping her perceptions of time and space, slowing her reactions. Rael felt the draining as Drapskii stole from her, hardly able to understand what was happening.

The draining extended through her, following a scent, clawing along a link.

Janac!

Suddenly her Chosen was *here*, confused but determined, answering instinct as well as her panicked summons. In turn, Rael fought to reach him, to protect him. They merged. Rael smelled fresh soil and flowers, knew the sun was warm, even as she accepted the power Janac gave her without question and used it to pull free of Drapskii's arms and . . .

. . . for an endless moment she hung suspended in the M'hir, one with her Chosen, feeling his wanting, knowing her own . . .

pain!

Rael nodded thanks in one space, eyes closed, mute.

Her lips formed a name as her mind lingered in that other space, reluctant to leave their Joining.

Words formed in her thoughts, warm with concern: *Are you all right? What was that?*

Janac. More than identification. Rael couldn't help but send her need along their link, sharing her emptiness and feeling his in return. They'd met once, in the Joining Chamber, yet he lived in her dreams. Was it love? She found she didn't care, knowing only that what they had was no longer enough. Barac, unChosen and *sud,* had been right.

Janac's sending became urgent, hopeful, almost desperate: *Has the Council finally given their consent?*

Do you want me to come to you? she asked her Chosen.

Always. Incoherence. Then, with a cold dash of rational thought: *The Council, Rael. Unless we have their permission, we can't—*

Life-changing moments have their clarity, Rael discovered, seeing everything she'd done, everything she believed, coming into focus. *We are Joined, Janac di Paniccia. We are meant to fulfill that destiny, to be one, not be bred at the whim of others. I've no longer patience for the Clan or the Council. This is our life, not theirs.*

Rael . . . a surge of wonder, of sudden determination that matched her own. *I'll be waiting, my Chosen.*

She hadn't expected the extent of his joy. It curved her lips and she sent, softly: *Soon.*

"Mystic One! Mystic One!"

Rael opened her eyes and peered at the ring of Skeptics, wondering which was Copelup. "I couldn't do anything—" she began.

"You must have," one said. "The readings are incredible. Drapskii is rousing—we can all feel it. You've beaten the Heerii!"

A little too late, Rael realized she'd never asked what would happen once Drapskii was reconnected to the M'hir.

It seemed she was in the right place to find out.

Chapter 22

IT seemed the Rugherans, strange and otherworldly
though they might be, still required a place of their
own. And I was invited.

The Heerii had finished *gripstsa*. It had taken a full
hour—an observation I might have found interesting,
under other circumstances. During that time, I'd wandered around the ship, seeing if I could find any way
to help myself, signal Morgan, or cause trouble. Everywhere I went, I found pairs of *gripstsa*-enraptured
Drapsk. I was tempted to play a practical joke or two—
Morgan had taught me a few—but it seemed too
important an occasion.

I'd become thoroughly lost, of course. Drapsk design tended to organic curves, including their ceilings,
which bulged downward, and their rooms, which
bulged outward from the corridors. There weren't features to be counted or used as a guide—that I could
detect, that is. For all I knew, there were signs and
scent trails throughout the place. I'd hoped, after this
hour of walking, to at least find myself back at the

.

bridge or in the cargo hold, being tired enough to look forward to lying down.

Instead, when the Drapsk remembered they were crew on a starship, I was somewhere down in the crew's quarters, investigating what I thought might be the Drapsk version of hammocks—little bags with holes that might fit antennae, suspended in rows from the ceiling. I'd have been more certain had there been any little bodies in the bags. There were hundreds—

"Mystic One?"

I jumped, having grown accustomed to ignoring any Drapsk in my vicinity. "Hello," I said inanely, looking down at the now-attentive creature. "Is this the crew's quarters?"

A politely subdued hoot. "No, Mystic One. This is the escape craft."

I looked back down the long hall, reinterpreting the little bags as crash protection, the curved walls as the inner surface of a pod's hull. "Oh. Have you ever used it?"

"To my knowledge, Mystic One, there has never been a need for a Tribe to evacuate their ship. But it's important to be prepared for any eventuality."

"True enough." I tried to imagine what it would be like in here, with four hundred and fifty Drapsk hanging in their bags from the ceiling, and shook my head. Were they bagged because of that tendency of Drapsk to roll when stressed? Some things, I decided, were better left unknown by aliens.

"Would you show me back to the bridge, please?" I asked.

"Are you sure? We are about to land. You would be more comfortable in your own quarters."

"Land—where?"

A tentacle popped in, and the Drapsk chewed vigorously. Perhaps, so soon after *gripstsa*, they needed to ponder their new roles. It didn't bode well for the species in an emergency. Yet they obviously succeeded. "The Rugherans have a name for their planet," the little being informed me at last. "But I can't imagine how to say it in Comspeak. You could call it—" he thought some more, "—'White.'" He took my hand and tugged me in a direction I presumed led to the cargo hold.

I went along with this remarkably informative Drapsk. "Is it?" I asked.

"Is it what?"

"White?"

He gave another hoot, rather cheerful for a Drapsk whose new role apparently involved being stuck down in the escape craft. "It's much like Drapskii, Mystic One. The Rugherans use terms equivalent to 'White,' or 'Fixed,' when they refer to this—" he slapped his palm against one wall. "They call the Scented Way: 'Normal.'" A series of hoots. "So we call their world 'White.'"

"Makes sense," I murmured.

"Maybe to them. We won't stay long—you'll see. It's not a good place for Drapsk."

The crewmember had said no more than the truth. The *Heerama*'s landing on White signaled a flurry of activity, all intended to get me off their ship as quickly as possible and their ship off White. Within minutes of the ship's arrival—despite vigorous protests and heel-dragging—I was hustled out the main port and down its ramp, clutching my keffle-flute and wearing my hated collar.

With nothing else besides the clothes on my back, not even shoes.

"Captain Heeroki!" I shouted, knowing he had to be among the many Drapsk who'd pushed me down the corridor to the airlock. "You can't leave me like this."

One Drapsk shouted back: "I would move as far from the ship as you can, Mystic One. There will be danger from the *Heerama's* engines."

I was tempted to stay right where I was, but there was something about their air of haste that convinced me the Drapsk wouldn't hesitate to take off even if they fried me. I didn't have to go far, at least. Their state-of-the-art freighter employed an antigrav thrust to push herself upward before ignition of the main engine—technology that allowed the Drapsk to come and go without damaging the landscape on worlds lacking docking tugs.

I lifted my flute case in mock salute to the Heerii, then turned and began jogging away.

So this was White. I hadn't known what to expect from the Rugheran homeworld, so I wasn't surprised to find it an ordinary-enough place. Breathable air, which I'd assumed given the beings had been on Drapskii and in both the *Fox* and *Heerama.*

And on Plexis, I thought, remembering that weight on my back. It could have been a Rugheran's arm.

No buildings or any structures in sight, which wasn't far—the horizon was obscured and everything closer was gray or black. Twilight, though the clouds overhead might be cutting the sunlight or White could orbit a dimmer sun than I'd ever experienced.

The Drapsk could have left me a light, I grumbled to myself. I added shoes to my list of Drapsk-neglect, finding the ground slippery-soft and chill. The air supported a rising mist, fingers of it stroking what might be trees, if I took the lack of leaves as temporary. Otherwise, the landscape was flat and featureless— presumably why the Drapsk chose this otherwise desolate and empty place for their landing.

As if the thought had triggered their launch, there was a shock of sound as the *Heerama* took off behind me. I dropped to the ground, instinctively digging my fingers into what felt like slick mud laced with tough fibrous roots.

Or, I thought, keeping very, very still, what felt like a Rugheran.

At that moment, when I was reasonably convinced things couldn't get worse, an appallingly strong something *pulled* my mind into the M'hir before I could resist . . .

. . . The Singer. More powerful, more potent than ever before. Chords vibrated through me . . . silent trills raced up and down my spine, seeking places where my body answered to such music even as my mind struggled to break free . . . I imagined a discordance, *played* it in my thoughts with all the power in me and . . .

. . . found myself panting and cold, my face pressed

against something that glistened like tiny scales in the retreating light of the *Heerama*'s engines. I lifted my head up, slowly, and looked around—taking advantage of that brightness. Nothing but glistening dark mounds surrounded by fibrous roots, as far as I could see—even where the Drapsks' starship had landed and launched.

This was not going well at all.

INTERLUDE

Things had gone well. Precisely for that reason, Barac was up at the crack of dawn—an hour his body normally found obscene, but it hadn't yet adjusted to local time—so he could survey their surroundings through a pair of mags.

The mags were just a sample of what was in the cupboards and bins below. Morgan had equipped his hole in the ground for a full siege, the Clansman thought, gazing at the magnified image of sand, more sand, and more sand after that. There was food and water—and beer—for months. Not to mention a selection of weaponry that had Huido's stamp all over it. Barac had had no idea Sira's Human possessed such thorough paranoia. It was quite refreshing.

It wasn't quite a hole. There were several of these black, has-been mountains, a chain that forced the dunes to curve around them—for now. Barac stood with one foot propped against an upcropping like a shattered tooth; below, huge, steplike terraces led down to the yellow sand. Behind him was another upcropping. Behind that? Well, Barac thought cheerfully, that was where

someone had shown pure ingenuity. Or insanity. Whatever it took to tunnel out a good-sized home in this
wilderness, complete with indoor shelter for two aircars.

Or one oversized Drapsk aircar, Barac chuckled to
himself, able to laugh about it now. Yesterday, he
thought he was going to have to bury the brute in the
sand. But somehow, he and Ruti had squeezed it
through the doors.

Ruti. Barac let out the finest of seeking thoughts—she
objected fearfully to any use of their Power—and withdrew it once he touched her sleeping mind. Good. She
needed the rest. He'd seen what she'd been through—
far more than anyone so young and inexperienced
should have to face alone. How could Acranam have
possibly imagined its children could survive, tossed into
the galaxy like that? Clan arrogance.

Amazing, really, how well Ruti had coped around
aliens without training. Probably would make a fine
First Scout, if Acranam was ever willing to look beyond
its own orbit. Of course, the continued existence of
scouts was something of a touchy issue, now that the
Clan was a full-fledged member of the Trade Pact and
was thus expected to stop influencing those weaker-
minded for their own gain. Ah, the good old days.

Barac looked at the rising sun, noticing an odd line of
yellow blurring the horizon. Clouds perhaps. If it was a
storm, he'd rather not try his minimal flying skills in
it. The two of them were here for a while longer, anyway.
He pulled the collar of his coat tighter around his neck.
There'd been clothing, Morgan's size and Sira's, to
which he and Ruti had gratefully helped themselves.
Now to wait for Morgan, who would be coming for

them once Symon was no longer a nuisance. Hopefully soon. That was the plan.

Barac found himself uneasy. Everything was going unusually well. In his experience, that wasn't a good sign.

Ruti buried her head under the sheets, unwilling to admit to being awake. The kitchen smells hadn't penetrated her room yet anyway. Kitchen? The events of the past days came back in a rush. She opened her eyes to stare at an unfamiliar ceiling, carved from black stone, a tiny portlight still obediently glowing in the upper corner where Barac had set it. In case, he'd said, she awoke in the night.

People who had been awake yesterday morning were dead today.

Barac had talked to her last night about those who'd died: the Humans he'd killed, as well as the life she'd ended. Not too much, but enough to reassure Ruti that what she felt was normal and right. Death wasn't to be taken lightly, even that of enemies. But she ached inside about Ansel. Automatically, Ruti reached for the comfort of her mother.

Nothing.

She stifled a yawn and tried to relax. This had happened before. She reached again, really trying this time, confident of success.

Nothing.

It had to be all this rock overhead. Ruti shrugged away her concern and climbed out of the bed, giving a little gasp of surprise as her toes found the cold stone floor instead of the rug nearby.

She liked knowing this was Morgan's house. His strength was here, in the stone and design; something of his kindness, too, in the soft blankets and well-stocked kitchen. There were vids and readers. Barac had told her there were other supplies—this was a fortress as well as a retreat—but Ruti did her best to forget all that.

It was easy here. Outside, the desert was quiet, except for a faint, steady susurration as the ever-present breeze rolled sand grains up the dunes to tumble down the leading edges. And she'd never seen a sky stretched overhead like a bowl in three directions, so full of stars you could almost see the yellow of the sand by their light. Inside? There were the paintings, above all else.

Ruti had never seen a home like this, where every surface had been used for art. Barac had said Morgan painted his ship as well, the *Silver Fox*. Some rooms were landscapes; others like being inside a burrow; most glowed with plant life. This was, Ruti decided, like being on a well-deserved holiday.

She couldn't fault her companion either, with the exception of his presumption in so abruptly scanning her thoughts in the aircar. They hadn't compared their Powers yet, and she hadn't any time to prepare herself. Her mind must have seemed disorganized and foolish. Still, Barac had apologized. If she were honest, Ruti knew it had been easier than trying to find words.

Otherwise, Barac sud Sarc had proven to be resourceful, understanding, and entertaining. It had been too long since she'd been around other Clan—not that Acranam had many with Barac's practiced charm. Ruti brushed her hair, feeling herself blush. He wouldn't be paying her so much attention if they were on Acranam, where there were older, more worldly Clan to talk to, individuals of Power and poise. Not to mention the Choosers, who always claimed center stage from everyone else.

Unless Council had moved them offworld already, she thought suddenly, trying to calculate the date. It had been the talk of Caraat Town, the new Council dictate to protect the unChosen. As if any of Acranam's Choosers would harm those they'd grown up with—no wonder, Ruti thought, pressing the brush in firmly enough to hurt, First Chosen di Caraat had insisted the fosterlings be sent in secret. How dare the Clan Council send Acranam an ultimatum! Even if Ruti's mother had told her Acranam would obey it, that it meant a wider range of Candidates for their Choosers. For Choice.

Ruti put down the brush, surprised to be a little breathless. She reached for her mother again, but was distracted by the sound of: "Breakfast!"

The rest had done her good, Barac thought, studying Ruti's face where it showed beneath the mags. There was some color to her cheeks, a rose-pink under that fine skin. It suited her.

"What do you see?" he asked.

She put down the mags and grinned up at him. "Sand. Huido would hate this place."

"And would make life miserable for anyone who had to be here with him," Barac agreed wholeheartedly. "What about that bank of cloud?" He pointed to the eastern horizon. The sun was well up, and blazing hot, but didn't seem to penetrate the ominous line of yellow-gray.

"I think you're right. It's moving toward us. It must be a storm." She sounded excited. "Will it rain?"

"Here? I doubt it. Probably a sandstorm." Barac, who preferred weather that behaved, felt a momentary alarm. Then he thought of the shelter behind them and relaxed. "I'm sure Morgan's house can withstand whatever it is."

Ruti fell silent, staring outward. Barac leaned on the outcropping, wondering what she was thinking. A dark curl of hair blew into her eyes, and he reached absently to brush it behind her tiny ear, his fingers lingering. She didn't move, but glanced sideways through her long lashes, a startled look.

Barac drew his hand away, startled himself. "Maybe we should head inside," he said quickly. "The wind is picking up already."

"I'll be right there," Ruti said. "I want to— I'll be just a minute more."

The Clansman nodded and left her. He'd walked around the concealing rock and was approaching the door when a surge of Power through the M'hir stopped him in his tracks. As he hesitated, unsure if Ruti meant him to detect it, he felt her sudden despair. Something wasn't right. Barac hurried back.

Ruti was leaning on the rock. Her eyes were troubled as she looked up at him. "Nothing," she gasped. "I can't reach her."

Things had indeed gone too well, Barac realized, his mouth drier than the desert air alone explained. "You can't reach your mother," he said, without any doubt at all, bitterly aware of the irony of his being here, now , instead of anyone else.

"No—I—" her eyes widened until he could drown in them. "What does it mean?"

Barac took a step back and swept her a low, graceful bow. "Congratulations, Ruti di Bowart," he said bitterly. "You are now a Chooser."

She'd 'ported to her room in the house. The threat of Symon and more violence was nothing compared to the look on Barac's face when he'd bowed. He hadn't been happy for her. He'd been sad and angry, as if this was all her fault, as if she'd done it on purpose, as if she'd wanted to lose her link to her mother and . . . and . . .

And want something to replace it. Must have something to replace it. Ruti stood in the middle of the room and lifted her right hand, suddenly understanding the only reason Barac would have reacted as he had.

He was unChosen.

She threw herself from her room and down the hall that stretched from the living area to the artificial cavern holding the aircar. "Barac!"

Where was he? Not in the kitchen or his room. She ran outside, growing more and more anxious. He wasn't there. But the sandstorm was. Ruti stopped, horrified by the oncoming wall of yellow. Already, the ledge where she stood was being scoured by the sand-heavy wind.

She rushed into the house and down the hall to the cavern. He was there, leaning into the Drapsk aircar, but straightened and turned to face her as she burst through the doorway. Ruti made herself stand still. "You aren't leaving—" she protested.

"How can I stay?" Barac said harshly. The M'hir heaved between them and Ruti winced. He saw and tightened his shields, tried to soften his voice. "Ruti. It won't be long now—you must know that. You must already feel it. I—" his voice lowered, and his eyes seemed burn into hers. "I do."

"The sandstorm's about to hit—and you don't know how to fly this thing. Not well enough for the wind," she added, in case the truth offended his pride.

"Ruti—" Her name sounded different from his mouth, as if it had another meaning now.

"Stay, Barac. Please. I won't hurt you. I promise."

"It's not something you can promise—"

Ruti fought back tears. She wasn't a child anymore; Barac had said so. That didn't make it easier. "You don't need to leave," she told him. "Don't leave me alone here. Everyone's left me—" she gulped. "I've lost the link before and got it back. How can you be sure I'm a Chooser already? And—even if I am, it might take a few more days. My friend Olea said—" She heard herself babbling and closed her mouth on the words.

Barac sighed and leaned back against the aircar, arms folded, eyes now hooded and inscrutable. "Ruti, do you now know what I am?"

"You're—you're unChosen." The word left a taste in her mouth, sweet and rich.

"I'm *sud*."

"Oh."

"Oh," he repeated, but gently. "I'm sorry to leave you. You've no idea how much I don't want to—but that tells me you are closer than you realize to Choice. A Choice I—a *sud*—can't survive, Ruti *di* Bowart. Is that what you want?"

Ruti wanted him to stay. She didn't care about anything else. "You can put me into stasis," she offered. "Knock me unconscious—"

Barac shook his head as he stood away from the aircar and went to the cavern doors. "It takes a healer to impose stasis, which I'm not," he said over one shoulder. "As for knocking you unconscious? That's hardly safe, is it? You'll be fine, Ruti. Wait here and I'll send help." A pause as he began to slide open the first door. "What the—!"

There wasn't a world outside. That was Ruti's first impression of the seething, moving darkness that had replaced the sky and rock ledge. Then she was choking in dust and sand, hearing Barac struggling to close the door again. Somehow, she found her way to him, lent her strength to shut out the storm.

They leaned against the door, side by side, panting and covered in sand. Ruti was shocked by Barac's low chuckle. "Glad Huido missed that."

Ruti couldn't laugh or smile, suddenly appalled by what she'd done. Her selfishness had delayed him—and now trapped him here, with her—against Barac's surely better judgment. She shouldn't have trusted her desire to have him stay. She'd thought it was because of her own fear.

But what if it was something else? What if it was what he feared from her?

"I'll be in my room," she said, feeling strangled. Not looking at Barac, not thinking about him, above all, not *wanting* him—Ruti made herself walk away.

The angry howl of wind and sand penetrated the stone walls. Not as sound, but as a vibration Barac could feel when he pressed his hands against the doorframe. A way out, he told himself.

As if he'd survive ten minutes outside.

He might not survive much longer inside. Barac leaned his forehead against the door, eyes closed. Ruti was trying. He could feel her effort to keep to herself, to contain the Power-of-Choice. How could she? It was so new to her, so strange.

It felt old to him, this game of his kind. Old and tragic. Barac had grown beyond simply wanting completion. He'd felt that with Drapskii—and knew there had to be more to a Joining. He envied Sira the happiness she'd found with her Chosen. He'd dared dream of such a thing for himself. Until today, when there was no way out.

The saddest thing of all was that he was half in love with Ruti already. More than half, he decided, knowing what it cost her to stay away so long—when it was all he could do to stay here. She was extraordinary.

Barac measured the rest of his life in breaths. Two more. Ten. Then, a footfall behind him. The whisper of cloth. She'd come.

Barac drew in one last quick breath and turned, choosing his most charming smile as his final expression. That smile died on his face. "No!" he cried, lunging forward.

Ruti stood before him, but her right hand wasn't outstretched in an invitation to her Choice. It held Huido's weapon, and she was pointing it at herself.

Chapter 23

IF I could have pointed to any one decision in the past few days—or weeks, since I still had no accurate accounting of the time I'd spent in stasis—as being responsible for my being here, it was probably the one that had me think it was safe to follow Ren Symon and his companion through Plexis alone. That was probably it, I thought, critically. Although the moment I'd first met the Drapsk had brought a certain inevitable complication to my life I could have done without.

/joy/satisfaction/~!~/joy/

"The same to you, I'm sure," I told the landscape from my perch. I'd made myself walk over Rugherans until I reached one of the trees, then climbed as high as I could before it started bending over. The trees weren't leafless, as I'd thought. The stems were covered with tiny, rolled-up tendrils. Perhaps it was spring on this part of White. "You know, a very similar thing happened to me on Ret 7," I continued. "Well, that tree had fallen to the ground already, but the basic principle of being abandoned in a hostile, alien environment was about the same. I seriously considered not climbing this tree, just to avoid the irony."

/attention/

"I'm glad," I said. "I'd hate to think I've been talking for hours without anyone listening."

I was, of course, not convinced anyone but myself was—but the sound of my own voice, however hoarse, was better than the alternative. White wasn't quiet. Once the roar from the *Heerama* had died away, I'd been able to hear it. Once I'd heard it, I was up the tree.

Imagine a sucking sound, steady, unchanging, as if the entire planet was an anxious Drapsk with a mouthful of tentacles. Worse, it came from below ground, beneath where I'd laid, as if the carpet of Rugherans was somehow sucking the life out of the planet itself.

Morgan would have laughed at me, I knew, and suggested the sound might be the result of some normal bodily function such as digestion or the Rugherans were singing to one another. He had the ability to look beyond the grotesque to the marvelous.

I didn't see much that was marvelous. Not to mention the ominous approach of sunset didn't help improve my opinion of White. Bad enough when I could see my surroundings.

"The Heerii talked to you," I said in nice, loud Comspeak. "At least, they implied they could."

/attention/curiosity/~meaning?~/impatience/

I wedged myself up a little straighter, daring to be encouraged by what might be a response. I did my best to sort out what I was feeling from the creatures, trying to compose something meaningful in return. First contact. Morgan, I thought with vast self-pity, would love to be here, doing this, while I was getting a stitch in my side from my deathgrip on a branch. "Why am I here?" I asked.

/attention/curiosity/~knownquantity~/impatience/

"'Known quantity,'" I repeated, elated. Definite progress. The Rugheran communicating with me, if it was one and not some communal effort, was reaching me through the M'hir—despite the Heerii's collar. I regretfully put aside the idea of trying to ask the Rugherans to remove it. It was far too complicated a concept for either of us. It also gave me an unnerving vision of a fibrous arm removing my head to achieve its goal. "What do you want from me?"

/curiosity/

It didn't understand. "What do you want with Drapskii?" I asked, for no particular reason.

That, the entire population understood. I hung onto the tree for my life as waves of disturbance crisscrossed the landscape, fibrous arms lashing in the air like so many whips. A blast of /attention/impatience/ ~notright~/responsibility/ coursed through my mind, then subsided.

"'Not right.'" I picked out, once my heart settled down again. "Something about Drapskii isn't right?"

/attention/acquiescence/ The landscape returned to dark and lumpy, with the occasional pulsation—as though some stayed unhappy longer than the rest.

Whatever my dear Drapsk had done, it had seriously upset this species. I could sympathize. The Drapsk—or their planet? A year ago, I would have thought the concept laughably bizarre. Now, having seen that Drapskii had a presence within the M'hir, a presence closer to life than any rock should be, I was prepared to keep an open mind.

"What do you want?"

/attention/impatience/~restore~/responsibility/

At this rate, I estimated, easing a cramp in my hip, I should have a clear, comprehensible answer to why I was up in this tree by the time I was a skeleton hanging from it. Still, I'd been right, in a sense. The Rugherans weren't helping the Heerii or the Drapsk, no matter what interpretation those self-centered optimists had put on their communications. The Rugherans had their own plans or needs—which seemed to involve the Drapsk's planet.

I hazarded a guess. "Do you want Drapskii?"

Another upsetting concept, given their reaction. When the arms stopped flailing, /attention/~permanencechangepermanence~/responsibility/

This wasn't helpful at all. Or was it? I'd been thinking like a Trader, like a Human. It supplied valuable insights, but I did have other ways to look at this, ways that might be closer to other M'hir dwellers. To a Clan, I reasoned, there was only one true change in life: between the seemingly permanent link between mother and offspring, to the truly permanent one between partners, forged during Choice and Joining.

The Rugherans and Drapskii?

Change. I drummed my fingers on the branch, certain I was close to some truth—or at least less confusion. Drapskii had changed years ago. The Drapsk referred to that event as when they'd lost the "magic" they desperately needed to somehow interact with the Scented Way. What if the Rugherans had lost something of their own at the same time, for the same reason?

Could both species actually want the same thing? To restore Drapskii?

If true, no wonder the Heerii had been willing, even eager, to risk holding me prisoner and bring me here. They might have believed they were supplying a Mystic One for the Rugherans, someone those beings could use to finish reconnecting their world for them. I could understand how that might seem quite reasonable to a Drapsk, if no one else.

Which didn't explain the Singer.

I surveyed what could be millions of Rugherans, given the entire planet was coated in the beings, unsure how to ask. Instead, I shouted: "Why me?"

/attention/curiosity/~causality~/responsibility/

Causality? There was more than the word. With each burst, I was getting an underlying sensation— less than language, more than emotion. A *push* to urge my thoughts down a necessary path, I decided. This time . . . I licked my lips, an odd memory come to mind, as if the Rugherans had taken me to it: I'd fought for my life in the M'hir long ago; a struggle I'd won by killing—damaging—something else.

Could it have been Drapskii? Was it why the Makii had picked me—not another Clan—as their Mystic One? Or was it simply that any passage through the M'hir was etched there, unforgettable and unforgiven, waiting to draw the traveler back? I'd read the work of a Clan philosopher who'd claimed our movements through the M'hir changed its nature, drew places closer together, inevitably reunited those who'd met in the past.

Had I done that to the Rugherans and the Drapsk?

"Did I cause the damage?" I asked desperately. "The 'notright'?"

/attention/confusion/

Perhaps this wasn't what mattered. But what did? "Why am I here? Why are you doing this? Why?" I shut my mouth to hold in what was becoming fear, not communication. The emotional load might have helped, because the next burst from the Rugheran was longer and more intense.

/attention/determination/~vulnerabilityconflict~/ impatience/

Then, it seemed they were finished talking to me, at least for the moment. I tried a few more times without success before resting my voice. Meanwhile, the sky continued to dim, chilling the air. The mist settled and fell, coating the Rugherans with a fine sheen. Perhaps that was how they drank, I thought, skimming droplets from the thinner branches with my fingers to put into my mouth. I rolled my ankles to keep checking there was something at the end of my legs, and tried to think.

However alien, the Rugherans weren't strangers. I'd sensed them before—when I'd 'ported to Camos and battled the M'hir to survive. The Singer? His first touch had come when I'd lost my mother's, even if I hadn't understood what I was feeling until my own desire for Choice became aroused. That need could have summoned him, without my ever realizing it.

Was the Singer a Rugheran?

No. It wasn't because part of me loathed the very idea, having seen and felt too much of the species already. I had a better reason. The Rugherans might be difficult to understand, but they had minds I could detect in the M'hir; what I called the Singer had a presence, but had never offered signs of discernible thought. It was as if I reacted to him, rather than interacted—like an instrument being played, not one musician meeting another. I was aware my mind clothed the unknown in safely familiar imagery, that music did not exist in the M'hir. But what I described did.

And thinking about it was dangerous.

I must have dozed, somehow, because I didn't hear the song right away. It woke me, gradually, as if whispered in my ear.

Even when I opened my eyes, I didn't realize what I was hearing at first, too startled by what I saw all around me. For it was no longer dark—every Rugheran fluoresced with a cold white glow. Bright dots were scattered over their bodies, but not at random. I could see the distinction between individuals by the whorls along their outer edges. Spirals and other shapes competed within, too complex to be sure if every decorated lump was an individual Rugheran, or if the pattern somehow repeated. I wasn't sure, after a moment, if the patterns stayed the same or were slowly changing.

There were species that communicated using visual cues. I sincerely hoped this wasn't the case with the Rugherans, having enough trouble with the burst of concept-laden emotions they sent into the M'hir as it was.

Then, I heard it. The Singer, faint but growing

stronger as I paid attention; impossible to ignore once I had. Somehow, he was reaching out to me, now, even though I was deliberately keeping myself from his portion of the M'hir. Were the Rugherans responsible?

"Make him stop!" I shouted.

/attention/determination/~nowurgentsubmit~/responsi-bility/

From not understanding one another, it seemed we'd leaped to a little too much comprehension. "Stop," I begged, part of me beginning to echo the song, straining to enter the M'hir, to answer the seduction. "It will kill me!"

/attention/~necessityregret~/determination/

My tree shuddered. I grabbed hold and looked down, horrified to see arms, trailing drips of fluorescence, wrapping around its base. As I stared, they began to pull.

INTERLUDE

"Pull or push?"

Morgan, wedged half inside the *Fox*'s translight drive, grunted something rude. He'd had other words when the *Fox* had plunged into normal space, malfunction alarms screaming and every console flaring red. "Pass me that spanner," he called out, stretching his hand out for the tool. Symon supplied it. "Thanks. I'd prefer a push from this engine," he replied grimly.

"How's it looking?"

"I won't know until . . . Wait. I don't believe this." Morgan fell silent, staring at what used to be the sequencer—the critical unit responsible for keeping all of the *Fox* within the null-zone during translight, not just the engine. The remnants of wire and plas showed how something else had been wrapped around it, something that had effectively chewed its way through an irreplaceable part.

The perfect way to stop the *Fox* without harming her crew. Morgan shoved his way back out, tossing the useless spanner into the box, and got to his feet.

"What is it? What's wrong?"

"The Drapsk." Morgan kept his face expressionless, but his voice shook with fury. "The *Fox* was in for repairs at Kimmcle when the Heerii showed up and oh-so-helpfully took over the drydock. Now I know why. Sequencer's fried." He made a quick gesture of negation with one hand. "All I can do is get on the com and see who can meet us here fastest. Bowman might be ready to lift."

"Bowman." Ren Symon's jaw worked, tightened. "I imagine the Enforcers will be interested to find me here." He spoke mildly enough.

"There's no need for them to know," Morgan replied. Blue eyes met brown, the blue determined. "It would just complicate things. I have to get to Sira."

Symon looked as though he wanted to argue, but settled for waving Morgan ahead. "Then go.

"The *Conciliator*'s on her way." Morgan announced, joining Symon in the galley. "Now we wait." He sat, trying to look at ease, but his every muscle was as taut as a bowstring.

The older Human raised one scarred brow: "Bowman launched just like that?"

"She was already enroute," Morgan said, taking the cup Symon offered and staring into it. "The Captain of the *Makmora*—that's Makii Drapsk—told her where we were going. A planet called White. The Rugheran homeworld." As he spoke, Morgan remembered that black glistening shape filling the corridor, his apprehension, and Sira's fear.

"How? We didn't even know and we've been following a tracker."

"The Heerii knew. They've been happily sending the information to every Drapsk, along with instructions to head for home. Something monumental is to happen on their planet—soon. And Sira is at the heart of it. The Heerii claim she'll be unharmed, but they've left her there—on that planet—with the Rugherans." Morgan couldn't stop his hand from crushing the cup, spilling hot liquid over the table. He *pushed* the mess into the recycler.

"How did you—" Symon stared at the space where the cup had been, looking amazed then thoughtful. "Jason—you have their ability to move through space?"

"No," Morgan said with deceptive calm. "I can do tricks." He looked at the half-filled cup in front of Symon, then *pushed* it into the M'hir.

Before Symon could do more than gasp, the cup reappeared, exactly where it had been. The other Human touched it with one finger, then picked it up and drank.

"See?" Morgan sneered. "Useless." He slammed his fist down on the table.

His companion frowned. "It seems useful to me."

"Does it? It can't take me to Sira. It can't bring her to me. It can't even fix the damn ship—" Morgan stopped midsentence, the strangest look on his face. "Pull or push."

"Pardon?"

"You said it. We need a way to move the *Fox*." Morgan made himself examine the idea from all sides, carefully but quickly. Time was not on their side—not with the Drapsk fleeing for Drapskii and whatever they intended for Sira. He made up his mind. "I want you to get off the ship. Take one of the life pods, Ren." he stated, getting to his feet, already gathering his Power.

Symon stood as well, close enough Morgan had to look up to meet his eyes. They were both still covered in medplas and bruises—their faces mirror images of yesterday's battle. "And I want you to tell me what's going on in that head of yours. Or should I look for myself?" only half-joking.

Morgan took a deep breath. "Size isn't what matters, not to 'porting something through the M'hir. The cup, the *Fox*. It's all the same. As long as I can know an object, keep my mind focused on it, I can move it."

"You aren't seriously—"

"Yes. You saw for yourself—the tracker signal has settled into an orbit. Sira must be on the Rugheran planet. It isn't far—not through the M'hir, not by what I've seen Sira accomplish. Distance there is all about subjective time. It takes Power to hold your mind together for long—that's the risk. But I have my Power—I have hers, too." Morgan seemed to be talking to himself as much as to Symon. "If I know where I'm going—if I have the strength? It's possible, Ren. I feel it."

"Why the hurry, Jason?" Symon objected. His big hands took Morgan's shoulders. "From what you've told me—from what I know—the Drapsk would never harm Sira. Why not wait for Bowman?"

Morgan hesitated, unsure how much the other Human would understand. "I can't wait. I know Sira's in danger. It isn't something I'm sensing through our link—what's left of it. It isn't a premonition or anything I've been told. But I know it, Ren, as surely as I know I can't abandon her." His eyes darkened. "I will get to Sira or die trying."

Symon gazed down at him for a moment, then said simply: "Then we'd better not stand here talking about it. And don't ask me to leave, Jason. Because I won't abandon you, either."

Morgan knew there was nothing in Sira's teaching or shared memories to help him. The Clan had apparently never considered moving their surroundings as well as themselves—perhaps another aspect of their disdain for technology. For all his confident words to Symon, he'd never moved anything larger than a pallet in the hold. He did have what Sira called a Talent for discrimination—an ability to *know* an object once seen, to identify it with his inner sense. It had been of great service in removing certain items, such as boots from slender feet.

Morgan *knew* his ship; that wasn't a problem. But he didn't know how much Power he had on his own in the M'hir, without his full link to Sira. And he didn't *know* where she was yet.

"A heart-search?" Symon repeated curiously. They'd gone to the bridge for no other reason than Morgan felt more confident there. Now, they each sat in an upcurled couch—Morgan in Sira's, Ren Symon in his—and prepared to do what had never been done before. It was, Morgan decided, either a stroke of genius or something neither he, Symon, nor Sira would survive. But he hadn't exaggerated. His fear for her was turning his blood cold, as if he shared something with her on another level than thought or Joining.

"I need to know where to 'port the ship," Morgan explained. "I can't visualize where Sira is—I've never been to White, and there's nothing in the ship's database. So I have to try and use Sira herself as the locate." He paused. "You're sure you don't want to take your chances in the pod?"

"And explain my reformation from evil to Bowman by myself? I'd rather have you scatter my molecules."

The tone was light, the meaning anything but. Morgan looked at Symon. "You could insist on a deep scan . . . truth drugs, if necessary. Bowman's hard but she's fair, Ren—"

"Don't, Jason," Symon said gently, his face weary yet peaceful. "I was a Healer before I was a psychopath. I know exactly what's on the plate for me. I deserve all of it and more. I'm grateful," he said, reaching across the distance between them to grip Morgan's arm, hard, then release it. "You made it possible for me to come out the other side, my friend, which includes facing what I've done. Let me worry about how I atone for it."

"Ren—" the words Morgan wanted to say seemed to bottle up inside him.

The older Human smiled. "Find your Sira. We'll talk later."

Morgan nodded, once. Heart-search. The technique to identify and locate another mind that could only be performed by those who knew each other emotionally as well as mentally. Soul-deep, Sira had called it. Morgan closed his eyes; forming the image of Sira was as easy as that. He poured Power into the memory of her smile, the feel of her hair against his throat, her scent, the sound of her voice, and felt the heart-search snap away from him to splash against a prickly, unyielding surface.

But she was inside. Good enough. Before he could lose it, he focused on that surface. *Here!*

Holding that place in his mind, uncaring if this feeling was enough of a locate for a 'port or if he was sending them all to die in the M'hir, Morgan concentrated on the *Silver Fox* and *pushed* . . .

This wasn't like walking on a beach. Surf crashed over his head, as though a tidal wave roared through the M'hir and tried to crush him. Morgan held his breath, fearing to drown. His image of Sira, his hold on the *Fox* were like strokes pulling him through the flood, powerful at first.

Yet each came harder than the one before, as if each stroke weakened him. Before he could falter, Morgan sought outward, tapping into the warm strangeness that marked the Power he now owned in this place. It responded, exploding through him, lifting him through the wave. Almost . . . almost . . .

The infusion of strength was gone. Morgan refused to give up, even as he felt his lungs screaming for air, felt his own life ebbing away . . . just a bit more . . . despair, as he knew he was sinking, his holds slipping away . . . Sira . . .

A second flare of energy struck him, painful and raw, as if he burned inside. Morgan didn't question its source. He added it to his own and *pushed* harder . . .

. . . opening his eyes to find himself in the copilot's

seat, the lights on the consoles blinking with the most peculiar normality, as though the *Silver Fox* journeyed through the M'hir every day. He rolled his head to one side. Symon was gone.

Morgan tried to get up, and found his hand trapped in a tight grip. Shocked, he looked down even as the other's fingers loosened and fell away. "Ren?"

Symon was lying on the floor, head thrown back, eyes half-closed and leaking tears of blood. His breathing was ragged and caught as Morgan dropped to his knees beside him. Then another breath and, "Are we there yet?"

Mogan glanced up at the panel. The tracker signal was steady and green. He sagged with relief. "We made it," he said unsteadily. "What were you thinking, Ren?"

"So that was the M'hir, huh?" Symon's eyes opened a little more, red and swollen as if burst from inside. Sightless. "Can't say I was impressed—" he coughed.

"What did you do?" Morgan demanded, his voice hoarse. "Why?"

"Why? Owed you. Owed Sira. And you know what I did, Jason, better than anyone else. It's what I did— to others. Seemed only fair to try it on myself, don't you think?"

With a sick certainty, Morgan did know. Symon had enjoyed killing this way, draining every particle of mental energy from a being, stealing what sustained life itself. The final energy that had brought them through the M'hir had been the theft of his own.

This was the price.

He held his hands above Symon, trying to summon

some remnant of his Power, then clenched his fingers into fists when nothing happened. "Hang on, Ren—" Morgan pleaded desperately. "Hang on, Ren. I'll get my strength back. I can help you—"

"You've already done everything I needed. Jason. Jason." Ren's voice faded. His head turned from side to side as though searching for Morgan's face.

Morgan rested his fingers on Symon's forehead, doing his utmost to will away the pain, unable to do anything about his own grief. "I'm here."

Stronger. "We did it, didn't we? Showed those Clan."

"Yes. But . . ."

"We showed them—but that has to be the end of it, Jason. You can't do it again. You can't tell anyone. Promise me. Any—" Symon coughed and spat blood, clearing his voice. "We both know what people will do to get what they want, Jason. This? Gods, if this gets out?" Another cough, the voice quieter, more strained. Morgan leaned closer. "Are you willing to trade the stars—your freedom and hers—for some hole in the ground? Because that's what it will take to hide from them. You promise me."

"I promise."

"Go. Save your Sira. Make this worthwhile."

"I will—"

"Go." Symon went so still Morgan reached for a pulse. He found it, then lost it just as words formed in Morgan's mind, ghostly faint, the voice as familiar as his own:

Stay as Human as you can, Jason, for everyone's sake.
And forgive me.

Chapter 24

I could forgive the Heerii. They'd only wanted to help their own kind. I could even forgive the Rugherans, since I had no real idea what they wanted.

But my imagination had definitely gone well beyond forgiveness. I stared at the side of the *Silver Fox*, close enough to touch, and knew I'd gone mad at last. It had just popped into existence, crushing a line of small trees, and stood there as impossible as . . .

As impossible as hope. My body swarmed with song, pounding, irresistible. The Rugherans pulled at my tree, swinging me back and forth. Perhaps I'd conjured up the *Fox* to as the ultimate distraction, so I could end this existence with thoughts of my . . .

The base of my tree disappeared in a gout of blaster fire, with the immediate consequence of my dropping to the ground through a spray of rapidly cooling ash. Rugherans collected their arms—seemingly none the worse for the blast—and moved back, leaving me lying sore and breathless on what I felt like a pile of rock. The Singer withdrew as well.

It had the feel of a very temporary reprieve.

Not that I cared at the moment, being too busy fending off an assault of another sort. Something or someone with hands was running them over my arms and legs as if I was unconscious, aggravating every tree-cramped muscle and new bruise I owned. "Stop that!" I snapped, wondering why this invisible someone hadn't thought to bring a light. My eyes burned with the aftermath of the blast.

As if I'd said something completely different, the invisible someone made an incoherent noise before pulling me into an embrace so tight I could hardly breathe.

This was too much. I'd had more than enough of strange beings trying to intrude where only my Chosen was permitted. I squirmed and shoved my way free, hauling the keffle-flute case out of my shirt and doing my utmost to hit whomever this was somewhere painful.

Strong hands caught and held my flailing arms. The case dropped and I heard a rather desperate voice say: "Gods, Sira! It's me!"

Morgan? I went still, unsure. The voice was familiar. But I couldn't imagine having him touch me and not knowing it inside, where it mattered.

He must have felt something of my distress. His grip eased, but didn't fall away. "I'll get a light. "Please, Sira. It's me. Jason."

My hair believed what I couldn't. It flowed over my shoulders and down my arms to reach his hands, seeming to paralyze us both with the possibility of truth. My eyes began to adapt to the Rugherans' glow and I puzzled out his silhouette against it. "I don't sense you," I whispered numbly.

The collar.

"Get the light," I urged him, already hearing the Singer returning. "The Heerii put something around my neck to lock me from the M'hir—from you. You have to get it off before the Singer comes back."

It must be my Human, for he didn't ask or delay, simply rose and fired his blaster along the side of the *Fox*. The resulting glow of heated metal reflected from the Rugherans surrounding us. I saw what should be Morgan look around, the realization of our situation dawning on his face. It wasn't him and it was. My Power strained to know the truth; I feared it would find the Singer first. "Hurry!" I cried, putting my hands under the collar to lift it toward him

He went to his knees in front of me, the light from the *Fox* catching the impossible blue of his eyes as they met mine, then dropped to the collar. "Hold still," he said. I felt the metal moving around my neck as he sought the opening.

"It takes a code to open it," I said, trying to be helpful.

What should be Morgan nodded grimly at our surroundings—and company. "No time," he replied. He altered a setting on his blaster, then picked up a piece of broken twig—hooking that under the necklace to pull it away from my skin.

Before I could do more than shout, "What do you—" he fired the weapon.

I found out later the heat had scorched my neck and cheek, though my hair pulled itself out of danger.

Later . . . because in that instant all I truly knew or cared was that Morgan, my Chosen, had reappeared in my mind as well as my arms.

There was no time for celebration either, after that one soul-deep embrace. I opened my thoughts to show Morgan what had happened with the Heerii and the Rugherans, what I knew of Drapskii. But when it came to sharing the Singer, I didn't so much falter as I felt shame.

Don't, he sent, with an undercurrent of understanding—and a hint of wicked amusement. I might have been starving, so rich was the feel of Morgan's sending in my mind. His amusement I would deal with later. *Know this,* he sent in return, wisely avoiding any further comment on my own experiences, and passing along what he knew about the Drapsk.

First things first. I gathered my Power, relishing the freedom to do so, and restored what I could of Morgan's. His Human strength was resilient, but even it had been tasked too severely to recover quickly enough. For once, he didn't argue about the gift, probably sensing I was in no mood to be refused.

Guard me, my Chosen. Without further delay, I drove my thoughts outward, reaching and finding Rael.

Heart-kin!

What's happening? I replied after the briefest possible reassurance.

Here! Her thoughts opened, clear and triumphant.

"Morgan!" I took his hand as I cut my connection to Rael, promising to come to her as soon as possible.

"It's Drapskii. Rael and Barac finished reconnecting it to the M'hir." I smiled with relief. "It's over."

/attention/impatience/~disagreement~/determination/

I glared at the Rugherans.

"They don't agree," Morgan said unnecessarily. "And I thought you told me the Singer was still here."

"This is their business, not ours." I tried to pull him toward the *Fox*. He wouldn't budge. I didn't need the faint glow of the waiting aliens to know that stubborn look was on my Human's face. "I can keep the Singer away," I assured him. "I have always."

"Have you?" No amusement this time.

/attention/curiosity/~!~/impatience/

"Of course I have. And as long as I don't play—" The words died in my throat as Morgan bent to retrieve my keffle-flute case. He opened it and took out the instrument. Its high polish picked up the Rugherans' fluorescence, producing tiny sparks. "What are you doing, Morgan?" I demanded.

/attention/satisfaction/~urgentcomplysubmit~/responsibility/

"What happens if she does?" Morgan asked almost idly.

Morgan! I sent, furious.

He winced, but shrugged. "It's worth asking."

/attention/joy/~survivalsuccesshomecoming~/joy/~!~/gratitude/

"Who comes home?"

/attention/anger/~trappedprisonersconfined~/determination/

Unlike me, Morgan seemed to have no trouble following the Rugherans' bursts of thought and emotion, turning this into some bizarre conversation. "Where are they now?"

/attention/anger/~trappedprisonersconfined~/determination/

"Why?"

The glow brightened, moved, as if the Rugherans heaved and pulsed like the M'hir when disturbed. The patterns on their bodies, I suddenly realized, reminded me of how I saw that other space.

/attention/sorrow/~invaders~/determination/

"The Drapsk?" I asked involuntarily, unsure who'd answer. "They weren't native to Drapskii. Did they move into Rugheran territory without realizing it? Was Drapskii yours before?"

/attention/acquiescence/~urgentcomplysubmit~/impatience/

Morgan ran his fingers along my unburned cheek. "I think I understand, Lady Witch."

"I'm glad someone does," I said ominously, sensing Morgan in full plotting mode.

"These fine beings want their colony—for lack of a better word—returned. Drapskii. Maybe it has resources they need, or stranded Rugherans living there. Or it's what you'd call property in the M'hir. The Drapsk want their access to the Scented Way through Drapskii restored—access, I believe, the Rugherans have tried to block in an attempt to get back what they consider theirs."

I'd have questioned his fast and furious interpretation if it hadn't been for the immediate burst of /attention/gratification/~!~/determination/ that followed it.

"The Singer?" I asked instead.

"Breaking the siege."

I loved my Human with all my being, but he was occasionally as difficult to comprehend as any other alien. "What?"

"Think about it. Drapskii has been a point of contention between these species—if not more—for years. You've told me Drapskii is itself alive and aware on some level. What if it's been held virtually under siege by the conflict? Doesn't it make sense that Drapskii would have tried to break free by forging a new connection?"

Nothing about this made sense, I thought, longing for the days when the Clan had believed themselves alone in the M'hir. "A new connection. With me. You think Drapskii is the Singer?"

"And has good taste." Definite amusement now, under the seriousness.

" 'He' being a rock." I wasn't sure why the notion that my so-alluring seducer was nonsentient offended me, but it did.

"The Rugherans seem to want the Singer to succeed, as if that will resolve their problem with Drapskii as well."

I didn't like where this was going. "What are you suggesting?"

"We are Traders, my Lady Witch." Morgan raised his voice, as if to make sure as many Rugherans heard him as possible. I didn't think volume mattered, but then again, I'd been the one shouting myself hoarse from a tree most of the night. "Drapskii wants its freedom. So do you. Promise to restore the Drapsks' access to the Scented Way and Sira will help you."

I will not! If Morgan hadn't strengthened his shields—with Power I'd given him—my outraged sending would have knocked hm to the ground.

Trust me!

"It's not about trust, Jason!" I stepped back from him, breathing heavily. "I am your Chosen. No other—pairings—are acceptable. I cannot offer myself to another—even like this—without losing myself. I'll die. You'll die. For what? To stop a war we can't see? It's impossible."

I felt his smile. "I've done the impossible today," the Human said calmly. "Hear me out. Of course I don't mean you to somehow submit to some creature—I'd kill it first." His voice carried utter conviction, conviction I could sense along our link. "You've shown me how Drapskii has been pursuing you—trying to use you—to fulfill its need. What if we can show it another possibility, guide it to another connection? There must be others like it. Perhaps closer than we realize."

/attention/acquiescence/joy/~!~/impatience/

I gazed over the dark humps and hollows, their shapes picked out in whorls and spirals of white. We could have been standing on some ocean, surrounded by shy creatures called up from the depths by night, reflecting the stars with their own soft light. Or stood in the midst of the M'hir as others of my kind would know it.

I spoke my thoughts aloud, courtesy, since we weren't alone. "Is it possible, Jason? Do other worlds have their mirror existence—do they seek one another, do they feel? Can they?" As I paused, I could hear the sucking sound again, low and strange, and imagined it the planet itself breathing, alive. I felt on the verge of grasping something large about the universe, something that might tie together the clues I'd be given, the hints from the Drapsk, from my life, from the Singer.

Before the moment faded—and common sense returned—I held out my hand for the flute. At the same time, I opened my awareness of the M'hir: first, to bring Morgan's glow close to mine, feeling his love and courage wrapping around me like a wall of protection; second, to seek the Rugherans in that other place. I *pushed* deeper, even as I lifted my flute to my lips, ready and waiting . . .

. . . I reveled in Power, finally free to go where I willed, as I willed. It wasn't the mobility of those around me, those others. Shaped like birds of uttermost darkness, they cavorted through the energy-soaked M'hir as if it were air, wheeling and diving in every direction while I clung to one place for safety, held to Morgan's mind as a lifeline, and poured Power into my knowledge of self, so I could leave this place once done. They viewed me as the intruder, the stranger, the unfit. Not unwelcome, but pitied.

Part of me was amused, understanding I had the Power to scatter these things like a predator among a shimmering school of smaller life. Part of me looked beyond, sought what gathered the Rugherans to this one place.

There. Morgan shared my astonishment as it appeared—as if summoned by my interest—a massive spherelike shape, like power coiled around itself. Massive, or was it infinitesimal? Size had no counterparts here. But this was White, the planet of the Rugherans.

I didn't doubt it. Arms, like theirs, reached out from the coil—arms of energy. They appeared to be feeling for something lost. Or desired.

Now, Sira. Morgan's voice, somehow here, with me.

In both spaces, I began to play—for Jason Morgan, not the Singer. The music started in the keffle-flute, drawn from my depths, my needs. It surged into Morgan, then back to me, then filled us both . . . passion and promise . . . need and completion.

It rippled outward, tumbling Rugherans midflight, as if a storm blew through the M'hir from my unseen lips, brightening the coil of their world, summoning the Singer. In an instant, he was there, demanding, desperate.

I stopped playing, Morgan so close we might have been one, the two of us as small a presence in the M'hir as I could manage and still be there. White blazed in front of us, echoing my music.

The Singer turned, lunged forward—scattering Rugherans who spun around and formed their own cloud around what began as two, then became one. The M'hir pulsed with dangerous, exhilarating darkness. Before it drew us as well, I *pushed* free . . .

. . . and found myself in my Chosen's arms, his eager lips searching for mine. Perhaps something of the music lingered in us both, or our desire was as ordinary as the joy of being one again.

Neither of us cared. For this moment, on our island in a sea of rejoicing Rugherans, what we wanted was each other.

And there was no reason to resist.

INTERLUDE

No! Ruti heard Barac in her mind. She closed her eyes and tried to block him out. This was the only way, she told herself. She wouldn't, couldn't . . .

As she tightened her finger, the weapon was knocked from her hand. "No!" he said in a terrible voice. "No, Ruti," softer, so softly she had to look at him.

Barac's face was so near her own. There was something wild in his eyes.

"I don't want to hurt you," she tried to say, but the Power-of-Choice robbed her of the ability to form words. She managed one: "Run!"

"I'm finished running," he said with a small smile. He took her right hand in his—as if accepting her Choice—but she felt his left hand slip along her neck and into her hair, as if to cradle her head. "And I admit to a certain curiosity, Chooser. I hope you will indulge me, since I doubt I'll have another chance."

Ruti didn't understand, until Barac's face came closer still. When she would have pulled back, his hand behind her head held her. She felt his lips touch hers, ever so softly. A kiss? The surprise of it made her heart pound even heavier.

And her hand clenched around his as the Power-of-Choice whirled them both into the M'hir . . .

She was glory and completion. She was everything and all things to be desired. Barac strained to reach the Chooser.

She thrust him back, her Power driving against his. *how dare he believe himself worthy!* Barac felt himself pushed farther and farther away and poured himself into somehow holding fast, knowing he'd passed the point of survival. Even if he could, to stop now was to die. UnChosen.

Worse—to die without Ruti. Writhing in the M'hir, shot through with pain and despair, on the edge of dissolving . . . Barac found himself suddenly reliving the sweet coolness of her mouth, the desperation in her eyes . . . reliving the feel of Drapskii, that wonderful moment of almost completion, the sense of Power flowing between himself and that other. Power he'd given—Power he'd received—Power that suddenly existed around him in the M'hir. He drew from it, making one more effort, knowing it was his last and . . .

. . . reached her. The Power-of-Choice that had tried to destroy him filled them both, forming a link, strong and sure, a link that drew Barac from the M'hir . . .

Finding himself holding Ruti in his arms. His—he could hardly form the word until he saw the wonder of it reflected in the glowing eyes and warm smile of his Chosen.

*　　*　　*

It wasn't easy to knock on a door made from stone, but Huido took it as a personal challenge. Not to mention he was determined to get inside shelter before any more sand insinuated its grit between his eyestalks. "Barac!"

Terk stood well back. Bowman hadn't exactly offered him a choice in this assignment. They'd been able to convince the Makii to trace their aircar before the Drapsk had lifted from Ettler's Planet. Once the sandstorm had settled, there remained the question of how best to get an unhappy Carasian into one of the *Conciliator*'s aircars. Terk was still sure it would have been easier to ram Huido into one of the cargo sleds and tow him. As yet another round of blows chipped the stone, Terk rubbed his left shoulder in sympathy. They'd compromised in order to fit inside the cabin—a compromise which included having that claw resting on Terk's shoulder most of the trip. There would be, he decided glumly, bruises.

"Ah!"

The door opened and all of Huido's eyestalks riveted forward. "What wonderful *grist!*" he roared incomprehensibly, surging inside before Terk could see who'd let them in. He'd hoped to find Symon here.

Obviously not. He sheathed his weapon and followed the Carasian.

"Constable Terk? Welcome! Welcome!"

The Enforcer blinked. He'd met Barac sud Sarc on several occasions. In none had the Clansman seemed, well, giddy. Not to mention rumpled. The Carasian was clanking happily to himself, already into a cupboard. "Are you all right?" Terk growled. "Where's the child?"

Barac had a charming smile at the best of times. Now, it was almost luminescent. Terk felt the corners of his own mouth trying to respond and shut down the impulse. They'd hurried out here to save these two from Symon and the elements. He wasn't the least impressed that Barac didn't seem to need saving.

"Hello."

Terk started, never happy to be surprised by Clan. This one appeared out of thin air in front of him, nodding her greeting, then rushed over to Huido. "Ruti di Bowart," Barac said with what sounded like possessive pride.

Not exactly the helpless child Terk had envisioned. Young, sure enough—the curves of adulthood only suggestions—but this Ruti looked back at him with an adult's assessment. Her dark thick hair was waist-long and gleaming. It also moved by itself in that alarming Clan way, locks sliding over the Carasian's carapace like silk over glass.

"And I would like to introduce you to my Chosen," she said just as proudly. "Barac di Bowart."

Huido snapped both claws, carefully, but making a ringing sound. "Congratulations to you both! Ah, there's nothing like the joys of your own pool, if I do say so myself. Where's the beer, dear Ruti—"

"Forget the beer." Terk glared at Barac. "I thought she was a fosterling—a child!"

Barac smiled even wider, if possible. "So did I! Isn't it wonderful?"

Before Terk could mire himself deeper in misunderstanding, the Carasian took pity on him. "Terk, Terk, Terk," he said, putting a claw over the Human's non-bruised shoulder and drawing him aside. Terk couldn't have refused without help from a servo or two. The effort at privacy was wasted, if that's what it was, Huido's voice being at its normal, robust volume. "I do believe your parental instincts have been offended, haven't they, Terk? How Human. Surely you know that Clan females do not mature physically until they have found and bonded with a suitable life partner. A very sensible physiology. So you see this is perfectly normal. Now be glad for the pair, or we'll find out how you like walking back to Rosietown."

"It's my aircar," Terk growled.

"I will be going home for the rest of my Commencement," Ruti offered with a blush. "Now that the storm is over. It's traditional to be with one's family." Barac's adoring eyes never left her. She seemed to feel his gaze, glancing at him every few seconds, her own eyes bold and sparkling.

"Congratulations," Terk grunted, pulled free of the Carasian's brotherly embrace. He didn't understand the Clan, but he did recognize the joy and preoccupation of these two with one another. Fine, as long as it didn't interfere with work. "But we're looking for Ren Symon."

A little less joy in their faces. "He hasn't been here," Barac informed him. "What's happened? Has there been any word from Sira?"

"More reason for beer," Huido rumbled contentedly. Ruti passed him a bottle and he poured the contents into his handling claw, then inserted it between his eyestalks with a slurp of delight. "Thank you, my dear. Cuts the sand, it does. Sira and Morgan are fine. He made it to the Rugheran homeworld just before the *Fox* broke down. Kimmcle can't be trusted. I don't know how many times I've told him." Another slurp. "Apparently they are now on Drapskii." The Carasian shuddered. "Better them than me, all this leaping through space. It's not good for the pool."

Barac and Ruti exchanged another look that left no doubt as to their opinion of matters.

Terk coughed. "So, we'd better get going—"

"Going?" Both Clan said the word with identical dismay.

Huido finished his beer. "What my fine friend Terk meant was that he and I must get going. Sector Chief Bowman will want his report, while I am long overdue at home. Our apologies for disturbing you. Is there anyone we need to—notify about the happy event?"

They both blushed. "No," Barac said. "It wasn't secret—the Watchers attend every Joining. They'll have informed the Clan Council. We'd just like to keep—"

"—to ourselves, a little while longer." This from Ruti, when Barac seemed to have lost the ability to speak. She smiled up at him fondly.

Terk shifted, apparently uncomfortable with so much happiness in one room. "Then we'll be off," he said. "I don't want to find out Symon has left Ettler's while we've been standing around."

"Excellent," Huido said, grabbing another bottle of beer. "And Terk—I really do think you should sit in the back this trip. I was quite crowded on the way here."

Huido hustled the now-speechless Human out the door, then sent three eyestalks to gaze back at Ruti and Barac.

"Make her an omelette," he suggested slyly. "The smart ones get hungry."

Chapter 24

THE M'hir seemed almost asleep, like a hungry beast that had eaten its fill. I had no difficulty 'porting Morgan and myself to Rael for our show-down with the Drapsk.

I did, however, have difficulty understanding what was going on once we arrived. "Where's Copelup?" I asked my sister as I extricated myself from her embrace, gently but urgently.

"More to the point—where are the Drapsk?" Morgan said, coming from the window. "I don't see anyone moving outside."

"Maybe we sent them all into the Scented Way," I suggested, only half-joking. We'd made an immense change in the M'hir without knowing the possible consequences. Morgan didn't mind tossing dice, but I did. I was anxious to do two things: find the Drapsk.

And then make sure the Heerii understood exactly how I felt about being their "guest."

Finding the Drapsk wasn't just to salve my formless worry that I'd done something dreadful to the creatures. The Rugherans were more than pleased with their end of the trade Morgan had arranged—it remained to be seen how the Drapsk viewed the result. Not to mention, Morgan and I didn't want the Drapsk to do anything to upset things again.

They were remarkably good at that.

"They left me in here hours ago," Rael said. "It was very confusing—except for the part where they insisted I wasn't to be near them. I thought I'd better wait."

I looked at Morgan. He shrugged. "I tried the com. No one's answering. I suggest we start looking."

"For Drapsk." I heaved a huge sigh. "Explain to me, husband, why I devote so much energy and time to these annoying creatures."

His eyes sparkled. "Because you like them. And you are Makii, are you not?"

Makii or not, I had no special insights into where we might find the missing beings. We could have split up in our search, but I had no intention of leaving Morgan and Rael, it turned out, wasn't about to leave me.

"It was—unpleasant—while you were out of touch," was all she said, but her eyes had filled with tears.

Incredible as it seemed, the three of us went hunting for Drapsk. To start our search, Rael 'ported us to the Skeptics' Hall, where she and Barac—and I— had contacted Drapskii. Her use of Power would have gained us attention, had there been any to notice. Once there, we were disturbed to find every machine turned off, as though no longer needed. Furniture had been retracted into the floor, curtains drawn, and nothing had been left lying on countertops and tables.

I'd never realized tidiness could be so alarming.

"It looks as though they were prepared," Morgan offered thoughtfully.

"For what?" Rael demanded. "Do you have any idea what's gone on?"

Morgan raised one eyebrow at me and I nodded. *Here,* I sent to my sister, and gave her my memories of what had occurred on White. Well, those memories she'd need to understand as much as we did; the rest I kept to myself.

"The Heerii," she said with disgust. "I never liked them."

"I didn't know you liked any of them," I commented.

Rael's face, always transparent, colored at the cheeks. "There are some individuals of the species worthy of interest," she admitted. "When they aren't being obstinate—or hiding." This last with more worry than exasperation.

"I suggest we look elsewhere," Morgan said, waving us toward the door. I started to follow, only to notice Rael hesitating. "What is it?" my Human asked.

I need to talk to you, Sister.

"Why don't you go ahead, Jason?" I suggested. "We'll catch up in a moment." Beneath the words, I sent reassurance and he nodded.

When Morgan was gone, from sight if not my thoughts, Rael sighed. "My apologies, First Chosen," she said with unexpected formality. "It's just that I can't wait any longer. I've made a decision—after what Barac said to me and what's happened here—a decision I believe you have a right to know as Speaker for the Council." Then she stopped.

And I blinked, trying and failing to imagine where this somewhat confusing beginning might lead. Unless. "Do you know about Barac?" I asked. A Watcher had told me of his Joining—as others would have told the rest of the Council. A cold, flat voice to deliver news of such joy. It was now up to the House of di Bowart to make the announcement to those they felt needed to know, although I'd planned to tell Rael.

Rael turned bright red and the M'hir flared with what I was surprised to feel as embarrassment. "He's told you what happened?"

"His Joining?"

"Oh!" she actually gasped. "It wasn't that. He pulled free in time, believe me, Sira. Even an unChosen would understand the feeling wasn't real—that it was a dangerous mockery of—"

"What are you talking about?" I demanded. "Barac joined with Ruti di Bowart—one of the fosterlings Acranam sent out. Turned out she was closer to Choice than the fools had anticipated." If Barac had died as a result—I stopped the thought where it was, unwilling to contemplate such a loss, knowing I could have done nothing to avenge it except try to protect the next unChosen.

I sensed Rael thinking rapidly, and politely kept my distance from her mind. I had enough confusion within my own thoughts. Then the M'hir between us calmed, almost miraculously. "My mistake, Sira," Rael said lightly. "This is wonderful news. I'd begun to wonder if our poor cousin would ever be Chosen. And to succeed with a *di?* How extraordinary." Her face darkened. "Do you know about the other fosterlings?"

I nodded, letting my grief meet hers. "The others are safe," I told her, having assured myself of that before coming to Drapskii. I hoped the loss of Nylis would be a lesson—for the Council and, hopefully, for the House of sud Annk and Acranam. There were too few of us—far too few children—to risk any. There would be cries for revenge, but I would prevent any attempt to retaliate against the Scats. The inability to understand other species that had led to putting a Clan child on a shipful of aliens terrified of any telepath? Our kind wouldn't survive such ignorance— here was tragic proof.

I hoped the disappearance of the Drapsk wasn't going to be more. "Rael, we'd better keep looking," I told her.

"Wait." I felt desperation in the M'hir, and Rael's hair began to writhe over her shoulders—something more typical of my locks than her usually well-behaved ones. "I am going to Janac," she asserted firmly, but with a suspicious brightness to her eyes. "To my Chosen. Without the permission of your Council, Speaker."

Rebellion from a most unexpected source. I grinned with delight. "You think I'm going to argue?"

Rael looked shocked, then, shyly smiled back. I opened my arms and my sister rushed into them. *I didn't know you wanted to go to him, Rael,* I sent. *But I highly recommend the experience.* This shocked her again, but not quite as much.

Then we both received Morgan's sending: *I think I've found them.*

The bowlcars had been the clue we'd missed. We hadn't seen any on the walkways, moving or still. Morgan still hadn't found them, but from the balcony of this building he'd spotted several of the larger Drapsk transports, parked and empty, at the base of the Drapsks' immense amphitheater. The amphitheater where I'd won their Contest to become a Mystic One.

Rael and I joined Morgan, then I took both their hands and concentrated, not without a shrug to the fates . . .

. . . the instant we materialized on the floor of the amphitheater, Rael gave a squeak, then subsided. I knew why. We had indeed found the Drapsk.

In fact, every row, of the hundreds upon hundreds of rows, were packed with Drapsk, clustered by Tribe so the whole looked like a mammoth mosaic, displaying a pattern the eye tried in vain to interpret.

And every Drapsk was silent, antennae pointing down at us.

"Sira," Morgan said very quietly.

Not at us, I realized as I turned. There , in a flower-petal-filled bowl easily as wide as the *Fox*'s cargo hold, sat a Skeptic. Behind that bowl was another, and another, until I counted twenty-four filling most of the floor of the amphitheater. There were, I'd been told, twenty-four Skeptics.

Meaning one of these was Copelup.

I didn't plan to ask which, since the Skeptics were very busy.

"Well, that answers a few questions," Morgan breathed in my ear. He sounded quite enthralled.

So was I. Each small Skeptic was, well, shedding even tinier Drapsk. The bowls were already half full of the little things: no more than balls with clear antennae to mark the end that presumably would become the head. They bounced and moved about on even smaller arms and legs.

"I don't know how you always get me into these things," Rael said, but with amusement.

I opened my awareness to the M'hir, slightly, careful not to disturb it. *Lar-gripstsa*, where Drapsk Tribes interacted. This was similar, but far more. There were connections between every Drapsk at this moment, mirrored by the lines of force that formed Drapskii in the M'hir. All focused on the Skeptics.

I withdrew and looked at Morgan. He'd seen it too, and nodded. "We never asked about the Skeptics," he noted ruefully. "And they were the key all along."

"Which one is Copelup?"

I shrugged. "I don't think it matters at the moment," I told Rael. But somehow I wasn't surprised to see the Skeptic two bowls to our right wave a greeting even as he/she gave birth to another hundred dear little Drapsk.

The clues, as Morgan told me later, had been there. The Drapsk hadn't been secretive—they'd just been alien. When the Blessed Event was over, the Makii had been quite surprised by our confusion.

Gripstsa. The changing of roles. Surely, they said, we'd realized that certain Drapsk would eventually perform *gripstsa* with enough others to know every-thing necessary within a Tribe. Such individuals would also—eventually—do *lar-gripstsa* with enough other Tribes to be everything. Who else could produce the next generation of Drapsk? It required access to the Scented Way, within which all might join the *su-gripstsa*. What could be confusing about that?

The problem, for the Drapsk, had been their re-liance on Drapskii for *su-gripstsa*. Each time they'd used it, for a new generation, their linkages had pulled some of Drapskii from the Rugherans. The Rugherans had reacted by sealing more of Drapskii away from the Drapsk. The Drapsk, believing they were under attack by some enemy, had developed technology to try and control the Scented Way. The meddling by both species had driven Drapskii into its search for completion elsewhere. Me.

"So you see, Mystic One, why we will always be grateful," Makyra, Captain of the *Makmora*, told me as we sat to supper in Rael's apartment. She'd packed her things and sent them to the shipcity before the meal. I understood completely.

"You will be more careful in the future," Morgan said sternly. "The Heerii made some serious mistakes. The technology to control movement in the M'hir mustn't be sold." My Human carefully didn't look at me, knowing I wasn't at all pleased that the Heerii Tribe was now in ascendance on Drapskii.

The Drapsk themselves had given up trying to explain to me why the Heerii deserved their new prominence—especially since I'd tried to insist they be punished instead. Apparently to the Drapsk, success was a matter of when, not how. The Heerii had been the Tribe to finish the task of saving Drapskii—with a little help from us—which meant they were the Tribe to be congratulated. That didn't mean non-Drapsk, such as Rael or me, had to enjoy the result. It also, I'd shared with Morgan, meant it was probably important to add abundant fine print to all dealings with any one Tribe.

"Oh, yes. I'll make sure." This new, yet familiar voice in the debate made us turn around. A Heerii Drapsk was coming in the door, moving with unusual determination. "Have no concern about the Heerii."

"And who might you be?" I asked suspiciously. I didn't think I'd met this Drapsk on the *Heerama*. That didn't mean I was prepared to forgive any Heerii.

"Heepelup. I am in charge of exports from this moment. I assure you, with the aid of the wondrous Mystic One, Rael, I will take every precaution—"

"What do you mean, with my aid? I'm going to Omacron—" Rael took a sudden breath and half-rose from her chair. I could feel her outrage turn to hope. "Copelup?"

Every Drapsk in the room stopped moving and tentacles popped into their mouths. In the ensuing, somewhat noisy pause, Morgan coughed into his hand, then said: "I don't think we need to ask, do you?"

I had to smile. There really never was another option with Drapsk.

"So. Barac found his Chosen, Acranam's remaining fosterlings are safe in Clan homes, and Rael seems content to return to Drapskii—some day," Morgan said, winding my hair around his fingers. I was fascinated by the way his voice vibrated through his chest.

"And Symon . . ." I added, because it had to be said. "You are both at peace now." An ending I'd never have imagined; a grief I never thought I'd share. We'd consigned his body to the M'hir—a final act of defiance to the Clan, who'd perverted him and damaged others. All to keep a secret. "Will you tell Bowman?" I asked.

Morgan's chest rose and fell slowly. A sigh. "I'll have to—otherwise Terk will keep tearing around the universe. Although that has its charm," a laugh.

I lifted my head to gaze into his blue eyes. "And what of your new Talent?" We'd returned to the *Silver Fox* with a replacement sequencer, supplied by the Heerii, and hadn't delayed lifting from White. As Morgan said, there were some species too alien for trade. We'd been lucky to do as well with the Rugherans as we had.

And there were others, waiting for us to meet. I found I wasn't afraid anymore. Morgan knew it.

"My new Talent? A fluke that cost Symon his life and perhaps saved yours." He reached for me. "Better forgotten, don't you think?"

We'd talked about it, knowing Symon had been right to warn Morgan of the risk. A Human? Moving a starship with his mind? Amazing—appalling. That was the sort of Talent other Humans could understand—and would do anything to obtain, if they knew.

A Talent that could start a war or worse between my species and his, just as we forged the first fragile links of trust. Morgan had wanted me to erase it from his mind and mine, knowing there was such a thing as too much Power, that peace was too high a price. And he was right.

But I was right, too. "It is never worth losing your past," I said again, brushing my fingers over his forehead, thinking of my music. "And if anyone can hold this secret, it's you." I followed my fingers with my lips.

He pulled me close. "So. What's next, my Lady Witch?"

I nestled into the arms of my Chosen, more content and whole than my wildest dreams and fantasies had imagined. "Is there a sun rising, somewhere, on some world, Jason? Right now?"

"I'm sure there is." Faint puzzlement. "With all the stars and worlds? Billions and more. Right now. Why?"

With an inner smile, I spun all those sunrises into music, to sing for my beloved.

Epilogue

A kitchen offered an array of potentially deadly objects, though none were as threatening as the natural armaments possessed by the two now inhabiting this one. Such weaponry implied a willingness to use it, but thus far, the two appeared content to merely glare at each other. Using a very large number of eyes.

"And why shouldn't I send you packing, Nephew?" An ominous rumble. "Did you not take advantage of my absence to destroy the hallway and the staff quarters to either side of my apartment? Not to mention rupturing plumbing systems through the next two levels below?"

Tayno crouched slightly lower. "The kitchen's still in good shape," he offered in a high-pitched squeak. Huido bent eyestalks to survey the emptied cupboards and drawers, the heaps of broken dishware and interwoven piles of cutlery. The congealing remains of food had been digested by the cleaning servos, but the machines had been confused by the presence of so many manufactured items on the floor. "I didn't do that."

Tayno added hastily: "Plexis security did that. I didn't. You can ask anyone. I didn't do that."

Huido waved a claw. "For which Plexis will pay—and handsomely. My good friend Sector Chief Bowman has already arranged for Inspector Wallace to take on new and hopefully onerous responsibilities on Kimmcle. One can only hope he leaves the brewers in peace. Yes, Plexis herself will ensure the *Claws & Jaws* reopens—with badly needed new crystal and a wealth of promotional advertising. But what am I to do with you?"

"As I have been assuring you, Uncle. I could be very helpful." Tayno said eagerly. "I have many skills. Besides, you must be exhausted from your adventures. Surely you could use a little assistance with your responsibilities . . ." his voice trailed away to a faint whisper as Huido seemed to swell upward. ". . . or not."

"Not," the rightful master of this domain emphasized calmly enough. "Still, you were useful, in a limited way. It would be uncivilized, though traditional, of me to rip your carapace into thirds simply to make ornaments for my pool—"

"Oh, I quite agree—"

"I wasn't finished. I admit, having you around has kept me slightly more alert than usual. My wives have commented on my usually amazing vigor becoming quite exceptional. Obviously, my previous lifestyle lacked the stimulation of ongoing conflict."

"Anything to please, Uncle." Tayno left it unclear whether this was Huido's pleasure or that of his wives.

"Since I have a couple of openings on staff, perhaps you could work off some of the repairs."

Eyestalks whirled hopefully. "Stay? Here? Near your pool?"

A warning snap. "Hardly. We would arrange quarters for you that were distant from such temptation. But you would be working in the restaurant. Besides," Huido added slyly, "it seems other species have some difficulty telling my magnificence from your lowly self—"

"Surely not—" the protest wasn't totally sincere, given the slightly smug cant to Tayno's head carapace.

"I know. It's incredible to me as well. But the sad fact exists. Making it rather convenient to have 'two' Huidos on-station. There are so many tasks I should do in person, you realize, time-consuming, tedious, yet necessary. Ansel," a sorrowful gong from one claw, "would ensure I attended all of these. Now, I have you." A castanet sound of delight. "Freeing me to spend more time in my kitchen, supervising these fools who claim to be chefs."

"And to visit your pool more often." Glumly.

"What a clever notion. It is so important to keep one's wives satisfied, isn't it?" The musing rumble deepened to something menacing. "I wouldn't become too clever, Nephew."

Tayno crouched as close to the floor as possible, claws disappearing under his body. "Never, Uncle. Never."

"Then we understand one another. It's good to have family close—do you remember the rest, Nephew?"

"And enemies closer," Tayno said obediently.

"Ah, there's hope for you yet, Nephew." Huido used a fine handling claw to topple a stack of pots. "Psshat. These can wait—I can't say the same for that keg of Kimmcle brew my blood brother sent."

Tayno rose, almost imperceptively, and ventured: "Uncle? I have a question to ask but no wish to offend your magnificence."

"Ask," Huido said magnanimously, but raised one massive claw, in case.

"This one you call 'brother.' Why consider a Human as kin? You are indisputably larger and wiser. These beings, as you rightly noted, cannot even tell us apart. Most of them," the Carasian added unhappily, apparently remembering a certain incident.

"You can't tell them apart either."

"I'm practicing." Sullen. "They are bland, unremarkable creatures."

Huido laughed. "Ah, you have so much to learn, Nephew. I think I will enjoy your education. Forget the Kimmcle—first we shall visit Keevor's disgusting establishment! After that, you'll appreciate a visit to purify your spirit and other parts with the Turrneds." Sudden seriousness. "Do not allow instinct and habit to blind you, Tayno. We are not alone in the galaxy. We are not even common. As our beloved wives gather in the pool, so must we gather with other species of the Trade Pact—to share our experiences and special knowledge."

"To what end?"

"Who knows?" Huido shrugged philosophically, dipping his carapace from one shoulder to the other. "I'd settle for an improvement in their *grist*. And reliable deliveries of good beer. I leave grander visions to the Humans. They seem fond of such things."

Tayno shuddered. "Better them than us, Uncle."

"I see you are becoming wiser by the minute, Nephew. This might become a first for our kind, two Carasian males remaining in such proximity without killing each other. Or not," Huido roared with laughter. "Which would also provide something Plexis has never seen before. Right, Nephew?"

Tayno was at least wise enough to know when silence was the safest answer.

Partial Genealogy of the Clan

This family tree includes events which occur in the two previous books of the Trade Pact Trilogy, A Thousand Words for Stranger and Ties of Power. Be forewarned that if you haven't read these yet, these pages contain significant spoilers!

Please note:

M — male
F — female
Name in ( ) refers to the House of the individual's birth, plus the di or sud reflecting their individual power. Following Choice and Joining, the name of the weaker individual in a pair is usually changed to that of the more powerful partner, with the permission of his or her House.

Not all of the individuals listed are still alive. Only those deaths occurring during the events of this trilogy are recorded.

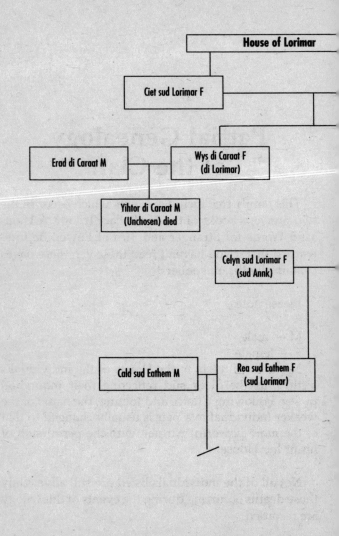

House of Lorimar

Ciet sud Lorimar F

Erad di Caraat M

Wys di Caraat F
(di Lorimar)

Yihtor di Caraat M
(Unchosen) died

Celyn sud Lorimar F
(sud Annk)

Cald sud Eathem M

Rea sud Eathem F
(sud Lorimar)

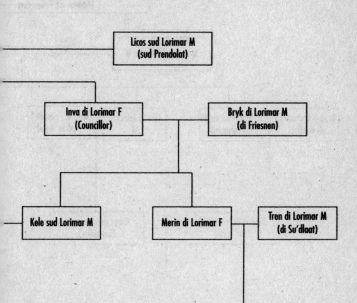

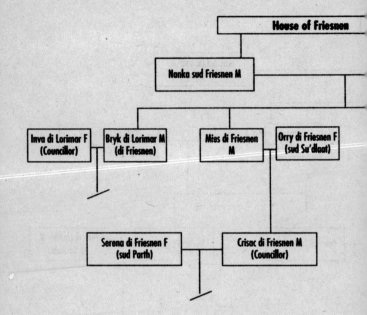

House of Friesnen

Nanka sud Friesnen M

Inva di Lorimar F
(Councillor)

Bryk di Lorimar M
(di Friesnen)

Mias di Friesnen
M

Orry di Friesnen F
(sud Su'dlaat)

Serena di Friesnen F
(sud Parth)

Crisac di Friesnen M
(Councillor)

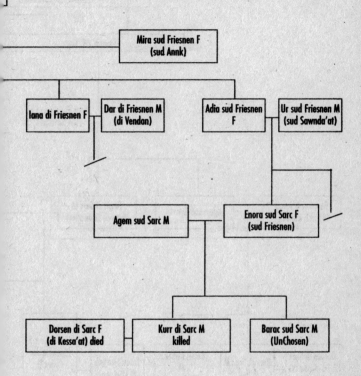

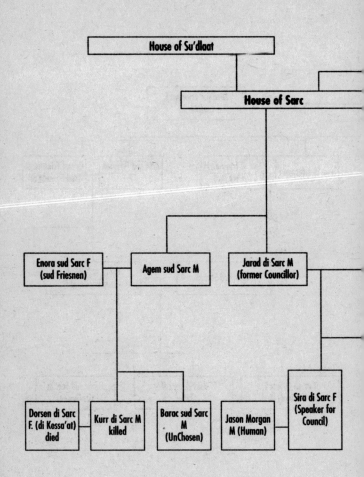

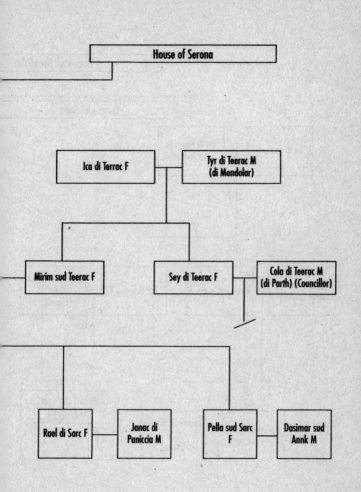

House of Serona

Ica di Terrac F — Tyr di Teerac M (di Mendolar)

Mirim sud Teerac F — Sey di Teerac F — Cela di Teerac M (di Parth) (Councillor)

Rael di Sarc F — Janac di Paniccia M — Pella sud Sarc F — Dasimar sud Annk M

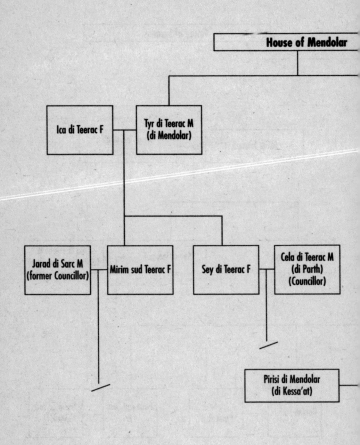

House of Mendolar

Ica di Teerac F

Tyr di Teerac M
(di Mendolar)

Jarad di Sarc M
(former Councillor)

Mirim sud Teerac F

Sey di Teerac F

Cela di Teerac M
(di Parth)
(Councillor)

Pirisi di Mendolar
(di Kessa'at)

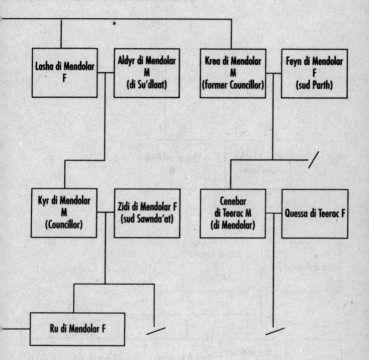

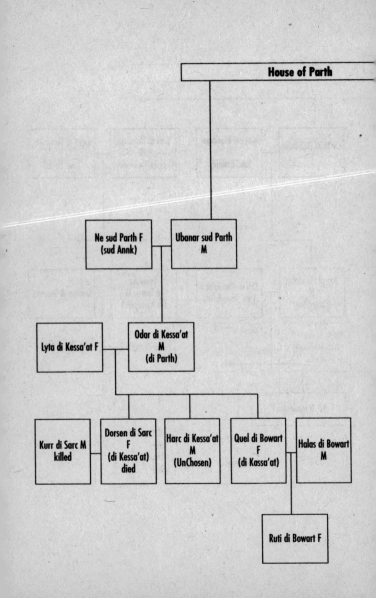

House of Parth

Ne sud Parth F
(sud Annk)

Ubanar sud Parth
M

Lyta di Kessa'at F

Odar di Kessa'at
M
(di Parth)

Kurr di Sarc M
killed

Dorsen di Sarc
F
(di Kessa'at)
died

Harc di Kessa'at
M
(UnChosen)

Quel di Bowart
F
(di Kassa'at)

Halas di Bowart
M

Ruti di Bowart F

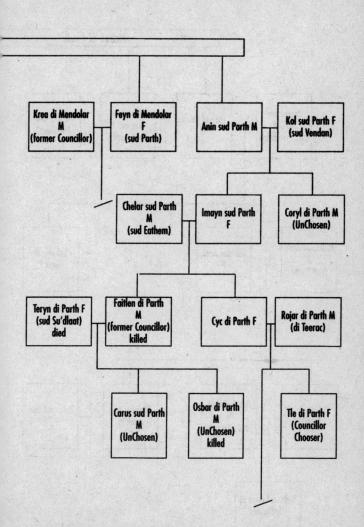

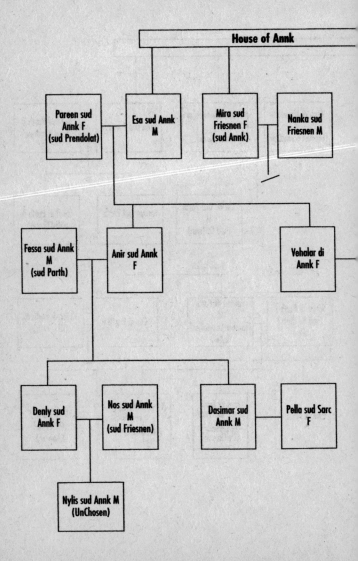

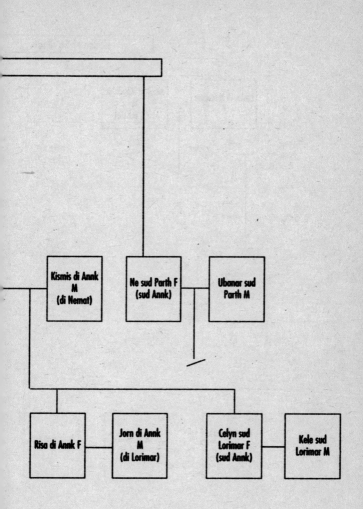

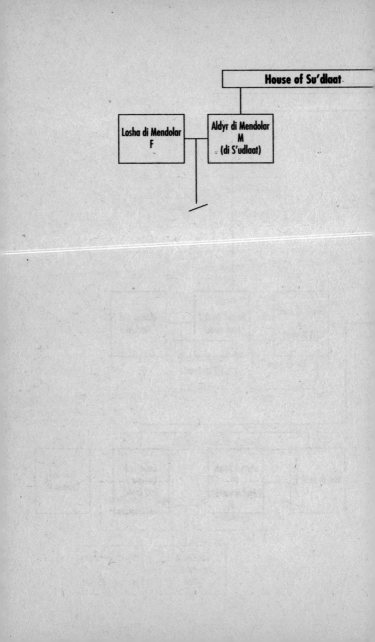

House of Su'dlaat

Losha di Mendolar
F

Aldyr di Mendolar
M
(di S'udlaat)

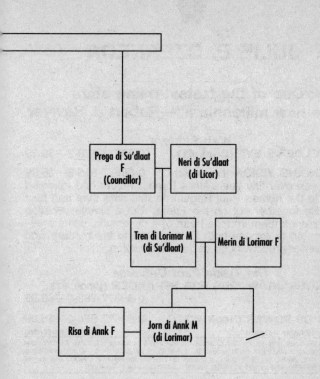

Prega di Su'dlaat
F
(Councillor) — Neri di Su'dlaat
(di Licor)

Tren di Lorimar M
(di Su'dlaat) — Merin di Lorimar F

Risa di Annk F — Jorn di Annk M
(di Lorimar)

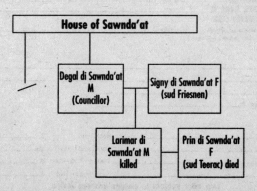

House of Sawnda'at

Degal di Sawnda'at
M
(Councillor) — Signy di Sawnda'at F
(sud Friesnen)

Larimar di
Sawnda'at M
killed — Prin di Sawnda'at
F
(sud Teerac) died

JULIE E. CZERNEDA

"One of the fastest-rising stars of the new millennium"—Robert J. Sawyer

Web Shifters

☐ BEHOLDER'S EYE (Book #1)   0-88677-818-2—$6.99

☐ CHANGING VISION (Book #2)   0-88677-815-8—$6.99

It had been over fifty years since Esen-alit-Quar had revealed herself to the human Paul Ragem. In that time they had built a new life together out on the Fringe. But a simple vacation trip will plunge them into the heart of a diplomatic nightmare—and threaten to expose both Es and Paul to the hunters who had never been convinced of their destruction.

The Trade Pact Universe

☐ A THOUSAND WORDS FOR STRANGER (Book #1)
                               0-88677-769-0—$6.99

☐ TIES OF POWER (Book #2)   0-88677-850-6—$6.99